AWARD-WINNING AUTHOR

QUINN COLERIDGE

VERITAS

Happy Reading!

♡

Quinn Coleridge

ISBN: 978-0-9988873-1-9 Print.
ISBN: 978-0-9988873-0-2 Ebook.
Cover Art by: James T. Egan of Bookfly Design
Brompton Road Literary, LLC Logo by: Green Cloak Design
Interior book design by: Bob Houston eBook Formatting

Contact the author for contests, giveaways, and book release news at her website: authorquinncoleridge.com.

Brompton Road Literary
Where art and commerce meet.

Dedication

Bear with me readers, it has taken many years to get to this place, and I have a number of people to thank.

This book is dedicated to…

My mother Elaine—you have been my rock and my dearest friend from the very beginning. Thanks is not enough, but I give it with a full heart.

Louis—I love you, Silver Fox. After a quarter century, you still show me the fairytale moments in life and keep me laughing. By the way, it was rain, not mist.

Jacob, Zachary, Taylor, Liam, Grace, and Owen—my greatest gift to the world is you.

Everett—welcome to the tribe, little one. And thank you to my son-in-law Cameron. Your smile is one of my favorite things.

Hester Grayson—for coming into my life at the exact moment I needed an invisible friend.

Lastly, I dedicate my first novel to those kindred souls who envision different worlds and then create them. Writers and dreamers, this one's for you.

Author's note

American Sign Language is a glorious, beautiful form of communication. I feel the utmost respect for those who sign and for the language itself. The main character in this book has difficulty speaking and learns ASL after reaching adulthood. It changes her life for the better, allows her to be understood as was previously impossible.

I have not adhered to the ASL grammar rules for this story, however. Yet I hope to illustrate how lives can be enhanced through sign. Authentic grammar is always desirable. Please pardon this exception to the rules.

 Prologue

Pulvis et umbra sumus.
We are but dust and shadow—Horace

Ironwood Lunatic Asylum
Ironwood, Colorado January 1892

Butterflies are my salvation.

Milkweed monarchs, to be precise. *Danaus Plexippus.* Though I may be trembling with fear, held captive in my subterranean cell, I summon the image of the butterflies with ancient magic, and they appear in my psyche, to bring a little hope, a little comfort within the confines of the Pit.

The monarchs are just as lovely as the day Tom sent them, via telepathic pictures, to my blind eyes. They came from a memory he had as a child of walking through a summer field of grain and watching the butterflies dance. By sharing the memory, Tom brought color into my world, showing me the brilliant shades and teaching me each name. Orange and black monarch wings, blue-purple evening skies, golden barley. He helped me understand the scene as a sighted person would, back when we loved each other, before all was lost.

My eyes feel dry and gritty, as though they have no more tears to shed. I lift my face toward the ceiling and the butterfly vision disappears as noise shatters my conjuring. Men curse. Boots scrape against the floor above. Metal grinds against metal and a series of shouted commands ring out as the iron lid of my cell lifts away. Like clockwork, the guards come for me on a madman's whim.

My cell, known within the asylum as the Pit, is usually a quiet place, except for the sound of dripping water and the scuttle-dash-whisper of rats and insects. But this noisy production is straight out of a penny dreadful—the ghastly novels once read to me by my friend Cordelia, for amusement's sake on slow summer afternoons. Only now I find *myself* cast as the hapless maiden in dire straits, and there is no hero arriving in the nick of time.

The Pit is stout and circular, and I lean against its rough, limestone squares as I listen to the guards move about. The stones are warmed by the kitchen ovens located on the other side of the thick walls. The heat here must be suffocating in the summer, but it's most welcome on winter days like this. I run my fingers along the nearest square. Is it odd that I am reluctant to leave this forsaken hole? My excursion into the world beyond can't possibly end well, after all. It isn't freedom, but merely a relocation from one chamber of horrors to the next.

A guard enters my cell through a hole in the ceiling, taking a set of iron stairs to the narrow landing below. He continues down more stairs another twenty feet to the dregs of the Pit. To my home away from home. Damn and blast, it's Titus. I know him by the squeaking heel of his boot. He kicks something across the hay-strewn floor—corn cobs or old chicken bones, most likely. Titus reaches me and grunts. A sound of disgust if ever I've heard one.

Yet I must look a little frightening, body and hair pale as an albino. Silver, iridescent eyes. At least that's the description I've heard others give of me. But lacking sight, and a mirror, it isn't as though I gaze at my reflection. Sometimes I imagine myself as a striking brunette, or better still, a redhead. Such vivid plumage is all the rage, is it not?

"On with your bracelets, princess," Titus says, latching a set of irons around my wrists and ankles.

So heavy and rough are they against the skin. And Titus doesn't need to use shackles—he knows I'll obey. Or I have done, for the most part, since my last failed escape when he nearly broke my jaw. Jackass.

"Up the stairs," Titus mutters, boot squeaking again. "We haven't time to waste."

How I wish I could tell him to go to blazes, but words don't come out, even when I try to scream or say no. They've stayed locked inside my head since I was a child. Hell if I know why.

I'm propelled toward the exit, clumsy and clanking. "Move along, your highness. Let's go."

I stumble up the stairs and out of the Pit. The asylum inmates are unusually loud, and their cries bounce from the rafters to the floor, settling painfully within my ears. They sound like a pack of wolves at the forest's edge. My senses shrink from them, their disease and misery thick in the air. Pray no one dies at Ironwood this evening. I'm sick to death of Death.

Our journey continues another twenty feet or so, footsteps ringing down the hall. Then Titus pushes me into a sharp right turn, and I enter a room of some kind. The atmosphere is astringent, as though carbolic solution has just been used to clean the place.

Hands big and blunt, he picks me up and lowers my body onto a hard surface. Without pillows or padding, it feels colder than the usual exam table. I run my fingers across the flat metal expanse, up the high sides. Not an actual table then, but a square trough of some kind. Liquid swirls and bubbles above me, and I begin to shake, chilled by the sound. A reservoir in the ceiling? Why does the madman need water?

As I consider these questions, Titus quickly hooks my shackles to the sides of the tub. Upon realizing my predicament, I kick and flail. Let me go, you fool. Release me.

Footsteps move along the corridor outside the exam room. *Deus misereatur,* I pray in Latin— Gods have mercy. He's here. Fifteen feet from me. Ten. Seven. My heart hammers inside my chest, and mere stubbornness keeps hysteria at bay. But the monster crosses the threshold, his French cologne arriving before him. While verbena does not begin to conceal the asylum director's rancid pomade and perspiration, it is his olfactory calling card.

"Why, Miss Grayson, you look unwell," he says. "Don't fret, my dear. We'll fix that. Water ready, Titus?"

"Yes," the guard replies.

I work the shackle on my right arm against the hook, pleading silently in my mind. I beg you, stop! Let's reconsider the situation. Over tea, like civilized people.

A loud scraping sound batters my head as a chair is pulled toward me. The doctor sits down and sighs. "You hurt one of my men the other day—clawed the side of his face rather badly. I can't allow such behavior to go unpunished, pet."

He deserved it, the filthy lecher. And I'm not your pet.

Faust leans in, his moist breath upon my cheek. "Rebellion equals pain and punishment, dear child. Obedience, on the other hand, brings relief." He waits for a moment—for what? for me to submit to his parent/child delusions?—and then turns back toward Titus. "Put the dowel in place. I'd hate for our patient to bite her tongue."

The doctor lies. Obedience won't lessen punishment. There will be pain no matter what I do.

Titus squeezes my jaw until I open my mouth. He pushes a slim piece of wood between my teeth, horizontally, and adjusts the connected straps behind my head. Similar to a horse's bit and harness. The splintery dowel rubs against my tongue, and I vomit.

"Clean her up," Faust commands. "Rinse the bile away."

Heavy material—like wool—is flipped aside, as though he has taken something from an inner pocket of his coat. I hear the creak of a worn leather spine and then the sound of writing. It's the Book. Faust always records our therapy sessions in his journal. He's does it religiously—*has* done it with every patient, since the beginning of his practice twenty-years-ago, when he started researching pain stimulus on aberrant personalities. The Book is famous throughout Ironwood.

Faust finishes writing and then begins a clinical description of the treatment ahead. "After the ten-minute mark, if the heart does not give out, the muscles will lose their ability to move. Some last half an hour, but I wouldn't expect that of you, pet. Not enough fat."

He's insane! Stark raving—

"Do the honors, Titus."

Like the removal of a sluice gate, I hear the channel open, and water rushes over me, rising to my neck in seconds.

So cold. Breathing too fast. Slow down, slow down.

Titus dumps a bucket of something—feels like snow—into the trough and icy fire slices through my skin to the joints and sinew, coursing through my veins to alternately scorch and then freeze muscles and organs.

"How remarkable," Faust says, documenting each second that I resist cardiac arrest. "But then you're a survivor, aren't you?"

Papers rustle within the Book. Pages turn. "Born blind and premature. Inadequate larynx. A bout of typhus at four—killed your nanny, the family maid, but not Little Hester. What a fascinating study! Water therapy alone may not be adequate. Perhaps you need more."

More? He's nonsensical. Body hurts everywhere. Might be sick again.

Water rises, covering most of my face, and I hold very still to keep my nose above it. Then Faust stands and pushes me under. Clamping my lips around the dowel, I manage to keep the water out of my mouth. Bubbles roll up my cheek, bounce against my closed eyelids. *Veritas. Dea.* Heaven help me. Need air. Air.

The madman brings me up, and I open my mouth wide, gulping oxygen. But the damned dowel's in the way, sliding to the back of my tongue. I bite against it and suck air in through my teeth, hissing like a snake. Then I go under again. And writhe. Kick. Strike against the sides of the trough.

Faust pulls me out a second time. I breathe … breathe … And silently scream for anyone who has shown me the slightest kindness. Cordelia. Willard. Even my dead mother. Mama, why did Father send me here? Does he really hate me so much?

The world seems to thunder in that little room as I fight Faust, as though the ocean itself crashes against my head. Weary from our battle, I grow somewhat detached and yet the physical sensations are acute. Pain is everywhere, so cold it burns. How am I alive? The blood which rushed through my veins earlier seems sluggish, and I can barely move my limbs, though my body shivers like it's having convulsions. Not dead or frozen then. The cold wouldn't hurt if I were ice.

"That's enough for the first session," Faust finally says, releasing me. "Return her to the cell, Titus."

O di immortales. Blessed heaven.

I barely feel the guard's hands as he carries me back to the Pit. Titus places my body on the wooden platform that I use as a bed, to keep me above the rats, and a nurse strips off my wet shift, replacing it with a dry one. Is she old or young? Someone's mother? Aunt? Her movements are so soft and gentle that it twists my heart, and I long to weep and weep. She drapes me in blankets, tucking them around my toes, and then follows Titus out of the Pit. The heavy lid drops into place with a thud.

My nerve endings grow livid as needles of pain shoot through my muscles and move upward, pulsing just under the skin. The shivering begins in earnest now. A blurry section of my mind knows this is not good, but I don't care. Death would be a welcome release.

And there He is, Sir Death Himself, drifting toward me. I sense His cool presence, see the tall, dark figure in my psyche and immediately feel the urge to live.

A swift, dry brush across my brow. It takes me a moment to identify the sensation. *The R-Reaper's k-kiss?* I ask telepathically.

Only a talisman. My brothers will see it and pass you by. Your time is not yet.

Very generous, Sir. But I can't help wondering why?

The insinuation of a laugh. *Are you questioning my judgment, Visionary?*

His voice is less substantial in my mind than a whisper. It is neither kind nor cruel, without apology or compassion. I shiver nonetheless. Fearing greatly, I suppose, because Death cannot help being what He is. Just as I can't avoid having visions of murder, cursed with the Sight by a fickle Roman goddess.

Death touches my jaw and the pain subsides, a soothing drowsiness taking its place. *Daughter of Rome, I think you've learned by now. There are worse things than me.*

———————— • ————————

I'm surprised, and a little dismayed, when I awaken in the piercing stillness. Checking over my body, I find breath in my lungs and a steady heartbeat. That Sir Death lived up to His word and gave me protection surprises me. It's splendid. *Fortunatus mea.* Adversely, my dismay stems from the fact that I am now in the Reaper's debt, confound it. When will He expect repayment, I wonder?

Unable to answer myself, I climb down from my makeshift bed and stretch. I circle the Pit several times, stiff and aching, and suddenly drop to the floor. My skull feels too tight, the bones of my body turn to fire. I hold the sides of my head and rock back and forth.

Stop! Not strong enough yet. Have mercy…

My prayer for relief goes unanswered, and faces flash through my mind. Those I saw in my last vision, the one initiated when the doctor touched my skin. Men, women, old, young—they appear and blur a moment later, shifting into the next person. All of Faust's victims are deep-branded inside me. They are angry, thinking I've neglected them.

Do not forget us, they call out from the grave.

I won't, I promise them. *Upon my life, I won't.*

The fingers of my right hand move apart, coerced by a supernatural power. They form the shape of a V—for Veritas, goddess of Rome. Burning within, like a human torch, I am now a prisoner of a different kind. Not of the asylum, but of the dead. My brain blossoms with the ideas they plant there, plans to make the guilty doctor pay. *Vindicta.* Vengeance. The ghosts tell me to find the Book and steal it. Escape the asylum and expose Faust to the world. Let him answer for every crime, they say, condemned by his own words.

If only these spirits could be a bit more specific. How exactly do I escape to do their bidding? Have they any suggestions? But the dead only wail and cry for justice. Blasted ghosts always leave the finer points of the plan for me to figure out.

Annoyed by my hesitation, they cause me to burn hotter. *All right*, I reply through my psyche. *As you wish, I do so promise.* Truth vibrates through the Pit, and the dead finally set my body free. They have accepted my vow, for the moment, but might be less forgiving tomorrow if I don't take action. I work for a very impatient crowd.

Most people belong to another in some capacity, as a daughter or son, a sister, spouse, or neighbor, but the inmates of this place have been forgotten. They have no one to speak for them, or to avenge their wrongs. And so I'm here, dumb and blind, to serve as the mouthpiece of the wretched, whether I like it or not. That brazen hussy Fate does love a paradox.

Ironically, serving the dead gives me a reason to live, to go on breathing each day. It answers Hamlet's eternal question of whether to be or not to be with an affirmative.

That is why I crawl about the Pit on my knees, searching for a palm-sized piece of metal. It has been hidden and used many times by the inmates before me. I find the broken iron strip and turn toward the northern wall. The rough surface is covered with spider webs and dirt, but something else as well.

Words.

Hundreds of them have been scratched into the crumbling stone with this strip of iron. I trace the curves and the straight lines of the letters, as I did with my alphabet stencils at home. Of sound mind, one inmate wrote, never insane. In another place, I find Hungry, God Sees, and Died Alone.

I scrape the iron against rock. Over and over, until each letter is formed, perfect and smooth. Wiping the sweat from my brow, I blow the dust away from my masterpiece, my call to arms.

LEX TALIONIS
YOUR DAY OF RECKONING AWAITS, FAUST

1

Arrectis Auribus.
With ears pricked up—Virgil

Three months earlier

A killing is certain tonight.

I don't know when or by whom, but it's a given. This is mad, bad Stonehenge, Colorado, and every other person in residence has a skeleton in their closet, or at least buried by the shed out back. Death's just a way of life here, and it is All Hallows Eve to boot. Quite the busiest season for a Visionary like me.

Waiting for the next victim to make contact—dreading the shock and unpleasantness sure to follow—I sit in a gazebo near the city park, where the wilderness begins to encroach upon Stonehenge. The air feels cool upon my face, smelling of pine needles and chimney smoke, and the ancient trees creak in the wind like bark-encrusted giants. Properly outfitted under my cloak with scads of ruffles and pleats, not to mention a bustle, a petticoat, and a damnable corset, my body doesn't feel the chill, just my soul.

I'm not alone this evening. Miss Cordelia Collins and I sip mugs of warmish cider with a shared plate of biscuits between us. People fill the enormous gazebo, celebrating All Hallows as though their lives depend upon it. They talk and drink, throw confetti, eat pie. I ignore most of these collateral sounds by subduing my ability to hear them. Not with ear plugs or cotton wool but through magic.

Until I grow careless and let my guard down. Then a hideous, unexpected noise crashes into my head, and I wince and rub my temples. The piano keys at The Red Rooster Pub are being brutally assaulted. The instrument is at least two hundred yards away but seems so much closer. Next there's a bit of playful gun fire, followed by singing. It's a felony against music, completely off-key.

Supernatural hearing can be such a pain in the tympanum.

Cordelia knows nothing of my enhanced senses—auricular range, olfaction and touch. Nor that I am a demigoddess of sorts, cursed with visions and ghost-sight, etcetera. She is decidedly un-supernatural, as oblivious to magical gifts as one can get. And I'm glad of it. I love Cordie for being a level-headed, no-frills human.

A credit to paid companions everywhere, she puts her mug down on the biscuit plate and begins to hover. "Are you warm enough, Miss Hester? We could have snow by tomorrow."

I nod that I am snug, but Cordie yanks my scarf up around my neck as though I am incapable, at twenty-two years, of discerning my own body temperature. Before I can pull the scratchy cloth away, she stiffens and sucks in her breath. She's finally noticed that people are moving to the other side of the gazebo, as though I am carrying the bubonic plague instead of being blind and mute.

The wind gusts around my companion and I, causing confetti to swirl against my cheek. I brush it away, and nudge my spectacles into place. Round, opaque lenses, they serve no real purpose other than to conceal my eyes from the superstitious townsfolk.

"We shouldn't have come," Cordie says. "They're so unkind."

She has a point. I might have remained with my parents tonight. But an evening out with neighbors who consider me a freakish anomaly of nature is preferable to staying at home. Either place, the sentiment is the same. It just feels less personal in town.

"Shall we leave, miss?"

I shake my head—not yet—and turn my face west toward Langtree's Music Hall. The jewel of High Street, it sits across from the park like a marble monarch on her throne. Cordelia does not share my interest in Langtree's. She sighs wistfully and taps her foot. Then she cracks her knuckles, drawing out the popping noise, and the whole process begins again. Sigh-tap-pop. Sigh-tap-pop. I cannot bear it! Something must be done about Cordelia's boredom if I am to concentrate on finding my ghost.

Fortunately, we are joined by Isaac Baker before I give in to the urge to strangle my companion and silence her forever. They make small talk for a few moments in the way of shy, young lovers, and it is almost worse than the sigh-tap-pop routine. Then, as Shakespeare would say, Isaac finally screws his courage to the sticking place and invites her to dance.

"A waltz, my dear?" he asks.

"No. I can't."

"Liar-liar. I've seen you do it. Quite well, as I remember."

I hear Isaac pull her up from the bench. There's sudden movement—twirling perhaps?—and Cordelia laughs brightly. Now the swish of long skirts, rhythmic stepping back and forth.

Dancing.

And then the motion stops. "You're being fool-headed, Isaac. I said that I can't."

Her voice is sorrowful—as though Cordie wants more than anything to waltz properly but knows she should stay. Young women deserve a little fun, though. I gently push her shoulder, encouraging her to accept.

Isaac squats down by my side. "She has nothing to worry about, does she? We have your promise. You'll stay right here."

Crossing my heart, I am the very definition of solemnity.

Cordelia sighs, nearly giving in. "But what if Mr. Grayson finds out? I'll lose my position."

I turn an imaginary key at my lips and push her again.

"Oh, all right. Who can resist the two of you?"

Cordie puts an arm around me. Her breath tickles my ear as she whispers, "Leave this bench, and I'll make your life miserable. Don't think I won't."

Oh, believe me, she would indeed. *Has*, in fact, on many occasions.

"Thank you," Isaac calls. He sounds so delighted that I can't help grinning in return.

As they walk toward the music hall, I remove two, button-sized pebbles from the pocket of my cloak. I shake them like dice, calculating actual waltz time with travel distance between Langtree's and the gazebo. I should have the next twenty-five minutes at my disposal. *Fortunatas mea!* Clutching the lucky pebbles against my palm, I unwind the scarf with my other hand, grasp my cane, and stand up. I thrust the end of the cane two feet ahead of me, and step toward the balustrade, savoring the aroma of dry corn stalks and candle wax.

Why was I drawn here? Where is that pesky ghost? It's out there somewhere, I can feel it.

As the minutes tick by, people leave the gazebo and filter into the night—for dance, for drink, for home—until only two of us remain. A gentleman and myself. I breathe in quietly, hoping to learn more of his character through the gift of supernatural olfaction. My sense of smell is as acute as my hearing, and most emotions have a distinct odor. Hatred is metallic, blood-like, and romantic love is a rich cocoa powder with hints of chili-pepper. Happiness is floral, fleeting.

Shaking the pebble-dice again, I read the most obvious scent first and then work my way inside this stranger. He smokes an imported cigar, the same brand my father uses. And I pick up the rich man's holy trinity: bay rum cologne, French pomade, and boot polish. He's also been sipping from a hipflask. Spilled a little on his coat, perhaps? Is that bourbon? A rather fine brand, I think.

Above all, however, this man is rank with feelings of inadequacy. It's a sour, curdled-milk scent. In addition I find more bitterness with the fear of failure, hard-pressed ambition, and an unfulfilled yearning to provide. These emotions permeate the atmosphere around him.

"Does the cigar bother you?" the fellow suddenly asks. "Would you prefer that I leave?"

I smile, startled by his polished American accent. No doubt my family would sound Welsh to him. Most Stonehengians do not talk like Americans at all and have roots outside the United States. Hoping to strike it rich in the mines of Colorado, they come from Canada, England, Scotland, and France. Predominantly European, but there are some from as far away as China and Russia. Regarding architecture, language and sensibilities, our city is an authentic international metropolis nestled within the Rocky Mountains.

Who are you then, mystery man?

The object of my speculation turns away and continues puffing on his cigar. Caught up in thought, I forget that I am holding my scarf. It slips from my fingers and drops to the floor. Drat. Cordelia's certain to scold if I lose the hellacious rag. I return the lucky pebbles to my pocket and squat down, patting the area around me, trying to find the scarf. A floorboard creaks, and the smell of tobacco grows stronger.

Mystery Man speaks again. "Where are my manners? Let me help you."

He gives me the scarf and pulls me up by the elbow. His hand brushes against the small patch of skin between my glove and sleeve.

Hells-bells!

A vibrating sensation begins in my bones, followed by an uncomfortable tightening of the cranium. Light shatters my peaceful blindness and a scene forms in my mind. In this psychic realm, I *can* see and speak, as I do not in ordinary life. Images slice through my head. Colors. Textures. Brilliance everywhere.

Just as I predicted. I *knew* a killing was certain tonight.

2

Deo dignus vindice nodus.
A knot worthy of God to untie.

The revelation drags at me, pulling me deeper, until I am lost in it. A part of the episode now, I hurry to keep pace with two people walking along a mountain trail. Tall and well-dressed, the man would be pleasant looking were his face not mottled with fury. His female counterpart has a smattering of gold freckles on her nose and wears a sly expression.

"You dare to threaten me?" he asks the woman, spittle flying from his mouth. "No one will believe the words of a lying cheat!"

"Don't worry, 'ee bleddy dobeck," she answers. "Folks'll know what's true."

The Mystery Man from the gazebo and a Cornishwoman? I hear it in the rhythm and intonation of her speech. And she's obviously lived a hand-to-mouth existence with little formal education.

I always warn the victim, though it does little good. "Leave," I beg her. "Go home."

We reach a rocky plateau and stop. Despite our beautiful surroundings, a figure waits silently, winding His watch in the shadows of the evergreens. I do not actually see Sir Death, but I sense the Reaper is there.

Mystery Man rubs his head, as though his temples ache. "This will kill my wife."

The Cornish woman is a redhead who seems to speak first and think later. "Your missus'll be fine. If 'ee pay, that is."

"I can't. I don't have the money yet."

His blackmailer frowns. "Then dead she be."

The words are barely out of her mouth before he strikes the woman. She loses her balance, falls headfirst onto a slab of stone. Quiet, no movement. Mystery Man kneels down and checks if she is still breathing. He looks thoughtful and then winces and rubs his head as he did a few moments ago. "I must," he murmurs. "There's no other choice."

Watching him lift the unconscious body from the ground, I smell his desperation and fear. It's rotten, like a decaying carcass.

"Stop," I say. "Whatever trouble you're in isn't worth your soul."

He brushes past me and carries the woman to the edge of a deep ravine. I follow after and nearly lose my footing, mesmerized by the jagged rocks at least fifty feet below. The woman's eyelids flicker open just before he throws her over the side. She falls forever, or so it seems, and my scream entwines with hers, echoing through the forest.

Until there is a thud and a terrible silence.

"Murder," I declare, my voice breaking on the word.

Mystery Man looks in my direction, as though he actually heard me. In all my years as a Visionary, this has only happened a handful of times. I think of the things I'd like to ask him, but the vision fades. Everything grows dark, and I return to my senses, back in the gazebo at Stonehenge, blind and mute once more.

The vision was lengthy in the psychic realm but occupied mere seconds of earth time. I cannot tell where the murder happened or when, but one thing is certain. The killer is standing beside me.

"Are you unwell?" he asks.

Trembling, I shake my head in response, the woman's scream still ringing in my ears. Remove your gloves, I tell myself. Steady now. Put them in your pocket and do it. Don't be a coward, you must touch him. I take a deep breath and grab the lapels of the killer's overcoat, my hands swiftly climbing up the heavy material to his face. His intake of breath tells me that I have surprised him. He doesn't know what to make of my behavior.

I feel his forehead and work downward, learning all I can. There's a scar by his right brow, and his cheeks are thin, more so than in the vision. Clean-shaven too, no beard like before.

"What are you doing?" the man cries, pulling away. "This is mad."

He shoves me aside, grinds out the end of his cigar on the handrail and pushes it into his pocket. "You're a menace to the public," Mr. Murder says. "Someone should put you away."

The killer leaves the gazebo quickly, and turns north. On impulse, I follow the sound of his footsteps, hands outstretched, but I stumble on the stairs.

No time to find my cane! He's moving too fast.

I draw myself up and go after him as music hall celebrants flood into the street. I grow disoriented amid the noise—lose my sense of the murderer's whereabouts.

Thunderation! He's gone. Escaped.

I don't know how long I stand on the sidewalk, surrounded by pressing bodies, bumping against me as they make their way past. The earth tilts crazily from side to side, and I grow nauseous.

"Miss Hester?" Cordelia gasps. "Is that you?"

She grips my arm, muttering her disapproval—each word a lecture in and of itself. "What a state you're in! Hands bleeding, dress torn. I knew I shouldn't have left you."

Now she's glaring at Isaac. I don't need seeing eyes to verify this. I feel him flinch under her scrutiny, poor lad.

Cordie gathers my cane, scarf, and reticule from where I dropped them at the gazebo. Teeth chattering, I shake uncontrollably, so she wraps me like a mummy in the scarf and buttons my coat as high as it will go. Cordie bids Isaac a crisp farewell and leads me back toward High Street. I do not wish to face my parents after the evening's debacle, so I drag my feet a bit. This elicits even more criticism from my companion.

After walking several blocks, Cordelia and I meet Willard Little Hawk, the family handyman, at the livery near city hall. "What in blazes happened to you, White Hair?" he cries over the All Hallows hubbub.

Impatient, geriatric, and possessing an arthritic hip, Willard has known me most of my life. I cringe at the volume of his voice, and the nickname he gave me long ago. It's Willard-talk for the color platinum. He sometimes adds Silver Eyes or Pale Skin to his repertoire.

Willard helps us into the buggy, and we ride for home as the clock tower chimes midnight. Usually the witching-hour is an ill omen, but perhaps not in this case. Instead, it feels fortuitous. My mother hears Cordelia's account of the Halloween party without interrupting once. Quite out of character for Mama. In addition, my companion does not embellish upon the tale. Rather, she edits things out with a vengeance, saying that I merely dropped my cane and fell, thus incurring the injuries to my hands and the rip in my gown. I don't know which my mother feels worse about—my scrapes or the ruined ensemble from Paris.

No, that's incorrect. I do. It's the dress.

"Carry Miss Hester upstairs, Willard," Mama says. "She's ill."

I wave my hands, but Willard scoops me up and follows orders. Traitor. Turncoat. He knows I hate being fussed over. Cordelia shoves aside the ridiculous mound of porcelain dolls that decorate my bed. Mama collects them for me, and no matter how often I hide the frilly ladies, they are returned without fail. Willard sets me on the mattress, and my mother closes the door after he leaves. Feeling stiff and sore, I let Mama remove my clothing until I am left with only a chemise and drawers.

She rustles through the armoire and chooses a nightgown. I know the exact one by its unfriendly, stiff-taffeta sound. The skirt is heavily embroidered, the neckline a volcano of erupting lace. It's utterly absurd to anyone with a lick of common sense and impossible to sleep in.

"Ready yourself," Cordie murmurs, and I feel awkward stretching my arms out into the air.

The nightgown is a fitting costume for Halloween, I suppose. Instead of resembling a real female, I am dressed like one of those porcelain dolls Mama values so much—perfectly groomed, impossibly stylish. Yet surface finery does not compensate for what I lack, or transform me into the daughter she longs for.

Mama makes a familiar, rattling sound—metal against glass, spoon to bottle. I scramble away, like a rabbit fleeing a fox. No laudanum! Leave me alone! But my mother catches me and pulls me back to the bed. As always, Cordie does as her employer demands and holds me down. I hate being reduced to this panicked state. Lack of sight and speech shouldn't take away one's fundamental right of refusal.

I don't want it! Please let me go.

After three failed attempts, they force a dose of laudanum into my mouth. I cough and sputter as the burning liquid slides down my throat, tasting bitter and sickly sweet. Rattle-clack. My mother returns the spoon and bottle to her pocket. She removes my spectacles and tells Cordelia to clean me up and change the pillowcase. Mama sets my eyeglasses on the table and calmly bids me goodnight, as though physical aggression has not just taken place. Cordelia wipes my chin and neck with a wet cloth, and I lift my head as she replaces the pillow.

"There," Cordie says, sounding apologetic. "Good as new."

But that isn't so.

I am not good or new, and never shall be. I hate my mother for what she did. I loathe being made weak and dependent. Even worse than the unclean feeling I get from the laudanum, I'm tainted from tonight's murderous vision. Now I must bring a killer to justice. That or suffer the freckled Cornishwoman's taunts until the end of time. Already, I hear her whispering in my head. *Do well of me, Visionary. You owe a body that.*

Then the ghost materializes near the window of my room, watching me with thinly-veiled contempt. Blood drips from a gash at the side of her head and stains her red and white checkered blouse. It reminds me of a picnic tablecloth. I see myself clearly through her eyes, as though I am she. Ghost-sight can be quite helpful with investigations, but it isn't always flattering. Laughter bubbles up in my chest, gets stuck in my throat. What a shameful picture I present! Idiotic nightgown, slack mouth, glassy expression. No wonder this ghost is upset. I'd doubt myself if I were in her place.

She begins to shriek, but I'm not over-bothered. I merely turn down my hearing and smile. With laudanum pumping through my system, I lose all sense of propriety and engagement. The ghost rants a bit more, and I notice again the charming sprinkle of freckles across the bridge of her nose. Of course they would be a great deal more charming if she didn't look as though she wanted to throttle me. Perhaps I'll call her Freckles as a nickname. I smile even more at this idea. Freckles must sense my levity despite her efforts to terrify me because the ghost stomps her foot and disappears with an angry pop. Ghost-sight leaves with her, and I am blind again.

Unaware of the spirit's departure, Cordelia brushes a strand of hair away from where it sticks to my cheek. She walks to the other side of the room, and the wooden chair creaks as she sits down. Soon there's a light clicking noise. Knitting.

Blast it, Cordie. Not another wool scarf. Kindly do the necks of the world a favor and cease.

She hums a lullaby, the Welsh tune melding softly with the air. I barely have a moment to think of the words to the song before my thoughts turn hazy, and I drift away.

3

Cura ut valeas.
Take care.

An opium-induced fog isn't conducive to real sleep. Therefore, I wake up later than usual and move sluggishly through my morning routine. It is Cordelia's day off, and a parlor maid has taken over her duties. The replacement's name is Martha. She smells strongly of linseed oil, sweat, and anxiety. A virulent combination in close quarters.

After stepping into the copper bathtub, I sink under the water and begin to wash, silently praising whoever invented perfumed soap, lord love him. I listen as Martha tidies my room like a dervish, shooting from bed to dresser to desk. A dusting, sweeping hurricane of cleanliness. "Well," Martha says, once her tasks are complete. "Are you finished?"

I shake my head and lie back in the fragrant water. My lethargy is not allowed to interfere with Martha's busy schedule, and she braids my hair as I sit in the tub, twisting it into a coronet and pinning it into place.

"Ring if you want me, Miss Hester, and I'll come back at once."

I continue to dawdle, splashing my tender knee and soaking the abrasions on my palms. The water cools far too soon, however, even with the heat-retaining copper. I reach for a bath sheet and freeze. A sound disrupts my peaceful interlude, a murmured sentence fragment followed by the scuff of a shoe against the floor. Gasping in shock, I cover my body with the sheet and sink under the water again. What the hell? Who's in my bedroom?

It takes me a few terrified seconds to identify my visitor—the way he shuffles foot to foot, talking softly to himself, confused and anxious. I collapse against the side of the tub.

Deo favente. It's only Carver.

Every Visionary deals with wayward spirits. They occupy a corner of one's mind—like a constant, low-level hum—and leave little room for personal privacy. This one fades in and out of my thoughts like Alice's Cheshire cat but with white, wispy hair and a three-button silk vest that must have been a lovely blue color once. Before he died last year, Carver spent his days at the Stonehenge saloons, gambling badly. Until he scored a perfect, unbeatable hand at the ripe age of sixty-five and had a massive heart attack before he could enjoy his winnings. Sir Death has no idea why this ghost is still here since haunting is typically done by homicide victims. He isn't decomposing like most who linger, losing his features and shape to become a gray formless cloud.

But then this is Carver we're talking about. At best, he is incompetent, stubborn and a rule breaker. At worst, delusional.

I've seen him in my psyche trying to hide a stuffed rooster in a banjo case. He's no more lucid now than when he was alive.

Go toward the light, Carver, I call telepathically from my cold bathtub. *You don't belong here. Embrace eternity.*

The ghost seems to consider this for a moment and then responds with a rude belching noise. Carver leaves as unexpectedly as he arrived, and I rub my face with my hands, wishing I could rid my brain of his memory. Why did the old gambler select me for his contact? What did I do to deserve him?

I step out of the tub and dry myself with another bath sheet. At the armoire, I choose a set of underclothes, feeling for the ribbons that decorate the front of these boxy garments, and pull them onto my body without any great difficulty.

Now to locate the corset, stockings, and petticoats. Bless you, Cordelia! They are all in their respective compartments due to her obsession with order. I throw the lingerie onto my bed, and return to the armoire for a gown. Since I can't see them, I choose clothes by the way the material feels. Should I pick the alpaca or the silk? Or would wool be better? Because my room feels drafty, I decide upon a heavier fabric for greater warmth. Cordelia has described the dress to me at length—bottle-green velvet with black piping at the hem, collar, and cuffs. Lovely-smelling, too. I hold the garment to my face and inhale the rose petal and cedar shavings scent.

Minding my own business, innocently enjoying a bit of potpourri, I hear my mother's voice, two floors above. She sounds angry and hurt. I do hate having magic ears sometimes. It's always awkward to eavesdrop on private moments.

"You can't send her off," Mama says. "I won't let you."

Father strides across the bedroom, his shoes pounding the floor with each step. "It's inevitable that she go."

"But this is her home. She's comfortable here. Don't you care about your own daughter?"

Sounding very Welsh, he mutters a few words, the kind I'd expect to hear from Willard after hammering his thumb. Then Father laughs. "What would you have me say, Lenore? That I cherish my life's trial? Feel affection for the thorn in my side? Be serious."

"I am serious."

"My dear wife, if you would only listen to reason— "

Mama throws something at the wall. "How can you be so cold? It's unnatural."

"*I* am not the unnatural one in this house…"

"We settled this long ago, John. While there's a breath in my body, Hester remains. I'm holding you to your word."

I have listened to at least a thousand variations of this argument. John and Lenore go round and round about my future every week or so, when they're alone and need something to fill the silence. I am all they share in common at this late marital date.

The air in my bedroom suddenly feels oppressive so I walk to the window, tripping twice along the way. It's absurd to let their comments upset me so.

My stupid ears hear Father walk down the gravel drive to the carriage house near the road. He's still obviously angry and seeking to vent his wrath on someone. Willard is the first person he encounters.

"Why hasn't the hog been butchered yet, Little Hawk?" Father yells. "You're robbing me of your wages. I should have the constable arrest you."

Father climbs into our buggy, and the horse takes a few skittish steps. "See to the butchering and fill in that old well. Otherwise, pack your bags and get out."

Back within the house, I recognize the parlor maid's heavy tread downstairs, moving in my direction. Martha enters the bedroom a short while later, smelling strongly of linseed. The oil has saturated her clothing to such a degree that I do not know how this woman has escaped spontaneous combustion. Someone needs to warn her to change into a clean uniform or avoid all sources of fire.

"Got worried when you didn't ring," Martha says. "Thought you'd fallen asleep in the bath."

I hold up the velvet gown, and point to the pile of under-things on the chair, beckoning for her assistance. It takes time to lace up my corset, tie on the petticoats and bustle, and affix the long row of buttons on the morning dress. Finally, Martha hooks me into a sturdy pair of ankle boots. She drops a shawl into my gloved hand and quickly clears the room of wet towels before taking her leave.

I throw on a cloak, pick up my cane, and step into the hall. The more genteel section of the manor lies to the right. I proceed in that direction, hoping to use the central staircase without notice. And luck is with me! The way is clear. After reaching the main floor, I turn toward the drawing room and listen to my mother playing *Moonlight Sonata* on the piano. It is perfectly executed, with the precise blend of technique and expression. I have no idea why, but even as a girl, it made me wish to weep. Is it the steady movement forward, the subtle persistence? Or just the lyric purity that touches my soul? Beethoven is one of Mama's passions—as well as Liszt and Brahms. She favors the German composers over their Italian and French contemporaries. It seems a waste of her talent not to love and play them all.

As the final note is struck, I leave my mother to her music—glad that she feels deeply about something—and walk toward the library. It should be empty since my father prefers to do his correspondence and business in his personal study. As I enter the library, it smells of hot-house flowers, furniture polish, and freshly-baked gateau. Chocolate, I think. Our dining room and kitchen are just down the hall, and evidently Cook is baking something delicious today.

The dessert makes my mouth water as I pass through the library, and I remind myself to have some when I return. Then I remember that Cordelia is not here and abandon the idea. She always sneaks treats to me from the kitchen, but I doubt Martha would do such a thing. Reaching the French doors, I open one and stroll out onto the patio. Weak November sun kisses the top of my head, and I smile at the sky. My parents are oblivious to these daily excursions for the most part. As long as I appear to follow their rules—keep to my set of rooms, don't cause problems with the servants, disappear when company comes— they stay clear of me.

Our arrangement works well, in my opinion.

Mahogany cane in my right hand, I reach out with the left, palm forward, and count the steps that I walk. Slow and steady progress, that's a girl.

It is a hundred feet from the patio to the formal rose gardens, most likely dreary and dormant at this time of year. Next comes the pond, a man-made pool that is fairly easy to circumnavigate if I stay on the right path. As yet, I have not fallen in, though I did come close a time or two. The pond now behind me, I continue forward... beyond the marble statuary, the outdoor chess board, the Italianate courtyard.

I pause and rest, stretching side to side at the waist. Sweet blazes! Corsets do not enhance oxygen intake one whit. Unlike the inventor of perfumed soap, I do not thank the person who created these blasted things. After a few more stretches, I continue on. It's still another three hundred and five feet to reach the maze and the conservatory at its center. Father calls this section of the grounds Mother's Folly because it was her idea to put in an evergreen maze. It occupies a dozen acres, has several dead ends, and features thousands of manicured shrubs. If one lined up all the twisting paths inside the maze, they would nearly run a mile. Many a servant has become lost inside the serpentine puzzle that is Mother's Folly.

The air grows cool when I arrive at the entrance to the maze. I pull the hood of my cloak up and give my ears free reign to sort through the layers of sound on the estate. It is reasonably quiet at the house. Except for Mama's playing—she's moved on to Schubert. The outbuildings and barn, on the other hand, are full of activity. Washerwomen snap wet sheets and peg them to the line. The slaughtered pig hangs from a hook, blood dripping—tap, tap, tap—into a pan. And a scullery maid is busy with the mid-day milking, berating the cow for kicking over her pail.

Amid this domesticity, I turn inward and listen to my heartbeat. The sounds of the world disappear as I call out telepathically to the other half of my soul. His response is quick.

Yes, Hettie. I hear you.

I smile at the voice in my head. *Sorry if I'm a bother—*

A pleasant distraction, maybe, but not a bother.

Could we meet this afternoon?

Reassurance and peace flow between us. *I'm just outside town. Be there as soon as I can.*

He leaves me with that promise, and I turn my hearing outward, cheered by our psychic communion. I stroll into Mother's Folly, feeling instantly at home, and run my left hand along the shrubbery. A haven of solitude and peace, away from spying servants and family troubles. Gravel crunches under my boots as I follow the narrow path. Move along, I tell myself. Left. Left. Right. That's it—ignore the false turn and go straight. Around the next corner, now take another right. And left once more... Yes. Almost there.

My tranquility is shattered when I hear someone speak. Not a ghost this time but a living woman. Voice brittle as dessicated leaves, she whispers from the forest that surrounds our estate. The sound cuts through the air like a razor blade, striking my ear.

"Come, child," the old woman says. "Tap your cane, that I might follow the sound and find you."

Tap my cane? I will do no such thing. I do not wish to meet this strange, bossy female. Yet my hand shakes when I resist, and fear ripples along my spine. I have no choice but to obey and strike the gravel. How can it be? Has she the power of Compulsion? That's forbidden magic. Evil.

Snap! A branch breaks at the forest's edge. The woman is now crossing our estate, walking toward the maze. She moves far too fast for an old person, faster than any human should.

Get inside the conservatory, my mind whispers. Flee.

I run along the curving path, cane swinging wildly, counting the turns in my head. But my feet grow heavy and slow, like they are caught in a vat of molasses. More dark power. I stick my cane into the earth and pull myself forward, only to slide back an inch or two. Forward, back. Forward, back. I must look as if I'm playing tug-o-war with my own body.

"Stop!" the stranger calls, reaching the entrance of the maze. "I mean you no harm."

Her cold magic disappears, and I sag against my cane, free of Compulsion at last.

The conservatory is directly ahead. Thirteen steps away. Heart sputtering, I run the distance to the copper and glass structure. The air inside is warm and smells of lilies. I shut the door, lock it, and shrink back against the wall.

My unwanted guest turns from the maze entrance. I hear her backtrack, walking along the outside of the hedge wall. Until she is directly across from the conservatory as the crow flies.

"I could reach you now if I wanted," the old voice whispers. "But I'll be patient and wait. Perhaps you're not ready to meet me."

Groping my way to the center of the hot house, I knock a plant off its pedestal, and the pot shatters on the floor. Sound waves tear through my ears, causing me to double over in pain.

"I'm Mary Arden," the woman says, as though she's calming a frightened child. "Just old Mary."

I lift my hand, perplexed. How odd. It seems I've taken the lucky pebbles out of my pocket without realizing it. I jingle them together and think of Mary Arden. Anyone who lives in Stonehenge knows of her. Some say she's a witch, a thief, a fortune-teller. A recluse who consumes absinthe in alarming quantities and hides deep in the wilderness—talking to bears, dancing under the stars.

Or so the fables go.

"It's an awful burden, being what we are," she murmurs. "The Sight can bring such pain."

Wait a moment. This person is a Visionary? Mad Mary of the forest?

Her voice turns hypnotic, intimate. "Life's never been fair for us, has it? Our gift is really no gift at all."

I'm being played like a violin at the music hall, but I cannot help listening. Is the woman friend or foe? Could she actually be what she claims? It is possible, I suppose.

Among the descendants of the goddess Veritas, the Sight jumps between members of our vast family tree, leaving the unchosen completely unaware of their lineage. The Lady gives her name to a select number of females in every era. They become the new Veritas, serving the people of their jurisdiction until death. Is Mary one of us?

Her crackling voice no longer floats in the air but lodges deep within my psyche, until I am unsure where her thoughts end and mine begin. *Come, sweet child. We must help each other. We have a common enemy.*

I squeeze the pebbles until my palm hurts. I do not wish to channel thoughts with Mary Arden, but I interrupt the fey woman's tidings, stifling her words with my own. *I have done nothing wrong. Who is this enemy?*

Archimendax...

The Great Liar? Impossible. He disappeared after the fall of Rome.

Mary paces outside the maze, skirts snapping in the wind. *Not Archimendax himself, Hester. His scion. He's threatened by you and covets your talent.*

What is there to covet? My power is small, limited.

She scoffs at this. *Are you so ignorant, girl? Your abilities are not limited. Who told you that?*

I just presumed.

You presumed wrong then. They evolve as you do.

I cannot help doubting her. Along with the unwashed skin and filthy clothes, Mary Arden stinks of ulterior motives. *How will my gifts change?*

Only time will tell. Maturity enhances them. And suffering. It shows the universe that we endure, that we're capable of bearing more.

In that case, I prefer to stay as I am.

Oh, child, you are naïve. Destiny is often thrust upon us. Mary Arden sighs and moves closer to the hedge. *You must listen now, Hester. Our enemy uses others to accomplish his evil work. Weak, impressionable souls who lack the will to resist. You'll hear it in their voices if you listen hard enough.*

Mary Arden pauses briefly and then severs our psychogenic connection.

4

Coniunctis viribus.

With united powers.

Why has she withdrawn? I lift my face, sensing movement and vibration within the maze. Footsteps. The tread is even and controlled, barely shifting the gravel on the path. Distribution of weight and length of stride suggest this is a male. He's nearing the center of the maze, still thirty feet from the conservatory.

Now twenty-seven. Twenty-one. Sixteen...

Mary Arden turns toward the forest as I silently count. She stomps her foot and mutters an oath against time, luck, and men in general. Rather timid for an alleged witch and former Visionary. Why not cast a spell upon the fellow? Why does she fear him?

The old woman reconnects with me briefly. *Consider my message, Hester. We'll meet again.*

Light on her feet, Mary Arden leaves her spot outside the maze and hurries into the forest. The air immediately grows warmer in the conservatory and tentative bird song erupts outside, squirrels begin to chatter. Hushed during Mary's visit, the animal kingdom returns to life all at once. I curl in on myself, wishing that I felt safe in my glass fortress. What to make of all this? I thought Mary was a myth until today. Is she sane? Trustworthy?

Gravel crunches nearby, and I cock my head toward the sound. My heartbeat quickens, growing light and fast when the door to the conservatory rattles. I step away from the wall and lift the latch. The man with the steady tread walks right inside, without an invitation.

"What's a nice girl like you doing out here all alone?" he asks.

I remove my concealing spectacles, tuck them into a cloak pocket, and smile. *Waiting for you, Tom Craddock. Or have you forgotten?*

Never, love. The words float through my mind. *How could I?*

Every Visionary needs an Interpreter, and Thomas Fearchar Craddock is mine. He is a gifted telepath and helps me analyze my dreams. Tom also teaches me about the sighted world by sharing pictures of his memories with my mind. This is how I know he has black hair and matching eyes. How I identify shades of color, symmetry, and visual beauty.

His father's people come from Scotland, and while there is not a drop of their Highlander blood in my veins, Tom and I are two halves of a whole. Since childhood, we have communicated with each other through clairvoyant thought—often using

Latin, a language we've never studied yet still understand. The side-effect of our ties to ancient Rome, I suppose.

Iam invenisti me, Thomas. It took you long enough to get here.

Tom laughs, the happy sound filling the conservatory. *Paenitet me fuisse serus. How shall I make amends?*

He lifts my hand and touches the lucky pebbles. "Worried about something, love? What happened?"

Putting the pebbles in my pocket, I smile at Tom. My distress over meeting Mary Arden burns away like dew in August, and I feel safe once more. Valued, loved. I am not the odd town's town oddity when we are together. My gloves warm from the outside as I touch his face. Strong cheekbones and jaw. Poetic brow. The full lips curve into a smile.

Kiss me, Hettie. I've missed you.

Salve, Temptatio.

Tom smells of the dried alfalfa he feeds to his livestock. He pulls me close, inside the lapels of his cowboy coat—a long, leather duster—and his arms and shoulders are work-hardened and muscular. I never have bad visions when I touch Tom. He cradles my head in his hands as though I am a delicate treasure. I marvel that such a rough and tumble man of action who wrangles cattle and runs a ranch can be so gentle.

Beginning slowly, Tom kisses my forehead, temple and cheek, working his way to my mouth, where he lingers for quite some time. I pull back, wishing that I could shout, make some assertion of my happiness for the world to hear. What would I say to equal the joy in my heart? Would it provoke the gods to wrath? They can be jealous, it's said.

The thought of the immortals sobers me. We have Visionary business to attend to, and we've put it off long enough. *Incipiemus?*

Tom releases me with a sigh. *I suppose we must, Hettie.*

I sense his feelings, the longing and physical attraction, inhale their scent as we separate. Rich and deep, like the finest cocoa with just a hint of chili powder. My favorite.

Tom claims a creaky wooden chair and provides me with a seat on his knee like Father Christmas. Smiling, I touch the rumpled material of his shirt, and tug at the thick lock of hair that always falls into his eyes when he leans forward. He unbuttons my glove like a man of leisure, gently taking his time and drawing out the process of removing it, as though nothing dark or evil awaits us in the moments ahead.

First I tell him of Mary Arden's visit, and I feel his surprise over the message she delivered. *Any sense of whether she's telling the truth, Hettie?*

No. I couldn't read much through olfaction or voice. Is it even credible, that the heir of Archimendax lives in Stonehenge?

We're here, aren't we? Who's to say there aren't more with supernatural gifts? Let's assume the threat is real, for now, and use extra caution where you're concerned.

Tom switches to audible speech. "I take it you've had another vision. Was it bad, love? Are you all right?"

My Interpreter has this habit of changing from telepathy to the spoken word. It's a breach of etiquette among clairvoyants, and technically against the rules. I let it slide because it's Tom.

Since I receive the visions through physical contact with a victim or perpetrator, I must also use touch to share the revelations. Tom can see them in no other way. Counterbalancing my skills, he shares his own memories through our psychic link at any time, over great distances. We clasp hands, and I show Tom the All Hallows vision several times. The Cornishwoman's blackmail attempt, the murderer throwing her off the mountainside.

He considers the crime scene, hoping to identify the location. "I saw something white behind those cedars. What do you suppose it is?"

After reviewing the scene again, I notice the blur of white. *Snow drift, maybe?*

"Not with columbine growing all over the place. Must be June or thereabouts. The weather's still cool then, but not enough for snow."

What if it's a house?

"Not many settlers in the mountains anymore, but it might be a building of some kind."

Ruminating, he plays with the fringe on my shawl. "According to the vision, the killer wears an expensive suit and a fur trimmed coat. Yet when he was with you in the gazebo on Halloween, he stubs out his cigar and takes the unused portion with him. The man's either *very* frugal or unaccustomed to wealth. I'm betting it's the latter since most frugal men don't own fur coats."

Tom drops the fringe and picks up my sash, probably unaware that he is even holding it. "Victim's thin, her clothing patched. Most likely unmarried, too. No ring."

Notice her hands? They're red, almost raw.

"My mother's look like that when they've been in hot water and lye. Perhaps our lady was employed as a laundress."

You didn't recognize the killer?

"Nope, but now that I've seen his face, I won't forget it. I'll keep an eye out; ask around about a woman matching the victim's description. Rancher's wives love to gossip."

I sigh and nestle closer to him. *If only Freckles could tell us her name or identify the man who killed her. But you know ghosts. They hate thinking about their past lives.*

He switches seamlessly into telepathic mode. *Who'd want to remember how they were murdered? With trauma too horrible to relive, the spirit suppresses the memory.*

Can't move on, can't remain here either. Believe me, I know. Nevertheless, a fully-cognizant ghost would be refreshing.

Tom sets me on my feet and stands. *You need to get back, carissima. Before your parents cotton on to the fact they have an escape artist for a daughter.*

We can't have that now, can we?

Laughter rumbles up from his chest. *Let's study the dream out a bit more, and then meet in a few days.*

Just tell me when, lover.

A ripple of wanting travels from him to me. Lust, respect, love, friendship. It's all inside my head, and I know my face is flaming. Which is an embarrassing thing for a near-albino.

Leaving the maze together, we converse in our unique way, and travel back across the grounds to my home. The exact route I took before but in reverse—courtyard, chess board, statuary, etcetera—until we finally arrive at our destination. Stealth personified, Tom and I sneak up to the less-frequented servant's entrance. I wait beside the door, listening as he walks away.

My smile grows smaller with each receding step.

"Be careful, Veritas," he whispers. "Remember what Mary Arden said."

I extend my hearing farther and farther until my ears hurt, but it's worth knowing when Tom reaches his horse, tied to a tree in the apple orchard. He climbs into the saddle and rides north at a fast clip, toward his family's ranch. How would it feel to be so free? To race the wind?

Then I hear my name being bandied about inside the kitchen. Cook is telling Martha that my dinner tray is ready. I subdue my magic ears, tiptoe up to my bedroom and shut the door. After throwing my cloak and shawl into the wardrobe, I jump under the covers of my bed, pull the blankets up, and turn to face the wall. The stairs creak as Martha climbs them with my dinner tray. She won't question my taking a rest. Why should she? I have no responsibilities or friends who would come to call. Nothing is expected of the infirm Miss Hester.

Yet if I seem too robust the servants will talk to Mama. She prefers me as a near-invalid. It's unacceptable to act wild or get excited—that's when the laudanum is brought out.

Martha walks down the hallway, enters my room, and places the dinner tray on a nightstand. "Warm rolls and a bowl of chicken broth today, miss. Cup of buttermilk, some shortbread. I expect you can manage that yourself."

Botheration. I hate buttermilk. And what of the chocolate gateau? The dessert I smelled downstairs? I'd trade my shortbread for it in a trice.

Gateau is not to be, however, and Martha fills my bed-side carafe with water before leaving. Perhaps a nice cool drink is what I need. My heart is thumping and my forehead is damp with perspiration after sneaking up the stairs. But I got out of the house and back in with no one the wiser for it.

An escape artist indeed.

5

De fumo in flammam.
Out of the smoke, into the flame.

C ordelia and I visit the Home for Orphans and Foundlings the next day. We sit at the back of a small classroom and listen to the children recite their history. It is a scene straight out of *Jane Eyre*. Cordie has read the book to me several times, and this sounds a lot like Lowood School.

The teacher raps on his desk, far too loudly in my opinion. Mr. Allen is a strict man who is inclined to punish first and ask questions later. My fingers are itching to touch Mr. Allen, but I haven't the nerve. There must be an intriguing secret somewhere in his past to make him crave structure and discipline so badly. People like him always come from something dreadful.

"What is the current population of Stonehenge?" he asks.

"Ninety-eight thousand souls," the students reply in unison.

"Very good."

Mr. Allen walks the length of the room, tapping an object against his palm. It sounds thin and flat—like a ruler. He stops at a desk near the front.

"Simmons Harrow, you will stand."

"Yes, sir."

At seventeen, Sim is the oldest child in the orphanage. He's shy and sweet, and Allen often singles him out for abuse.

"When was Stonehenge founded, Mr. Harrow, and by whom?"

I hold my breath, hoping he has the correct answer, but I needn't have worried. Sim clears his throat and recites with the skill of a seasoned thespian. "Eighteen fifty-nine, sir. Welsh immigrants camped in the foothills outside town, near a double circle of stones with lintels on top. Almost identical to the Stonehenge in England."

"Yes," Mr. Allen replies. "And what became of those immigrants?"

"They found gold, the biggest strike in Colorado."

"That will be all, Harrow," Mr. Allen says. "You there, Proctor. On your feet."

The child rises from his desk slowly. He is a new addition to the orphanage and possesses a terrible stutter. His fear has a sharp, vinegar-like odor and makes me feel ill. According to Sim, Proctor never knows the answers and spends most dinner breaks sitting on a stool with a dunce cap on his head. I'll sponsor the lad's extra tutoring, but how can I prevent Allen from embarrassing him today? A hamper sits on the floor to my right, filled with freshly baked rolls. I pick it up, having no better plan in mind, and rise to my feet, just as Allen reaches Proctor.

"Is there something you need?" Allen draws out each word as though I am the thickest person in the room.

His students titter as I shake my head, step forward, and hand him the basket. Allen sighs with impatience and puts it down. On a desk? A chair? I'm not certain.

"Will that be all? May I continue now, Miss Grayson?"

Not if I can help it.

Using my cane as a guide, I distract Allen from asking Proctor questions by wandering around the room. Allen thinks I am an imbecile and talks to me slowly, with simple words. He tries to guide me back to my seat several times, but I intentionally turn the wrong way at the last moment. The children laugh as I dodge their teacher once again and soon the noon bell rings.

Something lands with a clack at the front of the room, and I jump at the sound. Cordelia touches my arm, whispering, "Just Mr. Allen tossing his ruler to the desk. No need for concern, miss."

The bread basket creaks when the teacher grabs it. "I really should chide Miss Grayson for spoiling you with extra food. Perhaps I will forbid it in future, but as it is mealtime, we will adjourn for our repast."

I keep my face neutral as he threatens his students. Allen won't forbid anything edible—not if he gets a share. The linen tea towel is removed from the wheat buns, and the smell of yeast and sweet butter fills the air. Allen takes some buns for himself from the basket, gives the rest to Cordelia, and vacates the classroom.

We must steal the dunce cap while the coast is clear. And that hateful ruler as well.

The children form a line, whispering to each other about the food. Cordie gives each of them a slice of cheddar, a large bun and a dollop of strawberry preserves. I am thanked often. Twenty-seven times to be exact. They finish the rolls at their desks and then leave for the dining hall and the thin cup of beef broth the orphanage provides. I have Cordelia rewrap the remaining bread in the linen cloth and put it on Mr. Allen's table.

Hopefully, he won't notice the missing ruler and dunce cap.

Willard Little Hawk carries our empty baskets out to the wagon and Cordie and I follow him as far as the door. I am about to step outside when Sim Harrow touches my shoulder. He helps in the kitchens at the orphanage and smells like the broth they eat for dinner. "That sure hit the spot, miss. We never know what you'll bring, but it's always tasty."

I accept his appreciation with a smile. In a few months, he'll be too old for this place and will have to fend for himself. I can't imagine a bright mind like his being wasted at the button factory.

Schedule new project, I remind myself. Find quality employment for Simmons Harrow.

Willard returns and ushers Cordie and me out to the buckboard. It isn't a big rig, but sizable enough to pick up some crates of chickens at Hollister's Mercantile. Cordelia and I sit on the bench seat next to Willard as he drives down High Street, amid clatter and dust. We pull around behind the store, and our horse Jem comes to a stop. Willard jerks the brake lever into place, then flips the reins around the hitching post before going inside.

A special corner in my heart is reserved solely for Hollister's. I met Tom Craddock here. He was seven and I a year younger. Tom pulled my braid, asking if I wanted a piece of the toffee he had just bought. I replied in my head, *Of course I do, silly boy!* and he told me not to be rude. He's been hearing my thoughts ever since.

Cordelia pokes through her reticule. "I need some new ribbon and thread."

I nod, thoughts of love and destiny still warming my insides.

"And you're coming with me," she adds.

There are people within the store whom I don't especially like. I hear them chatting away near the bolts of fabric, and I would rather not deal with unkind townswomen today. I shake my head and yawn at Cordelia. She takes the hint, lickety-split, and climbs down from the wagon.

"All right. We'll do it your way, Miss Hester. I know I'll regret this, but I don't have the energy to fight you at the moment. I've a raging headache after listening to Mr. Allen all morning." Cordie leans in and lowers her voice. "Don't even *think* of leaving this bench. Or I swear before the Almighty, I will quit this very hour if you hare off again."

Now that's just throwing down the gauntlet.

Surely Cordie must know me well enough to foresee the effect of her words. I never met an ultimatum I didn't want to defy. But I decide to honor her wishes as I listen to my companion stomp toward the mercantile. I wouldn't want her to quit this hour or any other. She's the loveable sort, despite her pushy tendencies, and most days I almost forget that she's paid to be my friend.

Alone now, I stretch and listen to the surrounding streets. A few people are wandering about, no one too close. A catnap seems just the thing, like the ultimate indulgence. So I lean back, tilt my bonnet over my face, and concentrate on dozing. For all of five minutes. Sunlight engulfs my body, and I feel energized rather than fatigued.

Willard exits Hollister's with a crate of noisy poultry, causing our horse to yank against his tether. He's a gentle old love, the noblest of animals. Yet squawking hens can have a negative effect on equines, even a fine Welsh cob like Jem. Willard deposits the birds into the back of the wagon and returns to the mercantile for another brood.

A few minutes pass, then someone—sounds like a man— walks the length of the sidewalk outside Hollister's, directly to our hitching post. He does something with the reins. Slowly, quietly. Alarmed by his secretive manner, I shove my bonnet back into place and sit up. I smell strong emotion now and shrink from it. Blood. Hatred. Whoever stands at Jem's head is filled with the unholy passion.

Out of the wagon, Hester. Find help.

Before I can move, the reins are dropped and the brake lever released, followed by a brutal snap of a whip. Poor Jem takes off in a panic. I grasp the iron railing that runs along the bench and slide over to the driver's side. Everything is so loud it's difficult to think.

Be calm. Get Jem under control. The wagon pitches forward, and I'm almost tossed off. *Deus miserare.* That was close. Taking a deep breath, holding the railing for dear life, I squat down on the boards where Willard's feet rest when he's driving the wagon. Dirt and pebbles from Jem's hooves fly into my face. Calmness, be damned. Get those bloody reins, you fool! Slow the horse down! I run my free hand around the boards, but there is nothing. Then the vehicle slams to the left, and my body flips back up to the bench seat. I lie across it now, stomach down, feet hanging over the side of the wagon. How can I save myself? *O di immortales.*

The chickens in the wagon bed squawk an octave higher, and my eardrums feel as though they will burst. This situation would almost be comical. Except for the fact I'm in mortal danger and a threat to the pedestrians in my path. All the escape artist skills in the world won't help me here.

Is this my day to die? Does Sir Death wait for me just ahead?

I turn on my right side and draw my knees toward my chest. My feet no longer dangle in mid-air. As I sit up on the bench, we round the corner on two wheels and tear across High Street. Poor Jem is completely out of control and crazed with fear, the froth from his mouth flying back and hitting my cheek. People scream at me, as though I'm capable of fixing things. Children cry out in alarm.

If I survive, I will never live this down. Witnesses will tell and retell this tale forever.

The wagon swings wide, nearly turning over, and Jem jumps an obstacle in the road. I hear him crash against something and scream in pain. The crate of chickens topples out, and my head strikes the metal railing.

Blast it all but that hurt...

———— • ————

I must have lost consciousness, for how long, I'm unsure, but when my wits return, a horse and rider are bringing my wagon to a stop.

Curses! My top lip burns like hellfire. I spit the blood from my mouth and hear Jem swing his head, agitated and restless. His breathing is erratic, punctuated with shrill braying. I turn my hearing down while tears form in my eyes. Dear Jem. He must be in a world of pain with all that carrying-on. What can I do for him?

The rider dismounts and strides over to me. "Are you all right, madam?"

Slumped over the bench seat, I lift my aching head and nod once.

"Good," he says, touching my shoulder lightly. "I'll be right back. Don't move."

Don't move? But I must help Jem. Do I know this man?

It feels as though I've barely sat up when my rescuer returns. "Your horse needs to be put down," the low voice murmurs. "His front leg is nearly severed, and he has deep lacerations on his belly. I'm sorry, madam, but it should be done now. It's the merciful thing."

This news breaks my heart, for Jem has been my friend for many years. Even before Cordelia came, when I had no one else. Covering my face with my hands, I listen as the man leads his horse away. He returns to the wagon, unhitches Jem, and moves between the cob and myself.

I wish I could pet Jem or rest my head against his neck, as I have done so often. Smell that dusty hay and horseflesh combination. There, there, old dear, I'd tell him. I'm so sorry. You're a grand boy, and I'll always love you.

The stranger cocks his weapon and a shot rings out, shattering the air. Sound waves strike my ears, and Jem grunts briefly. His heavy body settles upon the earth. Oh, Jem. Farewell.

Dizzy, brain throbbing. Everything turns upside down again.

I resurface amid bits of conversation.

"You there, transport the remains of the horse. It's blocking the street." This person speaks with an official, constable-like tone. It's probably Wilkins-the-Younger—he comes from a long line of policemen.

Another person steps forward. "Did she strike the poor beast with this whip?" He rounds his vowels excessively and sounds so condemning that I wince. Must be Judge Phelan. He hangs everybody whether they're guilty or not.

"Miss Hester would never do that!" Cordelia replies.

Thank you, dear companion. That calls for a raise. And please don't quit. This wasn't my fault.

"There's a fresh lash on his back, I tell you!" the judge exclaims. He must be hoping to impress his constituents. It's an election year.

I shake my head gently, and sit up as Wilkins disperses the crowd. "Go home everybody. Clear out—"

The wood under my hand is rough. Where am I? How did I get here? The world spins like a top, and strong hands catch me, urge me back. Someone solid is sitting so close I can feel his warmth. In fact, I am lying across his thigh. He tilts my chin up and curses when I slap his hand.

"Stop struggling. Let me help."

It's the voice of the calm, reassuring man from before, the champion who saved me. Only now he sounds a bit peeved, and he's pulling off my spectacles.

This action dispels my hazy stupor. Nobody, but nobody, touches my glasses unless we've been introduced at the very least. I slap his hand again.

"I'm a doctor, Miss Grayson," he says. "I need to examine your injuries." Now he's at my spectacles again, this time successfully removing them. "The name's Kelly. Just arrived in town today."

Vulnerable, and therefore supremely put out, I gesture for the spectacles. Dr. Kelly returns my glasses, laughing softly. Even though this man has shot my horse and sworn at me, I do like his laugh. It's a smoky, whiskey-flavored sound.

"Where's your home?"

Raising my eyebrows, I gesture at my throat, implying that I cannot talk. And that he is a dunce. And quite probably medically incompetent.

Again, that smooth, dark laugh. "So you're mute as well as blind."

I clap and point at my nose.

"Right on the proboscis, eh?" Kelly checks my limbs for broken bones while he talks. "Let it never be said that you're uncommunicative. I'd rank your scowl with the best of them."

Cordelia joins us, climbing into the wagon bed, and sitting between the good doctor and I. Truly, it's rather crowded now.

"I'm so glad you're alive, Miss Hester." She puts her hand on my arm, turning me for a closer inspection. "You look horrible! Does your face hurt?"

What a ridiculous question. Of course it does.

Someone ambles over to the wagon and spits in the dirt. I know this man. He smells of chewing tobacco and sagebrush. "Yep, White Hair," Willard Little Hawk says. "You were born lucky, all right."

Dr. Kelly snaps his bag shut. "She'll be fine. Miss Grayson has a very hard skull."

He jumps off the wagon and walks south. His horse whinnies happily as the doctor approaches. Cordie immediately begins grooming me—wiping at something on my nose, fixing my hair, pulling my skirt into place. It has been a long, frightening afternoon, and my nerves can't tolerate much more. I think I'm being reasonable when I shove her away and stand on wobbling legs, ready to climb down from the wagon and walk home if necessary.

"You're a mess," Cordie whispers, brushing at my sleeve. "That Kelly's one fine-looking man, though."

I'm a mess? A mess? Doctor Kelly can bloody well—

These thoughts have barely formed when the man in question rides up alongside the wagon and grabs me.

6

Urbanus et instructus.
A gentleman and a scholar.

There are no words. No words even in my mind. I am so shocked by the indignity of being hauled out of the wagon like a sack of flour that I can't even think of what to call Kelly.

"Your friend Little Hawk told me where you live. Let's get you there, Miss Grayson."

We ride along with me sitting in front of the doctor, sidesaddle, with the pommel digging into my leg. Blasted uncomfortable. But Kelly cradles me with his free arm against the worst of the galloping motion, and my cheek rests against his chest. I haven't had any visions during this ordeal, even with the doctor's probing. Unusual. Must be the bump on my head.

The minutes drag by until we reach my family's estate. The manor house is called The Revels, which is incongruous since I have never heard the slightest bit of revelry taking place there.

Dr. Kelly speaks with a footman, telling him to notify my mother that we have arrived. From Mama's gasp, I'd say she's flummoxed. The doctor introduces himself, and describes the wagon accident in a matter-of-fact manner.

He hands me over to a stable groom, climbs down from his horse, and then takes me back in his arms again. It's similar to a slow game of hot potato, with me as the traveling spud. We proceed through the porte-cochere like incognito royalty, and Mama leads our entourage—housekeeper, butler, valet, cook— and Dr. Kelly and I to the second floor. I've always wondered what it would be like to be swept off my feet and carried to my boudoir by a gentleman. It's not at all as I'd imagined. The staircase is steep and long, and although Dr. Kelly does not sound out of breath, I'm sure he's regretting that he didn't just leave me with the stable groom.

Mama opens my bedroom door, and the entourage enters, Dr. Kelly and I bringing up the rear. He puts me down gently upon the mattress, and pushes me prone, taking off my glasses again without permission. Damnation, they don't belong to you. Give them back.

The doctor does nothing of the kind. Rather he clears the room of all bystanders except for my mother. Then Kelly unbuttons the collar of my dress and feels the pulse at my throat, the forward fellow. "Any nausea?" he asks.

I shake my head, causing it new pain, and hear the dreaded rattling in my mother's pocket. She sets the bottle and spoon on the nightstand.

Please, no laudanum. I'm not strong enough to wrestle with you and Cordelia now.

"What medicine is this?" Dr. Kelly asks Mama.

"The elixir of the poppy. It helps Hester to rest."

I hear the doctor pick up the bottle and uncork it. A moment later he puts the stopper back in. "I'll take this laudanum with me," he says. "It's the last thing your daughter needs. She must remain awake for a few hours, to ensure that her concussion is not worse than I suspect."

Much obliged, Kelly. I take back all the bad things I thought about you earlier.

"What if we require the laudanum at another time?" my mother asks.

"All your daughter *requires* is nourishing food and kind company. The repeated use of narcotics can lead to addiction."

Cordelia's footsteps hustle along the hallway. Willard must have borrowed a rig in town to bring her home. She opens the bedroom door and enters, quietly listening as the doctor gives further instructions for my care. He sends for water and clean towels and bathes my facial wounds—the broken skin on my forehead, the raw cheekbone and split lip. It is an odd, humbling situation for me, but the doctor has a soft touch. Checking his handiwork, Kelly leans over me again, cupping the side of my jaw in his hand.

Brightness and color explode within my head. Vignettes, not like a full-length vision at all, but a mental scrapbook of sorts. This kind of thing is rare for me, happening only a handful of times that I can remember. A flash of discernment without any scenes of death or crime. In theory, the revelation is supposed to help me understand people better, but I do not always know how to use the information I receive. And it can be quite disconcerting, to witness so much of another's life.

I can barely keep up with the vision, the images change so fast. A child plays at the seashore. He is golden-haired with heavily-lashed, hazel eyes and a faint cleft in his chin. A woman watches from a distance and calls him Noah, telling him to get out of the waves. The next scene shows an older version of the child—nine or ten, perhaps?—standing on the stoop of a brownstone with a toddler in his arms. Two people argue inside the building behind him; the man throws furniture about and the woman screams. Now Noah is a youth, at least five years older than the boy outside the brownstone. He runs through the night with a gang of hoodlums. They break the glass of a shop window, steal the jewelry on display inside, and flee. Except Noah is caught by a man wearing a top hat and carrying a doctor's satchel.

The last picture shows Noah Kelly at his graduation from medical school. Seated on a stage, he looks over the audience at the commencement exercises as though he is searching for someone, anticipating, a muscle working in his jaw. The strong, clean lines of his face are mature now, having finally achieved their full promise of rugged beauty. A stylish brunette waves at him from the crowd, holding an infant on her lap. Seeing them at last, the new physician smiles and waves back.

"You'll feel better soon, Miss Grayson," Kelly says, his deep voice sweeping into the vision and returning me to the present time. "I'll follow up with you tomorrow."

My cheeks bloom with heat, and I feel contrite, as though I've seen him bare, body and soul. After a few more words, he bids us farewell and leaves. Mama begins to give Cordelia instructions. Do not excite Miss Hester, see that she rests … I tune out their conversation and listen as a groom brings the doctor's horse to the porte-cochere. Kelly rides away, whistling the song "Oh, My Darling Clementine", and I smile inside at his choice of music. If my mother had heard it, she would have disapproved, but I like that the doctor doesn't take himself too seriously.

Mama kisses the top of my head before making her own departure, and Cordelia helps me undress. She chooses my favorite cotton nightgown—the soft, nearly-threadbare one. Bless her heart for putting my comfort before fashion.

"Shall I read to you?" she asks.

I smile with my cracked lip as Cordie takes a book from the shelf. It is most likely Mrs. Radcliffe's gothic masterpiece, *The Mysteries of Udolpho*. My companion smuggled the forbidden novel into my mother's fortress of propriety a few days ago, and it has proved gripping. I settle back against my pillow and she begins reading where we left off last time. And continues on, with only a few pauses to sip water or adjust her lap blanket, until the book reaches its conclusion. "Well, wasn't that something, Miss Hester?" she asks.

Nodding in agreement, I stifle a yawn. Despite my weariness, Udolpho was a thrilling tale which transported me outside my little world for a few hours. How I wish I could travel to far away places! Visit the Continent, the Far East, India and Africa. Even as I dream of it, I know I never will. My parents wouldn't allow me to go and neither would my magic. Stonehenge is the center of my power as a Visionary, and it sustains me in both the supernatural and physical sense. I can visit other places for a time, but I cannot remain there. If I do, I'll grow weak and eventually perish.

"How are you feeling, miss?" Cordelia asks.

She sounds worried. Does my face reflect my disappointment with the confines of life? I try to look cheerful, and it must be convincing. Cordelia decides that I am well enough to leave alone, says goodnight, and pulls the curtains around my canopy bed. The bedroom door shuts, and I listen as her footsteps turn toward the servant's quarters.

Snuggling under the satin duvet, I close my eyes, but sleep does not come. I toss and turn as the wagon accident repeats itself in my mind. Should I contact Tom? Would he mind the interruption at this time of night? I had planned to tell him tomorrow since he is likely asleep, but my reserves of pluckiness and strength are tapped out. I sit up and send Tom a message of yearning, pour my heart into each word. I share with him how scared I was in that wagon, express my sadness over losing Jem. He answers immediately with warmth and concern. We remain in this suspended state of mental togetherness, until Tom begins thinking rationally. He has me describe my experience again. The questions sound casual yet I know he is upset.

The horse was given a lash? You're certain of it?

Miles away in my bedroom, I nod, as though Tom is there with me. *Yes, just before Jem bolted. Was it a practical joke run amuck, do you think?*

Someone struck the horse and threw the whip back into the wagon, making it look as though you'd hurt the animal yourself. Nothing funny about that, Hettie. You might have been killed, as well as a score of other innocent people.

At Tom's request, I make a list of those who might want me dead. It's a miserable, horrible thing to do, but I begin with the obvious candidate. He who wishes I had never been born and has said so on several occasions.

My father.

It didn't sound like him walking toward the wagon. The emotion smelled different, more intense. As if it were usually contained and had suddenly broken free. Besides, Father doesn't hide his feelings. His distaste for me is obvious.

I'm sorry, love. John Grayson's a rotten, money-grubbing scoundrel. Just say the word, and I'll give him the trouncing he deserves.

No! No trouncing's needed at present. It can't be Father, anyway. He plans out every possible outcome. This was too spur-of-the-moment for him.

Tom's thoughts are a tapestry of frustration and fear. *What about our killer from the Halloween vision? He might have tracked you down, thinking you know the truth about him.*

I grab a pillow and hug it tightly against my chest. *Mary Arden warned me of danger, too. Let's not forget the heir of Archimendax.*

You communicated with the woman telepathically before. Why not try it again? Ask her about him. His identity, to begin with…

I doubt it will work, Tom, but I'll try.

Inhaling slowly, I listen to the beating of my heart. I reach out, calling her name with my psyche. *Mary Arden. Mary Arden…* Yet I hear nothing. Clairvoyant patterns are unique, and it's difficult to connect with a virtual stranger, like taking a handful of sand and searching for a specific grain. Unless there's an intrinsic bond, like Tom and I share—then it's as easy as breathing. The crazy witch woman and I do not have such an attachment, however.

Sorry. I'm not getting her.

How did it work before, love?

My exchange with Mary Arden plays through my mind again, leaving an unpleasant residue. *I think she used Compulsion.*

You're sure, Hettie? Forbidden gifts?

As sure as I can be.

All right then. We'll have to find old Mary's place in the woods. Until I locate her, stay inside, no more taking off on your own. Be cautious, for once.

I bristle at his reprimand. Why does everyone in my life imagine they can tell me what to do?

Fine, Tom. I'll do it if you insist, but boredom makes me grumpy.

Better grumpy than dead, love. I'll come to you tomorrow. See for myself that you're recovering.

I wish you could, but I expect Mama will hang about. And the new doctor is scheduled to visit.

Suddenly, I feel as though I cannot endure another moment of wakefulness. Sensing my fatigue, Tom fades away fast, but calls to me once more.

Be careful, heart of mine. Be safe.

7

Luctor et emergo.
I struggle and I survive.

It is early evening of the next day when Dr. Kelly returns. Cordelia has been my only source of entertainment, since Mama hasn't allowed me to leave my suite of rooms. We are now halfway finished with *A Sicilian Romance*, another of Mrs. Radcliffe's novels. The oldest child of two teachers, Cordie is well-educated, and her voice is smooth and expressive. Even so, my body is aquiver with untapped energy, and I fantasize as she reads, of escaping through my window and climbing to the ground on the thick vines girding the trellis.

If not that route, surely I could manage something.

Cordelia has just poured me a cup of Earl Grey when the doctor walks into my bedroom. The scent of fir trees, wet wool, and saddle leather clings to him. Kelly is literally a breath of fresh air.

He checks me over, asks pertinent questions, and decides I am shoring up nicely. Cordie fetches my mother, and she is delighted with the good news. Mama stays but a moment since my father is going over her household accounts in the study on the main floor. This is just a formality. My mother is an East-Coast heiress and has plenty of her own money—she doesn't drain his reserves in the least. Sounding impulsive, Mama invites Dr. Kelly to supper tomorrow.

"I would be delighted, madam," he replies. "Especially if Miss Grayson joins us. She's looking better every second."

Not a family meal. *Anything* but that.

Mama hems and haws and tries to avoid confirming my attendance while still encouraging the doctor to come. My father sends the butler to find Mama, and she leaves in a rush—after agreeing to Kelly's request.

Brimstone and hell-fire! Now I'll have to go.

Kelly wanders around my room snooping, as though he has nothing better to do with his time, and picks up one of the books Cordelia has been reading to me. "You're a fan of romance novels? I'm shocked by this, Miss Grayson. Absolutely scandalized." The doctor chuckles at his own teasing, replaces the volume, and continues to investigate the shelves. "Ah, but here's Jane Austen to balance things out. Bronte, Longfellow. And my old friend, Lord Tennyson. An excellent choice."

"'One equal temper of heroic hearts,'" he recites. "'Made weak by time and fate but strong in will ...'"

To strive, to seek, to find, and not to yield. Take that, Kelly, and—

I stop mid-insult when he asks, "Have you heard of Braille, Miss Grayson? It can help you to read these books for yourself."

Braille? What in blazes is that? Crossing my arms, I feel awkward standing there, still in my nightclothes. I shrug, having never given actual reading much thought. Why would I? I have Cordelia.

The doctor leaves the shelves and walks directly to me. "Through Braille, the blind use their fingers and touch a series of raised dots on the page. The dots represent words. A former patient of mine in Boston reads Braille. I could ask her for advice on your situation."

Overwhelmed, I retreat a few steps, back toward the safety of Cordelia. The doctor gives me no quarter and follows. "As a physician, I am duty-bound to improve your quality of life if I see a means of accomplishing it. I also feel some proprietary rights concerning you, Miss Grayson. I did save your life."

Guilt rears its ugly head. Without Dr. Kelly's heroic actions, I might well have died yesterday. I sigh and gesture toward the sitting room of my suite. We may as well be comfortable if Kelly is going to keep talking about this Braille business. Cordelia offers him a cup of tea.

"Thank you, Miss Collins, but I cannot stay," he replies. "Miss Grayson, we'll continue our discussion another time, I hope."

Kelly heads for the door and then pauses. "In future, may I have the honor of using your Christian name?"

My eyebrows rise of their own accord, but I nod, bemused by this question. No man has ever asked my permission before. Even Tom assumes things.

"Then good evening, Hester," he says, a smile in his voice. "And I'm Noah to my friends."

Twenty-four hours pass, and given that I have received no reprieve, the family meal is unavoidable. I've been bathed, doused with rose water, and powdered. Not that my skin could get much paler if popular opinion is correct.

Cordelia is working feverishly on my hair with the curling tongs. "Sit on your hands, Miss Hester," she barks like a soldier on campaign. "If you keep reaching up to your head that way, you'll get burned."

It takes forty-five more minutes, but my hair is finally done. Cordie steps away and sighs. "How striking you look! That dress, the oyster-colored silk. Just lovely."

My companion is doing double-duty tonight since Mama is between hairdressers, and she gathers her weapons of beauty and goes to check on my mother's coiffure.

"Don't move. Don't mess yourself up," she orders on her way out the door.

I fully intend to follow Cordie's advice, but it is so tedious to sit here, waiting to proceed down to the dining room. It's like passing time in a tumbrel when you know you're expected at the guillotine. I cannot stand the thought of descending the stairs under Kelly's watchful eyes. Or worse, with my father silently criticizing my every move. Better to go down now without an audience.

After slipping into a pair of elbow-length gloves, I choose my best mahogany cane, and take the stairs to the main floor.

I turn in the direction of the drawing room, but a rider gallops up the drive and stops at the front entrance of the house. I recognize his whistle, but it isn't the Clementine song tonight. It's "Sweet Rosie O'Grady". Our butler fails to appear so I open the door and smile at Dr. Kelly. He steps in, smelling of citrus linen water and newly ironed cotton.

"You do clean up nicely, Hester," he says, taking my hand and kissing my gloved knuckles as though I were a fine lady.

My face feels ten shades of red, but he continues chatting away. Even a novice can tell that Dr. Kelly is good with women. It does not stretch the imagination to suppose he has conquered more than his share of hearts.

Cane in hand, I lead Kelly to the drawing room. I hear him remove his overcoat and drape it across the sofa. The doctor admires the piano, fiddling around with the keys before breaking into a sprightly rendition of John Phillip Sousa's "Semper Fidelis". What in the world? I wasn't expecting this martial tune. For the hundredth time, I wish I could laugh. Instead, I grin until the sides of my face hurt.

My parents join us as the last note hangs in the air. Then there is an awkward period of silence. Kelly seems to have surprised them as well with his choice of music, but Mama recovers quickly and welcomes him with a flourish of friendly words. "You have real talent, Doctor. One doesn't usually hear marches performed on a Steinway. And a hero, too. I shall never forget the sight of you carrying my daughter into this house."

Kelly dismisses the praise, claiming that any able-bodied man would have done the same.

"Surely you know Hester is mute," my mother says, as though I'm not standing between them. "She won't contribute much to the evening's conversation, although she did talk as a child. Quite faintly, due to flawed vocal cords, but then illness struck and robbed her of what little voice she had."

This is precisely the scenario that I wished to avoid. Let me crawl under a rock. Or better yet, return to my room.

Kelly intervenes, however. "Words are not always necessary, ma'am. Hester and I communicate just fine without them."

"How kind of you," Mama says. "And forgive me for not inquiring before. Is there a *Mrs.* Kelly?"

"Not any longer. I'm happily divorced."

"Why happily, if I may ask? Most men would never admit to such a thing in mixed company."

"Then I must beg your pardon, good lady, but the institution of marriage holds no appeal for me. Although I am grateful my former wife and I had our Alice. My daughter makes the entire experience worthwhile."

This shuts my mother up. She expected something superficial, nothing so vulgar as an honest answer.

My father clears his throat and suggests that we make our way to the dining room. Kelly moves to my left, the opposite side of my cane, and tucks my hand into the crook of his arm. Father leads our group down the hall. The ice in his drink jangles against the glass as we walk.

"Where do you hail from, Doctor?" he asks.

"Massachusetts, sir."

"And who are your people? Have we heard of them?"

Kelly's arm flexes under my glove, but he otherwise seems unruffled. "My heritage, do you mean, Mr. Grayson? My illustrious ancestors?"

Father is a chronic opportunist. It's how he's made his money. I can almost hear the machinery at work in his brain—hoping to take advantage of this new connection if there is a profit to be made from it. "Exactly so," he says. "They must be an impressive group."

"No, Mr. Grayson. I'm a mongrel. We think granddad was partly Irish, having the last name Kelly and all. Still, no one is entirely sure as he was born on the wrong side of the blanket."

And *that* shuts my father up. He downs his drink in one swallow and walks ahead with Mama. Nicely done, Kelly!

I'm having a hell of a time keeping a straight face. This is the best family dinner I've ever attended. The doctor leans my way. "What?" he whispers, all innocence. "Did I say something amiss?"

Very amiss, and he knows it.

"Sorry, but I couldn't help myself. As the saying goes, you can take the boy out of the gutter but you can't entirely take the gutter out of the boy."

Kelly pats my arm as we walk. "You find me amusing then? You're enjoying my social disgrace?"

I nod without a bit of hesitation, and he laughs lightly. "As you should, dear girl. God's made your face for smiling."

The doctor slows the pace as we turn a corner, making sure that I manage it smoothly. "I know whereof I speak, Hester. I've learned something about those smiles over the course of our brief acquaintance. There is the polite, impersonal one, and the smirk that says *I-know-more-than-you-do*. I've seen both of them a number of times. But tonight you are mysterious, like Leonardo's *Mona Lisa*. I am lucky, am I not? For what man does not enjoy variety?"

My, my. I had not taken the full measure of Kelly's magnetism. He is a danger to the average female.

Fortunately, I'm not average.

After reaching the dining room, Father takes his seat at the head of the table. Mama and I sit on the opposite end and Kelly is stationed in the middle. The servants deliver a fragrant bowl of soup to each of us. Tangy, peppery steam rises to my face, and my stomach rumbles with nerves rather than appetite. Mama scoots her chair close to mine, the sound making me tremble. This is what I've dreaded most. Kelly may never think well of me again after witnessing my humiliation.

I listen as she scoops up a spoonful of soup, blowing on it several times. No, please don't make me do this. Not in front of the doctor.

But I am nothing if not well trained. I open my mouth and Mama slips the spoon inside. I normally would enjoy the creamy duck bisque, but it sours on my tongue. We repeat the procedure until the soup is gone. My mother then gives me a drink of water before turning to her own bowl.

For as long as I can remember, we have followed this procedure while dining formally. I can skirt around most household rules, if I am circumspect, but Mama doesn't budge here.

Dr. Kelly is quiet as a stone, but I know he's watching me. Tears of embarrassment fill my eyes, and I blink them away, thankful for the barrier of my spectacles.

Things deteriorate further as Mama cuts my meat, carrots, and potatoes. She gives me generous portions of all three until I shake my head, the signal that I am finished. Throughout the meal, talk has been meager at best, until Kelly asks what he must have been wondering all along.

"Why must you feed Hester, Mrs. Grayson? Why not allow her to do it for herself?"

"It is unseemly for a young woman to fumble about her plate, searching for nourishment." The chill in Mama's voice could freeze the blood of most men.

Kelly does not back down. "Improvement comes with practice, madam. Everyone should feel capable in their own right."

My mother doesn't back down either. "Hester need not be subjected to such experimentation while I am here to help."

"I see." He clicks his utensil on the plate once and mercifully, says nothing more.

Somehow we survive dessert, but Kelly is not invited to linger over port or coffee. My parents bid him adieu and then retire to their private salon, leaving me to show him out. Most young ladies of a marriageable age, such as I, would not be left alone with a bachelor of little acquaintance. However, I do not think that my parents consider my virtue tempting enough to the opposite sex to worry about protecting it.

Adding to my embarrassment, the butler has gone missing again. Kelly's coat is still draped over the drawing room sofa, and he shrugs into the garment without assistance. I feel my cheeks flame as I open the front door and curtsy for him. He doesn't say a word, doesn't move an inch to leave my home. I pivot toward the stairs, but Kelly's there before me.

"One question, Hester, if I may, and then I'll go." His whiskey-voice is low and serious. "Would you have tea with me in town on Wednesday?"

Does he jest? Scalding drinks in china cups with fairy cakes and cucumber sandwiches? Everyone in Stonehenge would be abuzz over it.

"Please say you will. It would be an honor to escort you."

I hesitate long enough that he feels the need to explain. "I have a sister who is dear to me. I left her at home with my parents when I went off to medical school, and I've always regretted it. Rachel has bloomed in the years since, but she was quite lonely then." Kelly clears his throat. "Such a waste, loneliness, and so easily avoided. Add another person to the scenario and you've got it beat."

Simple words, so genuinely spoken that I cannot refuse. Haven't I wished to be treated like other girls my age? They wouldn't fear an outing such as this. It would be a feather in their caps. I inhale, straighten my spine to its full length, and smile.

Kelly—no, rather Noah, just for this moment—squeezes my hand. "That's the spirit."

The doctor walks out into the night, whistling a merry tune, and I shake my head briefly, wondering what I have gotten myself into. Cordelia joins me, and we stand at the door together as Kelly rides away.

Ninety minutes later, I am tucked into bed, curtains drawn, telepathically sharing the details of my day with Tom. He is disgruntled, even a little bitter, and waves of jealousy transfer from him to me. *The doctor came to dinner? How cozy. I've never been invited.*

You know it's necessary for us to be discreet, and anyway, it's not like that with Noah.

You're on a first name basis?

We're friends. My mother only asked him out of gratitude.

How good a friend is he, love?

Stop being ridiculous, Tom. He's just a nice man who dined with us. You have no cause to worry.

If Tom and I weren't miles apart, I'd be tempted to box his ears. Instead, I kick a porcelain doll off my bed and hear a satisfying crunch when it hits the floor. Obviously, this isn't the time to mention that Kelly is taking me to tea.

After further reassurance, my love is finally appeased—how can such a strong, capable man be so insecure?—and then we make plans. Tomorrow, I will steal away at midnight, after Cordie has gone to sleep. He will come to the French doors in the library and wait for me there.

Once we disconnect, I fall into a dreamless sleep, and my world is fairly peaceful when I awake.

Until Mama makes her announcement.

8

Mirabile!
A marvelous thing!

“I am with child,” Mama says, sounding delighted. “Can you believe it, Hester? Over four months gone.”

Quite frankly, I can’t. She has had so many miscarriages over the years that I thought the childbearing season had passed her by. And being my parent’s child isn’t easy. I’m not sure I’d wish the experience upon another. Still, this little person will not be alone. I’ll help and protect him or her—assist in any way I can.

The more I think of this baby, the tighter my heart feels, as though there isn’t room enough for all the emotion. Hang it, I’ll call the little one Cherub. Gender-identification will be unnecessary, and I won’t have to resort to using “it”—a horrible term for an unborn child.

“Are you unhappy?” Mama asks, mistaking my thoughtfulness for dismay.

I shake my head and smile.

I cannot remember a nicer day in my household. It goes without saying that Father is away. He's at his club or business office or somewhere. Mama is feeling tired so she rests in her boudoir and invites me to sit at her side as Cordie reads the *Ladies' Home Journal* aloud. My mother laughs at the humorous articles and interrupts the more serious ones to discuss plans for Cherub's new nursery and wardrobe.

I finally understand about families—why they enjoy spending time together. It has taken me two decades to grasp the meaning of this bond.

At supper, I shoo Cordelia out of my bedroom so she might enjoy a meal with her friends in the kitchen. I tuck a large square napkin into the collar of my gown, and run my fingertips over the tray. Now to practice for Wednesday's excursion. There's a round plate flanked by a set of utensils. Fork on the left—knife and spoon the right. A ceramic mug containing buttermilk sits three inches above. I spill half my drink when I bump it with my wrist, but it's no great loss since I dislike buttermilk.

The entrée smells like poached chicken. No herbs or sauces, just a bland, rubbery thigh if this meal follows my usual menu. I touch the sides of the plate and find servings of rice and peas. Scooping at them with my spoon, I feel like I'm playing a game of chase. The peas bounce off the plate and the rice drops everywhere when I try to eat it. My stomach rumbles, and I stab at the chicken thigh. Hacking at the meat with the side of my fork, I cut off large wedges. I chew the chicken as quietly as possible, but it is hopeless with the size of the bites. Mama and Cordelia both would be appalled and rightly so. All things considered, supper is a failure. An especially messy one with my lap covered by rice and peas.

Thunderation. How will my clothes survive? I won't have the blasted napkin tucked into my collar when I'm at tea with Kelly. A frisson of excitement runs through me as I think of the outing—my first real meal taken in town. I have two more days to practice feeding myself. Forty-eight whole hours to ensure that this basic skill is second nature.

Won't Mama be surprised if I succeed?

———————•———————

It is almost midnight, and Cordelia is snoring like a banshee in the room next to mine. I worry for her nasal cavity. How does it hold up under the strain? Tom pushed me to have her move closer, as a protective measure. Everyone else in the house is asleep as well, except for the cook and the butler. They're being rather amorous behind closed doors in the servant's wing.

Well, at least the case of the missing butler has been solved.

I wear a wool gown and a heavy, hooded cloak to ward off the evening chill. Stepping as lightly as I can, I cross the library, carrying my cane under my arm. I pause at the French doors, and check one last time for any suspicious noises, but there are none.

Everything safe, love? Do you need my help?

No. Be there in a moment, Tom.

Once I am outside, I close the door, and turn to find him a few feet away. We embrace briefly and then walk to where he tied his horse in the orchard. Tom helps me step up onto a tree stump.

"We'll use it like a mounting block," he says aloud. "So it's easier for you to get on the horse."

He guides the animal over to where I stand on the stump. I pat the horse gently, missing my own poor Jem.

I don't think I've ridden this one before. Is it a he or a she?

"Technically a he. Dad bought some geldings at auction a few months ago."

I rest my hands on Tom's shoulders, enjoying my increased height while standing on the stump. We must be nearly eye to eye. *Would you please use telepathy? You know the clairvoyant rules.*

Sorry, love. I always forget them.

Yes, you do. What's his name?

Whose name?

The horse, Tom.

He laughs softly. *It's Banquo.*

Pulling some sugar cubes out of my pocket, I turn to Banquo and offer him the treat. The horse blows on my hand, his breath warm and moist. He eats the sugar and brushes my palms with his smooth, nibbling lips. Nice fellow. That's right. Tom trains his equines well, and this one is no exception. Banquo stands quietly as I take hold of his mane and swing my leg upwards onto his back. Tom gives my backside a boost until I'm sitting astride. No saddle for us tonight. I push my skirt down to cover my knees, and Tom hops up behind me.

He makes a clicking sound and the horse begins to walk. Tom's arms encircle me as he holds the reins. We're a good ways from the estate when we break into a gallop. I can't imagine anything more thrilling than this. I am speeding through the wind, arms outstretched, cloak flapping. Free of spectacles and stays, I might add. My hair is undone, flying out behind me.

And into poor Tom's face. He grabs some of my tresses, holding them with one of his fists. When I think up something especially mischievous, Tom laughs and gives my hair a slight yank. I do not know our destination, but the journey itself is pure joy.

The ground grows steep, and Tom directs his gelding to the right to avoid sliding backwards. Cool, damp air. Night creatures in the distance. Mountain sage.

Where are we going?

Stonehenge, love.

To town?

No. The rocks.

Why?

I prod him a few more times. Tom applies gentle pressure to my hair until the back of my head rests against his chest. I tilt my face up, and he kisses me.

Patience, Hettie. You've heard of that, haven't you? In theory at least?

Smiling, I relax my body, content to be held close and warm. After traveling east for a few miles, we arrive at Stonehenge, or Old Stoney, as the locals call it. I have only been here on rare occasions, and it is still relatively unknown to me.

"What a harvest moon," Tom says, as he dismounts. "The rocks glow in its light."

He helps me down, and we walk to the natural formation which many say resembles the Stonehenge in England. It sits atop a bluff and the wind sweeps down from the mountain above, blowing my hair in all directions. I shiver and pull up the hood of my cloak. Tom and I circle the area inside the ring of stones, and I create a kind of grid in my head to estimate its width and length.

Tom leaves me and goes back to the rim of the henge. I tune out the wind, kneel, and strike the ground with my hand. Vibrations spread outward, bouncing off the rocks, painting a sound picture in my head. Tom slaps the pillar closest to him and then moves on to the next one. What's he up to? I lift my face, tracking his movements as he hits each stone. What's the distance between us? Twenty-five, maybe thirty feet?

Returning to me, Tom drops something on the ground near my feet. It has a metallic rattle. I poke at it with the toe of my boot and find a rectangular case. Tom takes an object out of it, and slips a thin handle into my grasp. He guides my finger down the flat side of a blade, approximately six inches in length. The weapon is narrow and feels perfectly balanced.

A knife, Tom?

A throwing knife, love.

I cannot resist testing its sharpness. Just a little. The result is a tiny nick. It barely stings but Tom puts the tip of my finger to his mouth, sucks the blood away. Then he checks the scratch over and drops my hand.

Must you always touch things, Hettie?

You know I'm the curious sort. Why the knife?

I want you to learn to defend yourself.

Tom takes the weapon back, slides it into something. A sheath probably. He puts it into my hands, and I run my fingers over sleek leather. Two other knives are stored inside the sheath. Tom presses the attached straps and buckles into my palm.

Lady's boots aren't high enough to conceal this. You strap it on your thigh. Where it won't slip on the stockings.

How does one begin to respond to such a gift?

My love kneels down, and I hear a scratch, a flare, and then smell the faintest whiff of sulfur. It's a Lucifer being lit. Metal clanks and glass rattles. Must be the old bulls-eye lamp that usually hangs in the Craddock barn. How did it get up here? Did

Tom prepare this location ahead of time? I suppose that's romantic. In a way...

He switches out of telepathy. "I'll take those weapons, if you please." Tom puts the knives away and like a magician, returns with another trick up his sleeve. He hands me a cloth bag, tied at the top. The surprises just keep coming—I'm afraid to ask what's inside.

Tom loosens the top of the bag. "I know a group of seamstresses. They gather at the farm next to ours a few times a month, and I repair their scissors, sharpen them when they get dull. These are spare sets that I've taken apart."

And what do these women look like?

His gravelly-sounding laugh does things to my body chemistry. "Farmer's daughters, you know. Buxom, bonny wenches."

Buxom?

"Oh, yes, and grandmothers several times over. The youngest is sixty." Tom puts half a pair of scissors in my hand. "They pay me with pie, you goose. Though they have hinted at introducing me to a granddaughter or two."

Don't you dare!

Taking me by the shoulders, he spins me around. "Which way are you facing?"

North.

"Spot on. You're as good as a compass. Now let's have you practice throwing a bit before we use actual knives. Aim for the place where I slap the stones. That'll be the killer's heart."

I shake my head, disliking the thought of hurting anyone. *But I don't want—*

"It doesn't matter what you want right now," Tom says, interrupting the pattern of my thoughts. "An attempt was made on your life. Was it the murderer from the Halloween vision? Or the heir of Archimendax? Can't say as yet. But we need to surprise whoever's after you, and make them bleed first."

His serious manner dampens my mood, and I feel cold despite the cloak. Tom rubs my arms and sets me away from him. Then he teaches me a throwing technique where I begin with most of my weight resting on my back foot, until I bring the shear up and throw it while shifting the balance to my front foot. We discuss follow-through and blade rotation, with Tom counting off the circles the weapon makes on the way to its target.

"I'll take the lamp over to the rocks with me so I can see how precise you are. Throw the shears directly at the sound that I make."

How do you know about this kind of thing?

"I have an uncle in California. A blacksmith. He forges knives as a hobby, collects them, too." I hear Tom lift the lamp and walk over to the stone. "Taught me to throw when I was a lad."

Taking a few steps forward, I nearly jump out of my skin when he hits the rock. I'm not prepared at all, but I throw anyway.

"Low and wide. You've missed the baddie by two feet but the innocent fellow next to him won't be having children. Concentrate."

I do better with the next stone. I hit it at least.

"That's my girl," Tom says, laughing. "Scratched the villain's ankle."

Short. High. Plain feeble. This is how my further attempts are graded. Close. Not-even-close. Ugly. My shoulder is tired, but I rub the soreness away as Tom gathers the scissors.

"Again."

Over-heated and sweating, I remove my cloak after the next round. I throw until I can barely lift my right arm.

"You're doing famously, *vita mea*," Tom says. "They'll be calling you The Mistress of the Blade in no time."

I hate this. It's too hard.

He picks up my cloak, tucks it around my shoulders. "No. It isn't. We'll work on your left arm tomorrow and allow your right to recuperate."

There's no way I'm coming back here tomorrow. I haven't had a wink of sleep.

Tom swings up onto his horse and then reaches for me, telepathic once more. *You'll be fine after you've rested.*

Aren't you tired?

Aye, I'm weary. But the cows will need milking when I get home, and there are chores to be done. Don't worry about me.

We make the trip down the mountain and turn onto the main road. That's all I remember until I wake up some time later. Cordelia is puttering around in the next room, as though she has just risen.

I am lying in my bed wearing my chemise and drawers. No cloak. Or dress for that matter. And the green scent of alfalfa covers my skin. I suspect that Tom tossed my clothes under the bed or into the armoire. I don't know how he managed my slumbering bulk or why I'm surprised by his audacity, but this confirms what I learned years ago.

The man has magic in his hands.

9

Aliquis latet error.
Some trickery lies hidden-Virgil.

The next night is much like the one before. Tom and I meet at twelve, and ride to the mountains. I throw the scissors with my left hand until an hour or so before daybreak, and then we head home, like Romeo and Juliet after a romantic evening of weaponry.

We walk toward The Revels and Tom praises my efforts. *You're a natural attack artist, Hettie.*

He takes my hand and twirls me around. My feet get tangled, and Tom pulls me against him. We sway side to side, and it occurs to me that we're dancing. Perhaps it is my fatigue or the early hour, but this ridiculous gesture seems so sweet.

You know, Tom. Once I become the Mistress of the Blade, I could branch out and get a gun. Transform into the Countess of the Colt, the Dueling Duchess, the Baroness of Bullets.

His laughter is soft enough to be a short intake of breath. *I bow to My Lady Smith and Wesson.*

Actually, that's brilliant. How difficult can it be to shoot? I need a boot pistol immediately.

One instrument of death at a time, love. Let's not get ahead of ourselves.

Tom kisses me goodnight, and I leave him with reluctance. *You didn't take liberties when you brought me upstairs last night, did you?*

Absolutely not. I'm a country gentleman.

I squeeze his hand before entering my home via the library. Tom whispers in my mind as I close the door and lock it.

I did enjoy the lace on that chemise though. Very pretty.

This makes me smile as I tiptoe up the stairs and into my room. I can tell Cordelia is asleep, but luckily, there is no snoring. Thank heaven for small favors.

I undo the hooks at the top of my dress and slip it over my head, drop the petticoat, unlace my boots, and get into bed. I mean business now. I do not dream, or toss about. I sleep deep as the dead. Then I wake up briefly, feel the warmth of the flames in the fireplace, hear a few servants moving about the house, put a pillow over my head and doze again.

Unfortunately, Cordie must be worried that I have contracted some soporific disease for she keeps trying to roust me when I do not wish to be rousted—putting her hand on my forehead and testing for fever, calling my name again and again.

"You really must wake up, Miss Hester. It's near one o' clock. You're to meet Dr. Kelly for tea in a couple of hours. Wouldn't you like to use the water closet at least?"

Well, now that it's been mentioned…

Sitting up slowly, I stretch, then climb out of bed, use the WC, and take a rather chilly bath. Copper is not my friend when combined with cold water.

"It's your own fault," Cordie says. "The hot pails were brought in same as usual, steam floating all over the place, but Sleepyhead couldn't be bothered to bathe then."

Cordelia can be such a kind person. And then she has her Marquis de Sade moments. She's in a huff for some reason, and refuses to get me anything more substantial than a dry piece of toast.

"Breakfast was at nine. As always." My companion hustles about, getting my tea ensemble in order. "And you don't want to spoil your appetite."

Her quips continue as I get ready for my appointment, and for reasons unknown to me, I accept this reversal of power. Maybe it is penance for my assignations with Tom.

"Your escort has arrived, Miss Hester. Promptly, I might add. He knows how to follow a schedule."

And none too soon. Cordelia has almost reduced me to self-flagellation and haircloth. Dr. Kelly's voice at our front door signals a liberation devoutly to be wished. Cordie hands me my cane, makes one more swipe at the back of my velvet cloak, and follows me downstairs.

Mama has decided to overlook the awkward dinner with Kelly, letting bygones be bygones. He is unattached, has an education, and performs a valuable service within the community. Therefore, allowances for his behavior are being made. She now attributes his blunt speech not to rudeness but to a New England sensibility. Mama even visited Kelly's office and asked him to be her personal physician, given that her previous doctor retired and moved to Arizona.

She is feeling weary today, and Cordelia is remaining at home with her instead of chaperoning me at tea. My companion pulls the cloak's hood into place over my hair just before the doctor and I step outside.

Kelly takes my hand and slips it into the crook of his arm. "You look like a Dresden figurine that I saw in a shop window once—a skater named Snowflake. Everything she wore from her hat to her shoes was white. But you're all in blue, Hester. Perhaps I'll call you Violet."

I smile at this, and Kelly helps me up into his buggy, then claims the driver's seat. He throws a blanket over my legs and snaps the reins. The horse walks forward and breaks into a light trot.

"Borrowed this rig from a colleague," he says. "Speaking of which, I need to drop by the hospital on the way to tea. You don't mind waiting while I sign a few documents, do you?"

I nod in agreement. Kelly is paying for my meal later on, after all.

"So cooperative." He gently bumps my shoulder with his. "You are Hester Grayson from Stonehenge, Colorado. Not her doppelganger or long-lost twin?"

He banters this way, teasing me frequently, until we reach the mews near the hospital. We leave the buggy with a stable boy, walk a couple of blocks, and enter the building through the back. The physician's portal, Kelly says. He leads me down a long hallway and sees that I am comfortably seated on a chair.

"My office is just a few doors away. Thank you for being such a good sport about this, Hester. I'll buy you an extra scone."

I hold up two fingers.

"All right, make that two extra scones."

Kelly gives a good-humored snort and leaves.

Shrugging off my cloak, I hide my drawstring reticule in the garment's inner pocket. Kelly is inside his office, talking to another doctor about a recently discovered body. Female. Believed to be a suicide.

His voice isn't the only one I hear. The hospital is a loud place, conversations booming everywhere, but I tune them out. One person, however, cannot be ignored. The words are muffled, like they're traveling through deep water to get to me—nearly unintelligible, but so persistent. I stand and swing my cane out ahead of my feet, moving toward the sound. I detect a strong spoiled-joint-of-beef odor.

Turning right, I run my hand along the wall and find a wide, wooden door. I twist the knob and push the door inward with my knee. The spoiled meat smell is far more potent in this room than it was in the hallway. The whispering is still muted but more emphatic than before.

Why can't I understand the words when I'm this close?

It's all right, I say with telepathy. *I'm here. You're not alone anymore.*

As I follow the voice, I bump into an obstruction. My kid gloves are lined with fur and are a barrier to skin on skin contact. I lean my cane against the wall, remove the gloves and stuff them into my coat pocket. Nerves make my mouth dry. I lick my lips, but they feel sticky afterwards. Go on, Hester. A ghost can't hurt you.

I reach forward and touch the obstruction. Spacious, flat surface. Cool metal. An exam table? It's covered with a cloth. I pull the cloth away and hear it fall to the floor with a swish. The body on the table no longer whispers but chants inside my head. Other cadavers may presently be stored in this room, but this is the only one calling to me. I concentrate on the words and realize the ghost is a female.

Afraid-lost-help-me-help-me-forgive-please-forgive-help-me-lost-lost-lost...

She's wrapped in toweling. I walk along side the body, fingers searching for a gap in the fabric, until I come upon a human thumb sticking out from under it. I push the toweling away and grasp the entire hand. It almost flops out of my grip, long past rigor mortis. My skull tightens and my body trembles. Eyes hot and wet, I cannot ignore the piteous voice or release my contact with the corpse.

Mercurial. Perilous. The vision overwhelms me, and I travel to that realm beyond earth where past, present and future merge and the dead speak to the living. I sink toward the bottom of a murky pond. What am I doing underwater? My lungs burn, and I pump my legs, pushing myself upwards. The water seems to extend above me for miles. My eyesight sparks with electric pulses, and I am dizzy when my face breaks the surface. Retching, I thrash through the water like a fish on a line, somehow keeping myself afloat. I'm nearly to the grassy banks of the pond when I see a woman standing in the shallows under a willow.

She weeps silently, not bothering to wipe away the tears as they glide down her face. A large stone rests in her arms, the weight of it causing them to shake. Both the stone and the woman are bound together with a rope. Fragile-looking—thin and middle-aged—her face has an aura of faded prettiness about it. Like a watercolor painting left too long in the sun, the subtle tones of beauty are now bleached and drab.

Her forehead creases with pain. "Stop, please stop," the woman begs, stumbling further into the pond. "You're right. I deserve to die."

Maybe it's that I nearly drowned a moment ago. Or because I feel such pity for this tragic figure. Whatever the reason, she's going to listen. "Not another step!" I yell.

The woman looks up in astonishment. I'm surprised, too. Not so much over my ability to yell in this realm but by the fact we can communicate. Most people in my visions are oblivious to everything but their own pain. They don't listen to me. Have my powers begun to evolve as Mary Arden said they would?

Making my way through the water to the suicidal lady, I move awkwardly in a saturated dress, pond mud sucking at my feet.

"Who are you?" she asks.

I rub the stitch in my side, breathing hard. I really must exert myself more. "H-Hester. What's your name?"

"Marie-Louise Lennox."

"And today's date?"

The woman puzzles over the answer. "November. November fifth, I think."

Two days ago. She's probably the suicide Kelly discussed with his coworker. I move closer, until I am at arm's length. "Why are you taking your own life?"

Looking fearful, Marie-Louise steps back and shrugs.

I reach for the rope around her waist, but she evades me. "Don't do it. Please don't."

Then I cover my big mouth. Why did I say that? The woman's already dead. And what if she changes her mind and doesn't kill herself? I doubt the immortals would look kindly on my altering the past. Marie-Louise isn't paying attention to my foible, however.

Head cocked, she's listening to something else, eyes filling with new tears. "You can't change my fate, Hester. I must pay the price."

Her slim body bows as though she's been struck. "Oh, how my head hurts! He's so angry. He can't forgive me."

"Who?" I ask. "Who can't forgive you?"

Fresh agony strikes her. "I won't tell," she whimpers. "No more. I beg of you."

The woman turns, walks a few feet and enters deep water, throwing herself beneath the surface of the pond. I hurry toward the place where Marie-Louise went under but an unnatural current forms and pushes me back. Bloody hell. What trickery goes on here? Fighting the tide, I thrash-swim for several minutes, but I am swept out of the vision the same way I entered it. Sinking to the bottom of the pond, I pass a lifeless body tied to a stone, floating gently to and fro.

Marie-Louise.

Desperate for air, I writhe as darkness engulfs me. The psychic realm fades away and I return to myself, back at the hospital morgue, holding a cold hand. I release it quickly and step away. Patting my bodice and skirt, I find them completely dry. I am as I was before the vision. Well-dressed. Blind. Mute.

O di immortales. Take a moment and breathe, Hester.

I sink to the floor, onto the cloth that had covered Marie-Louise. Forcing myself to be calm, I cross my arms over my abdomen and exhale. The vision's done. She isn't your responsibility—it was a suicide, not a murder.

Although I feel for Marie-Louise, she can't assume ghost form and follow me from this place or haunt me like Freckles the Cornishwoman does. Those who end their own lives fall outside my supernatural job description. But why then did I hear Marie-Louise call? What does she wish me to learn from her death?

The voice is still speaking from the body on the table, calling out for relief that is beyond my power. I stand up and drape the cloth over the dead woman. Memory teases a corner of my mind. I'm missing something important about her. What is it? Flashes of color and motion appear. Mountains, early spring sunshine, a male voice. The scene repeats several times at high speed, so fast it barely registers... Now slower. Slower. It's of Freckles being murdered, just before she was thrown off the cliff. Then my exchange with Marie-Louise overlaps the Cornishwoman's death, like a dress pattern covering a piece of cloth. They must be connected somehow. Not at face value, of course, but truth vibrates through my bones at the thought of a common thread.

Comparing the superimposed visions, I find a link—Mr. Murder and Marie-Louise both seemed to converse with an invisible person. And they experienced pain. Almost like a punishment for disobedience.

What was it Mary Arden said? That our enemy uses others to accomplish his work? Weak, impressionable souls who lack the will to resist. She told me I'd hear it in their voices if I listened hard enough.

Inhaling slowly, I feel my skin go cold. The killer and the suicide were weak and impressionable. I heard it, smelled it on them. Mary Arden could be right about Archimendax's heir. He may be at work in Stonehenge.

I'm drawn out of my thoughts by sounds from within Kelly's office. Papers crinkle, a drawer closes. After grabbing my cane, I retrace my steps from the morgue to the chair in the hall. I sit down, weak with relief, and Kelly opens his door.

"What say you to three scones, Hester?" he asks. "You're a slight bit of goods, but you might be able to polish them off."

10

Amantes sunt amentes.
Lovers are lunatics.

We follow the waiter to our table in the hotel tearoom. I take my seat and listen, enrapt, as a harpist plays softly in the background. A beer garden does brisk business outside the windows of the tearoom. Between the two establishments, I smell lemon wedges, fresh cream, and Darjeeling, as well as pickled eggs and an overfull spittoon.

Stonehenge in a nutshell.

As always, I hear the townsfolk on the fringes. "Sapphire earbobs? Why would Lenore waste them on her?"... "Thank goodness for the glasses! Terrifying without them, you know... " Others are discussing Kelly. "Devilish handsome and a doctor, too. Rumor has it he's single."

How foolish of me to think I could do this. More foolish yet for them to think at all.

Kelly reads aloud from the menu and describes the variety of teas available to us. I barely pay attention as I listen to a group of debutantes at another table plotting to ensnare him. Still oblivious to the managing females, he makes suggestions from the trays of sandwiches and cakes, and I lift my hand when something sounds good, like a culinary auction.

Though I don't select many items. No scones, as it turns out. They're too crumbly. My entire side of the table would be a mess. Instead, I choose sandwiches—cucumber with dill—fruit and cheese, and my usual Earl Grey. My face feels hot as I eat in public. Do I look ridiculous? Is there something stuck in my teeth? I can't imagine ever wishing for the Cornishwoman's companionship, but wouldn't ghost-sight come in handy now?

I take small bites and chew slowly as Kelly tells funny stories about his daughter Alice. He's good company, and I begin to relax. Due to the late night meetings with Tom, I haven't spent much time practicing my table manners. Still, the sandwiches are dainty, crustless squares and not too difficult to consume. When a bit of cucumber drops onto my lap, I brush it off, hoping Kelly doesn't notice. I've just finished a slice of pear and hard Chesire cheese when Kelly offers me a petit four. The doctor shoves the little pastry into my mouth before I can decline.

"Bit of chocolate on your chin," he says, laughing. "Under your bottom lip."

Horrid man! The whole room must have seen.

My napkin is just large enough to hide behind as I wipe the melted frosting away.

"There's that expressive face," he says, once I've cleaned up. "I'm getting quite used to it."

Kelly leans closer and sighs. His breath smells of herbs and honey. "We'll have to do this again, Hester."

No, we will not. The townspeople are agog as it is.

"I want you to say to yourself, 'Noah, I've had a wonderful time. We must sup together anon.' That exact wording, mind you."

Apparently, the people around us are so caught up in this exchange that they've stopped gossiping. The room is quiet except for the clatter of silverware on china. I imagine what they see, and entertain the image of the doctor and I together at our table by the window, heads nearly touching. This might seem like a romantic engagement to those who don't know better.

"Say, 'Noah, you are a prince among men. High tea will never be the same without you.'"

Oh, for the love of heaven…

He takes something out of his jacket pocket. A rabbit, maybe? I hear a shuffling sound and feel a packet of paper sliding between my fingers. He turns my hand and kisses my knuckles before I pull away.

"You're welcome."

A resounding gasp echoes across the tearoom, as though someone has inhaled with shock after witnessing such forward behavior between the new doctor and the town deficient. The man coughs several times and several more after that.

My escort's tone is so smug that I am naturally curious to know what it is I'm holding, what he thinks requires my gratitude. I examine his gift. Stiff cards with cutouts in the middle.

"Stencils," Kelly announces proudly. "I had them made up at the stationers."

Ah, of course. Stencils. How lovely. Never heard of the blasted things.

But I pretend to know all about them for the doctor's sake and nod wisely as he explains. It's impossible to concentrate, however. The man on the other side of the room has increased the volume of his cough. Actually, it's become more of a distressed gurgle. A waiter is hurrying this way, straight toward Kelly.

"You'll learn your alphabet and eventually write—" the doctor stops speaking a moment before the waiter arrives and rises to his feet. "Hold on, that fellow's choking."

Kelly and the waiter rush the man out of the lobby, presumably to avoid distressing the other diners, and knock someone over in the process. Amid this confusion, I realize that I am in trouble. Big trouble. Well over six feet of angry Scottish trouble. *O di immortales!* I want to cross myself even though I'm not Catholic.

Are you coming out, love? Or shall I come in?

Let's talk later. When you've had a chance to get your temper in hand.

That may take years, Hettie. Go out the side door behind your chair. There's an alley on the right.

Standing slowly, I hug my cane for moral support. *It's not as it appears, Tom.*

I know what I saw through the window.

You won't understand.

Try me.

Following Tom's directions, I leave through the side door, but cowardice wins over valor. I swivel back toward the hotel before a hand grabs my arm and yanks me into the alley. Tom removes my spectacles before I can stop him.

Explain.

He knows how I hate having my glasses taken away and his blatant disregard of my wishes makes me seethe. I put my hands on my hips and thrust out my chin. *There's nothing to tell! Dr. Kelly asked me to tea, as a friend, and I accepted. Is that a crime?*

Tom crowds me a little. *Just for the record, which part was the most enjoyable, love? His feeding you the pastry or the knuckle kiss?*

Kelly just likes to be outrageous sometimes. That's all.

Oh please. He was looking for an excuse to touch you. And I didn't see any objection on your part.

This sparks my temper to new heights. I shove Tom's chest with my palms, but he doesn't budge. *Marry me then. I'm sick of waiting.*

All right, let's wed. We'll elope.

Having asked Tom to run away with me every year since I was eleven, I am filled with joy at this prospect, until I realize he's just being spiteful. I raise my hand to slap him, but Tom catches it and links his fingers with mine.

"What'll we do, once we're hitched? Live with my parents?" He whispers this against my ear, his brogue especially pronounced and husky. "Ma and Pa have the bedroom downstairs while the rest of us sleep in the loft. Splintery wood under our blankets, but never you worry, lass. We'll be right happy tucked in together. You won't mind the smell of the pigs outside the window, will you?"

I struggle against him, but he holds me fast. "Shall we honeymoon in the barn or the woods?"

Tears form at the corners of my eyes. *Don't treat me like this. You know I love you—*

"Aye, I do. The feeling's mutual, remember? You think I don't want you as my wife? That I don't dream of it?"

Then why are you being so mean?

Tom sighs and leans his forehead against mine, turning telepathic. *I can't afford to be a romantic, Hettie. Not about us. I care too much to see you brought low.*

Amor vincit omnia. Love conquers all.

He traces the side of my cheek with his finger, the touch devastatingly soft. *You say that now, but poverty can crush the strongest union. I won't bind you to me until I can provide a decent home for you. I won't have my children growing up as I've done.*

Cordelia once read Thomas More's *Utopia* to me and I remember marveling that gold meant nothing to the people within the book, so little that they made chamberpots out of it. Stonehenge is the absolute opposite of *Utopia*. It has a definite aristocracy, and it doesn't come from blue blood. It's entirely based on money. And wealth is just as important to Tom as it is to my father. The ironic thing is that Father was just like him once—before the gold rush.

I hold Tom close, wishing I'd never come to town. *Things are just things. They don't matter.*

Because you've always had them, love.

Tom allows me a glimpse of what's in his heart. Sorrow, aggravation, fear. These feelings are soon replaced by a different passion, and Tom sinks into me with a searing openmouthed kiss. I cling to him and weather out the storm of emotion, returning each caress.

Then he disappears from my arms.

Bodies roll across the cobblestones, fists strike muscle and debris crashes about in the alley. I switch down my hearing before my head explodes.

"You need lessons on how to treat a lady," Kelly mutters.

Tom laughs bitterly. "I was treating her quite well until you arrived."

The doctor grunts, as though he's been tackled and driven into the wall. He takes a good pounding before knocking Tom off his feet. The violence goes on for some time. They are gasping for air but still swinging.

No more, Tom. Please.

Tell that to your boyfriend—he fights dirty.

"I won't allow Hester to be taken advantage of," Kelly sputters, as though his throat is being squeezed.

"I'll kill anyone who tries it," Tom replies with a snarl.

After hitting the cobblestones, Kelly springs to his feet, the sound fluid as a cat. More punching follows. The moment there is a lull, I move between them and put a hand on Tom's chest.

Kelly steps back, and I sense him studying us. "You're friends with this man, Hester?" he asks, voice cool.

Nodding, I move closer to Tom, feel his arm slide round my shoulders. The doctor is quiet for a moment and then brushes off his coat. "A secret affair, is it? Well, to each his own, I suppose."

Tom's Scottish temper flares. "Careful, Doctor," he says. "Show Miss Grayson the proper respect."

Kelly moves past me. "Oh, I respect Hester. It's you I don't think much of. If she were mine, there'd be no sneaking around. The entire town would know I cared for her."

Tom curses through his teeth. "Son of a—"

I grab his arm tightly. *Let it pass. He thinks he's defending me.*

The doctor walks to the mouth of the alley and waits for Tom and me to follow. "I am Miss Grayson's escort at present," he says. "And when I take a lady out, I damn well see her home."

The body heat from the men at my side is stifling, and I want this encounter to end without further incident. *I'll go with him, Tom. It's only a short ride, after all, and my mother will ask questions otherwise.*

Fine.

Anger pulses from Tom as he hands me what remains of my spectacles and strides away. The frames are bent, the lenses broken. It's the topper to a hell of a day. As I despair over the spectacles, Kelly fetches my cloak from the hotel and leads me to the buggy, stiffly polite. Seems he's angry, too.

Kelly whistles for a while as the horse trots along before turning to me, his knee grazing mine. "I've known my share of deceptive females, but your skills are of the first water. The ice-angel, butter-won't-melt-in-my-mouth act fooled even me."

Reaching into my pocket, I turn away from him and hold the lucky pebbles inside, thankful for the breeze blowing against my flushed face. We finally arrive at The Revels and Kelly walks me to the front door. I curtsy because it's expected and thank him with a nod for taking me to tea.

"You're quite welcome, but it seems that trysts in alleyways are more to your liking. Had I but known you were in the mood for a tussle, Hester, I would have gladly obliged."

The treacherous cad! All that talk about friendship and loneliness. And to think I defended him to Tom.

I release the pebbles in my pocket as Kelly raps on the door, alerting the butler that I'm waiting to be let in. "At your service," the doctor murmurs.

I don't wait for the butler, for all I know he's visiting the cook again, and I push the door open myself. As I stomp into the house, I hear Kelly call my name and turn around.

"The choking man survived, in case you were wondering. And I'll see you in my office tomorrow. Your mother and I have made arrangements for your education."

He walks toward his buggy, and I pull back the door so I can slam it. I'll never go anyplace with him again, regardless of what he and Mama say.

But Kelly gets in a final jab before I slam the door. "Be there at one, Hester, and bring Miss Collins along to chaperone. I'd hate for your *reputation* to suffer."

Later that night, I try to contact Tom, without success. He's shut down our connection. I toss and turn for hours, fighting the urge to weep.

Things are no better the next morning.

I go to my mother's suite after breakfast, but she is still abed. The room smells musty, and I wish I could throw open the windows. Yet Mama complains her hands and feet are cold, even though Cordelia said she's covered in blankets and wearing a mink victorine. I gesture for my companion to add a log to the fire.

"Still under the weather, I'm afraid," Mama says in a faint voice. "All I want to do is sleep."

Cordelia places another blanket over Mama's legs. Then my mother explains about those educational plans that Kelly mentioned. I am to visit his office each day, blast it. There I will be instructed in a language of hand gestures tailored specifically for my needs. Modified sign language, she calls it.

Mama says that Kelly's younger sister Rachel is deaf. No wonder he wanted to be friends! It all makes sense now. He felt sorry for me because I reminded him of her. Evidently, Rachel learned to sign later in life and instructed Kelly in the skill.

What's this? In addition to sign language, the doctor wishes to teach me the alphabet, and later, Braille. I will be a slave to scholarship! And I did not ask to be renovated. I abhor change. The people I care about understand me. At least Tom does, when he's not upset.

I'm happy as I am.

My mother is not happy. "I should have thought of getting you a tutor before, but it didn't occur to me. You will try these lessons, Hester. The world is exceedingly limited for women. Why make it more so by being ignorant?"

She thinks I'm ignorant? My own mother? Well… I'll just refuse to go. The woman can't do anything to me if she's stuck in bed.

"I'm not to be agitated," Mama says, sounding tired. "It's bad for the baby."

Damnation. I can hardly say no to that. Curse you, Kelly, for stirring up my life and making a mess of things.

11

Experientia docet. Ipsa scientia potestas est.
Experience teaches. Knowledge is power.

We drive into central Stonehenge amid snow flurries. Kelly's practice is located on Black Swan Lane, and Willard drops us off there precisely at one. I follow Cordelia into a waiting room, and nearly slip on the wooden floor. It would seem that many a foot has crossed this threshold before us. I smell carbolic solution and mustard plaster. Funny that I never detect these odors on Kelly even when he's been surrounded by them all day.

Must be the fastidious sort. Always changing his shirt or overcoat after working in the surgery.

I still resent being forced into this, but I can act the part of an inquisitive student. That way, Mama won't be distressed, and I will have the satisfaction of taking the moral high road with Kelly. How much can he require in one measly lunch break?

A great deal, it would seem. He barely acknowledges my presence but explains the stencils to Cordelia, asking her to work with me on the alphabet. When that is done, I practice writing the letters with chalk on a piece of slate. All twenty-six of the confounded things! Over and over!

Life is easier when nothing is expected of one.

Kelly finally turns to me. I feel his steady gaze and shrink from it. Too bad we can't just send messages through Cordie without any personal interaction. He rolls his chair around the desk and stops at my side. "I'll need your hands now. No gloves. "

I shake my head, tucking my hands under my knees.

Kelly scoots a bit closer. Is he wearing cologne? Sandalwood, perhaps?

"I can be as stubborn as you, minx. Give over. Let's see them."

I shake my head again. I do not wish to make contact with this man's skin. Dealing with him is difficult enough without visions entering into the equation. I should know by now that Kelly won't be deterred, however. He reaches under my leg and grabs my hand, stripping the glove off in one motion.

Cringing, I fear the worst, but nothing happens. I am visionless. *Deo favente…*

"There, that wasn't so hard. What exactly are you hiding? Warts? An extra finger? Looks perfectly smooth and soft to me. Really, Hester, have you ever done an actual days work?"

Odious, insulting buffoon.

In addition to being odious, Kelly is also physically strong and he won't release my captive hand until he's good and ready. "I'll make a sign, you'll feel my fingers, and then you make the same gesture in return." He swivels to the side, still latched onto me. "Miss Collins, you need to learn these, too. I have practice cards with drawings of the signs to send home with you—finger spelling, new vocabulary, common phrases and such."

The doctor lifts my hand up by my face, pinky side forward and thumb nearest my nose. He straightens my fingers and pulls my thumb out a bit

"Keep those fingers straight and tap your chin with your thumb. That's the sign for mother," he says. "Try it again."

Kelly sits back in his chair. I imitate the sign, fascinated in spite of myself. Perhaps I was wrong about scholarship. It might be of some use after all.

"Fingers straight, Hester. Very good. You even mouthed the word correctly. How can you do that? Residual language skills from speaking in your childhood, perhaps."

Without warning, the room begins to sway. A vision. So dizzy. Falling through shadow, falling. Past an attic room. Open suitcase, boots with red heels on top. Heartbroken. Stop her. What can I do? What can I say? *Don't go, Evie.* I'm tumbling fast, out of control. *Some women aren't meant to be mothers, I told you that.* Angry voices shouting... *isn't yours... isn't yours... isn't yours.* Hard landing. Darkness everywhere.

What isn't his?

The revelation ends there, and I return to myself, as though my lessons with Kelly had never been interrupted. I realize then what isn't his. Or rather *who.*

He moves in his chair, the hint of sandalwood cologne growing stronger, and takes my hand. Kelly teaches me to sign *thank you* and *you're welcome.* I try to concentrate, but it's difficult to act normal, to not replay in my mind the moment when he realized he had been cuckolded, that his daughter Alice wasn't his own.

I quietly slip my fingers back into the kid gloves, a lump forming in my throat. I often hate being what I am. How I wish I were just a normal girl sitting here in his office, instead of the worst kind of thief, stealing privacy and secrets.

Unaware of the turmoil in my head, Kelly praises Cordelia's efforts. He doesn't mention my re-gloved hands and says little to me, other than the names of the signs I'm learning. *Goodnight, help, I am hungry, dinner was good,* and *I love you.* Quite unexpected, that last phrase.

"I love you," he says, making the sign against my palm. "Now it's your turn. Feel the shape I've made with my fingers, and repeat it back to me."

I manage to copy the sign correctly. "Once again, Hester. Excellent."

Thank you, I sign.

"Well done, minx. May come a day we won't be able to shut you up." Kelly rolls his chair behind the desk. "The hour's over. Thank you, Miss Collins. I'll see you both tomorrow."

Cordelia and I practice signing the entire way home, and for some reason this lifts my spirits. Each word is like a new discovery, and I cannot get enough of them. As soon as the wagon stops, I hike my skirt up to my ankles and climb down without assistance. Cordie runs to catch up with me as I hurry to the house, cane swinging before my feet.

I enter Mama's room at a gallop with Cordie at my heels. "Have you no manners, Hester?" Mama exclaims. "You mustn't rush about like that. It's undignified."

After giving her my best curtsy, I make the sign slowly, so she is sure to see it—**I love you, Mother**.

"What's she doing now, Cordelia?"

"She's telling you she loves you, madam."

"Really? Are you certain?"

I sign again. **Yes.**

My mother calls me, and I move into her embrace. "Thank you," she whispers.

Pulling back, I hold my hand flat, palm up, and bring it toward my stomach. "You're welcome," Cordelia replies as I mouth the phrase.

This small moment of understanding between my mother and me fuels my desire to learn more. I hope Kelly's up to the challenge for I possess perfect recollection. Every vision—everything I have ever experienced down to the smallest detail—is stored within my brain, waiting to be summoned for future reference. There is much I wish I could forget, but it will remain with me forever.

Perhaps this time, memory will be a blessing rather than a curse.

Meet me at twelve. Throwing practice.

Tom's words are direct and brief—in my mind one moment, gone the next. He's at the ranch shoeing a horse, an enterprise that requires his full attention, and can't elaborate. It was a great relief when we reconciled five days ago, after our quarrel over Dr. Kelly, and I am thrilled at the prospect of a midnight rendezvous.

Evening finally descends, and I meet Tom at the usual place by the French doors. Tom helps me onto his horse, and we fly away to the mountains. The night is so cold, I shiver despite my heavy, hooded cloak.

He insists that I exhaust both arms since I haven't thrown in nearly a week. When my muscles sing with exertion, he brings out a pair of saddlebags, hanging one on each of my shoulders.

What do you expect me to do with these?

"Walk around the circle. Fast as you can, *vita mea*."

This is not as simple as Tom makes it sound, but I apply my cane and complete the course. *What do you have in your saddlebags? Bricks?*

"Rocks, actually. Try it again, but keep your posture straight and tuck in your belly."

I don't like you very much right now.

His laughter sounds genuine. "That wounds, lass, really it does. Off you go."

Sweat films my face when I finish the next lap, but Tom has no mercy. He wants me to go twice more.

This dress will be ruined! I'll never get the smell out.

"And there's a hundred more just like it in your wardrobe. Pick up the pace."

All right, but you owe me a replacement. A new pair of glasses, too.

He kicks the dirt with his boot, cowboy language for *the-hell-you-say*. "I didn't start that fight. Ask *Noah* for your glasses."

Tom turns me to the course and pats my behind to get me moving. I promise myself that I'll finish this round if it kills me. The next one is worse. I dry-heave, stub my toe, and trip a few feet from the finish. Tom squats down next to me, and gives me a canteen. I gulp greedily for a few seconds and then he takes it away.

"Enough, love," he murmurs. "You don't want it coming right back up again."

Disregarding protocol entirely, I flop onto my back in the dirt. I have never in my life done anything so improper. Well, except for sneaking out of the house without permission, having a forbidden romance, and throwing sharp things into the early hours of the morning.

Was that really necessary, Tom?

He sits down beside me. "You need to build muscle and stamina. If you get attacked again, it won't be a drawing room musicale or a night at the opera. You can't fight like a lady—"

I've never been to an opera or a musicale, and you must admit, it's a stretch to call me a lady.

Tom laughs, and I take in the sound like a thirsty flower absorbing water.

"Just my way of saying that the killer isn't fooling. Fight him any way you can, Hettie. Knee him in the bollocks, gouge his eyes—whatever it takes to have you walk away alive."

I hold out my hand, and he accepts it, leaning down for a kiss. Tender, gentle. I touch his face when he releases me, and feel the dear, familiar lines of his jaw and brow.

Thank you for caring that I'm safe.

"Always, Hettie. Always and forever."

We hold each other, warm where our bodies meet, and listen to an owl hooting in the pine trees.

"I have a present for you," Tom says, reaching into his pocket.

He slips something over my head. I can barely feel the meager weight of it resting against my bodice. Taking the cool, delicate chain between my fingers, I find an oval attached in the center. A locket? *You didn't need to do this.*

"Yes, I did. It's a topaz. Belonged to my gran and her mother before that."

This is not a token gift. Few things mean more to Tom than kin, and the fact he's offering a family heirloom to me brings tears to my eyes. *I'm honored.* I send him an intense rush of emotion. *Gratias tibi ago.*

"You're welcome. Gran said the stone protected her from harm. Let's hope it does the same for you."

Te amabo semper, Thomas.

Te amabo semper, Veritas mea.

Time passes sweetly in his arms, and then he takes me home and we are separated until the next night.

From this point on, my life becomes an arduous routine. I strengthen my mind in the daylight, learning to sign with Kelly and Cordelia, followed by night practices which test the limits of my physical endurance. I struggle through it, sleeping when I can, and give my best every time. In an odd way, I feel empowered—as though I am gaining an edge I never had before. An advantage.

Who would ever think that a dumb, blind girl could be dangerous?

12

Caveat.

Beware.

D
r. Kelly visits my mother on Sunday evening. I sit in a chair near Mama's bed while they talk. He's concerned about her fatigue and swelling. "Not too unusual, I suppose, but most women feel more themselves at this point, once the early sickness is over." Kelly asks Cordelia for his coat. "I'd like you to eat foods that are rich in iron and protein, Mrs. Grayson."

Mama agrees, and Cordie and I walk with the doctor to the front door, where the butler is ready with his hand on the knob.

Maybe he and the cook have fallen out.

Kelly isn't prepared to leave, however. Instead, he asks after my studies. "You're being industrious, I hope?"

I nod and sign. **Work hard.**

"Here's an idiom, then," he says. "In keeping with your personality. My sister Rachel uses it a lot with me."

He makes the sign and describes the accompanying facial expression. I practice it a few times, knowing that I will use it with Kelly just as Rachel does.

"The sign means what precisely?" Cordelia asks.

"You're full of hot air," Kelly replies, deadpan. "Now, let's see. What's another? How about—I need sleep? You seem rather weary, Hester."

I perform this phrase until he's satisfied.

"A triumph, minx."

Full of hot air.

"I may regret showing you that one." The doctor laughs and squeezes my arm. "You winced just now. Are you hurt?"

Only the after-effects of knife-throwing… **Very tired.**

"I won't detain you further. Goodnight, ladies."

After Kelly leaves, Cordelia and I practice signing for a while, and then get ready for bed. I have my companion read from *The Histories* by Herodotus, expecting her to doze off immediately, but she is galvanized by his words, puttering around her room until nearly twelve.

I wait under my duvet for the snoring to begin. When at last it does, I gently push back the curtains around my canopy bed and climb off the feather mattress. Next come thick stockings, my oldest but warmest dress, and a pair of sturdy boots. I'll need the extra coverage since it's snowing outside. Cordelia looked out the window before reading Herodotus to me and complained about the snow. My companion never fails to surprise. I expected her to bemoan the ancient Greek historian rather than the weather.

When I am dressed, I wrap one of Cordie's wool scarves around my throat, drape another over the top of my head, and don my winter cloak. Tom is waiting for me when I emerge from the house, and we steal away like bandits through the night.

Once we reach Stonehenge, he places the case of throwing knives in my hand. "This is your own set, Hettie. We're trying the real thing now—letting you get some experience with an actual blade." He lights his clanky lantern and turns me north. "I brought up a bunch of burlap sacks earlier today and filled them with snow and dirt. Those'll be your fifteen targets. Each of the stone pillars has one. They sit at the base, 'bout three feet high."

The bit on Tom's belt clanks against the buckle as he takes it off and then he cinches the belt around my waist. Rather puzzled, I jump when my skirt is lifted, a gust of cold air blowing across my legs. Tom hikes the material up and tucks it under the belt. The length of my calf is exposed, woolly stockings and all.

Excuse me?

"Better access, love."

Access to what?

He removes one knife from the carrying case and gives it to me. The handle is so cold my fingers hurt. I touch the flat side of the blade. It's coated with frost, but I wipe it clean. My breath catches as Tom touches my garter, lingering there for a moment. Then his hand moves higher, and I feel him strapping the knife case to my thigh.

"Too tight?" he asks.

I swallow and shake my head. *No, but I'm freezing.*

"Sorry, Hettie. You'll warm up once we get to work." Tom finds a place to sit, far out of range. "You know the layout of the stones. Directly ahead of you is number one. Go clockwise, and I'll retrieve the weapons after the third throw."

The snowy weather heightens the sense of solitude and smothers sound. It makes things more difficult for me to locate.

"Hold the point between your fingers," Tom says. "It won't cut you if you're careful."

I'm assured by the solid weight in my hand, and I review the steps Tom has taught me, the moves I've been practicing. I lift my arm, draw back, and throw.

Tom claps. "Very nice. Severed an artery at the least."

Although my skirt is tucked up somewhat, it still covers the knife case, and I'm awkward at getting the blades from under the flounces of wool. Blasted clumsiness. I throw again and the knife just nicks the edge of the bag. But the third attempt slices straight through the middle.

"Dead center," Tom says, his voice dulled by the snow.

He brings the knives back, and I try again with mixed success. All the practice and trial-and-error kicks in on the next round. Every throw is golden.

Then I hear a horse whinny and extend my hearing to pinpoint its location. The animal isn't far distant, just past the clearing, but Tom seems oblivious.

A rider's coming from the south.

He grabs my arm, pushes me toward the nearest pillar. *Hide. I'll handle this.*

Slip-sliding, I make it to cover as a man rides out across the bluff.

"Is that you, Craddock?" he asks.

Tom returns his double-barreled shotgun to the holster on his saddle. "It's me."

"Where's Hester?" Noah Kelly asks. There's a metallic click, as though he's just slid the hammer of his revolver out of the cocked position. "I was on my way home from a late night call when I saw you two riding for the foothills. Didn't want to wake her parents so I followed you instead."

"Hester's here," Tom replies. "She's all right."

The saddle creaks as Noah Kelly dismounts. "I'd like to verify that fact, if you don't mind. And even if you do, for that matter."

I'll come out, Tom. We aren't doing anything wrong. He'll see that and go.

I leave my hiding place, and Kelly moves toward me, takes my arm. He flicks the hem of my tucked-up skirt. "Have you no shame, Hester? I would have expected more restraint from you than this. Exposing your leg like a common doxy."

"A doxy?" Tom repeats. "How dare you?"

And that's all it takes. They are fighting again.

Stop it. Right now. Stop it.

Tom doesn't respond, so intent is he on maiming Kelly. And vice versa.

Perhaps a well-aimed snowball will get their attention. I quickly make a pile of hard, packed balls. I listen to Kelly curse, finding the location of his head, and take aim a bit lower. There's a surprised yelp, and then Tom laughs. I throw at him, too. In fact, I pelt them both repeatedly, until Kelly calls a truce.

"Quite an arm there, Hester," he says. "Your aim is uncanny."

Did you have to throw so hard, love?

You wouldn't stop!

Neither would he.

I have one last snowball in my hand, and Kelly asks to borrow it. "To counter the swelling in my jaw." He laughs ruefully and takes possession of the orb. "You're rather beautiful when you're in a temper. I should provoke you more often."

This comment prompts another solid punch from Tom, and the doctor stumbles.

Last one, Hettie. And he asked for it.

"Let's call this a draw, Craddock," Kelly says, spitting into the snow. "You're a grand scrapper, but I've broken some fingers and your face is bleeding a stream." He takes a few steps and sits down. "Now that rusty lamp's a romantic touch. Adds atmosphere. But it's awfully cold for a tryst. Wasn't there a shed or silo somewhere closer?"

I am gripping Tom's hand, keeping him from making another fist. *Tell Kelly the truth—about the knife throwing and why we're here.*

"Burlap sacks?" Kelly drawls. "For the life of me, I have no idea what those are for…"

Does it really matter what he thinks?

After a moment, I nod. *Yes, it does.*

Tom exhales and hands me the knives. "Show him yourself."

Keeping one, I put the other two on the ground by my right boot, instead of returning them to the case on my thigh. I'd rather not have Kelly see me fumble under my skirt for the weapons. He'd only think me improper and inept. I concentrate on the stones and their burlap targets.

"Stay where you are, Dr. Kelly," Tom says. "If you value your life."

The knife flies from my fingers, whistling through the air, driving into the bag twenty feet in front of me. I don't need anyone to say it's perfect, I already know.

Tom whispers, "Stone number six, Hettie."

I swing about and release the weapon—clean and deadly. The third stone is next, and I hit that target just as well. Tom fetches the knives for me, and I continue on. Ten, four, seven. Not one wasted throw in the entire lot.

Kelly claps and whistles through his teeth. "You're remarkable, Hester. Absolutely amazing."

I smile and wipe the sweat from my forehead, trying to catch my breath. Concerned I'll catch a chill once I cool down, the doctor goes to his horse to get a blanket from the saddlebag. "And maybe a flask," he says. "For medicinal purposes."

Tom unhooks the leather case from my leg, puts the knives away, and pulls down the side of my skirt. A picture erupts inside my head, related to the Halloween vision. The killer walks up the mountain path, arguing with Freckles as usual, but in this rendition I am positioned at his side. So close it makes the hairs on my arms stand on end. I look down at Freckles as he slaps her when she says that his wife is as good as dead. She trips, falls, and loses consciousness. The killer checks to see if she is alive. A bluish vein pulses at her neck and her mouth is slightly open. How young Freckles looks in sleep—innocent and rather pretty, without the bitter lines around her mouth or the hateful tone of voice.

Would she have looked soft like this if her life had been easier? Was the harshness the world saw only a defense?

Sympathy grows in my heart, but I haven't long to examine the emotion. Mr. Murder picks her up and throws her away like so much trash. Standing on the cliff edge, he watches her hit the rocks below. Her screams echo in my head as he turns toward the path down the mountain, lighting a partially-smoked cigar. Mr. Murder takes a few puffs and the smoke wafts around his face. He notices a smudge on one of his cufflinks and rubs it on his jacket. What's that engraved on the cufflink? Are they initials? Before the killer lowers his arm, I identify three letters. D...T...P

Then the vision changes. I stand in the center of a wasteland with Sir Death. Freckles is at His side. She watches me with hard, glittering eyes and looks rather triumphant. As triumphant as one can appear while wearing a blood-stained gingham blouse and sporting terrific injuries after falling off a cliff.

Inky robes swirling about Him, the Reaper floats a few inches off the ground. He smells of marble, moss and damp soil. It isn't unpleasant, just a bit intimidating when one considers why He smells that way. The spirit world has many of His kind. They are immortal and legion in number, identical in appearance, purpose, and thought. All are called Sir Death, or the Reaper, and I have worked with this particular entity as long as I've been Veritas of Stonehenge. He supervises other Visionaries as well, covering the whole Rocky Mountain Sovereignty.

It's difficult to look into that pale, ageless face. He glances at His gold pocket watch, the chain glittering in the half-light. *What are you doing to free this ghost, Hester? She's been quite patient, I believe.*

Do I have anything to report? Even though Tom's been searching the foothills and talking to people in town, he hasn't discovered anything new. Cornishwomen with red hair abound in Stonehenge apparently, but none have been reported missing or dead. At least Tom has made an effort to move the investigation forward, in addition to meeting me at midnight. I, on the other hand, have been caught up with sign language and alphabet stencils and my ill mother, leaving little time or opportunity to sleuth. All I've got are those damned initals DTP.

I force myself to meet Death's blue, blue eyes. *We're still investigating, Sir. I'm confident we'll find the killer soon.*

Let us hope so. It's unfair to make the dead suffer longer than necessary. It makes me upset just thinking about this poor woman's plight.

Oh dear. Upset is a step away from angry. No one wishes to meet the Reaper in high dudgeon. Especially me. I enjoy living, thank you very much.

As I nod my head in agreement with Death, Freckles smiles at Him warmly. Why did she wink like that? Is the ghost infatuated with Death? The idea makes me shudder.

Her fair skin is growing translucent, looking more wraith-like than human. This happens when ghosts fail to cross over. Ripped from life in an untimely fashion, murdered souls are often hazy about their own mortality and death. The memory of dying violently traumatizes them and they subdue it. Yet ghosts are very clear about their desire to continue on to the spirit world. This cannot happen until the truth is revealed—about them *and* their killers. Only then will they move forward to the Judgment, where all of creation makes an accounting and justice and mercy await.

If the ghosts were good people in life then they are gentle and easy to work with. The bad ones are an entirely different matter. Despite my earlier sympathy with Freckles, I sense she is from the latter category. The friendly show she's putting on for Sir Death seems artificial.

But the Reaper appears to welcome the attention. He gazes at me in disappointment and fades away. I force myself back to the world of the living, back to Tom. It will become more and more difficult to separate myself from Freckles. The longer she stays here, the greater the risk her darker nature will take over. Visionaries have gone mad from such spirits.

We need to find our killer, Tom. Sir Death is upset. He wants justice now.

Tom puts his hand on my back, rubs gently. *What about that old chapel on Settler's Ridge? I haven't checked there.*

Our Lady of Sorrows? No. It's in ruins after the fire.

He slides his arm around my shivering body. *But the building was whitewashed, Hettie. It might look like a snowy mound from a distance, and there's a fairly deep ravine thereabouts. I think it's worth a try.*

When?

Tomorrow morning? We're lucky it's so windy up there. The snow doesn't stick for long, even after a storm. Maybe we'll find something.

Let's pray we do, Tom. Our ghost is trouble. She's trying to beguile the Reaper.

That's just wrong.

She winked and smiled at Him. Flirted even.

Tom's happy laughter makes my heart light. *The Shade and the specter? Now there's a love story to give you nightmares.*

I punch him on the arm. *Be serious. It's not love, it's manipulation waiting to happen. Let's help her move on, whatever it takes.*

Out of habit, he switches into speech, forgetting the rules of clairvoyance yet again. "*Fiat justitia ruat caelum.*"

"'Let justice be done though the heavens fall'?" Kelly asks, making both of us jump.

Wrapped up in our telepathic discussion, we forgot the doctor was still here. "Strange," he says. "I've been watching you two. It's as if you can talk to each other without saying a word."

"Such a wild imagination," Tom replies. "I wouldn't have expected it in a man of science."

"Most scientists agree there's much beyond our understanding." Then Kelly's pragmatic nature takes over, and he changes the subject. "Tell me about the knives, Craddock. Why is Hester learning to use them?"

"For self-protection. The horse was intentionally spooked on the day you saved her life."

Liquid sloshes inside a container. Is it the flask Kelly mentioned before? "Do you know who's responsible?" he asks, twisting a metal cap.

Don't mention the magic, Tom. Kelly will never believe it. Say I overheard the killer talking to himself. The doctor could help us search for evidence.

We've managed without him this far.

And we will again, but it wouldn't hurt to have someone with his training on our side.

I don't trust the man, Hettie.

Well I do, and we could use an extra person on Settler's Ridge.

Tom hesitates but still concedes to my wishes. "Miss Grayson overheard a stranger incriminating himself in the murder of a young woman. We think he is most likely the one trying to harm her."

Thanks, Tom. I'll make it up to you later.

"Is this true, Hester?" Kelly puts the flask in my hand. "You didn't recognize the voice of the killer?"

Shaking my head, I smell the beverage in the flask. Strong, alcoholic fumes singe my nostrils. I drink and liquid fire slides down my throat. It makes me cough and wheeze. I hastily return the flask to the doctor, but he pushes it back. "One more sip."

I do as he suggests and my insides are hot as hellfire. I remove my scarf and decline Kelly's blanket although he insists I take it with me on the journey home. My very innards feel flammable. Like the parlor maid Martha, I could combust.

Kelly passes the flask to Tom, who isn't shy about taking a drink. He has several before handing it over to the doctor. "The crime may have happened at a ravine nearby," he says. "We plan to go there tomorrow and search for clues."

"What kind of clues?" Kelly asks. "And why haven't you told the police about this?"

Taking Tom's hand, I give it a comforting squeeze. *Be as honest as possible. I won't hold it against you.*

He's angry inside—that he has to spell out my situation to the doctor, that the circumstances exist in the first place. "Hester can't speak for herself, and the people in town treat her like she's too impaired to function. We've worked with the police before, but they expect evidence, not heresay."

While Tom talks, Kelly has a drink and stows the flask in his coat pocket. "Crimes aren't solved unless they're reported, Craddock. Speak to the police for her, just as you're doing now."

Tom exhales with frustration. "We'll do that eventually. Right now we need an alibi for Hester to be away from home. You can provide that, Doctor."

"Why does she need an alibi?"

"To search for the murder site on Settler's Ridge.

Kelly shifts his weight and the snow under his shoe makes a crunching sound. "What are you thinking, man? It's dangerous up there. Hester could get hurt."

"That won't happen, Doc. I'll protect her."

"Perhaps you've been with cattle too long and have forgotten how civilized people behave. Gentlemen don't subject ladies…"

Not wanting Tom and Kelly to fight again, I interrupt and sign something the doctor recently taught me. He groans, and I sense that he has given up the fight. Irony is at last in my favor.

What was that you did just now? Tom asks, our minds linked again.

Smiling, I repeat the sign and translate. *It's an idiom. I told Kelly he's full of hot air.*

The doctor counts under his breath and paces. After a few minutes, he returns to Tom and me. "Answer me one thing, Hester. Will you continue with this scheme if I refuse to help?"

I nod and Tom says, "Hell yes."

"Just as I suspected." Kelly sighs like a man about to embark on a doomed voyage. "Very well then. I'm in."

The two men make arrangements as we pack up and ride back to town. The storm is nearly over and snowflakes fall sporadically, touching my face now and again like an icy kiss. Dr. Kelly follows Tom and me to the Revels. He leaves his horse and walks with us to the arbor.

Dulcis Domus. Home sweet home.

Goodnight, Tom. Thank you for doing things my way. I know it wasn't what you wanted.

Let's hope it works, love. Give me a proper farewell.

The kiss is possessive—leaving no room for misunderstanding on the doctor's part.

"Let the poor girl up for air, Craddock," Kelly mutters.

Tom releases me, but not immediately, not until Kelly grumbles a bit more. Something about Tom's parents being unmarried at the time of his birth or some such thing.

"Better go, Hester," the doctor says, taking my elbow and turning me toward the house. "We've got big plans for tomorrow. We may even catch a killer."

13

A fronte praecipitium a tergo lupi.
In front a precipice, behind, wolves.

A large group of people stand at the back door of our kitchen. It's free-dinner Monday. This culinary noblesse oblige has been a tradition since The Revels was built. It is my mother's way of sharing her bounty with the deserving poor. Father wants nothing to do with it. He thinks that the words *deserving* and *poor* are mutually exclusive.

Cook has made an enormous kettle of venison stew, and skillets of corn bread. The hungry come with bowls, tin coffee cups, and once, even a straw hat. Cook fills the containers to the brim until the food runs out. It's fortunate for our visitors the snow has stopped. My mother said the clouds departed early this morning and that the sun had finally come out.

Members of the Ladies Charitable Works Association have come to call on Mama, and Father is entertaining some of his cronies from the gentlemen's club in his study. Listening to the grandfather clock chime, I realize that Kelly will be here soon, ostensibly to pick me up for lessons. My mother is quite happy about this. It must not have occurred to her to question that Cordelia is staying behind. Secretly, I think she's hoping Kelly compromises me so he'll be forced to ask for my hand and give me his name.

It's a sad day when a mother aspires for her child's corruption in order to secure said child a hearth and home. I guess a simple dowry doesn't suffice in my case.

Cordelia pushes the tea trolley into the winter parlor where a fire crackles in the grate. The scent of burning juniper and imported perfume floats into the hall. I smile to myself and tip-toe past the parlor. It's nice to hear Mama chatting with her friends. She must be feeling better.

"Is that you, Hester?" Mama calls.

I stop tip-toeing and put a hand on my hip. How did she know I was sneaking out? And why ask for me today, why now? She's never brought me to the attention of visitors before. I go to the parlor doorway without entering the room.

Leaving, I sign. **Good afternoon, Mother.**

The women murmur among themselves after seeing this. The essence of their comments boils down to "What *the devil* was that?"

"Hester is learning sign language," Mama says. "It replaces speech. She works so hard at it and learns faster than anyone Dr. Kelly's ever seen. He was just saying so the other day."

Feminine voices break out again. "Well I never *heard* the like… Can you *imagine*… The *miracles* of the modern age…"

These same ladies gossiped about me when I went to tea at the hotel with Kelly. Now they are merely showing support for their rich friend Lenore Grayson. I could be a performing monkey for all they care.

Our butler steps into the hall and announces the doctor's arrival. Kelly joins me a few moments later. "Ready to go?" he inquires loudly enough for all my mother's friends to hear.

I turn to Mama and sign quickly, **Nice-party-you. Me-home-soon.**

My mother insists on introducing Kelly to all of the Ladies Charitable Works Association. They praise his skill as a teacher and a few ask if he would privately tutor their daughters. Mama excuses us before Kelly can give them an answer. He leads me out of the house by the elbow.

"That was interesting," he says, sounding relieved to be outside. "I was afraid those invitations entailed more than just tutoring."

Probably marriage, I sign. **Single daughters.**

"Really? In that case, my tutoring schedule is full."

I smile at Kelly as he leads me across the drive, toward the stables. Why are we going this way? Usually buggies wait in front of the house.

We stop near the corral. It sounds as if some horses are tied to the fence. Kelly pushes me toward one of them. "We're doing something different, Hester. You'll ride alone today."

It takes a second for the words to sink in and then I give him a scowl. Oh, ha, ha. Tease the blind girl. Ride alone, indeed!

But he's dead serious.

Despite my opposition, the doctor helps me onto the horse and gives me the reins. "You're slipping a little to the left, minx. Move back. Good." He walks around the animal, gives it a pat. "Your cloak is long enough to cover your legs, but a riding habit would be better."

A *riding* habit? My wardrobe is extensive but Mama never thought to get one of those.

I rub the horse's smooth coat and it whickers softly. Oats, dry hay. I love his smell. Kelly mounts his own horse.

What's happening? I ask, trying to sign and hold the reins simultaneously.

"Hmm," Kelly replies. "Are you referring to our riding arrangement?"

Of course.

"Let me introduce you to your noble steed. Jupiter meet Hester. Hester, Jupiter."

My mouth falls open. Jupiter? My steed?

Kelly seems amused by the situation. "They were going to ship the beast to a glue factory in Colorado Springs, but I bought him for you instead. Just a few dollars, really. He's been hitched to a wagon at the mill his whole life."

It bothers me that Kelly is so nonchalant. Jem died not long ago, and I still feel terrible about it. Besides, what would I do with the animal? **No horse for me. *Blind,* remember? Crash, fall off, die.**

"I have created a monster," Kelly says. "You can be quite sarcastic at times."

His mount takes a few steps and Jupiter follows, as though there is no other option for him but to show obedience. I am terrified initially and then I remember the reins in my hands. Leaning forward, I reach out and find a lead rope connected to my horse's bridle.

"Don't worry, minx. I have the other end. You're safe."

I feel better now. Kelly can be exasperating at times, but I trust he will keep me from harm. We use side streets—where there isn't much traffic—and I sigh in relief once we are out of Stonehenge.

The world smells clean and new. Sunlight warms my cheeks and the wind whirls about me, tossing tiny particles of ice into my face. I pat Jupiter, thankful he and I are both alive to enjoy this day.

I hear Kelly turn in his saddle. "Would you like to gallop a bit?"

Smiling in confirmation, I can barely contain my excitement. Our horses spring forward and their hooves churn up the slushy ground.

Oh, it's marvelous! My eyes water, my heart thumps. I've never felt so alive.

"Too fast?" Kelly yells over the noise. "Shall we slow down?"

I shake my head, and he laughs. "All right then. Loosen your hold on the reins, and let old Jupiter have his way."

We ride for another mile or so, nearly reaching our meeting point with Tom. He might even see us galloping along the road. Horrors! He does.

What are you doing, Hettie? And why are you sitting on that pitiful nag?

I refuse to honor Tom's last comment with a response. Jupiter is not pitiful. Or a nag.

Kelly groans, evidently at the distant sighting of my love, and brings his steed to a trot. I pat Jupiter and turn to the doctor. If I had any reservations about accepting this horse, they've since vanished. He isn't Jem, but he's a good old fellow.

Thank you, I sign. **Love him.**

"My pleasure," Kelly says. "As they say, don't look a gift horse in the mouth. Who knows if Jupiter even has teeth?"

As we draw closer to Tom, I register how displeased he will be that Kelly bought me such a gift. **Don't tell Tom,** I ask surreptitiously.

"It'll be our secret," Kelly answers, bringing our horses to a full stop. "Hello, Craddock." His greeting to Tom is as bland as unsweetened porridge. "Your eye has a nice shiner from our bout last night."

"I've had worse," my love replies with the same dull intonation and helps me down.

They stake the horses nearby. "Is that one new?" Tom asks Kelly. "The animal Hester rode?"

"Jupiter was a bargain."

"By bargain, I hope you mean free."

We climb to the top of the ridge. Tom remains at my side, telling me what he sees, and I get a vague idea of my surroundings. Our Lady of Sorrows chapel is nothing but a pile of charred timbers, except for one remaining wall. Tom says it is remarkably unscathed.

"There's still some stained-glass in the window," Kelly observes.

A strong wind blows from the north, pushing against us. *See anything, Tom?*

Lots of trees yonder. Could be those from the vision. Are you tired yet? Do you need to rest?

I grin, not the least bit tired. *'Lay on, Macduff, and damn'd be him that first cries, "Hold, enough!'*

Tom laughs, shouldering a branch aside. *Shakespeare this early in the hunt? Deo favente. What kind of day lies ahead?*

Passing through the conifers, I hear the wind shake the old giants. I marvel at the dance going on between the elements and the mighty forest until we're out in the open once more.

"Careful, Doctor," Tom says. "The ravine's up ahead."

We walk another ten yards, and skirt around a few boulders. "How can you be sure this is the one?" Kelly asks.

"Call it intuition."

Tom goes to the edge of the ravine and looks down. "I should be able to make it. There are plenty of outcroppings and shelves for climbing."

Kelly joins him on the rim. "All yours, Craddock. I'd help if it weren't for my broken fingers. You might tie your rope around that stone pillar over there. Seems sturdy enough."

The doctor gets his pack and takes something out of it. The object clacks together, like a handful of metal parts. Kelly tells me they are stakes. He gives them to Tom and asks him to pound the stakes into the earth near any evidence he comes across, to mark his findings. Evidently there's also identification tags involved and twine to outline the area so the police know where to look for further clues. If this practice of staking and tagging seems strange to Tom, he doesn't mention it to Kelly. Even though my Interpreter had qualms initially about having outside help, he seems rather intrigued at the idea of applying scientific methods to our supernatural investigations.

After securing the rope, Tom tosses it over the side. It bounces several times against the hard mountain face, and his boots grind into the shale as he takes hold and begins his descent.

Sitting on a nearby boulder, I listen to his journey into the ravine. *How are you holding up?*

He grunts from exertion as he climbs. *I'll pass on the pie next time the sewing circle offers it.*

Please eat the pie, I answer. *Skip the climbing instead.*

"A fine effort, Craddock," Kelly says.

Gravel pelts Tom a moment later and he curses softly. "Is the strain of watching too much for you?"

The doctor laughs. "For a lesser man, maybe, but I could do this all day. Don't hurry on my account."

It takes a while, but Tom makes it to the canyon floor. "Safe and sound," he yells.

Tom searches for Freckles for hours. To pass the time, we argue telepathically about politics, quote poetry, and discuss things of interest in the canyon. He tells me the creek has chunks of ice floating in it, the rocks by the water frosted and shining. Leaning back, I close my eyes and listen to his movements.

Kelly sits across from me, sorting his pack of medical wonders. He explains each item: the magnifying glass, tweezers, envelopes and linen sheets, glass specimen jars, scraping tools, thin cotton gloves and several chemical compounds. Is such a collection typical of most doctors? I admire individuals who prepare for all possibilities, but this is a little unsettling.

"We have bones down here, Kelly," Tom suddenly shouts. "Bits of an arm or leg, I'd say. I've put a stake nearby. Don't see any other parts as yet, but I'll keep looking."

Kelly hustles to the edge of the ravine. He and Tom call back and forth as more discoveries are made. Quite a few bones, a ring, and scraps of gingham.

In spite of the wind, I hear a sly, cunning presence creeping through the cedars. I rise to my feet, facing west. *Not alone, Tom. Bad feeling...*

He immediately disconnects from me. "Watch your back, Kelly," he calls. "Protect Hester."

But Tom isn't fast enough with his warning. Footsteps rush up behind Kelly and the doctor cries out in surprise, as though he has been pushed toward the ravine. I cover my mouth in terror and wait for the crash of bone and muscle striking rocky earth. It doesn't happen. Rather, Kelly makes a guttural sound, like he's holding on to something for all he's worth.

Tom? What do I do? How can I help him?

"Forget Kelly," he yells. "Run!"

I reach for my cane, but I am grabbed from behind and spun around. The strong fingers are swathed in wool, and my attacker clamps them around my throat, almost lifting me from the ground. I claw at his face. But my gloves are soft and slide over his flesh, allowing me no purchase. He swings me to the side and squeezes harder. My eyes stream with tears.

Help me. Can't breathe...

Fight, love—buy yourself time. We're coming.

In desperation, I pound on my attacker—his sternum, throat, and nose. Then I kick him hard with the pointy tip of my boot. He flinches and his fingers go slack. My topaz necklace catches on something—his wool mitten, perhaps?—and breaks just before the man throws me to the ground. I fall flat on my back, and immediately reach for the knife under my skirt. The blade flies straight and true, finding its target.

A low whimper, and seconds later, the knife drops to the ground, clattering between some rocks. My enemy steps toward the fallen blade, no doubt with the intent of retrieving the weapon and using it against me. Fearful, I scoot back, trying to put some distance between us. This fellow hates me. His emotions smell like a sea of blood. I reach under my skirt again, take out the second knife, and hold it between my fingers, tracking the villain by the sound of his breath. It smells faintly of food, some kind of meat.

He pauses, and I feel him watching me, as though he's weighing his options. Then he turns and flees toward the forest, breaking through the trees. Suddenly exhausted, I lie back on a patch of stony earth and wipe the mucous from my nose.

Alive, Tom. Alive.

While I was being attacked, he climbed desperately. I heard him in my mind, bartering with the universe for a pardon. *Spare Hester. Take me instead.* Kelly, on the other hand, muttered obscene phrases that I never dreamed existed. The man is a cursing wordsmith. Had Willard been there, he would have erected a bronze bust in Kelly's honor.

The doctor hoists himself over the ledge. He examines my throat, and checks for other wounds. "Hester Grayson," Kelly says, breathing heavily. "One day you'll give me a heart attack. Followed by a stroke. A nervous tic. Gout—"

Tom clears the rim, scrambles to my side, and interrupts Kelly's list of grievances. He hugs my quaking body for a few minutes, stroking my hair—*I'll be back, my brave, bonny lass. Keep a knife in your hand and wait here*—then leaves with the doctor to search for my attacker.

———— ● ● ————

I worry for what seems like an age and then they return, discussing the would-be killer's footprints. "Average size,"

Tom says. "Common brand of boots. No distinguishable markings."

"Wish I'd seen the bastard, but he was so quiet. Didn't hear a thing until he shoved me over the side."

I share what I remember of the assailant with Tom. *Strong build but slim. Tall, though not quite your height. Smelled of meat, like he'd recently eaten it. And his hands had the same odor. As if he'd made food and failed to wash afterward. Pungent emotions, too. Lots of rage.*

Tom shows my knife to Kelly.

"The depth of the bloodstain on the blade is shallow," the doctor points out. "I think you winged him, Hester, and he panicked."

Kelly wipes the dagger clean and hands it back. Slipping it into the sheath on my leg, I remember the loss of my necklace.

Tom, your grandmother's topaz—the attacker broke the chain. He may have taken it. I didn't hear the necklace fall to the ground.

He tells the doctor about the topaz, and they search the immediate area. Despite their efforts, the heirloom remains unfound. I feel awful for losing something so dear.

Me paenitet. So sorry.

You're safe now. That's all that matters.

Sitting down beside me, Tom squeezes my hand, and then reaches for his pack. "Kelly, take a look at these. I should have left them in the canyon like I did the rest, for the police to document, but the bones were on the creek bank. The soil was crumbling into the water, and I was afraid we'd lose them in the drink."

"Did you stake the location of your discovery?"

"As close as I could get to the bank, Doc, and tagged it as well. Just like the other remains I found down there."

"Show me your treasure, Aladdin."

A quarter hour passes as Kelly deliberates over Tom's findings. Waiting for the doctor to share his theories, I feel cold, hungry, and bruised—not a combination to encourage patience, especially when I lack that quality on a good day.

What? I finally sign. **Tell now!**

"Sorry, Hester. Tom brought us an incomplete hand— partial carpal and metacarpal as well as proximal and intermediate phalanges. Lucky the mud by the creek kept them together. I assume the whole appendage was separated from the body and dropped there, stuck, and decomposed. Some of the hand might have indeed fallen into the creek, as Tom surmised. Though small, the bones are not immature or childlike. They belong to a woman."

I huff out some air and turn telepathic. *Is Kelly going to tell us something we don't already know, Tom?*

He nudges me. *Be quiet. I'm trying to listen.*

"She's delicate," Kelly observes. "Like you." He lowers my palm to the bone puzzle, comparing my frame with that of the dead woman. A flash of supernatural heat and truth vibrates between the victim and me. This is Freckles all right.

"Aside from the traces of mud, the remains are quite clean," the doctor says. "Partly, I assume, because they've been exposed to the elements for a while. Well over a year, I'd say."

Now Kelly moves my fingers to another piece of evidence. "The tibia is a part of the leg. Feel that indentation?" I wince and pull my hand out of his grasp. "Too squeamish? Never mind, then. This tibia's covered with notches. Animal bite marks, would be my guess. One set of teeth is bigger, but the others are little. Maybe a family of mountain lions? A mother and her cubs? Lady X is probably scattered all across this range."

Bile rises in my throat. *Stop him, Tom! I don't need to know more!*

Tom covers his laugh with a cough. *As they say, be careful what you ask for.*

The doctor is on a deductive roll. "I doubt she was alive at the time the animals fed. No bites on the phalanges to indicate she fought against them. The creatures most likely found her later and then nibbled away." I hear Kelly scoot back on his heels, a man in thought. "Wish I had the skull. Death by falling? Is this what you overheard the killer say, Hester? That he'd pushed her?"

Another nudge from Tom. *Stick to the story we told him, love.*

Correct, I sign to Kelly. **She fell.**

The men discuss the shredded square of gingham next, saying it's spotted with tiny flecks of blood. "Where did you find it, Craddock?"

"By a cave. Some rocks blocked the opening, like there was a landslide recently, and made the hole too small for me to go inside. But the gingham was fluttering in the wind, caught in the branches of a dead sagebrush. I couldn't see it until I bent over to drive a stake into the ground. I suspect we'll find more gingham in the cave. Might have been where your cougars lived, Kelly. "

"I'll put the cloth in an envelope and store it in my bag."

Tom reaches for something else in his pocket. "What about this ring? Saw the gold shining under a thistle. Ever seen the like, Doc?"

"Not an expert on jewelry, I'm afraid, but it's definitely a man's ring. Looks like good-quality gold, too. It might have slipped off the killer's finger."

Kelly drops the thing in my lap. "Have you an opinion, Hester?"

I feel the band. Raised rectangle on top, etched with a symbol. I've come across one of these before. *Look at the etching, Tom. Does it have an eagle's head and a lion's body?*

Yes, it does.

That's the symbol of Griffin House, my father's club. Members wear those rings.

Tom is not even remotely involved in fashionable society. The concept of people wasting money and time on a stuffy, elitist establishment must be foreign to him. However, for the doctor's sake, he feigns a sudden burst of inspiration.

"I'd check at Griffin House. I recall hearing the members are given similar rings after joining the club."

"Good memory, Craddock," Kelly says, moving the bones back into Tom's pack. "Now we know where to begin the search."

"The search?" Tom helps me to my feet. "Shouldn't we give this information to Inspector Jones? He'll listen now that we have some evidence."

"Certainly, but I'll look into it as well."

"What are you talking about, Kelly?"

"You and Hester haven't heard the news yet?" He gives my right hand a quick shake. "Newly appointed coroner of Stonehenge. How do you do?"

14

Nec mora nec requies.
Neither delay nor rest.—Virgil

We emerge from the trees, cold and wet, and return to the horses. Holding onto Jupiter's lead line, Tom rides a little ahead of the doctor and me. I turn to Kelly and sign. **New job. When?**

"Official as of this morning," he says. "If I were the medical examiner in Boston or New York, more would be required of me. But I can wear an additional hat here and maintain my daily practice. That's the idea anyway."

We ride on for a moment and then Kelly exhales. "I have to ask you some questions, Hester—about Lady X's death. When did you encounter the man who killed her?"

I scrunch up my nose, thinking of how to answer. **Three weeks**, I sign.

"About twenty-one days ago?"

Correct.

Kelly guides his horse around something in the road. "On Halloween?"

Correct.

Tom shifts in his saddle. *You okay, Hettie? Is he bothering you?*

No. I can handle him. Just slow down and give us a little more time.

As you like.

"Where were you when you overheard the alleged killer?" Kelly asks.

I try to set the scene, hoping he gets the gist. **Town party. Alone. Park.**

"You went to the town party and ended up alone in the park," Kelly says, voice harsh. "Must you always do the dangerous thing, Hester? Wherever was Miss Collins?"

Dancing.

He makes a disparaging noise. "Companions aren't paid to dance."

My idea.

"On top of my future heart attack, you'll give me wrinkles and gray hair," Kelly mutters. "Did he sound familiar?"

No.

"Describe what you remember about him, Hester."

Drinks liquor. I point to my hip, like a flask rests there. **Sad man.**

"He had a hip flask and was drinking? Sounded unhappy?"

I make an effort to share the content of what I know, without revealing how I came by the information. Helping the new coroner isn't as bad as I feared. He wants the truth, and I wish I could tell him everything. As open-minded as this man is, I doubt he would believe I am a Visionary.

"What did he say?" Kelly asks.

Threat. Must kill.

"Afraid of a little redhead, eh? Why?"

Blackmail.

We arrive at the crossroads between Stonehenge proper and its outlying homesteads. "Thank you, Hester," Kelly says. "The police will want a statement., of course. You and Tom can go down to the Metropolitan Office together. Have him repeat what you've told me. Tomorrow, though. You've had enough excitement for one afternoon."

Tom and I are not strangers to the Met. We've been there a number of times over the years with other investigations. At first, the officers considered us a nuisance. Now we're crime hobbyists—civilians who sleuth for the fun of it.

"She'll need protection," Tom says. "The killer wants her gone."

They talk across me, discussing my fate. "Hester will have it. The Inspector should have a constable patrol the area around The Revels. Have him pass by every so often to ensure that she's safe."

Completely unnecessary.

Tom makes a rude choking sound. *Of course it's necessary, love. You are the moth and danger is the flame.*

The harness on Kelley's horse jangles, a cheerful noise amid such dark conversation. "You did well today, Craddock. I'll send some detectives out to scour the ravine and see if there's anything else to find."

The air feels frigid—like the sun is setting. I pull up my cloak hood and Tom leans in his saddle, touches my face gently. Kelly groans, turns his horse, and trots away.

I'll visit a few of the big houses in the area, describe Lady X to the servants, and see what they know. Shall we meet tomorrow evening?

Agreed.

His mouth brushes mine. *Cordie's your shadow, love, and keep those knives sharp and handy.*

Tom leaves for his family farm. He has neglected his usual work there and must catch up tonight. Kelly whistles as we ride in the opposite direction, and I feel at ease in his company.

"Want me to put in a word with the inspector and have Tom deputized?" he asks.

Won't change jobs, I sign. **Loves ranch.**

"Well, he's a fine fellow. There's just one thing I don't like about him." Kelly's voice doesn't sound happy. "She comes yea high to my shoulder. If not for her, Tom and I could be friends."

My blithe attitude is temporarily diminished as blood rushes to my cheeks. Nevertheless, I am cheered by a fleeting thought. While Tom and Kelly were off searching for my attacker, I nicked a piece of the Lady X mystery for myself, tucking it away in the pocket of my cloak, next to my lucky stones. I smile and rub my finger against the narrow strip of gingham, torn from the piece of evidence now hidden in Kelly's bag.

———————•————————

Cordelia is not feeling cooperative this morning. Nothing new, of course, as she's rather outspoken for a paid companion. To her mind, the gingham material is hideous, and I must be insane for wanting more of it.

"Red and white checks?" Cordie asks again, as though the very existence of the pattern offends her. "You do get funny notions, miss."

New dress, I sign.

"You'll look like a walking picnic table."

Picnic tables and gingham do go together. I thought the same thing about poor Freckles.

My companion accepts the inevitable with a modicum of grace. "Oh, all right. We'll go into town and look for the gingham. We have to collect your new spectacles, anyway. I'll go tell Willard."

An hour later, the three of us are parked in the center of Stonehenge. The streets sound busy, and I inhale the brisk air like a woman on a mission.

I didn't sleep much last night due to awful nightmares involving Lady X, or rather, Freckles. I stood in a room of mirrors, and the ghost appeared in every reflection, shrieking like a Fury, clawing at the glass. When I awoke, there was an angry scratch mark on my neck. I touch the scratch and shiver—ghosts aren't supposed to cause physical harm. Drive someone mad, yes, but not hurt their bodies. What will she do to me in a month's time if I haven't found her killer?

Or maybe it's nothing at all. I might even have scratched myself while sleeping.

Shivering even more, I am determined to meet with success today. Our expedition begins at the Emporium—my old stomping grounds from childhood. I can't help feeling somewhat optimistic. The store smells of freshly ground coffee, walnuts, and new leather. Using my cane, I walk to the counter and take out the scrap of gingham. Cordelia stands at my elbow, ready to act as the middleman—middle*woman*—in our exchange.

"We're interested in some material," she says to the clerk. "Do you have any of this on hand?"

"No. Just in summer," he replies. "For tablecloths."

I feel Cordie turn my way, certain that she has a smirk on her face. The know-it-all.

We move onward to the Ladies' Dress Shop. In fact, we tromp all over creation, but there's no gingham to be had. Obviously, Stonehenge has passed a seasonal moratorium against it.

Close to giving up, Cordie and I visit my eye doctor and get the spectacles.

He tells me that the glass in the replacement pair is black instead of the usual brown. "You're fortunate, Miss Grayson. That's a finer set than most people can afford."

This comment bounces around inside my brain, and it finally occurs to me that I have been approaching my task in entirely the wrong way. Lady X, a-k-a Freckles, was 'most people.' Her clothing budget was limited.

I turn to Cordelia and smile. **You buy clothes**? I sign, filled with excitement. **Where? Where?**

"At a secondhand place," she replies. "If you spruce up the old gowns, nobody can tell the difference. Unless they owned the dress before you, that is."

Show-me-store! I ask. **Show-me-store!**

"What? Slow down, miss. I can't understand."

I try to calm myself. **Show me,** I sign slowly. **Favorite store.**

The owner of Willoughby's is kind enough to spare us a moment. Cordelia gives him the fabric, and I tell her what to say.

Woman. Red hair. Buy shirt?

Cordie sounds puzzled as she relays my message. "Have you sold a gingham blouse or shirtwaist to a woman with red hair?"

"Not in winter," he says.

Last year?

Mr. Willoughby thinks long and hard. "No, wait. I *did*, now that you mention it. The garment was poorly made, quite tacky, in fact. I gave it to her for next to nothing. I remember the lady because she had airs, and I found that inappropriate in one lacking style and good taste."

Name! I sign. **Name! Name! Name!**

Cordelia releases an embarrassed cough. "You wouldn't know her identity, by chance? Apparently, it's important."

He goes into the back room, mumbling phrases like, "highly unusual" and "better buy something."

Fortunately for us, Willoughby values order above all else. He proudly reads the date on the merchandise receipt, the 21st of April, 1890. His customer is identified as one Maude Lambson.

Her work? I ask. **Where?**

But Cordie has reached the limit. "Jumping Jehoshaphat, what does it matter?" she inquires, turning to me.

This comment is rhetorical so I don't waste time on it. Instead, I point toward Willoughby. **Ask! Her work where?**

My companion sighs gustily. "Miss Hester wonders if you know where the lady worked."

The storeowner has no idea, but I feel indebted to him anyway. I gesture to Cordelia. **Clothes**, I sign. **You buy. My treat.**

She clears out most of the high-end items, and Mr. Willoughby writes a rather extensive receipt. An embroidered shawl, silk gloves, ankle boots, muslin nightgown, feathered hat, and a day dress.

Reminder to self—Cordie cannot be trusted with carte blanche.

I hand over every dollar on my person to the shopkeeper. He promises to box up the goods and hold them until Willard arrives. Cordie and I exit the store, walking half a block before Mr. Willoughby hurries outside, his memory enhanced by hard cash.

"There was something odd about Miss Lambson!" he exclaims. "She had very dirty hair. Lots of coal soot near the roots."

Smiling, I elbow my companion, encouraging her to express my appreciation.

"Thank you, sir," she replies woodenly.

"Not at all, not at all. Come again. Should you need another receipt, my collection goes back five years."

Willard Little Hawk told us he would be at the saloon, so I give a lad my last coin to go inside and fetch him. Cordelia tells the handyman about the shop and asks him to pick up her parcels in an hour or so. She orders two baked potatoes from a street vendor and then loans me sufficient change to pay for our meal. With sign lessons beginning soon, Cordie and I hurry to Black Swan Lane, eating the taters on the fly.

Five blocks later and Stonehenge begins to change from humble to posh. The smells alone prove that we're moving uptown. Midden piles and rotgut saloons give way to restaurants, teahouses and bakeries. I know we're close to Black Swan because of the chocolatier with it's rich, box-of-candy scent and the perfumery which evokes a summer garden of lilies even in winter. I savor the aromas of the rich as we stroll along.

Two Cockney women pass Cordelia and me, chattering like magpies. "There's no satisfyin' Ol' Archie," one of them says.

"Garn," the other agrees. "'E's bad to work fer."

I listen as the girls walk through the side entrance of the Windsor Hotel, complaining about their boss the entire time. The grande dame of Stonehenge accommodations, the Windsor sits two doors away from Kelly's digs, frequented by those willing to pay a fortune for discreet luxury. In short, this is my father's sort of place. Enjoyed by the rich and made ridiculous by the poor.

A thought strikes me, and I stop in the middle of the sidewalk, upsetting Cordelia and a few other pedestrians. Lady X/Freckles/Maude Lambson must have lived nearby, certainly within walking distance of Willoughby's store. She couldn't afford to hire transportation and wasn't the type to go too far afield for shopping—Maude liked things to come easy, after all. Assuming that she worked as a maid, a fancy place like the Windsor would have brought her into contact with the rich on a daily basis, and there's a Cornish community not three minutes away on Falmouth Road.

The scratch at my neck suddenly stings, and I pull my scarf even higher. Miss Lambson worked at this very hotel and met her killer here.

She begins to weep inside my head, confirming my latest clue.

Kelly sighs and shuts the door to his office. "All right, Hester. We're alone now. Tell me why I had to send Miss Collins on an unnecessary errand."

For pipe tobacco? I sign.

"I don't smoke, you ninny." He sits down in the chair opposite me, and leans forward. "We haven't long until your companion returns. You asked for privacy?"

I take the ill-gotten piece of gingham out of my reticule, and hold it out to the doctor.

"Did you remove this from the evidence we collected yesterday?" he asks.

Maybe, I reply.

"Which means yes. Are you aware that tampering with evidence is a criminal offense?"

Know name. Lady X.

The side of Kelly's jacket swings open and hits my arm. I hear a light ticking. He must have taken out his pocket watch.

"And you deduced this in … nineteen hours? Fairly quick for a novice crime-fighter."

I reach inside my bag again and bring out the chalk and slate. I write the letters slowly—according to Cordelia, my chalkmanship leaves much to be desired. Not enough flounces and swirls for a female.

MAUDE LAMBSON

Kelly takes the slate, reads the name aloud. "This is Lady X?"

I gesture for the tablet, and he returns it.

CORNISH/MAID AT HOTEL

"Which hotel?" Kelly asks.

I return the writing tools to my reticule and stand. **Show you**, I sign quickly.

We are out of the office in seconds, and Kelly doesn't think to question how a blind girl can show him anything. He merely informs his secretary to give Cordelia a cup of tea should she return before us. After stepping out of the medical building, I turn my body to the right and point with my cane toward the Windsor.

The doctor links his arm with mine and leads me forward. "Stonehengians aren't known for cooperating with the police, Hester. I may stretch the truth a bit as I question people. Don't let it alarm you."

We cross the street and arrive at the hotel.

"I'm looking for my niece, Maude," Kelly lies to the doorman. "She worked here as a maid, I believe."

"You should talk with Archibald Evans," the fellow replies. "He's in charge of all the cleaning staff."

Evans must be the one the Cockney servants were talking about. The "Archie" who's so difficult to satisfy.

Crossing the threshold, Kelly and I enter the Windsor lobby. The room is filled with voices, echoing through the rectangular space, saying little out of the ordinary. We stop at the concierge desk, and Kelly asks for Mr. Evans. "I'll send for him," the clerk replies. "Please wait over there, in the alcove."

The overseer joins us promptly and Kelly repeats that Maude Lambson is his estranged niece. Archibald Evans accepts his claim without question. I'm a little uncomfortable with how well the doctor fabricates, actually. I may never believe another word that comes out of his mouth.

Archibald takes the seat next to Kelly, his old joints creaking. He smells like liniment, ulcer powder, and laundry starch. A curmudgeonly combination.

"Lambson left our employ some time ago. She was the *worst* maid I ever had." Evans stops there, appalled by his own candor. "Beg pardon, sir. That was a terrible thing for me to say, you being her family and all."

I feel Kelly lift the hand resting on the arm of my chair. The air stirs as he waves it magnanimously. "Don't give it another thought, man. We aren't close. Why did she leave?"

"To marry, of course. You surely must have heard that news. We had no inkling Lambson had a beau, let alone a fiancé. Took a break one afternoon, without so much as a by your leave, and sent for her things the next day."

"Who collected them?" Kelly asks.

"Wouldn't know. A hired coach arrived and the driver took her belongings."

Kelly reaches into his pocket. I hear paper moving, being unfolded, and passed to Evans. Must be money. "Any hint where he delivered Maude's possessions?"

"As I recall, the man complained about having to drop her suitcases off at the train station. In the public cloakroom where any Tom, Dick, or Harry could take them. An irregular situation, to be sure."

"Ah, I see," Kelly murmurs, slipping Archibald another bill. "And when was this?"

The elderly man pauses. "Over a year ago. Beginning of June, I think."

That fits. It sounds right.

Kelly rises to his feet, then takes my arm and helps me up. "This may seem strange, Evans. But how would you describe Maude Lambson to me?"

"Well, I suppose that she was small, had reddish hair. Came from Cornwall."

Kelly withdraws something from his pocket again. Doesn't sound crinkly, not like money this time. "Did she wear gingham similar to this sample?"

"Quite often, sir," Archibald Evans replies. "She had it on last time I saw her."

15

Quo fata ferunt.
Whither the fates bear.

We leave the Windsor, and I am thankful to be out in the open air again, until we pass the chestnut vendor. The nuts smell foul in my opinion, but Kelly feels the opposite. He's quite enthusiastic about them, and stops to buy a bag, crunching the odiferous nuts for the rest of the trip.

Cordelia greets us the moment we enter Kelly's medical building. "Where have you been? I've drunk enough tea to float away. Oh, here's your pipe tobacco, Doctor."

Kelly takes the tin. "Right. Thank you, Miss Collins. You were very kind to get it for me."

"Easily done, sir." She touches my shoulder. "It's Ma and Pa's anniversary tonight, miss. Do you remember my mentioning it?"

I certainly do—although I had forgotten. Cordie scheduled the evening off weeks in advance. She had planned to leave for the family get-together halfway through our signing lessons, but Kelly and I threw her schedule into chaos by interviewing Evans at the hotel.

"Dear Miss Collins, please make haste to the celebration and wish your parents well," Kelly says. "Our apologies for having caused you distress."

Cordelia begins to button her coat and turns to me. "Willard's at the tavern. He'll drive you home."

"Be at ease," Kelly replies. "I'll make certain she returns safely."

Have fun, I sign. **Go.**

The doctor tells his secretary to send a message to Willard, informing him that his services won't be needed. I must look surprised.

"I'll take you home after lessons. I'd like to pay a visit to your mother and see how she's feeling. You don't mind spending a little more time with me, do you?"

I pretend to be dismayed and Kelly laughs. He leads me into his private office and drops the tin of pipe tobacco on the desk. We work for over an hour on signing, adding more words and phrases to my reserve. Since our second lesson, the doctor has allowed me to keep my gloves on. They are made of thin cashmere and fit my fingers well—that way I can easily feel the position of Kelly's hands without actually touching any skin.

"You really are the brightest student a teacher could have," he says. "How do you pick things up so quickly?"

Because I hail from a Roman goddess, Doctor, and there's magic in my blood. I give Kelly a little smile, the Mona Lisa one that he enjoys.

"You're a mystery, minx," Kelly says, rising to his feet. "No doubt about it."

He waits for me to stand. "Much as I would like to linger here with you, we'd better be off. I'd hate for your mother to worry."

Kelly pays a coachman to drive us to The Revels. Once we arrive at my home, he climbs out of the vehicle and asks the driver to wait. He lifts me down, escorts me into the house. We enter the foyer, and remove our winter things, handing them to Martha. Kelly follows me up to Mama's boudoir. She is resting quietly, and I sit in the chair by the fireplace while the doctor gives her a quick assessment. Mama's voice is breathy as she answers his questions.

"Well, Mrs. Grayson," Kelly says. "Your heartbeat is rather fast, and you still exhibit unusual swelling. This is the beginning of your fifth month, correct?"

"Yes," she murmurs.

"Is the baby active? Kicking and moving?"

Mama's voice brightens. "He did near somersaults after dinner."

"That's good," Kelly replies. "Are you comfortable?" I hear him adjusting the blankets on the bed and fluffing the pillows. "Would you be willing to see an obstetric specialist? I have a colleague at the hospital vastly more experienced with troubled pregnancies than I."

My father strides into the room now, smelling of spirits. "Troubled? What do you mean by that?"

Kelly proceeds to share his concerns about my mother, but Father isn't impressed. "Maybe a bone-cutter like you isn't up to the job."

"That's exactly what I was saying to your wife, Mr. Grayson. It might be in her best interests to make a change. I can refer you to the most qualified physician in the county. He has an office in the same building as mine."

Up until this point, I have remained in my chair in the corner, calling as little attention to myself as possible. Then my cane slides off the chair arm and clatters to the floor. I sense that Father has turned my way. Anger. Embarrassment. Those are the emotions I smell on him, in addition to lots of brandy. He stumbles and the liquor sloshes within his glass.

"What's this I hear, Hester, about you traipsing around the city today? Are you too simple to know your place is at home?"

Kelly steps between us. "Your daughter's *place* is wherever she wishes to go, sir."

Father takes a drink. "Ah, I see," he says at length. "Can't find yourself a normal woman so you take what you can get. There's a good dowry, too. I'd pay a high price to be rid of her. "

I hear the doctor move close to my father. There can only be a few inches separating them. "I'd call you out this minute, if I didn't think it would upset your wife and daughter. You're in their debt today, Mr. Grayson."

Kelly's voice is so quiet and controlled. But scary too.

Grabbing my cane from the floor, I stand and walk out of the room, hoping to reach my suite before any further words are exchanged. Kelly catches up with me in the hallway.

"Wait, Hester," he says. "Wait. I'm so sorry."

I bristle at the sympathy behind his words. I would have preferred a witty, off-the-cuff remark instead. Angry words may hurt, but I'm accustomed to them. Receiving another's pity is far more painful. I won't have Kelly feeling that for me.

"Come downstairs, won't you?" he asks. "Walk with me to the door?"

Absolutely. Why the hell not? My pride's in tatters, but I'm still a good hostess.

Turning around, I follow the doctor down to the foyer. Martha helps him into his coat and Kelly sends her away with a curt expression of thanks.

"I feel badly, Hester—about what was said upstairs."

I give a small shrug and then sign, **Father jackass.**

The doctor laughs softly. "That he is."

Go home, Noah. Fine.

"Yes. I can see that you are." He pauses briefly. "I've been meaning to ask you something for hours. Do you have plans for tomorrow night?"

Plans? Me?

"I discovered a bunch of old mail behind the trash can in my office this morning. As I sorted through the mail, I found an invitation to the Fall Cotillion at Griffin House. James Scarlett, the owner of the place, has invited me to many such occasions, but I've resisted. I thought I might escort you to this one, Hester. As I said, it's tomorrow, which gives you very little time to prepare."

What time?

"Eight." Kelly puts his hand on my arm. "Maude Lambson is likely tied to Griffin House, given the ring found near her remains. Hopefully, we can identify the killer at the dance. Would you recognize his voice if you heard it?"

Immediately.

"Then tomorrow at eight, it is."

Kelly leaves me with a kiss on the top of my head. And a new situation to explain to Tom.

I meet him at midnight, and all the worries of the day fade into nothingness. I can deal with the challenges of life when he's with me.

Tom brushes the hair out of my face, tucks the strands behind my ear. *It's too cold to go up to the rocks tonight, love. Do you mind practicing with the knives at our barn instead?*

Feeling sorry for other women, I count my blessings—because he's mine.

Sounds perfect.

Tom nudges his horse to go faster. *You're certainly easy to please.*

No. I'm just happy right now.

"Bad day, love?" he asks, going vocal.

There's no reason to rehash the situation with my father. Tom already hates him, and it wouldn't change anything.

No, just busy. Lots to tell.

"That's fine," Tom murmurs. "We have all night."

So I share almost everything. How I learned Maude Lambson's identity and met her employer at the Windsor Hotel. I tell him that I am attending the cotillion with Kelly, as a means of finding Maude's killer, and he reluctantly admits it's a good idea. Once the perpetrator is brought to justice, Lambson's spirit will move on to the afterlife, and she won't haunt me anymore. Then Tom and I will be able to focus on finding the heir of Archimendax.

I don't share that the doctor gave me a goodbye kiss on the head. Tom thinks the cotillion is dangerous enough as it is. Knowledge of the kiss would only add fuel to the fire of his discontent.

"I'm going," he says. "I'll stay outside Griffin House, in the shadows, but I'll be there to help."

Thank you. I won't be afraid if you're near.

We ride across the Craddock ranch, and I sense Tom's pride of belonging to such a spread. After reaching the stable, he tells me he has brought the targets down from the mountain. The barn is a large structure, far bigger in every way than his house. Tom helps me gain a sense of dimension and space in an isolated section of the building, and I throw my knives well. Arms aching, I finish with a flourish by hitting three bags within seconds of each other.

Tom picks up the knives and returns them to me. "Now you're ready, love."

———————— ● ————————

The next day is a blur of activity. Cordelia and I visit the orphanage in the morning and practice signing for a few hours afterward. She finds me a dress in the armoire that I can use for the cotillion, adding a strip of black lace to the hem since I've grown an inch or so over the last year. Cordie says it's midnight blue and has bits of jet beading sewn here and there. Around seven, I slip into the gown and my long evening gloves, and she gives me one final inspection. With my hair smelling of orange blossoms, ornate combs holding it high upon my head, my companion's work is evidently finished.

The moment of truth has arrived, and it's time for Cinderella to depart for the ball. I find a comfortable chair in the library and wait for Kelly, mink cloak draped across my lap. I check that my lucky pebbles are in the pocket and smile at myself for being silly. They're just stones from a creek bed in the woods, nothing extraordinary. Except that they came into my possession during my first escape, when my nanny fell asleep in the rose garden after a picnic. Counting my steps, I walked the length of our property and ended up in the forest. I fell a few times but it didn't matter, I was free and happy. I dunked my feet in the creek and found the pebbles, napped in the sun, and listened to the birds sing. My life at The Revels felt small and cold by comparison and I realized there was much more to experience than my parent's home had to offer.

Yet I believed I could escape my sterile existence, if I was clever enough. Such knowledge brought a confidence, a boldness which I lacked before.

Rising to my feet, I pat the lucky stones in my cloak pocket and smooth my layered skirts. No use looking like a wrinkled fool at the cotillion. Upstairs, Father shouts for the butler to bring him his tonic, and my muscles automatically tense. I remind myself that I need not worry. He won't be attending the ball tonight. His stomach is ill, the old ulcer flaring up again.

Don't think of how angry he'll be in the morning.

Without doubt, some sort of punishment looms in my future, but I would hate to be discovered now. Banished to my room without even completing this investigative mission. Leaving the library, I walk to the front door, open it quietly, and go outside. There are three steps ahead of me. I hold the handrail and descend them, using my cane only when I am out of earshot. Night sounds fill the air—the snap of a twig, fluttering wings, branches scratching a window pane.

And weeping.

A shiver runs up my spine as Freckles, or rather Maude Lambson, materializes. *Do your job, Visionary. Or Death will come for you.*

Maude begins threatening me with the worst kinds of torment. Is she telling the truth? Is the Reaper under her control? Knowing Maude's tendency to blackmail, I think not or not yet at any rate. As an immortal, He's seen most of the subterfuge the world has to offer, and I doubt a hotel maid could pull the wool over His eyes.

Maude/Freckles abuses my character even more, using bad language and Cornish insults. Then I begin to wonder if she really wishes to pass over to the other side or if she just enjoys the power of haunting. I feel Maude's breath against the side of my neck. The ghost is standing a few inches away, temporarily exhausted from her tantrum. The scabbed-over scratch at my throat burns like it's new.

Shut her out, Hester. Get to the cotillion; that's your next step.

Maude Lambson suddenly gives me breathing room. She is distracted by the appearance of Carver, the old gambler ghost whom I last saw when I was bathing. I focus on his presence with my mind and envision him strutting about the driveway in his blue silk vest, marching like a soldier on guard detail. Carver pretends to carry a rifle. He tips an imaginary hat my way and points the invisible gun at Maude. She flies at him, thrilled to have a new victim to abuse.

The rewards of a Visionary are not worth this level of distress. I pinch the bridge of my nose and exhale. Are there any rewards? Have I ever received one? Carver interjects at this point. *Skedaddle*, he whispers in my head, sounding half sane. *Go while the redhead's occupied.*

I nearly fall while counting my steps to the end of the drive. I call out to Tom telepathically. He seems harried, too.

On my way, love. I'll be at Griffin House when you arrive.

His affection and comfort surround me, and for a split-second, my anxiety disappears. I am so enthralled by our mental connection that I do not notice the doctor's arrival and give a little jump at the sound of his voice.

"What are you doing out here by the road, Hester?" Kelly asks.

Ghosts, my father, nerves... **Hello**, I sign.

"Let's get you into this carriage and be quick about it."

Thank you. Kind gentleman.

The coach is a luxury model, large and comfortable. It must have cost the doctor dearly to rent. We travel to Griffin House, and I sense Tom's presence, hidden away in the garden. A fashionable fifteen minutes late, Kelly and I climb the steps to the gentlemen's club. By all accounts, this establishment is sumptuous. It has billiard rooms, a chess salon, an in-house barber, fencing practice, and a pugilism ring. Not to mention a library for the cerebrally inclined and a saloon for those who prefer to pickle their brains instead. Most well-to-do Stonehengian males over the age of eighteen dream of being members of this place.

The entry way is redolent with the smell of evergreen boughs and crushed cloves. I feel Kelly take something out of his vest pocket and hand it to the butler. We are then introduced at the ballroom door. "Dr. Noah Kelly and Miss Hester Grayson."

I subdue my ears to better tolerate the quartet playing in the musician's gallery above. The waltz is slow and lilting, and I wish I knew the dance steps to accompany the tune. Voices whisper on all sides, and I listen to one after another.

But nothing signifies, just a lot of idle conversation.

"Let's have some punch, Hester," Kelly says. "Circulate a bit."

He puts a cup into my hand. The liquid inside is flavored with citrus, cinnamon, and honey. I take another sip, and Kelly leads me about the room, chatting with the other partygoers and allowing me to hear their voices.

"Anything?" he asks an hour later.

I shake my head. **Sorry,** I sign. **Not yet.**

A man steps up and joins us. Kelly seems to know him. "I must admit, Mr. Scarlett. You throw as fine a party as I've ever attended."

"Thank you, Doctor," an attractive voice replies. "It's high time you joined us."

Kelly puts his hand on my back. "May I introduce you to Miss Grayson? Hester, this is Mr. Scarlett."

"An absolute delight," Scarlett says, taking my hand.

I smile and offer a small curtsy. So this is the owner of Griffin House? Our younger maids whisper about him with the greatest reverence. According to them, he's God's gift to women and quite without equal in degrees of handsomeness and sophistication.

He turns toward Kelly. "How is it that I've never met this lovely creature? Been hiding her away, have you? Keeping her all to yourself?"

Kelly laughs. "I'm afraid she's spoken for, Scarlett. Your hopes are dashed."

I ignore the banter and use my gift of olfaction. Interesting.

No scent to Mr. Scarlett at all. No emotions of any kind, no sweat on warm skin. Not even a drop of liquor to his breath. If I hadn't heard his footsteps and voice, I'd swear Kelly and I were standing here alone. Of course, there are exceptions with olfaction, rare people whom I find difficult to read. Perhaps this man is one of those.

Out of the blue, Scarlett asks for a dance. What? How *embarrassing*. Does he not realize I am blind? A bolt of terror runs through me and my limbs feel gawky and uncoordinated. I turn to Kelly, seeking rescue, but he does not intervene. The doctor takes my cane.

"It's a party, Hester. Enjoy yourself. I'll give the cane back when your dance is finished."

Scarlett puts his hand at my waist and draws me onto the floor. "It's easy, Miss Grayson," he says in a kind voice. "Just follow my lead."

My partner is a sublime instructor. He negotiates the floor effortlessly, skilled enough to put a sightless neophyte at ease. At last, a town rake who lives up to his legend!

"Thank you," he murmurs, when the set is finished.

We are walking back to Kelly when another fellow steps forward. He returns me to the dance floor before I can refuse. The night goes on forever, or so it seems according to my dance card. I must be a novelty to the men of Stonehenge. Yet we have accomplished nothing in regards to solving Maude's murder, even though I have listened to most of the men in the room.

Kelly has not returned with my cane, and my feet are aching. Cursing the inventor of high-heeled shoes, I limp off the dance floor with the help of my last partner. He is anxious to conquer the next lady and leaves me in a quiet alcove. A curtain divides the tiny space from the rest of the ballroom, and I pull it aside, desperate for a moment of relative peace. The silk sofa cushions feel like heaven beneath my weary back. Dancing is hard, dangerous work, and I want nothing more to do with it. Let Maude haunt me all she likes.

"Parties can be so tiresome," a voice says from the other side of the sofa. "Especially if there's dancing."

The woman sounds friendly. For want of a better reply, I point to my throat and shake my head.

"Oh, you don't speak? That's all right. My husband says I talk enough for ten people."

I smile at her self-deprecation, and she laughs softly.

"My name's Cecily Thornhill. I was a Vaughn before I married my David." Cecily pats my knee, laughs again. "Forgive my tendency to ramble. I haven't been out in public since Junior was born."

I like this lady. She has a genuine, endearing quality about her. Like a child with an enormous amount of love to give and not enough people to give it to.

"Have you always lived in Stonehenge?" Cecily asks.

I nod in reply.

"Perhaps you could visit our place in Summerton when the weather improves? It's only twenty miles by train. We could make a day of it and—" She stops midsentence and releases a happy-sounding sigh. "I always get carried away. David says I'm far too enthusiastic, but it *is* so nice to make a new acquaintance."

Cecily talks for twenty minutes straight, and I find we have much in common. Both of us like having books read aloud, the smell of lilacs, and cashmere blankets. But neither of us enjoys liverwurst, oysters, or dentistry. While I am pleased at the prospect of gaining a friend, I remind myself of my true purpose in attending this party. I try to think of an excuse that would allow me to go in search of Kelly.

Then Cecily turns toward the left and fairly quivers with excitement.

"Oh, David," she says. "There you are!"

"It's getting late, darling. We should go. Can't having you tiring yourself."

I freeze in my corner of the sofa.

David Thornhill is Mr. Murder.

16

Quem di diligunt, adulescens moritur.
He whom the gods love dies young. —Plautus

Pulling the alcove curtain forward, I hope to conceal my profile, but Cecily pushes it aside. "Let me introduce you to my new bosom friend. Don't be bashful, dear. Show yourself, and meet my David."

I feel his gaze running over me. "Do we know each other?" he asks, a puzzled note in his voice.

As soon as I shake my head, I sense a new tension in the air. Thornhill remembers Halloween night. Will he tell his wife about our encounter in the gazebo? When I touched the killer's face and he thought me mad?

No. He ignores me instead and chats with Cecily about Junior needing her at home.

"Would you like a last glass of punch before we go, dearest wife?" Thornhill asks. "It's rather good."

"Oh, I've already had too much, David." Cecily stands and touches my arm. "I hear Mr. Scarlett built a ladies room for this event. Marble floors, golden sinks. Why don't we visit it together?"

Yes, let's do that. I'd like to get away from Mr. Murder now that I have his real name. Pushing up from the sofa, I turn toward Cecily, as though I intend to leave with her.

"Your friend needn't follow you to the lavatory," David Thornhill says. "Run along, sweetheart. I'll keep her company until you return."

She laughs, apparently chagrined. "Bossiness is one of my worst faults. If you don't wish to go, I won't make you."

What I don't wish is to remain here with her husband. I move to follow Cecily, but Thornhill grabs my waist and pushes me in the opposite direction. Unaware of his actions, his wife continues on the other way.

We leave the ballroom through a side entrance, and I call out for Tom in my head.

Killer's here! West end of the building.

Right. On my way, love.

"Damnedest thing," Thornhill mutters, as we travel down the hall. "What are the odds?" He suddenly stops and pulls off my glasses. "I read the newspaper only this morning—sensational story about a blind girl who overheard a murderer's confession. But I didn't believe it."

Seconds tick by as Thornhill studies my face. Emotions swirl around him. He's terrified of being exposed for his crime and completely baffled as to how he ended up here with me. "How could you know? I never said a word to anyone. Not a living soul."

A sliding, metallic sound. Like the hammer of a revolver clicking into place.

Take care, Tom. Gun.

"Don't move a muscle," Thornhill says. He presses the hard nose of the weapon into my hip. "We're going to the stables now, and you'll do just as I tell you."

We take a few steps and something big hurtles past me and tackles Thornhill, knocking him to the ground. Things happen simultaneously—an awful popping sound, the smell of gunpowder and sharp particles bouncing off the wall next to my head. They puncture my cheek in several places. I stumble, fall backwards, and hit the floor. My ears are bleeding from the sound waves, and I retch, willing myself not to vomit as I subdue my hearing.

Holy hell.

Humanity floods the hall—still so loud, so loud—and Kelly calls my name. People shout complaints as he pushes them aside. "Where's the fire?" "Look out, good fellow!" "Who do you think you are?" My head pounds with the noise.

"What happened?" he asks, reaching me. "There's blood on your face. Are you all right?"

Still a little dazed, I nod and point to where Thornhill fell. The killer is crying. "An accident," he wails. "Didn't mean to hurt him."

He smells of terror and regret. This clears the confusion in my head, replacing it with panic. *Tom? Dearest? Are you there?*

Aye, love. Don't worry.

Deo favente. Thank the gods you're safe!

A great commotion erupts as David Thornhill is taken through the back exit. "Help me," he says. "Send for my attorney."

Kelly kneels down beside Tom, and immediately begins cursing. "I'll need my medical bag. Craddock's been hit."

What? The bullet struck you? How bad is it? Why didn't you say something?

K-knew... you'd...fret.

I crawl forward and grasp Tom's leg, working my way up his body. The leather duster—Tom's cowboy coat—feels slick in some places. Blood, so much blood! I find his hand and lift it to my heart. *Hold on, sweetheart. That's it. You're going to be fine, I just know it.* Kelly shouts orders—has the crowd disbanded and clean linen brought. The doctor is strangely quiet as he works on Tom.

My beloved coughs. Wet, sputtering. "*Amor vincit omnia,*" he whispers.

A tear rolls off my chin, drops onto our threaded fingers. Another cough breaks through Tom's lips, and a horrifying realization strikes me. He's saying goodbye.

You can't leave, Tom. What an idiotic notion.

But his thoughts grow hazy, and he shudders under my hand. I kiss his forehead, eyelids, and cheeks, over and over, blood soaking through my gloves and smudging my chin. I would gladly sell my soul to the highest bidder, if it meant saving Tom's life. I send message after message, pleading for him to live.

Breathe, darling! Don't give up. You're all I have in the world. Can't you see?

So cold, Hettie. Hold me tighter.

I cradle him as close as I can, but he doesn't respond. *Don't you dare quit, Thomas Craddock. You stay and fight.*

Lifting his knuckles to my mouth, I close my eyes, and listen, until the whole universe narrows to the beating of just two hearts. *Thud-thud. Thud-thud.* His grows slower and slower and finally stops. *No, stay. Stay here.* Then my body seizes, as though I'm drowning, and I can't get any air. I rock back and forth—*Wait, Tom. Wait for me*—keening in my head, still clutching his hand. But Kelly interrupts and hauls me to my feet. He hits me hard on the back, and shocked, I gasp in oxygen.

"Get her out of here!" the doctor yells.

Someone takes me to a nearby room. Is it James Scarlett? Whoever the fellow is, he puts me on a chair, and shoves a drink into my hand. I don't know what to do with the scotch so I rest it on my thigh. *Tom? Tom?* He doesn't answer. Why would he be so cruel? His silence is enough to kill me. I drop the drink and the glass bounces away. Rising to my feet, I feel unmoored and adrift in a life that makes no sense. What do I do now? Where have they taken Tom that he cannot hear?

Oblivion embraces me and I succumb.

* * *

The smell of lye is strong, like the laundering house after a busy day of cleaning sheets. Other scents permeate the air, more medicinal in nature, and my tongue tastes bitter. What are those sounds? Horses? Carriages dashing down the street? They're driving so fast. At first, I am befuddled by these unfamiliar conditions, but memory has a way of catching up with one.

Heavy as a stone, it presses against every cell in my being. Yet I feel empty, too—like a fruitless, hollow pod waiting to be cast into the fire.

Tom, my love. Tom…

Nothing. Just the painful clarity of my own thoughts.

This private grieving is interrupted when someone walks down the hall toward my room. It's a woman, I think. She moves slowly, side to side, as though each step brings discomfort. Old age, perhaps? A bad back? Turning my face into the pillow, I stop myself. I do not wish to play this idiotic guessing game. What's the point?

The door to my room opens, and a woman shuffles over to the bed. "Good," she says. "You're awake. I'll get Dr. Kelly."

I roll over and draw my knees to my stomach. If only Kelly would stay away. Leave me alone for a while. But he comes quickly and makes a racket, pulling a chair to the side of my bed. He sits down and waits for half a minute in silence before touching my shoulder.

"Stop pretending you're asleep, Hester," he says. "You're at Stonehenge Hospital. I brought you here last night and removed the splinters from your face. Particles from when the bullet hit a wooden beam in the ceiling. Looks worse than it is at the moment, but I doubt you'll scar."

His voice is tired, as though he's barely scraping along on adrenaline. Perspiration, dried blood, and coffee. For the first time since I've known Kelly, he does not smell nice.

"I don't want to offer you false hope, but Tom Craddock is alive. For now anyway."

I sit up and reach for the doctor—clutching at his arm—and silently beg him to continue.

"He *was* dead. For nearly three minutes, I tried everything I knew to bring him back, and then I pounded on his chest with my fist. Repeatedly, not even expecting it to work. But Tom inhaled after the fourth blow and kept right on breathing. I didn't think he would last through the next hour, but he did. Doubted he'd survive the night. He did that, too."

Visit him? I sign.

I can feel Kelly nodding his head. "Later this afternoon. We'll have to watch for infection, and see how he progresses. I've never had a patient survive this kind of trauma."

Lambson's killer?

"In jail. He went mad once they locked his cell, confessed everything before the lawyer arrived. David Phillip Thornhill, if that's his actual name, is a con man with a long list of aliases. When he visited Stonehenge, Maude Lambson recognized him from a job he did a few years ago and wanted payment for her silence."

David Phillip Thornhill. It matches the initials on the engraved cufflinks from the vision—DTP.

Maybe Kelly's learned more details about the killer's motive. **Why murder? Why not leave town?**

The doctor's hands make a scrubbing noise as he rubs them over his face. "I asked Thornhill that very thing but he said he couldn't leave."

Because?

"Because he loves his wife. Thornhill wanted to be the man she thought he was, to make his new identity real. Claims he heard a voice in his head, urging him to do away with Lambson in order to protect his family. The fellow must be insane."

After hearing my stomach rumble, Kelly decides that I need sustenance. He insists upon a cup of tea with sugar when I decline food and goes to find the old nurse. Poor lady. She'll have to walk all this way with her bad back just to deliver my tea.

Leaning on my pillow, I consider Kelly's inaccurate assessment of Thornhill. The killer is not insane but selfish, weak and impressionable. He was used by the heir of

Archimendax due to those very characteristics. But why influence David Thornhill to murder Maude Lambson?

Her ghost has finally moved on to the spirit world with the assistance of Sir Death. I saw her departure in my rather troubled sleep.

Not yet, Sir Death, Maude begged. *That Visionary should pay. I've been so patient.*

You have, Death agreed. *What price do you ask?*

She leaned against the Reaper and smiled. *All I deserve.*

Death's blue gaze turned shrewd—perhaps He wasn't as taken with her as I thought. *Oh, Maude. I'm afraid that's not my judgment to make. You'll get what you deserve on the other side.*

No, Death. You owe me.

If Maude imagined treasure or wealth untold, she was disappointed. The ghost pounded on Sir Death's chest, but He only smiled, pulling out His pocket watch. *It's time to move on, Maude. Your eternal reward awaits.*

He encircled her with his billowing cloak, and that was the last I saw of Freckles.

I touch the scratch on my throat and wish her well in the afterlife. Something tells me she's going to need all the positive thoughts she can acquire.

The blanket makes me feel closed in, so I push it off my body. I wonder where my clothes might be. Should I feel my way around the room and search them out? Are they here? Halting footsteps and sweet-smelling tea arrive as I move my legs to the side of the bed. The nurse enters my room and I gratefully accept the cup she puts into my hands. Kelly was right when he insisted on the tea. It's hot and strong and restorative. I may even feel human again soon.

The doctor comes in next and returns to the chair at my bedside. "I had to get these for you. Thornhill carried them in his suit pocket."

Patting the area on the mattress where he placed the object, I locate my glasses. **Thank you, Noah**, I sign.

"I shouldn't have left you alone at Griffin House, Hester. Will you ever forgive me?"

No blame.

"I was foolish. I told Scarlett I suspected one of the fellows in his club of committing murder, and he said that I could look over the membership records. I thought it would only take a few minutes to scan through the names, but I lost track of time."

While I listen to Kelly's explanation, something doesn't make sense. Not about him leaving me to go with Scarlett but about Thornhill. He was confused when we met at the ball, as though he didn't quite know me at first. But that doesn't sound right. *If* he had made the recent attempts on my life—the wagon accident and the attack near the ravine—surely Thornhill would have recognized my face immediately. I share these impressions with Kelly.

"It could be that the man was just stringing you along. His wife was standing right there, after all. Obviously, he would go to great lengths to keep her in the dark."

I shake my head. **Didn't know me.**

"I'll consider it," Kelly replies. "Right now, I want you to be clear on Tom's situation."

I reach out and hug him as he's babbling on about survival percentages. This quiets the doctor and for a moment, we just hold each other. Until he pushes me away, back to business once again.

"Miss Collins is coming within the hour, bringing you clean clothing and the like. Before she arrives, I'll have the nurses get a pitcher of hot water and some soap. That way, you can wash and make yourself presentable. Wouldn't want Craddock waking up to a grimy mess, would we?"

17

Dum spiro, spero.
While I breathe, I hope–Cicero

Newly washed and wearing a clean gown, I follow Cordelia to the men's ward on the south side of the hospital. It's the treatment hub for those patients likely to die. Nurses move between the beds. Changing sheets and dressings, removing bedpans, administering medication. I detect the haunting scent of laudanum—something I never wanted to smell again in this life. Some of the sick murmur in pain, while others are deathly silent.

Tom? Can you hear me?

His mind is quiet and unresponsive. There is no communication between us, but I am content he is still among the living.

Cordie seems unhappy we are here. I know this from her tapping foot and near-constant sighing. She figures she knows everything about me and cannot understand how I came to be friends with this undisclosed male.

"Who is he?" she finally asks. "The fellow you wish to visit?"

I finger spell, **T-O-M C-R-A-D-D-O-C-K** and then show Cordie my usual sign for his name. My companion flags down a nurse and asks for his location.

"Oh, yes," the woman replies. "Follow me."

She leads us to Tom's bed, and Cordelia informs me that there is only one chair. This situation makes her tap her foot again.

I sit down and wave her away. **Come back later. Four hours.**

"What would your father say?"

Don't care. Go.

"I'll tell you what he'd say. You're fired, Collins! Collect your things and depart!"

Calm down. Father won't find out.

"Remember Halloween night? What a disaster that was! I barely escaped with my employment intact." Cordelia turns toward the bed and surveys Tom. "He does have a nice face though, Miss Hester. Kind-looking, strong."

Yes.

"Wish I had those lovely lashes. Good jaw line, too."

I nod, eyes misting up behind the black glass of my spectacles.

"You're sure you'll be all right?" Cordie murmurs, cracking under my will at last. "Can I get you anything? Water? A handkerchief?"

No. Thank you.

"I'll be back at five. Willard can cool his heels 'til then."

Cordelia leaves the ward, and I reach for Tom's hand. His pulse feels weak, so different than it did before. I remove my glove and touch his face, running my fingers along his cheek, smoothing the laugh lines around his eyes.

A clock chimes downstairs in the next hour of my vigil, and again sixty minutes later. A nurse wants to check Tom's wound and asks me to step away for a while. I use my cane and walk to an empty corner of the men's ward. Kelly joins me, sandwiches in hand.

"Thought you might like a bite," he says. "I have bottles of lemonade in my pockets, too."

Not hungry, I sign.

Kelly takes my arm, turning me toward the door. "Well, I am, and I don't care to eat alone."

We leave the ward, turn right, and walk for several yards. Then the doctor stops and leads me through a narrow doorway. "Sorry," he says, as I step inside the room. "It's a tiny place, but it works when I need a quick wink. No chairs, I'm afraid. You sit on the cot, and I'll take the floor."

The rope and canvas bed groans loudly as I rest my weight on it. I scoot to the edge of the feather tick, face hot.

"Never mind, Hester. It always does that. Here's your sandwich and some dried apples. Eat up."

I bite into the thick, buttered bread and taste a delicate slice of ham inside, a daub of grainy mustard layered between. The dried apples stick to my teeth, and I roll my tongue into the crevices to capture the last of their sweetness. So much for not being hungry.

"Hit the spot?" Kelly asks, a smile in his voice.

Thank you. Very good.

Once our early supper is finished, Kelly delivers me back to my chair near Tom's bed. "Craddock's quite pale, but I haven't seen any infection or fever, which is a marvel. Have faith, Hester. Your fellow's a tough one. He obviously has something to live for."

I smile, skimming my fingers along the edge of the bed until I find Tom's hand and link it with mine. Kelly turns to the patient across the aisle and asks the man about his level of pain. He calls for a nurse and prescribes a different medication. From there, Kelly wanders among the suffering, making every effort to ease their discomfort. He fights a losing battle but does so valiantly.

Having returned from taking Maude Lambson to her afterlife, Sir Death hangs about these people—a long shadow stretching toward their sick beds. I feel Him biding time, waiting beyond the room's threshold.

In the corner of the room—approximately thirty feet away—I hear a soft, convulsive groan, followed by stillness. Sir Death hovers no more but enters swiftly and flies to the bedside of the dying man. Though it is rare, some humans see Him in their last moments, when the veil separating mortality and the after-life grows thin. He appears to them as a family member or an old friend, come to bring them home to the other side.

The Reaper draws the man's spirit from his body and glances over. I reach across Tom, shielding him from Sir Death. *No shadow on this one. Pass him by.*

He rolls His eyes, gently mocking. *If it's Craddock's destiny, I will come. You cannot stop me, Lady V.*

Damn, He's got me there. Death is always in cahoots with the clock. I watch the newly departed soul looking about the ward in confusion. The Reaper takes his arm and draws the fellow upward, toward the ceiling, as though he weighs no more than a feather. The dead man does not call out to me for justice or retribution, but journeys easily to the other side. Death isn't gone for long. In an instant, He's back at the threshold.

———————— ● ————————

"Hello!" Cordelia exclaims.

I nearly spring out of my chair. Confound it. How did I not hear her approach? Angry squirrels are usually quieter than my companion.

Tsk, tsk, Visionary. Sir Death laughs at His post near the door. *Am I distracting you?*

Not at all, Sir.

He can be so egotistical, this Reaper. Still, I prefer egotism to His anger—it's far better for my health.

Cordelia scoots by me and picks up my cane and reticule. "We have thirty minutes to get you home, miss. Willard's waiting out front."

All right, I sign.

After kissing his hand, I stand and touch Tom's face, feel his motionless features. He could be a marble statue, except for the warm skin and the slight stirring of breath at his lips. I don't know why I do it, perhaps it's Sir Death being so close, but I make a sign upon Tom's forehead—marking him with a V.

Deus tibi faveat. May the favor of the gods be upon you.

———————— ● ————————

I nod at the Reaper as Cordelia and I exit the men's ward. Kelly told her about the cotillion and she peppers me with questions the entire trip home, especially about David Thornhill.

"Why ever did he try to kill you of all people? It seems so farfetched."

Kelly's explanation didn't cover all the details of our night out, but I am too tired to explain. **Ask Doctor**, I sign.

She snorts with feeling. "Our next appointment isn't 'til Monday! Must I wait that long?"

See him tomorrow. Hospital.

"We're going back?"

Appealing to her romantic nature, I suggest that Cordelia and her sweetheart Isaac spend time together while I'm with Tom. "Hmm," Cordelia replies, after some consideration. "That might be nice."

My father was still ill when she left this morning, and I can't help saying a prayer of thanks. Fate plays havoc with my life most days and this development is like a gift from above. We reach The Revels before the appointed supper hour, but I have no appetite, since Kelly fed me a short while ago. Cordelia removes the untouched tray from my room and leaves for the servant's dining area below stairs. I grow restless, trapped within my little suite. I take up my cane and walk through the house, ending up at my mother's chamber. She greets me in a quiet fashion, but doesn't mention the splinter marks on my face. Did she even look my way? I doubt it, caught up as she is with her own worries. Cherub moves less and less, and Mama says her new doctor isn't optimistic about a full-term delivery.

My mother reads aloud from the *Ladies' Home Journal*, but Mama doesn't stop to comment on a certain article, as is her habit, or make further plans for the nursery. She doesn't ask about the drama I experienced yesterday. Does she even know? Has my father learned of it? If not, he soon will, and I hope to be several counties away when he does.

After an hour passes, I seek my bed, and fall asleep quickly. My subconscious replays the fight between Tom and David Thornhill. Blood is everywhere, splattered on the wall, dripping from the ceiling. It gushes from Tom's abdomen, forming a pool at my feet, glazing my shoes and ankles.

Lips blue, he looks at me balefully. "I did it for you, love. All for you."

"No," I cry. "No."

At lightning speed, the scene moves back to the point before Tom comes to my rescue. I alter my circumstances and wrestle with Thornhill, try to wrench the gun from his hand, and throw myself against him.

It doesn't matter what I do, the end is always the same. Tom enters the dream and dies to save me.

* * *

I go through the motions of my morning toilette in a daze, but then Cordelia takes over. She does my hair, sees that the pleats of my dress are just so, and fetches me a set of gloves to match. I hear hooves crunching up our driveway. The horse sounds large and its bridle jingles. Is it the one belonging to Kelly? I step into the hall, filled with dread. He can have no other reason to be here now than to tell me something awful.

The front door opens and a person enters the house without invitation, bounds up the stairs. The scent of horseflesh and pine resin swirls about him. It is Kelly.

"Into your room, Hester," he whispers, guiding me by the elbow.

Once we're seated in my bedroom parlor, my head grows light, and I have trouble breathing. The doctor rubs my back vigorously. "Exhale, woman. Don't pass out on me."

I rally at his words, trying to regain my composure and lung function.

"Prepare yourself for good news, minx. Craddock woke up this morning. Ate, drank. The nurses even got him to walk a few steps. All positive physical developments."

I lift my face at Kelly's tone. His use of tact is frightening—it doesn't become him at all.

What? I sign. **What else?**

Kelly keeps his hand on my back. "In addition to the obvious wounds, it would seem that Tom sustained further injury. I don't know how to soften the blow, Hester. I performed some tests this morning, and the results were disturbing. Tom's brain has been affected. His memory, to be precise."

Tom can't remember?

"Everything exists for him only in the present tense. No past, little comprehension of the future. Just here and now. I can't explain why—it might be due to lack of oxygen after his heart stopped. Or there could be psychological issues involved." I feel Kelly shrug. "I've seen it happen before, with the patient recovering his full faculties. In a few cases, however, the situation is permanent."

No memory? None?

"Tom didn't recognize his own mother an hour ago. Wasn't even sure what their relationship entailed. But once Mrs. Craddock was identified, he accepted their connection. That's promising."

The doctor settles back into the sofa cushions. "If Tom can relearn things, we have hope for recovery. Are you up to the challenge of teaching him?"

How? I ask and point to myself. **Dumb. Blind.**

"You love the man," Kelly replies, exasperated. "Craddock knew it once, and if you're brave enough to stick it out, he'll know it again. Are you willing to try?"

Yes. *Yes.*

"That's the answer I expected. Are you coming to the hospital today?"

Cordelia bring me.

Without further comment, the doctor rises, and we walk to the front door.

He mounts his horse and says farewell. "I'll see you soon."

Soon, I sign in return.

18

Alea iacta est.

The die is cast—Julius Caesar

I have Cordelia run into Hollister's, the place where Tom and I first met. She hurries back with a pound of English toffee—his favorite treat—assuring me that it's tastefully wrapped.

"I added a small note," Cordie says. "To wish him a speedy recovery. I signed your name at the bottom, miss."

Ambivalent about the note, I thank her anyway and hold the parcel on my lap as we drive to the hospital. Willard drops us off and Cordelia goes with me to Tom's floor. She says there's a screen drawn around his bed, so I take a seat a short distance away. We arrange to meet at five and then my companion leaves.

Sir Death is at His post by the door. He must visit often. Stonehenge boasts the biggest hospital in the area, and patients are brought over from every town in the county.

I listen for anything that might concern Tom.

He has a visitor with him now. A female. I know this by the creaking of a tightly laced corset, and the mothball smell of her dress. I assume it's a rarely worn garment, brought out after months in storage.

"You were named after my great-uncle," she says. "He was a good, hard-working man, too."

Tom's mother? I feel a sudden kinship, bound by shared love and grief. Not wishing to infringe upon a family moment, I stand and turn toward the door. I intend to wait in the hall, but a nurse takes it upon herself to divest me of Tom's English toffee.

"You needn't be shy, dear," she says, removing the box from my hands. "I'll deliver it to Mr. Craddock."

What? No! Unhand that toffee!

But I'm too slow to grab the parcel back. With the best of intentions, I assume, the nurse moves the privacy screen a few inches to the right. "Sorry to interrupt, sir, but you have a present from an admirer."

Mrs. Craddock leaves her chair and asks for the box. On pins and needles, I hear her remove the ribbon, lift the lid. "Why, it's candy. The store-boughten kind."

Grunting a little from exertion, Tom shifts on his bed. "Who's it from?"

Joy surges through me, and I bite my lip. His voice is quiet, weak even, but any words from Tom are more than acceptable. I didn't anticipate how happy I would be upon hearing them.

Now there's a bending-paper sound, like the card being opened. "Hester Grayson," Mrs. Craddock murmurs.

Is that disappointment in her tone? And the scent on her skin? Surely, it can't be jealousy.

"Is this person a friend of mine?"

"Just a girl from town," Mrs. Craddock says. "Follows you around like a puppy. It isn't healthy, in my opinion, having someone like that at your heels. Handicapped, you know. Still, her family is rich."

I follow him around like a puppy? At his heels?

"Miss Grayson's right outside the screen," the nurse says, ever helpful. "Waiting for a visit."

Tom moves on the bed again, groaning in pain. "Bring her over. So I can say thank you."

Beyond embarrassed now, tears forming, I step back and bump into the wall. Kelly's private room is just around the corner, and I hurry into the hall and count the doors until I reach number five. Thankfully, the room is empty, but it smells of peppermint, like Kelly often does. My thoughts return to Mrs. Craddock as I climb onto the squeaky cot.

After all these years, I never knew she felt that way. She seemed uncomfortable around me at times, apologizing for the state of her clothing or the messiness of her home—as if I could even see those things. Despite our differences, I thought we were friendly.

Don't blubber, Hester. It won't help.

The urge to reach out to Tom and test our clairvoyant bond is overwhelming, but I decide to wait until he's stronger. Fatigued myself, I pull the blanket to my chin and doze. Then I hear Kelly's voice.

"Wake up, minx," the doctor says. "I looked everywhere for you and finally thought of this place. I'm tired of hide-and-seek."

I prop myself up on one elbow and sign, **Tom's mother**.

"Scared you off, did she?"

I nod, caught out with the truth.

He squats down by the bed. "Can you blame the woman? It's obvious she's played second fiddle in her son's affections for years."

Hurts.

"Undoubtedly, but she's gone now, home to cook dinner for her brood. Let's reacquaint you with Tom." Kelly pulls me up by the hand. "You might want to fix that collar first and pin back the hair drooping over your ear."

With the doctor's help, I make myself more presentable.

Look, I sign, and point at the puncture marks on my face. **Ugly**.

Kelly merely laughs. "The scabs from the splinter wounds, do you mean?

Yes. Must be terrible.

"Oh, come now. Even with a few of those, you'll do."

We leave the little sleeping chamber and walk toward the recovery ward. After a few steps, I panic once more and turn back.

Kelly hauls me around. "Wrong way," he mutters. "I would have thought you'd be plowing people over to reach Craddock's bedside."

Mother hates me. What if Tom hates me, too?

"Where is your spine, Hester? You'll never know what he's feeling if you remain in this hallway."

To blazes with Kelly. I have spine to spare. Answering the challenge in his words, I finish the journey to the sick room without stopping. The doctor stands with me just outside the door.

"He's worth fighting for, I presume?"

Yes.

"Then take a deep breath and square your shoulders."

I follow the doctor's instructions and actually feel better. "Good," Kelly whispers. "Let's go."

Our approach to Tom's bed is unimpeded now that the screen has been removed.

"Well, Craddock," Kelly says. "How are you this afternoon?"

"How do you think?" Tom replies, a sullen note in his voice.

"Those stitches burning? Stinging yet?"

"Yes. Both."

Kelly pulls over a couple of chairs. "Sorry, old boy. You're at the most painful stage in the mending process."

"When can I get out of here?"

"Not for a while, I'm afraid."

A nurse gives Tom another dose of morphine, at Kelly's suggestion, and then the doctor turns to me, placing a hand on my arm. "I've brought you someone special. Can you guess who she is?"

I feel Tom study me. His gaze is like the sun on my skin, and I know my cheeks, forehead, and neck are flushing a vivid rainbow of pinks, reds, and purples.

Please let his memory return.

My love sighs. "Can't you just say her name? I didn't know the other one either, the man from this morning."

"James Scarlett?"

"That's him. Offered to pay the hospital bill, my being hurt in his club and all." Another belabored sigh. "You must like putting me on the spot, Doc."

"One of the many perks of being your physician. Now back to my question, Craddock. Who's our lovely lady?"

I could kill the doctor for making this introduction so difficult. A rather convenient homicide since Sir Death is only half a room away and seems bored.

Tom grumbles about needing a drink, and the nurse brings a pitcher. Liquid spills into the glass, making a happy sloshing sound. He spends a full minute drinking the water, stalling for time. Then he speaks to me as though I am a stranger.

"I'm sorry, but who are you?"

Over the years, I've learned to school my features, showing the world an impassive face. I have not learned to school my heart. It is rent into a thousand, throbbing pieces.

"She's your good friend," Kelly says. "Hester Grayson."

Tom leans forward. "The one who sent the candy? I thought she was younger—a little girl who follows me around."

"Where did you hear that, Craddock? As you can see, Miss Grayson's fully-grown."

My spectacles attract some interest at this point and Tom inquires about them. Kelly points out that I am blind and mute—also that I sign, ride a horse named Jupiter, and throw knives.

"Knives, did you say?" Tom asks.

"You taught her how. Hester can hit the wing on a gnat at fifty paces. It's amazing."

"What else did I teach her?"

"Hmm." Kelly deliberates for a moment. "You two kissed a lot."

Tom sputters. "Excuse me?"

"You loved her."

I make a fist with my left hand and spread the fingers of my right, bringing my palm down and touching the fist. **Enough!** I sign.

The doctor doesn't agree. "It had to be said, Hester. Every word's true."

Tom curses as he turns my way again, his wound protesting the movement. "What's she doing with her hands?"

"That's sign. You didn't like me teaching her the language, but you tolerated it. Barely. I'm afraid you're the jealous type."

"Where did we meet?"

"Let's have her answer that, Tom. Ask her questions, and I'll translate. And remember to look at Hester, not me. I'm her voice, but she's the one doing the talking."

I inhale, afraid yet excited.

"Where did we meet?" Tom asks again.

My face breaks into a smile at the memory and I fingerspell the word. **H-O-L-L-I-S-T-E-R-S.** I cannot sign fast enough as I share the story.

"In front of the dry goods store," Kelly says. "Six years of age. Hester wanted a piece of your toffee and you offered her some. Friends ever since."

"Why aren't we married then?"

The smile disappears from my lips, and I worry for a moment that he won't understand our situation. Kelly clears his throat, a gentle reminder that Tom is waiting for me to continue, and I fumble through my reply.

"You work hard on the ranch. Family needs you. Good son."

Tom kicks something off his bed. Might have been a quilt from the sound of it. "After listening to my mother go on and on this afternoon, you'd think I was an indentured servant in my own home. Maybe I don't want to remember any of this."

I shake my head and keep signing, trying to convince him that his life wasn't all bad, that our future was worth the work.

It's funny to hear Kelly speak such words for me. "I would have married you. Lived in a shack and been happy. But you wanted more for your wife and children."

Tom thinks a spell and then sighs. "The nurses said I saved my lady friend from a murderer and got shot. I must have loved you to do that."

Kelly reads my response and then puts it into words. "Brave man. Strong. Would have done it for anyone."

"I might think of my own skin next time. Safer that way."

I've never heard Tom say a cynical word in his life. He bears his challenges with grace and humor, and his capacity to love, soothe, and protect are nearly inexhaustible. I sense a hardness, an anger, in this person before me—as though he is the negative reflection of the man I know and love.

I picture the world as New Tom must see it—poor family, sick father, work always looming on the horizon, and a handicapped sweetheart who depends upon him heavily. No wonder he's reluctant to pick up where he left off. It's easy to imagine those beautiful black eyes turning as cold as his voice.

A nurse requests Kelly's help, and he leaves with her. I take a deep breath, hoping it will bring me inner peace. Should I reach out to Tom now? See if we're still telepathically joined? I hear him remove his glass from the side table and drink again. Closing my eyes, I focus on the sound of my heart. I send him all the love and concern welling within me.

Tom? My dearest, are you there? How I've missed you!

The words catch him mid-gulp, and he sprays water all over the place—his blanket, my lap, the floor. The glass hits the tile and shatters. Sound waves bounce around my ears and into my head. *Ouch.*

Tom moves about on his mattress, obviously searching the room. "Who was that?"

Kelly returns from his errand a moment later, and takes the other chair. Dash it all! Why did he have to come back so soon? Impatient and a little desperate, I try to contact Tom again.

Please remember. I need you, like air and sunlight.

Tom flings himself out of the bed, stumbles against my chair, and falls across me. A moment later, he puts his hand on the back of the chair and pushes away. His stitches must hurt because he groans in pain. I hate that Tom hurts, but it feels so sweet to have him close. Kelly tells him to remain still and calls a nurse to sweep up the glass. Amid the chaos, I smell fear on Tom. All-consuming, smothering.

The doctor gets him back to bed and begins checking his stitches. I remove my right glove and reach out, finding Tom's hand dangling over the side of the mattress. Our connection is open! Yet I see violent images surge through his head—a soft, beguiling voice attached to them. *Stay away from the girl*, it seems to say. *She's the root of your troubles. Her fault, all her fault.* Then Tom slams the telepathic door closed.

No. Let me in. Let me help.

I try to reconnect and fail. Try many times but nothing works. What was that awful thing inside Tom's mind? How can he stand it?

"You're rubbing your temple, Craddock," Kelly observes. "Does it hurt?"

I lift my head when the doctor's comment finally sinks in. *O di immortales.* Please, not Tom. But truth tightens my bones, and I realize what has happened to the person I love most. That horrible, irresistible voice in his head is the heir of Archimendax.

My love mumbles incoherently for a moment before returning to audible speech. "Take her away. I don't want company."

The doctor puts his hand under my elbow and helps me to my feet. We leave Tom and walk out of the ward. "He's just tired, Hester," Kelly says. "Come back tomorrow, after lessons at my office. I'm sure Craddock will feel better then."

He leads me to the stairs, toward Cordelia and Willard and my life at The Revels. I turn my head, hoping some miracle will grant me a glimpse of Tom's face before we part.

All is darkness.

———————— ● ————————

I feel numb throughout the next day, even when Kelly teaches me new words and proper signing techniques. My hands follow his instructions, but my mind is thinking of more important things. How can I find Mary Arden? She'll help me save Tom, won't she? Archimendax threatens us both, after all. But Cordelia makes it difficult to concentrate, conversing so cheerfully with the doctor that it's impossible to ignore her chipper voice.

"Your heart isn't in this, Hester," Kelly finally says. "Why waste my time if you'd rather mope?"

"She's been sad all morning," Cordie replies. "Anxious about her friend, I think."

Kelly walks to the coat rack briskly. He smells of dried ink and tea leaves. I can't even enjoy these wonderful scents, worried as I am.

"There's no reason for sadness, minx. Give Craddock a chance to recover. He's only human." Kelly slips on his jacket, coins jingling in the pocket. "I haven't said anything to either of you about this, but I'm leaving for Boston tonight. To collect my daughter Alice from boarding school."

Is she coming to visit? I sign.

"No. To live with me. We've been separated for too long."

Wonderful! Congratulations!

"Thank you, Hester." He opens the office door and twists the knob a few times. "Shall we take a walk? A little fresh air might do you good."

Snow swirls against my face as I walk with Cordelia and Kelly. The air smells nondescript, just of clean, sharp winter, and I hunch my shoulders against the cold. As we amble down the sidewalk, I imagine this is simply a brief constitutional to clear the cobwebs from my mind before returning to Kelly's office for more signing practice. But the doctor has a softer heart than he lets on and leads us exactly where I've wanted to go all day. Kelly's a good friend, and I'm glad Alice will be a greater part of his life now. He deserves some happiness of his own. The wind picks up and my feet are sopping wet by the time we reach the hospital. I stomp them against the boot bristles in the lobby and follow Kelly to the men's ward.

As always, Sir Death is waiting in the shadows. Cordelia stands a foot away, practically touching His elbow. Out of fondness for her, I indicate that she should go first through the doorway, giving her a chance to put distance between herself and the Reaper. But Cordie halts a few feet over the threshold.

"The screen is up around your friend's bed again, miss. Shall we sit and wait?"

Yes, I sign. **Thank you.**

This is when I hear Tom whispering to Kelly. "I don't care if she's out there or not," he says. "I don't want to see her."

"Why, Craddock? Is your schedule full? To the best of my knowledge, it has nothing on it but a dose of cod liver oil and a sponge bath."

"Doesn't matter," Tom grumbles. "It feels wrong. *I* feel wrong when she's around."

"That's ridiculous. You adore the girl."

"I can't explain, Doc, but I don't trust myself. I want to lash out, to hurt her."

"That's a strange reaction, I must say." The doctor scribbles on something, maybe a pad of paper or a chart, and drops it on the table. "All right, I'll talk to Hester. She's my friend, too. I'm sure she'll understand if you aren't able to see her now."

"Not now, not ever. A fresh start's just what I need."

Kelly yanks the screen out of his way. "You shouldn't burn your bridges, Craddock. I'll send Hester home today, and then you and I will talk again when I get back from Boston. You'll have time to cool off and clear your head."

"I won't change my mind," Tom replies.

My heart begins to pound, and I wish for the lucky stones in my pocket. Tom's right. He won't change his mind. Olfaction reveals genuine hostility, to the point of violence. It's physically painful to feel this emotion directed at me, coming from the person who has been my beloved protector. I rise from my chair and put a hand over my aching heart, needing to leave the ward before I faint. Kelly calls my name and hastens to join Cordelia and me. The doctor lies to spare my feelings, making excuses for Tom that I know to be untrue.

Don't worry, I sign. **Understand everything.**

"Give him a couple of weeks, Hester. I'll get you in for a visit when I return from my trip. Afterward, I'd like you to come to dinner at my home. To meet Alice."

Thank you. Honored.

Cordie takes the lead as we make our departure, and I accidentally brush up against the Reaper at the door. The contact chills like ice water and lingers unpleasantly. His voice is a cool whisper in my mind. *Careful, Visionary.*

Pardon, Sir. I'm having a bad day.

His dry laughter scrapes against my bones. *Oh, believe me, it could get worse.*

Cordelia tugs my hand and I follow her to the stairs, stumbling on the first one. I do believe Sir Death, and it frightens me to the core.

Life can always get worse.

19

Bellum domesticum.
War among family.

Willard draws the horses to a halt at the porte cochere of my home. The animals whinny and stomp as they wait for a good brushing and a bucket of oats. It's supper time for their humans as well, although I lack Cordelia's appetite at the moment. Eager to get inside, she climbs out of the carriage first and then helps me down. Wintery air surrounds us as we walk toward the house. It pushes under our cloaks, swirls our petticoats.

Cordelia opens the heavy door and cries out in shock. It seems that Cook is sitting at the entrance to the servants wing. I know it's she from the sound of her fitful weeping. Hoping that her tears are a result of an argument with the scullery girl or a fallen soufflé, I walk toward the front of the house where masculine voices are conversing in somber tones.

Something terrible *has* happened. I shut down my ears, afraid of what I might hear. Where shall I go? The library is located on my left, so I walk inside and close the door. It smells of antique leather and dusty books, of comforting, familiar surroundings. The fireplace is cold, but I sit at its marble base and pull my knees to my chest. Cocooned in this room, I prepare for the worst and let myself listen.

My mother's obstetric doctor is here, talking with my father in his study. They discuss phrases like "massive maternal hemorrhagic stroke" and "fetal mortality". Poor Cherub is no more, and Mama is unconscious in her bed upstairs, never to awaken.

A train whistles at Stonehenge station, echoing through the woods outside, through the forested space between High Street and The Revels. I've heard this same, lonely noise every night of my life. It signals the last departure—for the train Kelly's taking back east. I imagine him settling into his seat, anticipating the reunion with Alice.

Chest burning, I lean against the hard marble, longing to weep. But I can't produce a tear. Cordelia opens the library door and comes to my side.

"It's your mother, miss. She's in a bad way."

My mind goes blank during the trip upstairs, until I cross Mama's sitting room, and bump my foot against something hard and heavy. I reach down and touch a smooth, enamel-covered figure with bulging eyes and flaring nostrils. It's Mr. Ming, the Chinese dragon doorstop. He's sat here, keeping watch over Mama's boudoir, for as long as I remember. Bigger than a housecat, made of iron, Mr. Ming was once a playmate of mine. When isolation was overwhelming, I pretended the dragon was a baby and swaddled him in blankets or dressed him up in a hat and one of Mama's fur stoles for impromptu tea parties.

I haven't thought of my dragon friend in years, despite his constant presence. Funny, what one remembers of childhood... Yet tonight's not the time to reminisce about my life, rather it is Mama's moment of summation.

No one is keeping her company or speaking words of comfort when I enter her inner chamber. Surely everyone deserves that, at least? Rose water perfumes the air and the room feels steamy, as though my mother's body was recently washed. I find a footstool, pull it up next to the canopied bed, and sit down. Her small hand fits easily into mine, and I clasp it tight. So finely-boned and elegant, even now. Strange that I never thought of Mama as petite with her commanding, larger-than-life presence.

After taking a deep breath, I sit up straight. I may be dumb and blind, but I can do this well. I can be here when Sir Death comes.

My thoughts travel back, revisiting the happy moments Mama and I shared. It is far too short a trip, with little to remember until recently. She was a formidable, complex woman who focused on causes rather than her own child—a socialite, a philanthropist, a suffragette. And without ever truly knowing her heart, I have loved and hated her all my life.

Leaning forward, I rest my head on the edge of Mama's pillow, our hands still entwined. Cordelia enters a few moments later, placing a shawl across my shoulders. "In case you get cold, miss."

She sits on the sofa near the fireplace and begins to knit. Click-clack-click.

Still nestled close, I almost hear my mother whisper, *Bury me with my baubles, Hester. You know the ones I mean.*

Bury me with my baubles. From girlhood, I've heard her say this. In Mama's mind, a lady doesn't go anywhere without her favorite trinkets, even if she's meeting her Maker. It would be disrespectful both to her and the Almighty.

"I'm taking them with me," Mama would declare, in that sure way of hers.

With a safe full of jewelry to choose from, her baubles consist of three pieces. The small ruby pendant my father gave her on the day of my birth. A silver bangle that once belonged to my grandmother. And Mama's wedding rings. The necklace and bangle are quite plain when compared with the elaborate wedding set. Regardless of the difference in cost, each of her baubles meant something significant to my mother.

I hear the servants downstairs preparing for the passing of their mistress before she is even gone. It is quite an undertaking. They send for the priest to administer last rites and hang black crepe about the windows and doors. Mourning armbands are given to the men as a sign of respect and memento mori, a reminder that all must die. The maids turn the mirrors against the walls, for vanity is not proper now. And also because there is the superstition that a reflection in a house of mourning brings further death. I imagine this would make the Reaper smile. He finds such things amusing.

Cook brings me a tear-catcher. I run my fingers over the ornate crystal vial and wonder what I shall do with it if I can't cry. Cordelia asks whether she should cut some of Mama's hair for a keepsake, but for some reason, I can't bear the thought of it. I touch one of her long soft waves, pooled on the pillow by her head. It would be a shame to remove even a strand.

Father and the obstetric doctor come and go but neither bothers to stay until the end. Only Cordelia and I remain, and my companion is snoring softly when Sir Death makes His entrance. He says nothing to me, but steals across the room, that thief of souls, calling my mother from mortality. His voice is hidden by the labored gasps rattling within her throat. She is alive one moment and then, in the beat of a hummingbird's wing, she's gone. Her body but a shell upon the bed.

I hold Cook's tear-catcher in my hand and wait, dry eyed. Nothing happens until Cordelia stirs and stretches. "Is she... ?"

Nodding wearily, I cover my mother with a thin lace shroud.

————————● ●————————

After another sleepless night, I throw off my covers and dress in a simple day gown. It has one row of buttons on the front that are easy to fasten but my fingers fumble despite this. I walk downstairs, sans corset or petticoats, and listen for Cordelia. Instead, I find Simmons Harrow eating breakfast in the kitchen. He's helped himself to a roll—tossing the hot bun from one hand to another before dropping it on his plate.

"There you are, miss," Cordie says, joining me at the kitchen door. "I brought some clothes down from the attic for the funeral. We should be able to get a dress fitted for you by tomorrow."

Thank you, I sign.

I sit next to Sim while Cordie fetches me a piece of toast. Sipping a cup of chamomile tea, I listen to the staff talk, but Sim's enthusiastic chewing overrides the surrounding voices.

Too old for the orphan's school, he is now employed as my father's financial clerk and lives in the attic. Father wanted someone with a neat hand and a head for figures post haste. So I had Cordelia gossip with Cook about an educated lad who could be hired on the cheap. Cook then told the butler who in turn passed the news on to his master. Father couldn't resist. He loves a bargain, especially when it comes to his employees. I'm relieved that Sim isn't wasting away at the mill, or the button factory, or the mines.

Solving his problem was easy. Everything else in my life is not.

Surrounded by hothouse lilies, my mother sleeps in the formal parlor, waiting for her friends to pay their last respects. I'm not required at that gathering, my father told me yesterday. Therefore, Willard is driving Cordelia and me into town. Perhaps we'll find something special to add to Mama's funeral attire—new gloves or a fine set of combs. It isn't necessary, but I know she would like them anyway.

Cordie is my rock during this undertaking. At each shop, she speaks to me gently and with great patience. "That's a lovely ribbon, miss, but maybe this one would serve better." Or … "An embroidered shawl is too much, don't you think?" I can barely form a coherent thought, and everything Cordie says is right. We return home after a few hours, and I shut myself in my room. Pulling the heavy curtains around my bed, I lie down on the feather mattress. In the past, I could always call out to Tom, and he would be there to help. But the fellow over at the hospital is not *my* Tom. He's the polar opposite. What Old Tom once loved, New Tom hates.

Curse the spawn of Archimendax forever.

The next twenty-four hours pass slowly. I don't know how to behave in a house of mourning. My frequent exchanges with Sir Death never prepared me for this. On a superficial level, perhaps, but not deep enough to truly affect the heart. Father doesn't handle the situation well either. Between receiving visitors and making plans with the mortician, he drinks copious amounts of alcohol. After supper, Cordelia and I retire early. It wouldn't do to look haggard in the morning. The Stonehenge elite don't tolerate women who show real emotion in public, even at funerals. It simply isn't done. Thankfully, there are no rules to govern the sleep of those who grieve. And I do grieve for Mama. She was the closest thing I had to a parent.

Next morning, I bathe in the copper tub, and then Cordelia helps me dress. I wear an itchy crepe gown, taken from the steamer trunks in the attic and hastily fitted to my proportions. The crepe distracts me from dwelling on the upcoming funeral, but not for long. Within the hour, Cordie meets me on the landing and hands me the velvet pouch containing Mama's jewelry. I undo my drawstring purse and slip it inside.

"Ready, Miss Hester?"

The heavy, mink cloak that I wear makes my shoulders ache, but I straighten my back and ignore it. Cordelia and I walk down the main staircase, across the foyer, and through the front door. She puts her hand on my arm and describes the inky swags that hang from the carriage, the horses in their black feathers, looking like rich old ladies wearing hats. We climb into the vehicle where my father silently waits. He's quiet as the grave as we travel into town.

The funeral director takes my cloak and accidentally touches the back of my neck with his fingernail. A vision forms behind my eyes where a man closes and locks the door to a sleeping chamber. He removes a dead woman's valuables and then seals the casket. "The dead don't need gold," he says. "I do." I see this scenario repeated with a different corpse each time—the last one is my mother. Is it true? Our funeral director is a thief?

Well, he won't rob the dead today. I'll make certain of it.

I am expelled from the vision and thrown back to the present. Cordelia and I stand beside Mama's coffin in a viewing room, Cordie weeping softly.

Need privacy, I sign to her. **Leave. Close door.**

She hesitates a moment. "Are you sure, miss?"

Yes. Go, please.

After a few seconds, I hear the door shut and turn back to the casket. Forgive me, Mama. For not honoring your wishes. I reach down and touch the glove covering her hand, trace the wedding set beneath it. Her body feels so strange and cold, but I force myself to pull the glove off. A few tugs, and the rings slide from my mother's finger and land with a plop in my palm. I tuck them into the jewelry pouch within my purse, and replace Mama's glove. Not long after, Cordelia knocks tentatively and opens the door.

"Shall we start with the necklace?" she asks, putting her hand on my back. "Mistress Grayson will look grand indeed."

I shake my head firmly. **Changed mind**, I reply. **No jewels.**

"What? But I thought—"

Don't argue. Let's go.

Regretting my sharpness, I follow Cordie into the chapel. The smell of incense mixed with burning tallow hangs about the room like a dowager's robe. We wait in the section of the chapel reserved for the deceased's family and Father joins us seconds before the program begins. We sit through a poetry reading, an address by the minister, a violin solo, and an elegant eulogy, but I am moved by nothing until we reach the final hymn.

Amazing grace, how sweet the sound,

That saved a wretch like me...

Breaking my own rule, I remove my glasses in public, and wipe my eyes. But I can't keep up with the moisture they manufacture. Where is that damned tear-catcher now? I could fill it to the brim with liquid misery.

But I sense that Fate isn't done with me yet. These tears could be just the beginning of what she has in store.

20

Facilis descensus Averno.
The road to hell is smooth—Virgil

After the entombment at the mausoleum, Father shuts himself in his study with a bottle of scotch and remains there for hours. Why is he drinking so much? There must be more to it than Mama's passing. I haven't detected a bit of sadness on him through olfaction. Rage and desperation, on the other hand, are quite evident. Cordelia brings a tray of food to my room, which I consume out of necessity and follow with a nap. When I awaken, the house is filled with men's voices. My companion taps gently on my door.

"Sorry, miss, but Mr. Grayson would like to see you."

I climb off the bed and yawn, groggy and disoriented from my first real sleep in days. Cordie hands me my cane, and we go downstairs together. She does not rush me as we walk across the foyer. Any interaction with my father is undesirable, and even more so when he is intoxicated. It sounds as though he has company—five males in all, at my count—discussing the recent drop in the value of silver.

Our butler is standing nearby and opens the study door.

"Ah, Hester," my father murmurs. "Come here."

Realizing that I left my spectacles in my bedroom, I pause at the threshold, considering the best course of action to take. Should I return and fetch them? Send Cordelia instead?

"As I said, gentlemen, she is slow-witted and disobedient."

I lean against the door frame, stunned at my father's words. He describes me as slow-witted? On the day my mother is put in her tomb? This is low, even for him.

"There are treatments available," a man replies. "To cure aberrant personalities."

I do not know the person connected to the voice, but he is an idiot. I can tell that much already.

"Exactly, Doctor," Father agrees. "That's why I contacted you."

The stranger moves to my side, and I catch a whiff of dried sweat and verbena cologne. I feel Cordelia's body swing toward him. "What are you doing?" she asks, voice strident.

My father backs away, smelling of hatred, like a vast pool of congealed blood. "Take her."

Someone grabs me about the waist, and I cannot manage more than a few poorly aimed kicks. A cold metal band snaps around my right wrist, followed by another on the left. What are they? Handcuffs? No! Please get them off! Cordelia begins arguing with my father.

"As of this moment," he announces loudly, "you are fired, Miss Collins. Pack your things and leave my house immediately."

My fur cloak is slung over me—I believe it is the butler who does this—and the ribbons at my throat are quickly tied.

Father's voice is flat and hard. "I've honored your mother's wishes, but now you're going where you've always belonged."

Is this a nightmare? It must be. Wake up, Hester. Wake up!

A cloth covers my face, held firmly in place by a beefy hand. I scratch and pull at his arm, but I'm overwhelmed by a strange chemical odor. My thoughts grow abstract, and I have the sensation of sinking further into the arms that hold me, of losing the will to fight.

"See here, what's all this about?" Sim Harrow cries.

Help me, Sim. Don't let them…

Dizzy and nauseous, I wake up on a smelly blanket. After listening for a few seconds, I realize that I'm riding in the back of a wagon. My hand pushes against a canvas tarp, fastened over the top of the wagon's bed. The violent bouncing of the vehicle matches the pounding in my skull, and I cannot sit up or move more than a few inches from side to side. More blankets are spread across my body, nearly smothering me, but at least I won't freeze to death.

It sounds as though I am accompanied by two men—one is driving, the other riding shotgun. According to my traveling companions, I have slept the night away and it is midmorning. They are disgruntled that someone named Dr. Faust has taken a train while they are forced to plod along with me in the wagon.

"Will you be adding her to your harem, Roy?" the passenger asks, as though he is bored and making routine conversation.

He can't be serious.

"I am, Titus," the driver replies. "Never had a rich girl."

"Won't be much different than a poor one. They're all the same with your eyes closed. When's it happening? I'd like to make myself scarce."

Roy snaps the reins. "Be obliged if you would."

The more they converse, the more I hate them.

"Let's take a break in that canyon up ahead." Titus coughs and blows mucus from his nose. "Food first?"

"Sure," says Roy.

I shove the disgusting blankets away and turn on my side, searching for some kind of weapon. There must be something! If I didn't give myself to Tom, whom I love, I certainly won't be despoiled by a pathetic deviant smelling of pickled onions. Of course, the two imbeciles pay no attention to my movements under the tarp. They continue to talk. About their wives and children… the pitfalls of working for Faust… saloon rotgut versus home-brew. And Roy's superstitious fear of his next birthday.

The wagon turns in a half circle and stops. Titus and Roy climb out, and I hear them shaking something. Heavy fabric? A wool blanket, perhaps? They collect their dinner pails and the tarp is untied and thrown back. I am pulled up by my elbows and then lifted from the wagon. The wind whistles and whines against the mountains and smells of wet sage and mud. It makes my eyes water. I can't detect any sounds of life or civilization nearby.

"Calm down," Titus says. "Stop that kicking!"

Roy instantly takes charge of me. "Oh, she'll cooperate. Won't you, honey?"

Like hell. I spit at his face.

He curses and drags me away by the hair. At first I'm shocked by the pain but the rage sets in a few seconds later. How dare this man hurt me? Fear churns in my gut and my scalp blazes, nevertheless I scratch, pound at Roy's hand. Then I change tactics and make myself dead weight. Roy throws me to the ground. As I kick at him, I scoot back over the snow and grass until I bump into a gnarled tree trunk. It's dry and brittle—like an old juniper that's seen healthier days. Roy pins my legs with his knee, unhooks one of my cuffs and attaches it to a juniper branch.

"Ain't no point in fighting," he says, slapping at my boot as I jab the tip at him. "Hear me, wild cat? You're never going back to how things was."

I spit at Roy again, and he leaves in a huff, stomping over to Titus. Breathe now, I tell myself. Just breathe and think of an escape. The guards spread the wool blanket on the ground and open their dinner pails. Titus belches often, giving me an easy reference point for judging distance. Sound waves form a picture in my head, showing me where Titus is seated. He's seventeen feet away, facing south, and Roy sits across from him at a right angle. Their meal smells strongly of liverwurst and pickles, and I test the branch as they eat. It's not as solid near the middle—the bark feels bug-ridden, as though termites have gnawed through a few spots.

Roy gets up from the blanket and walks over. Sweet blazes. Get away, you stinking louse. I lift my chin in defiance when he squats down by my hip. "Got some bottled pears here. Awful sweet."

I feel him twist around. "Toss me your knife, Titus."
Knife?

Titus throws the blade to Roy. It hits the ground, bounces twice and comes to a stop. The pears slosh back and forth as Roy spears them in the jar.

"Try some," he murmurs, running a piece of the ripe, dripping fruit along my bottom lip.

I shake my head and move as far from him as my cuffed arm will allow.

Roy laughs like I've made a good joke. "See that, Titus? She don't want any."

"Women never know what they want," Titus replies, rising to his feet.

He's tall. Six two? Six three? And the heel of his boot squeaks when he walks.

"Come on, Roy. You'll have your fun after we've rinsed out these dinner pails. Don't want them attracting vermin."

Too late. The vermin are already here.

"All right, all right. You sound like my mother, Titus."

"Only I'm not as ugly."

"No argument there," Roy says, chucking me under the chin with a callused thumb. "She could scare the stripes off a skunk."

He walks over to the spot where he and Titus ate. I hear him rub the knife in the snow, and toss it on the blanket. Then Roy picks up his pail and follows Titus, and his squeaking boot, to the creek. As soon as the men leave, I begin to work on the juniper branch—sitting on it, pulling, even hanging from the thing with my full weight. Damnation! I thought the branch would break at once, but it's refusing to cooperate.

Lifting my face, I listen for Titus and Roy. They're telling obscene jokes and dumping out the unwanted bits of food from their dinners pails. I stop and rest after another attempt at breaking the branch. The two guards have moved on to rinsing out the pails. Given their overall lack of cleanliness, I can't imagine it will take much time.

This juniper has my begrudging admiration. Who knew it could withstand so much? My wrist hurts like hell with all the jerking and pulling, but I keep at the branch. A few minutes later, Titus tells Roy he's going for a walk and strolls off into the wilderness. Roy heads back up the hill. Horrors. It sounds as though he's unhooking his belt. The clinking of the metal bit makes my heart pound in the worst possible way.

Hurry up, infernal tree. Break!

"Be there soon, darlin'," Roy calls. "Don't worry."

He stops some thirty feet south, and I detect the light splashing of liquid. Is Roy making water? Yes, I believe so. With his back to me if my judgment is correct.

Crack!

The branch splits in half sending me sprawling to the snowy earth.

"What was that?" Roy yells.

I scramble forward to the blanket, snow scraping my fingers, and grab the knife. It doesn't have the perfect balance of a throwing blade, but I still like my chances.

"Put that down, sweetheart," he says, moving closer. "You don't want to hurt no one."

Oh yes, Roy. I really do.

Rising to my feet, I judge him to be at ten paces. His pants must be around his ankles, since he's shuffling awkwardly. I put a mental target on the spot I want to strike, step back, lift my arm at an angle, and throw. Hard. Roy sounds like a slaughterhouse on butchering day. Except that would be an insult to the pigs.

"You cut me," he screams. "You really cut me. Help, Titus! I'm bleeding."

"What's all the ruckus?" The other guard crashes through the trees and hurries over. "It's just a flesh wound. Stop causing such a fuss."

Making himself scarce, my eye. Titus was right there, ready to watch.

"I'll be a eunuch," Roy sobs. "Look at all the blood."

"Pull yourself together, man. It's just a hell of a nick."

"How'll I explain it to Lucille? She'll kill me."

I hear all this as I'm running away. Actually, running might be too strong a word. I am walking quickly, hands extended, bumping into every blasted boulder, shrub, and snow bank in Northern Colorado.

"Rip off a piece of that blanket and wrap it around the wound," Titus tells Roy. "Where's the woman?"

"How should I know, you moron?" Roy answers. "I'm busy here bleeding to death. Anyway, she can't be far."

Immediately after this comment, I hear Titus sprinting through the brush and increase my pace, tripping over a log several steps later. He reaches my spot and slams his fist into my jaw. *Deus misereatur!* My back tooth cracks and the bones in my face feel like they've caught fire. I can't breathe properly and fall backward, over the same damn log but in the opposite direction. Titus squats by me and holds my body down with one arm, punching me again. Hot blood runs from my nose and fills my mouth. I nearly choke on it.

Thunderation…

I come to under the wagon tarp in a haze of pain and wish I'd remained unconscious. Lying across the filthy-smelling blankets, I test the movement of my jaw several times. Bruised, enormous in size, but not broken. My left eye is swollen shut, though, and my ribs ache, like I was kicked a few times after passing out. I can't bend one of my fingers. Curses but it *throbs!* Must have been stomped on, too.

Roy is moaning loudly from his seat next to Titus, and I can't help thinking that my injuries are worth his present torment. Roy may still have the inclination to molest, but his equipment won't perform. A temporary solution, but better than nothing.

A ball of wadded up material pushes against my ribs. Criminy, it hurts. With all the discomfort going on, I'm surprised I even notice. Is it another dirty blanket? I reach out to shove the material away and grasp the silk liner of my mink cloak. How soft and lovely it feels. Thank you, butler at The Revels. For bringing me my mink cloak when I was being kidnapped. It makes me dislike you slightly less for not stopping them, you bloody idiot.

I rub the silk lining with my thumb, as though it is the cure to all injuries, and find there's a bulge within the cloak pocket. Could it be? Is the purse still there? I lift my hips a half-inch and use my good hand to yank the cloak free of my weight. This is no easy task with my hands cuffed near my belly.

Reaching into the cloak pocket, I catch a silken tassel and pull. My drawstring purse! I tucked it into the pocket yesterday after leaving the mausoleum, worried I would lose Mama's belongings. I'd completely forgotten the purse was still inside my cloak. After setting it on my stomach, I remove the jewelry. Nothing has been lost, not even the tiny pearl earrings I grew tired of wearing and slipped into the bag. And here are my lucky pebbles. Hope blossoms inside me as I feel the cool, smooth stones in my palm. How can I hide the purse? Surely Roy and Titus will want it.

My drawers have two pockets, just above the knee, concealed behind panels of lace. They were designed to store emergency items of the feminine kind, but I'll use them today to smuggle treasure instead. I kiss Mama's ruby necklace with my swollen lip and put it, and Grandmother's bracelet, into the pocket on the right. The pearls, wedding set, and lucky pebbles go inside the left one.

The cloak still smells of cedar shavings and potpourri, of my life before this nightmare began. I pull a section of it up to my face and rest my battered chin on the soft folds of mink. How surreal that I am in this state. I stroke the fur, hugging the symbol of my past and trying not to weep, afraid that I'm not up to the challenges of the future. We travel for some time along a country thoroughfare, and then turn onto a sloping road. Gravel crunches under the wagon wheels.

"Sure would like to drive into the city," Titus says. "I could use a drink."

Roy snorts. "You and me both."

What city? Where are we?

I hear the distant bustle of carriage wheels rolling down streets, a train whistle, and a smithy at work with his hammer and anvil. Yet new sounds capture my attention—twittering birds, wind gusting through tree branches, softly falling snow, and the mournful call of a mountain lion. Every time I hear a big cat make that sound, it reminds me of a human baby crying for its mother. This notion destroys what little composure I possess. How could Mama leave me without some sort of protection? Didn't she guess what Father would do? Were there no provisions made in her will on my behalf?

Tears sting my eyes, and I summon a borrowed memory. Butterflies dance and float with brilliant color across a blue, cloudless sky. Like a gift from the gods to the world below.

When Tom was young, he saw these very monarchs—a cloud of orange and black flying across the sky—and years later transferred the image to me with a tender wave of emotion, saying *I love you* for the first time. They bring assurance on a deeper level than even my lucky stones can.

As the butterflies dance, my stinging eyes cool, and my brain begins to calculate. Breathe and think, that's it. What can you do to survive?

But the wagon takes a turn and gravity rolls me toward the right. My ears pop with increased altitude. I'm being taken into the wilderness?

Count to sixty, Hester. Good, now begin again.

It takes over an hour to reach the top of the mountain. Seventy-two minutes by my count. But the wagon went so slowly at times, I think I could have passed it on foot. We come to a lurching stop, and I hear the squeak and groan of a pulley system lifting something heavy. A door? A gate of some kind?

"Enter in," a man says.

Titus talks with him for a moment, and then drives the wagon through the entrance and parks it. The canvas is drawn away, and Roy pulls me upright, crushing my throbbing hand. I squirm in agony, close to fainting.

He puts his stinking mouth next to my face. "I'll be back in a few weeks. You think on that."

Titus fastens leg irons around my ankles and puts his hand on my back, pushing me out of the wagon. "Ironwood Lunatic Asylum. Welcome to your new kingdom, princess."

21

Infernus.

Hell.

What did he say? Where am I? No, *no*... I can't have heard right. Titus and Roy are playing a trick, that's all. I'd rather die than be at Ironwood.

But what they tell me feels true, and I can't escape the testimony of my own senses. I pound at my ears and shake my head, trying to block out reality. *No*, no. Not Ironwood, not that place. Yet I'm surrounded by half a dozen men. They chew tobacco, walk around Titus and Roy, and talk about Faust's newest patient—who is she? Is it I they speak about? No, no. It must be a joke. Blast you, Titus. You're too cruel to laugh at me like this. After fearing the asylum most of my life, my brain can hardly process the possibility I might actually be there. Didn't Father say it would happen, that I belonged at Ironwood?

One of the men brushes against the back of my dress. I whirl around and slap at him. Don't touch me, filth!

"Come on, princess spitfire," Titus says. "Let's go."

He takes my arm, but I claw at him and fight like an animal despite my shackles. Biting, butting against the guard with my head. I won't go inside. You'll have to kill me first.

Titus doesn't punch like he did when I tried to escape. The other guards are laughing, and he is the center of attention now. Roy tells them about my shenanigans on the trip to Ironwood as Titus grapples with me. Right shoe squeaking, he evades my fists and sharp-toed boots, but grows tired of it quickly, despite the cheering men. Done with entertaining the masses, Titus throws me over his shoulder, walks up a flight of stairs, and crosses the threshold. Unclean humanity assaults my senses, along with the metaphysical stench of fear, sadness, anger, shame. People murmur behind the thick walls—some of them pray for death, some hallucinate and laugh wildly, and others despair of ever leaving this place.

No. *Not* here. Never Ironwood.

Then I remember Cordelia reading from an English translation of Dante's *Divine Comedy*. It was years ago, on a rainy afternoon, and I was bored and being difficult so Cordie turned to the *Inferno*. "Abandon hope, all ye who enter here," she recited dramatically, expounding upon the nine circles of hell.

Limbo. Lust. Gluttony. Greed. Anger. Heresy. Violence. Fraud. Treachery.

All exist in this place—completely overlooked by the outside world—for Colorado boasts a Bedlam of her own. Hell is here on earth, here in Ironwood.

Trying to ignore the sounds of the broken and insane, I slow my breaths and concentrate on my own heartbeat until two women approach. Who are they? Titus puts me down and one of the women excuses him and leads me into another room. Will she be kind? Will these women help me?

"You need to change," one says, sounding old as dirt. "Don't give us no trouble."

Both women discuss my clothes and grab at the cloak, untying the ribbons at my neck. I step back, shocked by the boldness of their hands. These women do not ask if they can touch or take. It's as though I am a subhuman species, and they need not bother with such courtesies.

Removing the handcuffs, but leaving my leg irons in place, they peel away whatever dignity I have left. It is the final straw, as they say, and I lose my fighting spirit. My gown, bustle, petticoat, and corset are taken. Yet I can't seem to scratch or kick the nurses as I did Titus. Rude and ignorant though they may be, we are of a gender. I don't wish to hurt another female.

"Never seen a real mink cloak before," the old as dirt one says. "Matron should get a handsome price for it at resale."

"Thank goodness the fur is brown," the younger nurse replies. "There's spots of blood everywhere."

"Didn't your mother teach you? Cold water removes blood stains. We'll clean the fur real carefully."

They're gentle with animal pelts but unfeeling toward humans? It makes no sense.

Young Nurse sighs with longing. "Her cameo's sure nice. I'd buy it if I had the means."

Take the cameo, I plead silently. It's yours. Only let me free.

"Hush, she's coming!" Old Dirt barks.

The new woman's step is fast and hard, like she's crushing grapes instead of walking into a room.

"Good afternoon, Matron Latham," both nurses say together.

The matron walks around me. "Strip off her underclothes and cut her mane. The wig-maker will like that whitish blonde color."

My braid hangs down to the middle of my back, and Old Dirt strokes the length of it before hacking across the top with a pair of scissors. "Finish this for me?" she asks Young Nurse. "My arthritis is bad today."

Between them, they get the job done. I reach up and feel my jagged hair, judging it to be an inch or two below my ears. I don't mind overmuch, I guess. Could be rather liberating, and hair grows back. I do mind when they try to take my camisole.

Get your hands off me. How can you do this to another woman? You should be better than a man. Old Dirt repeatedly slaps my bruised cheek, and the young one pinches hard enough to break the skin on my arms and legs.

No tears now, Hester. Don't let them win.

"Everybody's the same at Ironwood," Young Nurse says. "Right down to their drawers. No lace and satin for you here."

She grabs the drawstring ribbon on my drawers, and I remember the treasure in the pockets. Bending over myself, I hold the underwear firmly in place. These she-devils won't touch Mama's things! Old Dirt smacks my back now, until she's breathing heavily. "Foolish, foolish girl."

Latham steps in from the hall. "What's all the fuss about? Dr. Faust will be here soon."

The nurses tell her that I won't surrender my drawers. "Well, let the girl keep them then. We don't have time for this. Get her dressed."

I exhale in relief as a linen shift is thrown over my head. It smells of soap flakes, hard water and iron laundry kettles. The neckline exposes the top of one shoulder, but at least the coarse material covers my legs completely. I receive a pair of canvas slippers and put them on, too. Dr. Faust enters a few minutes later, on a waft of verbena, and Matron encourages him to inspect the new me.

"Doesn't look so haughty now," observes Latham. "We'll sell the hair tomorrow."

"Excellent," Faust replies.

He leans close, but doesn't touch any part of my body. "You used a knife on Roy this morning, Miss Grayson. What shall we do about that?"

I turn my face toward Faust, as though I am looking right at him with my sightless eyes. If I'd meant to kill Roy, Doctor, he'd be dead.

"Is that defiance I see? How unwise," Faust murmurs. "I'm putting you into the Pit for now, but tomorrow, we'll begin therapy. You won't be so proud then. In fact, I think I'll have a new pet by suppertime."

New pet? I don't think so.

Faust leaves and another set of guards march me to the basement. They secure my handcuffs to an iron ring attached to the wall. A scraping noise hurts my ears, like a heavy lid being lifted off a pot. One of them unhooks me from the wall, and I back away, nearly plunging through an opening in the floor. He turns me around and tells me about the stairs before us. My foot misses the first step, and I begin to fall, mouth open in surprise, until the guard grabs the back of my shift.

"Careful," he says, releasing my shift once I've found the step.

His voice is gentle. The type one could imagine calming a wild colt or a lost dog. He leads me down the stairs. My bones grow hot, and I have a vision, a testament of truth. Unlike my clothes, the nurses cannot strip me of my psychic gifts. This revelation is brief, a mere glimpse of a gangly young man saying grace over Sunday supper, eating his meal in a sunny kitchen surrounded by family. He's younger than me by a few years and still has the face of a child. Ginger hair, blue-green eyes. New to Ironwood, this fellow is a decent person. I know I need not fear him, unlike Roy and Titus.

"The bucket under the stairs serves as a toilet," he says, bringing me out of the vision. "And that table over there is what most people sleep on."

He removes the cuffs from my wrists. The metal loops have rubbed my skin raw, and I wince and blot the sores against my sleeves. Oh, blast. They sting something awful.

"Doctor Faust hasn't used this place in months, but the female wards are all full. You'll be stuck here for a while, I'm afraid. Take it from me, the conditions up there aren't much better."

The guard kneels and frees my feet from the irons. "I know how Roy is. He deserves what you did to him."

I hold my painful jaw and nod. His kind words weaken my resolve to be strong. I am so weary of fighting tears and grief, but I keep nodding like a fool, hoping to regain control.

"We're not all like that." He turns for the stairs reluctantly and pauses on the bottom step. "Leave the table by the south wall. It gets the heat from the ovens in the kitchen, and the stones are toasty."

Don't go. Please don't leave me here. Removing my hand from my jaw, I point to him, hoping to learn his name.

"It's Davis."

Thank you, I sign.

This gesture means nothing to the guard. He climbs the stairs and steps out of the Pit. The iron cover is slid back with a hard thud. It is an intimidating sound, and I panic, rushing up the stairs. I pound on the lid but no one answers or even yells at me to stop. Exhausted and sore, I fall asleep, slumped over the top two steps.

My bladder brings me fully awake, and I climb down into the Pit to search for the bucket. It smells as though it hasn't been emptied in months, and I'm suddenly grateful it's December instead of July, when the odor would be worse with the warmer weather. Yet the bucket's acrid scent competes with the overriding essence of mildew, and the air feels dank, like the old cellar at home that I was afraid to enter as a child.

After relieving myself, I investigate my new surroundings, using my hands and feet to gather information. The floor is liberally covered with straw, and former tenants have left other debris—small, hollow bones, a pile of corncobs, a torn shoe, and filthy-smelling blankets.

The wooden table feels rough, but I scramble on top and sit cross-legged. Something must be done about my broken finger. It inhibits the movement of my entire hand. What would Kelly recommend? The doctor had the same injury after fighting with Tom, and he tore off a piece of his shirt and wrapped his hand with it. I rip some lace from my drawers, and push my aching finger straight, using the lace to tie it to the next healthy digit.

Terribly painful, but I hope it works.

Leaning back against the warm stone, I sigh and enjoy the heat for a moment, until I feel something strange in the area of my shoulder blade. I turn and reach out with my good hand, touching the wall. Letters? Carved in the stone? I slowly trace them, the curves and the straight lines. Thank you again, Kelly—for insisting I learn the alphabet.

I get down from the table and touch other parts of the wall. Carved words are everywhere. The writing varies in style but the overall theme is the same. The Pit is steeped in wretchedness, past atrocities screaming from its very stones.

What will I carve during my time here?

I wander about the cell, left hand pressing against the lucky stones in my pocket. The space is round, no more than fifty feet in diameter, and I continue to walk until I weave and sway with exhaustion. How many times did I circle it? A hundred? Two hundred? Then I climb the stairs to the iron door in the ceiling and touch the metal. A brittle substance breaks off in my hand. Rust, probably. I wipe my fingers on my skirt and take the stairs back to the cell floor. Up and down them I go. My legs burn with fatigue, and my belly aches. I will go mad if I remain in the Pit much longer.

Recognizing my own desperation, I force the panic aside. Stop thinking that way, Hester. Get warm. Go back to the table.

Atop the table once more—pressed against the heated stones—I recline on my less-bruised side and tune out the anguish of the others in the asylum. Their suffering is no longer palpable, clinging to me like a filmy sweat. I sleep for a time, how long I'm unsure, but I awaken feeling weak and tired. I extend my hearing by slow degrees and find that the cover is being removed from the ceiling of the Pit. Someone comes half-way down the stairs, boot heel squeaking. "Here's your meal," a familiar voice says. "Eat up, Your Majesty."

Titus.

He drops something at the bottom of the stairs, but mercifully, does not stay. Titus leaves the cell and shuts the lid in the ceiling. I cough several times, chilled to the bone, and clutch the wool blanket around my shoulders. Influenza must be common at Ironwood, with freezing temperatures, inadequate clothing, and impure air. Many patients probably die because of it. But what can I do to keep warm? Light exercise, sporadically walking around the Pit, perhaps. Keeping my body against the heated stones. I have little knowledge of how to care for myself, but I will have to learn quickly. I cannot afford to get sick.

The straw on the floor is damp, and I slip on it, jarring my already stiff joints. I stretch for a few moments, but hunger becomes more important than sore limbs. After reaching the stairs, I grope around them until I find a small pan and a canteen of water. I pick up the canteen and drink until it is empty. Afterward, I dry my hands on the blanket around my shoulders, wishing, not for the first time since this ordeal began, that I could wash myself.

The substance inside the pan feels cold and lumpy. I take a handful of the mixture and smell it—just oats, no milk or honey. I place a small amount in my mouth and chew. Crunchy bits scrape against my tongue. It doesn't require more than a quick touch of my finger to know the pan holds as many dead weevils as it does oats. Horrible! I will not eat this! After spitting the cereal out, I return to the table. The warm stones feel good against my back, and I push my spine into the heat. My fingers land upon some sort of indentation hidden behind the table lip. I stick three fingers inside the hollow space.

Dominus providebit! The gods do provide.

Taking Mama's jewelry from the pockets in my drawers, I slide it into the groove under the tabletop. Hopefully, this hiding place will protect the treasure. I doubt there's a single person in the asylum I could trust to keep it safe. Although, given my situation, maybe greed trumps trust. Surely somebody here will accept a bribe.

For I must escape, and soon. I sense the Reaper upstairs, reaching from the shadows for another lost soul.

I am only twenty-two. I don't wish to die alone, hidden away in a cell. Yet, conditions as they are, it is only a matter of time before Sir Death pays a call to the Pit.

22

Pulvis et umbra sumus.
We are dust and shadow.

Ironwood Lunatic Asylum
January 1892

T he guards come for me on a madman's whim.
Over and over again.
Faust knows just how long to chill a body without killing it, giving me time between therapy sessions to recover. Either that or the Reaper was right when He kissed my brow, and His brothers have seen that I am marked and are allowing me to live a while longer. Two of my toes are numb though, and it worries me that they will require amputation. Not so terrible, if you consider how much worse it would be to lose a whole foot or a leg. I'm also quite fond of having arms and hands.

It seems that Faust is bored with water therapy, however, and we are trying something different at our next visit. What this new treatment is I have no idea. It could be hypnotism, but that would be too kind for a sadist like Faust. Part of his strategy is to let me stew in the Pit, giving me time to imagine the terrors ahead.

Titus brings me a meal, and under his watchful eye, I eat it all. I do not spare the energy to think upon how far I have fallen that I grovel like an animal and eat slop with my fingers. My past life is over. I left it beneath the freezing water in Faust's therapy room, and those days are as dead to me as my mother.

To keep myself sane, I summon the details of Tom's face—the hard angles and smooth planes that I've seen in dreams. I obsess over his image. Are his eyes really so dark? His teeth so white? Using telepathy, I've chanted his name for hours, but he never responds. What did Heathcliff say in *Wuthering Heights*?

> *Be with me always—take any form—*
> *drive me mad!*
>
> *Only do not leave me in this abyss,*
> *where I cannot find you!*
>
> *I cannot live without my life! I cannot*
> *live without my soul!*

Exactly right, Tom. Precisely so. Howl at me, haunt me, drive me to distraction. Do anything you like, except nothing. It's the lack of you I can't abide.

But Titus does not care about me and Tom—or Heathcliff and Cathy. Nor anyone else for that matter. Heedless of his cruelty, he leads me upstairs to the main floor. But why? Our sessions are always held in the basement.

Of course, I understand now. There's a cemetery in the grove of trees behind this building. I heard a nurse saying that it's a pity there are no markers to identify the dead. She sighed afterward, her point moot. If no one cared enough to claim the deceased, they wouldn't bother to purchase a tombstone. Is Titus taking me to the grove? I conjure the image of my body tumbling into a dark hole without a casket, swallowed within the earth's gaping maw, soil filling my nose and ears.

But Titus turns down a different hallway, bringing me to the front of the asylum. He opens a door and pushes me forward. The room's warm temperature reminds me of how cold I've been. I move toward the hearth, hands extended, absorbing the fire's snapping heat. The scent of verbena enters before Faust. He shakes himself, snow sliding from him to the floor like a small-scale avalanche. "Thank you for joining me in my office, Miss Grayson."

There was a choice?

"Move along," Titus says.

He propels me over to a cot—narrow and hard—unlocks the handcuffs, and pushes me down. Titus fastens the left cuff to a rod of some kind and drapes my right arm over a pillow. Dr. Faust draws up a chair beside me and sits. He caresses my hair lightly. "I think we'll bleed you this afternoon, my dear. It could be just the thing to dispel your ill humors."

My ill humors? Perhaps you need a good bleeding, Doctor.

"I prefer using a scarificator when perforating the skin. It's an ingenious device—far better, in my opinion, than the fleam. Who wants a single blade when one can have many?"

Who, indeed?

The smell of burning cotton. "I must warm the glass cups," the doctor says. "They are applied to the incisions, forming a vacuum of sorts with enough suction to draw out the blood. Leeches can be so unreliable and inconvenient to deal with."

I hear the doctor take something from a bookshelf, then walk to the desk and unlock a drawer inside it. He removes an object, and by the fluttering of paper, I would say it is the Book. Faust must document his research, after all.

"Come, Titus. I'll have you apply the cups, but be sure to check the temperature of the glass first."

I turn on my side, away from the doctor, and try like mad to pull my hand out of the left cuff. I yank against the metal as Faust primes the scarificator, winding the gadget to the desired level of tension. He grabs my shoulder, repositioning me on the cot, and pushes the scarificator against my upper arm. At first, the metal is just very cold, and then there is a loud snap, an intense stinging, and the sensation of fluid trickling across my flesh. A hungry predator, Faust goes into a frenzy and barks orders at Titus.

"Bring the cups!"

The guard shuffles to my side and presses the hot glass over the wound. Ahh, take it off! How it burns! I kick my legs wildly, dislodging the cup and sending it to shatter on the floor.

"Much too hot!" Faust says. "Try again, Titus."

Although I continue to struggle, the scarificator is used on my other arm, and another cup is applied. I do not know if it is real or imagined, but I feel myself fading, becoming less with the loss of blood. The doctor touches my throat, presumably to check my pulse. My body goes rigid against the restraints as images of the Book fill my psyche. It rises up, suspended in the air, and opens. The pages turn, revealing identities, giving me specific dates for those Faust has treated at Ironwood. They are etched in my memory, and I could spout them off like a catechism twenty years from now. Yet all the information in the world will not help if it isn't recorded in Faust's hand—only then will it condemn him. Ghosts circle about me, impatient and angry. There are so many of them that they blur into a scarlet mosaic.

My own blood spurts and pools in the shallow glass, as I realize what I've learned today. I now know where the doctor keeps the key to his desk. The key which protects the Book.

"Remove the cups," Faust cries, bringing me wholly back from the vision. "Bind her incisions. Hurry!"

Davis is wiping my forehead with a cool cloth when I awaken in the Pit. The guard puts a thick wedge of jerky in my hand and helps me sit up and lean against the wall. I tear into the dried beef like an animal. It tastes salty and abrades the sides of my tongue. I chew so hard my back molars ache.

The young guard gives me a cloth-wrapped bundle once I'm finished with the jerky. "Here's the sorghum cake from my lunch, too."

He fills my canteen with clean drinking water and then returns to his post upstairs.

Bless you, Davis. You won't last long here.

The other guards will make the boy brutal like them. Inevitable, I suppose, but it feels like the fall of Adam repeating itself to think of this kind, soft-spoken lad becoming hardened and cruel. Another mark added to the tally of sins hanging over Faust's head.

I lean against the warm bricks, despairing, but the glimmer of a memory flits through my mind. Closing my eyes, I surrender to the past, to my thirteenth year. When a woman of regal bearing appeared to me on my birthday in a vision. I could not guess her age, for she looked neither old nor young nor in between. Her eyes were a color that I still cannot name, having never seen their like before or since. They mirrored unfathomable wisdom and sadness, and the garments she wore were Roman in style.

The voice in my mind was quiet but powerful enough to shake the world. *Do not be afraid, Hester. I am Veritas, daughter of Saturn. Mother of Virtue.*

She shared the history of our cursed line. *Rome loved truth once, in ancient times, but the people were led away by false voices. Their hearts grew cold.*

A name formed in my psyche. *Archimendax?*

Veritas nodded. *The Father of Lies. He convinced them to spill innocent blood, commit vice, usurp without mercy. As a result, Rome decayed from the inside and fell to ruin.* Resting her hand on my shoulder, the immortal smiled at me. *You must succeed as I did not, filiola. Bring truth to the world.*

But I'm blind outside of the visions. I have no voice. How can I do what you ask?

All Visionaries have challenges to overcome, and you will be given an Interpreter.

My chin dropped in surprise as I thought of my dark haired friend. *Tom?*

Yes. He is the first.

Will there be others?

If you require them. Her smile held the mysteries of the universe. *Have faith, little one. The good will find you beautiful—the bad, fearsome. All is as it should be.*

She visited several times throughout my youth, and then no more, allowing me to fulfill my destiny in my own way.

Mulling over the memory, I remove my lucky pebbles from their secret place within the table. They feel good in my hand,

and I shake them as I circle the Pit, ending up at the bottom of the stairs. I lift my face toward the iron lid in the ceiling. It taunts me, a symbol of the many things blocking my escape. Maybe there *is* a little magic in these stones because I suddenly feel hopeful when there's no reason for it. I extend my hearing out into the asylum and the doleful sounds of the inmates enter the Pit and settle on my shoulders. Pierce my heart.

They're my people now, my family. Times haven't changed so very much since ancient Rome, I suppose—even the fight between Veritas and Archimendax continues today. Except I will not neglect my duty as the great Lady did.

I will not let the world fall to ruin.

23

Socius. Patronus.
Comrade. Protector.

Everyone works at Ironwood asylum. If they're lucid and able-bodied, that is. The cuts from the bloodletting are now scabbed over so there's no excuse for me to lounge about in the Pit. Not when I could haul wood. Wearing a heavy wool shift, knit stockings, winter gloves, and a moth-eaten shawl, I wait for orders in the courtyard at the rear of the asylum. Matron gave me an old pair of men's work boots yesterday. Despite the fact they slap about my ankles when I walk, the footwear is certain to create a barrier between my extremities and the snow. Surprisingly, I am not as cold as I imagined I would be. Perhaps physical tolerance develops with regular exposure to low temperatures. Or I could just have nerve damage.

"There's dry kindling across the way," Titus says. "Bring the wood in and fill the storage bins on the main floor. Needs to be finished by sunset or you'll lose your rations. Get started."

Extending my arms, hands splayed, I begin walking in the same direction as the other inmates. A path has been cut through the drifts, and I follow it as carefully as I can before slipping on the ice. The sharp point of a tree branch gouges my cheek an inch below my eye. Criminy! That's all I need! I wipe the blood away and reach up to the branch, snapping it off and tossing it aside.

"Here," a female inmate says. "I'll guide you."

She has a smell of old age about her but it isn't unpleasant—rather comforting instead, like the tapioca I always liked the idea of but never actually ate. I grasp the woman's arm and we crunch along over the ice for several minutes and then she introduces herself. "My name's Anna. Anna Loveridge."

Pointing to my throat, I mouth two words. Cannot. Speak.

Anna faces north again, shakes her head, and begins walking. "Mute and blind both," she grumbles. "Better stick close to me."

After reaching the shed that houses the firewood, my new acquaintance takes the two front ends of my triangular shawl and wraps them about my waist and back, knotting the remaining material above my navel.

"Frees your hands for work," she says. "And you can use this scarf. It'll warm your ears."

We wait in line as those ahead of us get their wood—the smell of sap penetrating the air. Anna makes conversation with the person to her left.

"Good day, Isabelle."

"And to you," a timid voice replies.

"Feeling all right?" Anna asks. "You look pale."

Isabelle groans softly. "The babe has a foot in my rib."

"Sorry, dear. Stretch a bit, why don't you? That always worked for me." Anna coos and clucks over Isabelle like a mother hen. "They shouldn't give you chores like this. Got to carry that child a month yet."

Why, they're completely rational, I think to myself. Not the least bit insane.

I feel Anna stiffen when she turns around. Surprise must be evident on my face. "What? You think Ironwood's just for crazy people? There's nothing wrong with me. I'm paying off my debts working here."

She hunches closer, forced to whisper so Titus won't hear. "My man got sick, and doctors are real expensive. Died anyway, but I had to try, didn't I?" Her bony knuckles brush against me as she gestures toward Isabelle. "Izzie's family threw her out."

"Never guessed Ma and Pa would do it..."

I feel the young woman's anxiety and heartbreak as though they are my own. She seems so fragile for the burden of motherhood. I shiver and pull Anna's scarf tighter around my neck. This is a debtor's prison, and a home for social outcasts? Are there petty criminals here, too? The asylum must be the human dumping ground for three counties.

Titus shouts at us, and we go to work hauling wood. I am very slow at this, but Anna fills my arms—then does the same for the struggling Isabelle. We begin the long journey back to the asylum. The women flank me and describe the rough terrain ahead so I won't fall. After making at least two-dozen trips to the shed, Anna, Isabelle, and I fill a quarter of the bins on the main floor, and then take our dinner break. Isabelle rests on a chair inside the building, but I stand on the covered porch with Anna, drinking soup from a tin cup.

"You need this more than I do." She shoves a piece of bread and chunk of cheese into my hand. "They give bigger portions if you're a hard worker—to increase productivity. Lost a stone of fat since coming to Ironwood, but I'm stronger than I've ever been."

I nibble on the stale rye as Anna eats her meal.

"Sit down on the steps, girl. Take off your shoes and socks and use that scarf to dry your feet. Warm them with your hands as best you can."

My two toes are still numb, but I heat up the rest of them as I follow her instructions. I hear Anna doing the same.

"Wish I knew who you were and why you're here," she says. "It's obvious you aren't defective, apart from sight and speech."

I stand and walk to a window, feel the thick frost that covers it. I spell out HESTER GRAYSON, hoping the ice won't melt before Anna reads my name.

"Your writing is better than mine!" she says, laughter in her voice. "Hester's a right pretty name, too. But where have I heard Grayson before?"

A large part of me resents any association with my father, and I wait on tenterhooks, dreading the moment Anna makes the connection.

"There's a family lives yonder, in Stonehenge. You belong to them?"

I nod, wishing I didn't. She sobers quickly, and I feel her turning and surveying the area before scrubbing the words from the window.

"What are you doing in Ironwood? Your father's rich as Croesus. He could buy this place ten times over."

I write on the opposite corner of the window. ASHAMED OF ME.

Anna makes a huffing sound, her expelled breath hitting my neck. "Keep that last name to yourself," she mutters. "You don't want anyone thinking they could sell you for ransom."

A lot of good it would do. Father wouldn't pay them a cent.

The old woman is quiet for a while and then she takes something from her pocket and presses it into my palm. Feels like a pencil.

"Hide it in your shoe, Hester. Paper's hard to come by around here, but my son sends me letters each month. I'll give you the envelopes and you can write on them—to visit or just to tell me if you need something."

Thank you, I sign, a huge smile on my face.

She adjusts her shawl, pulling it tighter against the wind. "We'd better get back to work before Titus notices we're happy."

Miracle of miracles, I have found an ally in this hellhole. And maybe even a friend.

———————— ● ————————

The following night, I'm given supper with the general population as a reward for working well. I learn to avoid the west side of the dining room, the section assigned to the especially violent or demented inmates.

"Stay away from Harry," Anna whispers. "He's killed people, I'd swear to it. That's him talking now."

I turn toward the voice and listen. Harry repeats five female names without ceasing, and there's something familiar about them. I bite my lip and think. Yes, I remember Cordelia reading an article to me out of the newspaper. It detailed the fate of five prostitutes killed in London. Exhaling slowly, I try to calm myself. Harry's women have the same names as those killed by Jack-the-Ripper.

The Butcher of Whitechapel? Here in Colorado?

Harry continues his incantation, and a chill runs up my spine. If this fellow isn't Saucy Jack then he's doing a fine impression of him. And isn't a sick, violent man as bad as the actual criminal himself—if he truly believes he's the Ripper? I squeeze Anna's arm and point in Harry's direction.

"What's that?" she asks, still puzzled by my gestures. "Oh! How long has Harry been here?"

Isabelle puts her cup down and burps daintily. "Just a week. He attacked a soiled dove in Ironwood City and pulled a knife. Crazy enough to scare the town jailer so they brought him to the asylum after hours."

Anna clears her throat. "Don't be afraid, Hester. Between the two of us, we'll keep you safe."

"That we will," Isabelle agrees.

The meal is strangely tense after this exchange, and I understand why. No one can keep that sort of promise. Not in Ironwood.

———————————— ● ————————————

After considering all the staff at the asylum, I finally select Hershel Watts as the perfect candidate for bribery. A night watchman, he is unpopular among the other guards with his rotund figure, slowness of speech, and fondness for chewing tobacco. Anna says that he couldn't hit the broad side of a barn when he's ready to spit. Best of all, he's fallen on hard times financially. Hershel might end up in debtor's prison if his creditors have anything to say about it. Hence, he's primed for a good palm-greasing, and I couldn't be more delighted. Mama's jewelry should pay for my freedom with sufficient left over for Anna and Isabelle.

At supper, Anna and I ponder how to go about enlisting Hershel Watts. "I could deliver the message," she says. "I'll leave it for him when I clean the guard's rooms."

I unfold the paper and wonder if Titus or Roy are watching me. Careful, Hester. Keep your head down.

The envelope smells like tapioca, like Anna. GOOD IDEA, I write.

She erases the message after reading it, saying nothing more for several minutes. I touch her arm, and feel her muscles tense. Taking the paper and pencil back, I write again.

IT WILL WORK, ANNA.

She swivels around, glances across the dining room briefly, and erases my words. "Let's see what Isabelle thinks."

I follow her toward the counter where the dishes are piled up after meals and deposit my plate. Another inmate shoves his way between us and I stumble, pitching into a stout male figure. Did it have to be Titus? He laughs and shoves me in the opposite direction, toward the side of the room I've been instructed to avoid. Someone else passes me further along, and I feel an assortment of groping hands making free with my person. I slam my knee into the male groin at my right and rip out a chunk of hair belonging to the fellow on the left. Bloody perverts.

"No!" Anna screams. "Let her alone!"

A distinctive voice cuts through the noise, and I identify the man standing a few feet away. He shakes the chains girding him to the table, and the other men release me.

"Tell me yer name, luvvie," Harry Swinton asks, a true East Londoner.

The smell of his rotting teeth makes me want to retch so I turn my face away. Harry reaches out, caresses my cheek, and screams bloody murder a second later. I feel a strange fatigue creep over me, as though our connection is siphoning strength from my body. He jumps back and drops to the floor. I hear him writhing there, bucking against the wood, chains clattering loudly.

My head pounds with the noise, but no vision is prompted by our physical contact, just an overwhelming sense of evil. Calculating, highly-intelligent, possessing a hatred of all things feminine, Harry is more deadly than the crazed Faust because, unlike the doctor, he is compos mentis. Or at least more sane than many of the patients here. To him, killing is an exercise, a game.

"Damn witch!" he rages in Cockney. "Burned me fingers!"

Everyone in the room is yelling now. I try to remain calm and decide what I should do next when a huge form steps up. Turning in fear, I measure its height in my head. Seven feet? *Seven*? I must be wrong, but I know I am not. The walking mountain puts his body between Harry Swinton and me.

"Nuffink to do wiv you, Lazarus," Harry sputters, standing up. "Move on."

My shield stands his ground. "You move first."

"What 'appens if I don't?"

"I'll snap your neck, and you'll be dead," says the deep voice.

"Thee can always try, Frankenstein. 'Ave a go."

"Hester!" Anna calls, and I turn my face in her direction.

Harry laughs in triumph at the sound of my name. He recites the list of murder victims again, adding me in at the last as a future casualty. "Put 'er to the knife, lads, and she'll wear red ribbons like the rest."

Then Lazarus picks me up, his hands big as serving bowls. My feet dangle above the ground as the behemoth carries me away, and I am pinioned against his massive chest. Reaching up, I touch him, knowing his entire life in a flash.

Originally named after the archangel Gabriel, he is now called Lazarus. His glorious cerulean eyes are the only reminder of his ruined beauty, although his intelligence remains intact. Deep scars run across his forehead and down both cheeks to the strong chin and lips. One side of his face hangs lower than the other, a result of shoddy reconstructive surgery. I see the carriage accident that caused his wounds. He was a magnificent fellow, barely out of law school, when the vehicle rolled, tossing him to the ground in time for the spinning wheel to grind his flawless features into pulp. His appearance became the stuff of legend in the little hamlet where he lived. Even his parents couldn't bear the sight of him, and he lashed out in frustration, becoming the creature they all feared.

Deep down, you aren't Frankenstein though, are you? Or Lazarus. Inside, you're still Gabriel the archangel.

I reach around his neck and embrace him. I know what it's like to be unloved by a parent, to feel so alone in the world. He's experienced nothing but cruelty for decades, and, somehow, I care for this person, even if he does frighten the hell out of me. Placing my palm on one of his shoulders, I notice that it feels horribly twisted. A sudden surge of warmth transfers from my body to his. It does not harm Gabriel, as it did Harry Swinton a moment ago. Instead, the power seems to heal.

The giant puts me down. "What did you do?" he murmurs, a note of wonder in his voice. "Where has the pain gone?"

I'm as surprised as he. My world's turned helter-skelter within the asylum, and I have no idea what I'm capable of anymore. Mary Arden did tell me of evolving powers, how they grow with suffering. Perhaps that's what is happening now. I smile at Gabriel, bone tired, and then Titus blows his whistle, disrupting any further communication between us. The guards begin herding the inmates back to their wards. Anna arrives at my elbow and pulls me way.

"Don't go near Lazarus again, Hester," the old woman says. "Everyone's afraid of him—the patients, staff, even Faust himself."

Isabelle steps around to my other side. "You know why they call him Lazarus, don't you? It's an old Ironwood myth."

"No," Anna interrupts testily. "I don't care and neither should you."

"They say he's been touched by God, Hester," Izzie whispers. "Even death can't hold him."

I have no time to learn anything more from the women. Titus makes his way through the crowd, takes my arm, and walks me back to the Pit, thoughts of archangels and miracles dancing in my head.

As I'd hoped, Hershel Watts takes the bribery bait like a hungry sturgeon. The night guard quickly seals the deal with me—his unknown, unnamed partner-in-crime—using a clumsy code of sorts.

Anna reads the message again. "I will take your sister to the dance, as you suggested. Plan on it."

Watts isn't exactly a sonneteer, but his words stick with one. Especially the last three—plan on it. I've been singing them in my head for at least five minutes to the tune of *Jingle Bells*.

Anna folds the paper and stuffs it into her pocket for safekeeping. We are in the laundry room today, surrounded by steam and soap flakes, using our dolly sticks to beat tub after tub of soiled linen.

"A wagon goes into Ironwood City once a week," Anna says softly, working her dolly stick. "We could hide in the back. Escape that way."

I smile at her, adrift in my own dreams of leaving the asylum, until I hear a familiar voice arguing with Dr. Faust upstairs.

O di immortales. Noah Kelly has come to Ironwood!

Relief surges through me, and I give Anna a hug, despite her protests. The smile fades from my lips when I recognize an odiferous blend of stale onions and unwashed hair, coming from the person walking through the laundry room door.

Roy's back.

24

Aut viam inveniam aut faciam.
I will either find a way or make one.

nna lets out a cry of alarm when Roy takes the dolly stick from my hand and pulls me toward the door. "She has a visitor," he says. "I'm to bring her up." When we reach the top of the second flight of stairs, Roy shoves me into a strange room. It smells musty and unused, forgotten for generations. I fall to the floor and dirt rises in the air, coating my skin.

"I've thought about this for weeks!"

I actually haven't. I guess my schedule has been busier than his.

Roy brags of the vile things that he intends for me. I do not smell lust on him, but rather fear and anger. Roy's working himself up to perform, requiring verbal reassurance of his potency to fulfill his dreadful promises. Look skeptical, Hester! Keep him talking. My brain hurtles ahead, whirring through the information I have on this man from the moment I became aware of his existence.

Ah, here's something I can use.

During our journey to Ironwood, Roy told Titus that he feared his next birthday. The fifth of June. He's superstitious, worried he'll die at thirty-nine years of age, just as his father and two uncles did.

Roy's voice grows louder and more confident with each description of degradation and abuse. "And I won't stop. Not until I've had my fill... " He's almost ready to attack.

I quickly choose a course of action. My eyes have an iridescent quality that disturb some people. Cordelia's told me more than once that they remind her of a cat at night, the pupils reflecting light in the darkness. Lifting my face, I use my strange appearance to my advantage and gaze at Roy, as though I am a seer with a deadly premonition.

"Afraid?" he asks with some pride. "You should be. I said I'd kill you after—"

Eyes wide, I go rigid and pretend to be in a trance. I crawl toward Roy and write in the dust on the floor. I'm counting on his irrational fear and innate stupidity at this point. Which he exhibits on the grandest of scales.

"What's that you've written?" Roy asks, leaning over me. "Why, it's the number thirty-nine."

His physical proximity unleashes a rage so thick I could choke on it. Unfettered, white-hot. Who is this reprobate? That he can prey upon the weak? Violate the innocent? The heat grows until I fear my very flesh will be consumed.

Vindicta.

Vengeance.

I feel my face glowing, energy burning beneath my skin. I continue to write the number thirty-nine. In fact, I cannot stop. My hand flies in a frenzy, going faster and faster until I nearly collapse. Then I crawl to Roy's feet and spell DEATH upon the floor in slashing letters. He stumbles back, landing hard on the wood. The pounding of his heart fills my head, and I savor the perfume of his fear. Rising to my feet, I tower over Roy as he lies on the floor. I lift my right hand, fingers dividing into the shape of a V—the symbol of a curse or blessing.

"Stop it," Roy whimpers. "Put your hand down!"

Listening to the tattoo of his heart, I bore into him with my gaze and my body grows light. I raise my fingers higher, drawing the V across my throat. Truth makes my bones tremble, and I know Roy will not die on the fifth day of June. Sir Death will come for him in April. The heat inside flares and it feels as though everyone Roy has ever victimized is here, adding their strength to mine. Suddenly I lift upward, I leave the floor entirely, floating a short distance above it in the air. I hardly notice this as the rage courses through me.

"What the hell? How did you do that?" Roy screams and scrambles toward the door. "Take the curse back," he begs. "I didn't mean no harm."

He dashes into the hall—the liar—and runs for the stairs, leaving me in the filthy room. Tired, weak, and afraid, I lose the power to levitate and drop down slowly. My feet touch the floor, and I fall in a heap. How *did* I do that, lift into the air and float? I have no idea—it's never happened before. What started as playacting, in order to scare Roy away, became something different. Something terrifying.

Was it brought about by the victim's wrath? I could swear they empowered me. Or was it a new gift, the kind Mary Arden said would develop over time?

I don't know how long I cower there in the dust before Titus-of-the-squeaking-boot finds me. "Well, Roy's upstairs hiding in the water closet. Won't listen to nobody."

He squats down. It sounds as though he's eating an apple, and I smell the sweet/stale fragrance of cellar-stored fruit. Leaning forward, mouth slightly open, I yearn to taste it, but Titus pushes against my chest with the back of his apple-clutching fist. "Been asking myself, princess," he says. "How'd a little thing, bones no bigger than a bird's, scare a man so bad? Roy could crush you with two fingers."

Titus finishes eating and throws the core away. My body turns in the general direction where it landed. I wish I could snatch up the remains of the apple and gobble any bits of left-over fruit. But before I can crawl after the core, Titus fastens a pair of irons around my wrists and yanks me close. "Tricks are over for today, you hear? I'm nowhere near as dumb as him—and lots meaner."

It's difficult to keep a straight face. Don't flatter yourself, Titus. You are just as dumb as Roy, if not more so.

The worthless oaf does not read my mind, however. Instead he stands and rattles my chains. "Boo! Her Majesty's a ghost."

He continues this mockery for quite some time, and I plan his entire funeral and obituary as we walk to the reception hall. I imagine bagpipes playing on a hill at sunset, smoke billowing from a flaming pyre as his body turns to ash. It is a grand, hollow affair, sadly lacking in mourners.

For his wife has run off with the milkman, his children gone to their friends. And all their acquaintances are drinking a toast at the pub, using his obituary for privy paper, saying, "The lad's gone *forever*. But *not* soon enough!"

I smile to myself as Titus leads me along. It's a better service than he deserves.

———————■ ● ■———————

Noah Kelly gasps aloud at the sight of me.

"You have thirty minutes," Titus says, retreating to his place by the door. "No more than that."

The doctor leads me to a chair, smelling of everything good and normal in the world. Cinnamon, chocolate, cold wintry air, dried lavender, pine needles, healthy horseflesh, and a male body kept clean with the daily application of warm water and soap. It's an unbefitting thing to admit, but I could sit here and inhale Kelly for hours.

Tucking my shift around my knees, I wait for something from the doctor—swearing, dark humor, comfort of some kind—but there is only silence. I've thought of this visit, dreamed of it for weeks, and now that it's finally here he's at a loss for words? Using my gift of olfaction, I find Kelly's in quite an emotional state. Anger, a desire for violence against those who hurt me, guilt over his absence and profound relief that I'm still alive. My mostly healed jaw gives me a twinge as I smile at Kelly. I'd like to beat Titus to a bloody pulp as well.

He clears his throat and sits forward. "My heart fails me to see you thus. I was stuck in Boston far longer than I expected, tying up loose ends, and returned to Stonehenge only yesterday. Miss Collins informed me of your situation, and I left for Ironwood within the hour. Unfortunately, Faust is determined to keep you here, the bastard."

Yes, well, I am his new favorite.

Thank you, Kelly, I sign. **For trying.**

He leans close, touches my jagged hair gently and whispers. "Take courage, Hester. I spoke with a fair-minded judge in Stonehenge. The news wasn't good at first. He told me that as your sole guardian your father was entitled to commit you by law. Grayson also has Faust's documented diagnosis of your supposed mental illness."

Guessed as much.

"The judge did mention that your situation might change if you married."

Married?

Won't work.

"Of course, it will. Your husband could sign your release papers and free you from this place. It would also help if he had another medical opinion contesting Dr. Faust's verdict. I can do both."

You're saying...

"I'm *saying* marry me, Hester, and let's get you the hell out of here."

You hate marriage.

Kelly pats my knee. "Don't worry, we'll get an annulment in time. And it wouldn't really be a marriage, would it?"

Other choices?

"Only those that will take years to achieve in court, without any guarantee of success." His laugh is short and sardonic. "Of course, I do have a pistol in my boot. I could distract the guard and knock him out. We could make a run for my horse. Probably both get shot."

I think of Tom briefly, stunned that doing so doesn't hurt as it once did. He had years to wed me and always found an excuse to avoid it. Yet here's Kelly, with his own marriage ending in a painful divorce, ready to step in and save the day.

The doctor leans back and sighs. "Miss Collins said she would stand as your proxy at the Stonehenge courthouse. Once the ceremony is complete, I'll ride for Ironwood with the license hot in my pocket."

Good old Cordie.

"Should I find another alternative, I'll pursue it."

Haven't said yes yet.

"You just did." Kelly stands—evidently thinking the matter is settled—and walks to the window. "David Thornhill lives in a far better institution than this, you know. It's a tourist resort by comparison. His father-in-law convinced the jurors Thornhill had suffered a complete breakdown."

Maude Lambson's killer? I sign, relieved we are no longer discussing matrimony.

"Precisely. Last time I saw him, he said he never intended to hurt you. Swore to me that he only meant to take you to the stable and tie you up so he could fetch his wife and ride for Mexico. According to Thornhill, he never made any attempts on your life and had not laid eyes on you since Halloween."

Like I thought!

"Which means someone *else* spooked your horse and tried to choke you. Psychotic men seem to follow you in droves…"

Not my fault. They're crazy.

Kelly leaves the window and picks something up. Sounds like his hat, the way his fingers trace the brim. "I must ride to Stonehenge—get going on our plan for your release."

But it won't work, despite Kelly's good intentions. Faust will never let me go, not in a million years.

My pseudo-betrothed kisses the side of my head and puts his arms around me. The fraternal tenderness in the embrace makes my eyes sting. We remain like this for a while, until Titus tells us visiting hours are over. Kelly releases me and walks toward the guard at the door. "I'm the coroner of Stonehenge," he tells Titus. "I'll be back to claim my future bride, and you'll be accountable for what happens here. One bruise on her is ten on you. For your own sake, keep her healthy."

He turns to me again. "I'll visit in a week or so, Hester. You have my word."

Kelly squeezes my hand and walks out of the room. Please keep your promise, I silently beg. A week is a long time here.

Extending my hearing, I listen as the doctor strides through the asylum. He exits the building and walks across the courtyard. Then Kelly stops and turns back toward the asylum, as though he is torn over his decision to leave me. I'm torn as well. I don't want him to go. A few moments later, he curses under his breath, mounts his horse, and trots past the watchmen. The sound of Kelly's departure brings on temporary moral weakness. I almost forget Anna and Isabelle and Faust's ghosts, nearly abandon my mission at Ironwood.

All I want is for Noah Kelly to come back and make me safe again.

———————●•●———————

"Time for another session," Davis says the next day, interrupting my work at the wood shed. He sounds quite sorry to bear such tidings.

I give the kindling in my arms to Anna and follow the guard to Faust's office. I feel a strong urge to apologize to Davis for causing him distress. The boy has shown me nothing but kindness, and it isn't his fault that I am here.

As usual, a fire is burning in the hearth, probably fueled by the wood I carried into the room a few hours earlier and stacked in the large copper bin. I'm always surprised by how normal this room seems. If I were to visit it, having no previous knowledge of the acts performed within these walls, would I think it had a quaint, cozy atmosphere?

No. Evil leaves a mark, and any person with a shred of sensitivity would sense the darkness here.

Davis helps me onto the cot, and we wait for Faust to arrive. It is a short interval. The doctor walks into the office with something rattling in his portmanteau. Sitting at his desk, he takes the Book from the drawer, his flowery cologne drifting across the room. Faust removes several items from his bag— glass clinks against a hard surface, a liquid of some sort gurgles. Curiouser and curiouser...

"I've missed you," Faust finally says. "Our time together is the highlight of my day, Hester."

Does he think to flatter me? I may vomit on his cravat.

He opens the Book and makes a contented sound. "Yes, here it is."

Belonging only to Faust, the patients of Ironwood are his trophies, and he relives our sessions by reading them over in private. It's his way of taking us down from the display case, to polish up and admire.

As he sits by my cot, I smell the new leather of his shoes. "So sorry to hear of the commotion with Harry Swinton," Faust declares. "He was burned so badly he lost all the fingers on his dominant hand. I had to cut them off. He can't write or hold an implement properly, as a result. Be careful, pet. Harry bears a grudge against us both now."

Faust adjusts his body to a more comfortable position. "I experienced something similar to Swinton when I came into contact with the skin on your face. My hand grew terribly hot and later I found blisters between the fingers. Why is that, do you suppose?" He turns to Davis and orders him to wheel a cart over to the bed. "That will do. Back to your station."

The doctor goes to get my medication. His movements sound practiced, belonging to one experienced with filling syringes. Faust ties a cord around my arm above the elbow and flicks the glass barrel a few times with his finger. The needle punctures my skin, followed by a burning sensation as the drug enters my body. Faust unties the cord and sits back in his chair.

"Many of my patients need this sort of encouragement, to allow their real selves to emerge. You will tell me everything I wish to know, Hester. There will be no secrets between us."

This is not my mother's laudanum. Whatever it is works faster and takes me to a whole other sphere. Wishing to be everywhere at once, I feel like a fly caught in amber, like lightning frozen in the sky. I sense all that occurs in Ironwood simultaneously. Anna works over a steaming cauldron, cursing Matron under her breath. A man chokes on his own saliva in the east wing. Titus corners Isabelle on the stairs.

A sense of detachment fills my mind, and I have no loyalty to any other being but myself, no need to conceal my thoughts. All is open wide, without any measure of self-preservation.

Faust looms over me, his head next to my lips. "The barriers you have built around yourself are gone. You spoke as a child. There is nothing to prevent you from doing so now. What is your name?"

"Hester," a faint, rasping voice replies, less than a whisper. It is soft enough to be a figment rather than an actual sound.

"Very good. Why does your touch burn others? Do you use an ointment that causes inflammation? Is it a chemical compound? Where did you produce such a weapon?"

"*Veritas.*" Another nearly indistinct utterance. "Harms the evil, heals the good."

"Who is this Veritas?" Faust asks, sounding impatient. "Are you schizophrenic? Is she your other personality?"

"No."

Swallowing against the raw pain in my throat, I realize that the frail voice is mine. The world turns, like a wheel rolling madly down a hillside. Topsy-turvy until the vision grows detailed and clear. I am at Griffin House, back in Stonehenge. The ballroom is filled with people wearing hooded cloaks, dressed for an elaborate Venetian masquerade. We are dancing the waltz, and tall candelabras stand in every corner. Their light is weak, barely penetrating the fog and darkness that swirls about the floor.

My partner wears the mask of a horned beast. His jaw and lips are exposed, but the rest of his face is hidden. Who is it? I feel I should know him. We waltz over to a Harlequin, his diamond-patterned domino glowing in the candlelight. The beast releases me, and the Harlequin takes his place.

He mumbles something, and I snatch the domino away. David Thornhill gazes back at me. "Throw her off the mountain," he says. "You'll lose everything, if you don't."

Thornhill twirls me around and around, until we reach a small figure swathed in red, the entire face covered in black leather. I remove this mask as well and find Marie-Louise Lennox under it. "No reason to live," she whispers.

The woman's face is pale and wet, and weeds tangle in her hair. I look down and see a rope cinched about her waist—still tied to the stone at her feet—as if Marie-Louise had just been found in the pond where she took her own life.

Then I am caught by strong, calloused hands. I cover them with my own, knowing their shape well. They have held me a thousand times, but I am frantic to get away now. Heedless of my resistance, he refuses to move, wearing the gold, weeping face of Tragedy.

"Quickly, Tom," I whisper, his soft, alfalfa scent filling my lungs. "Run for your life."

"I can't, love. He won't let me."

As soon as I embrace my Interpreter, he becomes insubstantial, dissolving into the air. The crowd parts with one accord, revealing the horned beast seated in a chair on a platform. I walk toward him, sensing his eagerness and pleasure. His mouth turns up into a welcoming smile. I recognize him now.

The heir of Archimendax.

Fog rises suddenly and cuts me off from the dancers, sweeps me into the darkness. The beast laughs from his elevated throne, and the vision ends. I return to Faust's office, gasping.

25

Solamen miseris socios habuisse doloris.
It is a comfort to the wretched to have
companions in their sorrow—Virgil.

The guards are late to fetch me the next morning, so I
follow a routine I've developed for days when I am
stuck in the Pit with nothing to do. I walk around my
cell quickly, then up and down the stairs as fast as I can, until
my muscles grow hot and tired. Despite this, they feel good
after the exertion and will not atrophy for lack of use. Each time
I finish this routine, it feels like a triumph against Faust. His
drugs muddle my brain and the exercise counters their affect
somewhat.

As my body cools, I sit on the table and try to make
weapons out of a few old bones. They are rather brittle and
small; about the right size for a chicken. I grind their edges
carefully against a piece of iron. The same bit of metal I used to
carve words into the cell wall, when I vowed to stop Faust.

Some of the bones shatter. I push the useless fragments away and run my finger over the two successfully sharpened pieces. The little knives aren't for throwing, but if I were very close to a villain and struck a jugular vein forcefully, I could kill. Or I might take one of their eyes. Yet even if I never actually use the makeshift weapons, I feel better knowing I have some sort of defense. Supernatural gifts cannot always save me. The new ones haven't shown themselves since my encounter with Roy when I burned with power and levitated.

Slipping the bones into the secret pocket of my drawers, next to my lucky pebbles, I stand and roll my shoulders, deciding to work my arms next. I pick up the remaining bones from the floor, the ones that feel knobby and round and gather bits of plaster that have fallen from the ceiling and rotten wood. Then I stack the ammunition at my feet and throw at various points in the Pit. Not like when I worked with Tom, but just as a reminder of an old skill. The daily chore of hauling wood has developed my upper body and although I am still thin, I possess a sinewy strength.

What is that murmuring sound behind me? Spinning about, I come face to face with Carver, the vagabond ghost from Stonehenge. The confused soul pops in on occasion and always leaves in tears. It's rather depressing to watch him cry over my current state. Ghost-sight is even worse. I hate what it reveals.

My blindness disappears and I see myself and my surroundings through Carver's eyes. It is not an attractive picture. The atmosphere in the Pit is gloomy, but I can still see myself standing next to the pile of bones and rotten wood, wearing a stained shift. My eyes look too large for my face and even with the shadows, the dark circles under them are evident.

Gaunt cheeks, paler skin than before and dry, cracked lips. Is it any wonder Carver cries?

Turn off the ghost-sight, I ask him.

Oh, yes. Sorry about that, Hester. How have you been?

I gesture around the Pit. *As well as can be expected, I suppose. Thank you for visiting, Carver.*

He tips his hat to me and tucks his thumbs into the pockets of his dirty blue vest.

Why has Carver followed me here? He cannot help or get me out. Is the incompetent gambler my self-appointed guardian angel?

The ghost circles the Pit, shaking his head. What can one say about such a dreadful place, after all? He takes a handkerchief out of his pocket, blowing his nose and accidentally passing wind at the same time.

I snort with mirth. Once I thought Carver was a nuisance, but perhaps he is a blessing in disguise. Who else could bring humor to the Pit?

Pardon me, he says, cheeks blooming with embarrassment.

Carver fades away, and I shake my head at his absurdity. A sound near the iron lid of my cell makes me lift my face toward the ceiling. Davis walks along the corridor upstairs. I know it is he because of the unhurried, simple stride—the way a child moves without thinking much about it.

The lid to the Pit lifts. "Brought you something," Davis says, cheerily descending the stairs. This is what my young friend always announces before handing over a gift. Brought you something.

He unveils the bowl with a flourish, snapping the cloth that covered it. "Chicken noodle! But there's only one piece of cornbread. Sorry."

Thank you, I sign.

Davis knows this gesture well by now. I perform it for him several times a day. Thank you for more jerky... clean blankets... a new shift.

"Think nothing of it," he says, casually sitting on the table and swinging his leg. "I threw away Faust's schedule this morning. I hoped he'd forget your appointment if he didn't see it on paper, but my idea didn't work. He always remembers you."

Come hell or high water.

Faust has injected me each afternoon for six days straight. As a result, my brain feels fuzzy, and I find it difficult to concentrate and plan my escape. I hate to admit it, but I'm beginning to enjoy what the drugs do to me. I'm intrigued by my ability to speak while under their influence. It must be all those ideas and opinions whirling about in my head, waiting for the chance to be heard.

I finish the soup, and swallow the last bit of bread, wishing there was more. That's your problem, Hester. You've always wanted what you can't have.

Davis gets to his feet. "We better go, before Titus or Roy come looking for you."

We climb the stairs leading out of the Pit. I lower my chin, hoping to appear submissive to the other staff members as we walk to a new location—Faust's temporary office. Davis tells me that the usual treatment rooms are being painted. Evidently, the evil doctor chose a warm, buttery yellow.

Davis opens the door, and I follow him inside. He takes the cuffs out of his pocket, once I am stretched out on the cot, and slips them around my wrists. "I'm afraid I must," Davis whispers, the metal ratchet snapping into place. "They're as loose as I can make them."

Having caused little trouble recently, and by working well at my assigned tasks, I'm no longer forced to wear heavy irons. Should I thank Faust for this? I shake my head, fearing I have actually gone insane.

Faust disrupts my thoughts by storming into his office.

Doctor's tardy—ten demerits.

He despises lateness of any kind, especially in himself, and goes about readying the syringe. The needle plunges into my arm without preamble, and then the fun begins. Except this time the dosage is off. I pull against the restraints, filled with aggression. It is a thrilling, terrifying experience.

"Now, Hester," Faust says. "You claim that you reveal truth. I'd like to test this assertion. Tell me something about my childhood."

Manic energy runs through me, and the raspy voice emerges from my throat. "You were punished. Harsh and often. Didn't know what you'd done to deserve it, or how to please her."

Faust does not respond for some time. "Who told you about my mother?" he finally asks. "Was it Harriet? I mean, Matron Latham?"

The doctor stands, knocking the Book to the floor, and tells Davis to fetch a vial of another drug. He injects it into my arm, lacking his usual finesse with the needle. Within moments, I feel such fatigue that breathing is nearly impossible. Head spinning, I concentrate on sucking air into my lungs, exhaling it a few seconds later. What's happening, Faust? Help me. But he never helps anyone. Instead, the doctor opens the door, calls for Titus, and walks out. If this is how he treats his favorite, how do the neglected ones fare?

"You okay?" Davis asks, patting my shoulder. He gives my arm a shake, and I nod in response.

Titus enters the room, picks me up, and carries me to the Pit. I hear Faust upstairs, stamping into the staff quarters for women. He slams through a door, and Matron lets out a shriek of surprise. Before she can utter a word, Faust strikes her. He hits the woman repeatedly, and I listen to each blow.

"Please, stop," she begs. "What have I done, darling?"

Faust abandons his lover without a word.

I cannot feel victorious over my involvement in this. I close my eyes and strange dreams come—images of the people in Faust's Book. Stuck in limbo, they do not rage like Maude Lambson, appearing dramatically when I least expect it. But they haunt me nonetheless. Like a sorrowful Greek chorus, they prophesy of doom from their little corner of my mind.

Promising to drive me mad if I fail them.

———— ● ● ————

"Everyone's scared to death because of the murder."

Davis sits with me in the Pit, sharing Ironwood gossip as I eat the leftovers in his dinner pail. He mentions the murder while I chew a piece of gingerbread, and I choke on a wayward crumb. For a moment, I worry that Matron Latham was fatally injured during her encounter with Faust and that I will burn in hell for causing the fight.

Davis slaps my back a few times to dislodge the crumb. "It was a new nurse. Margaret Hotchkiss, I think. Titus says Lazarus strangled her to death."

Although the whole asylum calls my friend Lazarus, I never shall. He is indeed Gabriel, like his namesake, and Titus is wrong. The man who saved me from Harry Swinton would never kill a woman.

"Oh, and you're being moved to the Unresponsive Unit in Ward E," Davis adds. "With everyone else being catatonic, Faust thinks that you won't be able to cause trouble in there. They need the Pit for Lazarus since he broke the door on his cell upstairs."

I don't like the idea of Gabriel living in this horrible place. Taking up my pencil and paper, I write Davis a note.

CAN I VISIT MARGARET? IS HER BODY STILL HERE?

"What?" he asks. "I could get fired for helping you do that."

I erase the words and write a quickly formulated excuse. MUST PAY HOMAGE TO HER. RELIGIOUS CUSTOM AMONG FEMALES.

"Never guessed you for a churchgoer."

Davis mutters for a while before telling me what I wish to know. "She's laid out in an examination room nearby. They're taking her to the funeral home tomorrow."

He is obviously giving me the once-over, so I try my hardest to look pious, like an Ironwood Joan of Arc. Perhaps he has noticed his womenfolk visiting dead acquaintances in the past, and this small coincidence gives enough validity to my request for him to consider granting it. Regardless of his reasoning, Davis finally relents.

"They'll hold a trial in a month or so, but it's always a sham. Poor Lazarus is as good as hanged." Davis pauses briefly, and I hold my breath, hoping he hasn't changed his mind. "I'll come to the Unresponsive Ward at midnight to get you, but your religious thing for Miss Hotchkiss better be quick."

He walks up the stairs, empty dinner pail rattling. "This goes to prove that you're trouble in any ward you're transferred to, catatonic neighbors or not."

I rather enjoy this quip—Davis delivers it with such wry warmth.

Thank you, I sign. **Thank you. Thank you.**

"Right," he replies. "That's what you always say."

Davis closes the lid quickly, once I indicate that I must use the chamber bucket. I accomplish the repugnant task, slip my writing tools into my boot, and remove Mama's jewelry from the hiding place in the table, stowing it again in the secret pocket of my drawers.

My friend then opens the lid again and escorts me to the laundry room where Anna is slaving away. I go to work beside her, but there isn't an opportunity to learn more about Margaret Hotchkiss until we stop at noon to eat. We sit at our table in the corner of the dining hall, and I take the envelope and pencil from my boot and write.

A NURSE WAS KILLED?

Anna reads my message, erases it. I cringe when the precious paper tears. "I liked her," she says. "Margaret was a nice girl."

She scoots a bit closer. "Lazarus was found dragging the body down the hall. Her limbs had locked up."

Rigor mortis? She'd been dead for a while then.

The old woman seems puzzled by the crime. "I could imagine Lazarus killing somebody. Just not Margaret."

WHY? I write.

"Because he was sweet on her. She had him wrapped around her finger without even trying. Must have been one of them crimes of passion."

Regardless of what others think, I know he didn't do it. I must work fast though and gather what information I can to pardon him. If not, then Davis is correct. Gabriel is good as hanged.

Isabelle has hauled wood for hours by the time Anna and I join her. The mother-to-be drops the kindling once we arrive and reveals that she's in labor. "Can't have him now," Isabelle moans. "Too early."

Anna laughs at this. "Early or not, the baby thinks he's right on time. Take that other arm, Hester, and we'll get her to the doctor."

Isabelle pulls away. "Won't you do it, Anna?"

"Be sensible, child. I've delivered calves, foals, and a woman or two, but I'm no midwife."

"I don't care. I want you. The nurses will just take the baby from me."

"Not for a few weeks, Izzie. You'll have him until he goes to the orphanage. You've seen it happen a dozen times."

"It's different when the child's yours."

The old woman grinds her teeth. "Even if you keep him, you can't leave until Faust is repaid—for your room and board over the last few months. And with you earning pennies a day, it'll take years to work off that sum. Add a baby and interest to your balance—it's doubled again."

We begin walking toward the asylum, and Isabelle starts to weep.

"Do you really want him raised here?" Anna asks. "An orphanage is the lesser of two evils."

The entire situation sickens me. I cannot allow this to happen to Isabelle and her baby. And what good is having a diamond ring in your drawers if you don't use it? I pull out the pencil and paper and scribble a question.

HOW MUCH?

"To pay Isabelle's rent?" Anna asks. "They charged the last girl thirty dollars. Took four years 'til she was free of Faust. I'd count on thirty at least."

I write as quickly as I can, and Anna reads my message aloud. "Will sell the diamonds. More than enough."

The laboring mother bursts into tears again. "Oh, Hester…"

"It just might work," Anna says. "My people in Denver could sponsor Isabelle so Faust can't keep her here on the grounds of future vagrancy. You could stay with them, child, until you get back on your feet." She steps lively after this, and Isabelle and I make an effort to keep up. "Come on. We'll go in the west entrance. There's a room there, behind the laundry. It's small, but I reckon we'll have enough hot water for washing and clean linen."

Davis opens the asylum door. He must have guessed our predicament in a glance because he obeys Anna's orders without question—checking the hallway is clear, raiding the drying racks for a few clean quilts, and keeping watch outside the improvised birthing chamber.

Isabelle stretches out on the bed we throw together, and I kneel nearby, holding her sweaty hand in mine. Blood-scented air flows over us as Anna checks her progress and gasps.

"Don't know why I'm even here, Izzie. You've done most of the work already. This baby's ready to come out."

As a new life is pushed into the world, I have a vision of a dark-haired baby perched on my lap. We sit on a rocker in the garden of a brick row house. "I love you, Ollie," I whisper, smiling at the little one.

"It's a girl!" Anna exclaims, tearing my attention away from the vision and grounding me to earth.

Anna wraps the baby up and hands her to Isabelle. Soft infant breathing and a tiny hiccup. Isabelle counts ten fingers and ten toes. Wiping my wet eyes, I feel almost new again. To think mere diamonds are valued above this.

"What'll you call her, sweetheart?" Anna asks.

Isabelle sniffles a bit. "My mother's name is—"

Olive.

———————————•———————————

Our euphoria over Ollie's birth is nearly ruined by Hershel Watts. Even though he rode into Ironwood City, sold Mama's wedding set, and made it back to the asylum by suppertime. Greed makes haste, I suppose. Unfortunately, it also breeds deceit. The guard has pocketed an extra ten dollars, money that rightfully belongs to Isabelle and her baby.

Curse that ungrateful, lying schemer.

Standing beside me on the covered porch, Anna pulls out a new envelope from her pocket, and tears it in half. "There's nothing on the back, Hester, and nobody should recognize the color either. Plain white."

I smile and take the paper rectangle. Anna keeps watch as I put my tiny nub of a pencil to work.

MR. WATTS,

LEAVE THE FORTY DOLLARS UNDER THE COPY OF OEDIPUS IN FAUST'S LIBRARY. ONE HOUR, NO LATER. DON'T THINK OF STEALING FROM ME AGAIN. THAT GUNSLINGER AT THE SALOON IN TOWN IS STILL LOOKING TO BREAK YOUR CHEATING NECK. GOOD THING HE DOESN'T KNOW YOUR ADDRESS ON CHERRY CREEK. I'D HATE TO LOSE YOU HERSHEL, I HAVE LOTS MORE TO TRADE.

I would never turn Watts over to the gunslinger—I need him too much. But maybe this note will remind the guard to stay on the straight and narrow. He does, in fact, owe a substantial amount to that fellow in town. On his days off, it's said that Watts hides in his house by the creek, afraid the man will find him.

Anna enters the asylum quietly, slips inside the guard's sleeping quarters and puts the note in Hershel's supper pail. "Staff eats in ten," she says, returning a few minutes later. "He'll read it on the sly, and then we'll see what he does."

Crossing my arms, I imagine leaving this horrible place. It's a pity I cannot send all of the inmates home. Many patients here require supervision, however, to prevent them from hurting themselves or others. They need genuine care—not experimentation, neglect, or torment—and once I get out, I hope to help them.

But I must free Isabelle, Anna, and Gabriel before I go, and I cannot escape without the Book. So much to do, so many at risk.

26

Quod me nutrit me destruit.
What nourishes me also destroys me.

The Unresponsive Unit isn't nearly as tranquil as Davis led me to believe. While oblivious to their surroundings, most of my fellow patients are far from quiet. I sit on my bed and listen as they groan, snore, and gasp. Tuning out the noisy patients, I concentrate on the night crew patrolling the other wards. Asylum staff is much smaller in the wee hours. I hope this will make things easier for Davis and me.

He arrives when the clock chimes midnight. "All set?" I nod and he puts my hand on his shoulder. "Follow as quietly as you can."

As we make the trip to the basement, I hear Roy talking to himself just around the corner. I tap Davis's shoulder in alarm and he pulls us into the stairwell to the basement before the other guard starts down the hall.

"How'd you know he was there? I didn't hear a thing."

Smiling, I shrug in response as we take the stairs to the lower floor. As luck would have it, there is a problem waiting in the basement. Titus is patrolling the area near the Pit and blocks the path leading to Margaret Hotchkiss.

"Hide in that nook under the stairs," Davis whispers. "It's dark, and you won't be seen. I'll get rid of him."

He opens the door to the stairwell and walks forward to greet Titus. "Slow night?"

"Sure is," Titus replies.

"I'm sick of the main floor. You want to trade for a while?"

"Sorry, Davis. Can't muck things up now that I'm head guard."

"What's to muck up? It's the same job."

Titus has received an advancement? Was it based on his high standards of cruelty? And Faust must have given him a raise along with the new position because his boot heel no longer squeaks. He's either bought another pair or at least waxed the old ones. Now if only he would bathe...

A chill begins at my toes and moves upward, running the length of my spine to my neck and face. I've felt His constant presence at the asylum, but there has been no direct contact between us. He is not my Death, not the Reaper I usually work with, but one of His brothers. I climb out from my hiding place under the stairs and stand.

It's good to see you, Sir.

Death seems surprised, as though He expected me to be more intelligent than my comment would imply. *Few would agree, Visionary, but then you wear my brother's kiss. Do not think I will always spare you. His protection will not last forever.*

Your generosity is greatly appreciated, but may I ask a question?

I am working. Would you make me late?

This Death is more imperious and career-oriented than most. Nevertheless, I press on. *Who killed Margaret Hotchkiss?*

The space around me warms as He draws away, melting through the walls with a whisper. *That is for you to discover.*

Blast. How uncooperative.

Davis opens the door and walks into the stairwell. "Sorry. Titus isn't budging. I can't help you, after all."

Double blast!

We sneak back to the Unresponsive Unit, and I thank Davis before we part. But I am no closer to solving Margaret's death than I was an hour ago.

Noah Kelly sits on his horse, arguing with Titus in the courtyard. Their conversation is public domain due to its sheer volume. Standing at a second-story window, I am agitated and sick, trembling with fever and nausea. The blanket I wear about my shoulders falls to the ground. I leave it there, and listen to the exchange below.

"If you don't step aside," Kelly says, "I'll move you myself."

"You'll be shot if you do," Titus replies. "We're quarantined with measles. Have been for two weeks. I told you that the last time you came."

"I'm a physician, you imbecile. Let me enter and be of service."

"Faust said, 'No one in or out until the ban is lifted.'"

But Kelly wouldn't be Kelly if he let it go at that. "I want to see my wife. *Immediately.* If this fails to happen, I will bring charges against you, Faust, and this institution."

We are indeed married now, thanks to a civil service with Cordelia standing as my proxy. While there's no ring on my finger, Kelly did buy one. He just can't enter the asylum to give it to me due to the measles outbreak. I wasn't even aware our marriage had taken place until Kelly notified Faust of it, coming to the asylum and showing the other doctor the license. All it did was enrage Faust.

I'll never be free of him. Not until one of us is dead.

Kelly dismounts his horse and approaches Titus. "Get out of the way."

I feel his anger escalate. Even at this distance, it could melt an iceberg. Abandoning the window, I walk toward my ward, palm sliding along the cool wall. Kelly continues to fight with Titus for some time, but leaves eventually, promising retribution if I am damaged in any way.

Tears hang about my eyelashes, and I brush them off with the back of my hand. What Kelly doesn't know could fill an ocean. I am already damaged goods.

Ward E sounds like it always does, gasping and groaning, and I crawl under the blankets on my bed. Usually I can ignore the noises made by my unit mates, but I find them intolerable now. It has been two days since my last session with Faust, and I know exactly what is wrong with me. And it isn't the measles. I've grown dependent upon his special mixture of drugs. If I weren't so miserable, I'd think it was funny.

What I once loathed, I now embrace.

Davis leads me into the treatment room, and I climb upon the bed meekly as a lamb, obediently holding my wrists out for the cuffs.

"Sorry," he says, as demoralized by his duties as always. "Faust should be here soon."

Not soon enough.

"Did you know the storm's passed? That's good news. I saw blue sky this morning."

I nod, aware that Davis is trying to comfort me with optimistic chatter, but I turn my face to the wall. In my hunger for the needle, my senses are jumbled and distorted. I cannot trust them. At first, I believe Faust is beside me and then I grow distressed, thinking I hear him leave the asylum. But both impressions are wrong. I gain clarity for a moment and realize he is speaking to Matron in the office next door. She's writing something down for the doctor.

"Send a telegram to Miss Honeycutt," he says. "Say that we're expecting her in two days."

"Consider it done," Matron replies.

"And don't mention the quarantine. Our ban was lifted days ago."

"Of course."

Faust fiddles with something on his desk. "Doctor Kelly is unaware of that fact, and let's keep it so, Harriet. I won't allow him to interrupt my sessions with Miss Grayson."

Matron opens the door a crack. "It's said he has powerful friends. I've heard talk of an injunction."

"Idle gossip, my dear. Make certain you send the telegram."

"First thing in the morning."

Details grow confusing once more, until I feel the hard metal pricking my skin, the sweet heat in my arm. Euphoria and physical relief follow as the narcotic flows through me. I can function for another forty-eight hours if this dose is like the last.

"Good afternoon, pet," Faust says, untying the cord at my elbow. "You've missed me, I see."

He gives the drugs a few minutes to work, pulling the Book from his desk. "Answer my questions with the first thing that comes to mind."

Faust has not asked me to reveal anything more about his personal life. He would rather listen to my childhood trauma instead. So I spin him a yarn for his record book with my raspy, drug-induced whisper. All of it is true. I *did* have a lonely childhood. My father *is* cold and distant. I did *not* learn about healthy relationships from my parents, and then there are the trust issues. My dark side runs deep, and Faust eats it up like caviar on toast. As he should. I've learned to be a good little actor to satisfy my chemical cravings.

The session eventually ends, and Davis leads me back to the Unresponsive Unit. Matron gives me permission to skip my chores and rest. After sleeping through the night, I awaken with a start in the early morning, when the clock chimes three.

I know who killed Margaret Hotchkiss.

———————— • • ————————

Faust mentioned a Miss Honeycutt to Matron Latham while dictating the telegram to her yesterday. I've heard the name before. It's Miss Amelia Honeycutt, to be exact. I know her because she came to my family home on several occasions. She was my mother's friend.

A New York heiress, Amelia Honeycutt is also a generous philanthropist, an emerging mental health advocate akin to the great Dorothea Dix. In years past, I remember Mama speaking with her about the need for reform in asylums such as Ironwood.

"I will guide the leaders of the industry, Lenore," Amelia said. "All they need is incentive and proper instruction."

I think of the repairs the asylum has recently undergone. The painting of Faust's office and a few other rooms, the improvements upon the façade and the dining hall, but nothing to actually benefit the patients themselves. The exterior is pretty while the inside rots. All to make a good impression on Honeycutt, I'd wager. And what would Amelia Honeycutt offer Faust as an incentive for reform? A cash reward, of course. Faust loves money almost as much as he enjoys inflicting pain.

By all accounts, Margaret Hotchkiss was a caring nurse, a good woman who followed the dictates of her conscience. If she wanted to reveal the truth about the conditions at Ironwood, Faust would kill her to avoid exposure and still retain the prize from Honeycutt.

Then why was Gabriel carrying the body away?

That's easy to understand as well, I suppose. He found Margaret before Faust could dispose of her and could not bear to leave his love behind. That's why Gabriel allowed himself to be captured when Titus saw him with the corpse in the hallway. According to Anna, the giant sunk to his knees cradling the body, weeping like a child. Truth vibrates through my bones, and I know these deductions are correct. An innocent man is trapped in the Pit, wasting away in the darkness.

You and Margaret deserve better than this, Gabriel.

I rub my clammy palms together, feeling a bit like Lady Macbeth. A party to murder until I reveal the sin. But weak and sick and addicted, I can barely save myself, let alone anyone else.

Libera me ab sanguine. Deliver me from blood. Make clean my hands.

Isabelle has regained her strength after giving birth. She and the baby also avoided catching the measles during the outbreak, thanks to Anna's vigilant care. Mother and child left Ironwood after breakfast this morning, their dues paid in full to Faust. She rode into town with Watts and according to his conversation with Davis, has settled into a hotel in Ironwood City to await the arrival of Anna's son.

The Loveridge family is sponsoring Isabelle's transition from the asylum to regular life—offering her housing and assistance with finding employment. The sponsorship was one of the contingencies of Faust letting her go. Before Isabelle's departure, I slipped my grandmother's silver bracelet into her hand—a gift commemorating baby Olive's arrival into the world. Should things take a bad turn, and I never see Isabelle again, she can trade the bracelet for cash, and use the funds to care for the child.

Now that Izzie and Ollie are free, we can move forward. Hershel Watts has agreed to help Anna escape if I give him the ruby necklace. The plan seems risky, but he assures us it will succeed. This isn't much comfort, since Watts is the mind behind the plan itself. He has also upped the ante, demanding more compensation if I escape as well. I hope to go with Anna, but that hinges upon whether I obtain the Book beforehand.

With Gabriel condemned to hang in a week, I cannot wait for Kelly to come back. I have no idea when that will be. Watts' greed, however, is a sure bet. The price for my freedom? Two small pearl earrings. The last of my loot.

But what if we're caught or punished? What if Hershel fails?

Time passes as I fetch kindling and restock the firewood on the main floor. Then the dinner bell clangs, and I make my way into the dining hall without giving my appearance, or hygiene, a second thought. I don't have escorts anymore—the asylum guards only come for me if I have a session with Faust. Otherwise, I am expected to show up for chores and meals on my own.

Ironwood has become familiar. I am accustomed to the layout of the place, the smells, the spoiled food, the brutal behavior of its occupants. With one hand extended, I keep next to the wall, measuring the distance before me. Twenty feet to the dining hall entrance. Eighteen. Twelve. Seven.

I cross the threshold and find the end of the serving line, waiting for my portion of the usual midday fare. There's the wet plop of barley stew hitting my tin plate. With a spoon in my hand, nothing extra is required for consumption of the stew but the will of iron to eat it. I find a table and sit down. The air is musky with body odor, which doesn't help anyone's appetite. Certainly not mine. Anna is too busy to join me. She has extra laundry to clean due to Miss Honeycutt's forthcoming visit. I divert my brain from listening to my taste buds complain about the stew and analyze Hershel's route for our departure.

He and Roy just cleared the weeds that grow in the irrigation canal on the north side of the property. It must be done before the gardeners open the spillway from the lake and use the canal to water crops the asylum sells to grocers in Ironwood City. Even with the cold weather, they hope to plant rows of spinach and green peas soon. Nutrition-rich foods the inmates help the gardeners tend but will never eat, planted only to benefit Faust's already fat wallet. Nearly as deep as Hershel is tall, the clean canal bottom is hidden from the asylum windows, even the guards in the watchtower can't see it.

My thoughts are interrupted when I gag after trying to swallow the last bite. After wiping my mouth, I exhale slowly, forcing my stomach to relax. Fortunately, the nausea passes, and I pick up the puzzle once more. As Watts suggested, Anna and I will use the north exit tonight and climb down into the irrigation canal. We will follow it to the edge of the property, to the asylum wall. This is the end of Hershel's involvement. He knows nothing beyond the door, canal, and wall. Doesn't want to know, either. Evidently, bartered jewels carry no guarantee of good service these days.

Anna's son is made of entirely different cloth than Hershel. Already in town to pick up Isabelle and Olive, he will throw a rope ladder across the stone barricade and we will climb up and over. The three of us will dash to Ironwood City, meet Isabelle at the hotel, and separate for our various destinations. Anna, her son, Isabelle, and Olive are bound for Denver. I shall take a train to Stonehenge.

It might just work. If the stars are aligned and the gods are on our side. Sweaty and hot, I reach down to my boot and remove the pencil and paper. My corner of the dining hall is quiet, but the rest of the room is filled with movement and noise. Sickness descends upon me again. Trembling, I place the smooth, clean paper on the bench and write a line. Davis will transport this message when he takes the supper tray to the Pit. He's delivered several of them already.

DON'T GIVE UP, GABRIEL. DO NOT DESPAIR.

It's medication time for the Incurables Unit. I sit in a corner of the stairwell, squeezed into a tiny nook beneath the landing—where, hopefully, no one can see me. Sweat streams down my face and neck, but I shiver and rub my arms for warmth. Heart pounding, I count off the seconds in my head. Time passes quickly when there is little to waste. Missing from my work detail, I could be found and punished at any moment.

I listen to Matron advising a novice employee. She's a young thing just arrived to replace Margaret Hotchkiss.

"Be organized and efficient," Matron intones. "Prompt, precise. The entire staff is only as good as it's weakest member, my dear."

Then Matron, or as I like to call her, Lucifer's Concubine, leaves the new nurse to carry on and walks directly toward my hiding place. Frantic, I try to make myself even smaller and pray I escape her notice. She passes by me and climbs the stairs to the third floor, rose attar blooming behind her. I finally exhale, weak and shivery.

Fifteen minutes, that's all I have until Titus returns from his smoke break. *Think.* Surely your brain is good for something. Light a fire in the stairwell garbage bin? Throw a rock through the window and hide until the nurses run past? What to do to empty the Incurables…

Concentrating on the nurses in the next room, I learn the exact location of the medical cart. It's at the top of the second aisle, twenty feet from the entrance. Three women are working the ward together, and presently, they are preparing syringes for rapid injection among the patients.

The more experienced nurses begin administering the medication, but Novice stays at the cart. Is she distressed? Yes,

I definitely smell anxiety. Her hands must be trembling too, because she drops a vial and knocks some of the prepared syringes to the floor. They roll in various directions: near her foot, next to the cart, in the center of the second aisle. As the new comer, she obviously doesn't wish to call attention to her mistake and picks them up discreetly. But she misses one.

Good girl, Novice, remain just as you are. Intimidated, slightly incompetent.

"Help me with this fellow, Hanks. He's too strong for me."

Evidently Hanks *is* Novice the new girl, because she runs to the older woman when called, leaving the last fallen syringe behind. It calls to me from the aisle. I had hoped to steal some vials from the trolley through some hastily-orchestrated ruse, but this is so much more convenient. All three nurses are facing the opposite wall, concentrating on their patients—I can tell from the direction of their voices and breathing. You know, being bad isn't so hard after all. I'm rather adept at it.

Opening the door carefully, I cross the threshold and take several quiet steps. The room stinks of bedpans and lye, the sour smell of near-death. No one seems to notice my progress with all the groaning and suffering going on among the sick. I move quickly, counting off the distance between me and the desired bed, holding my breath as I creep. This must be the center one. I lower myself to the tile and turn on my stomach, sliding under the bed. Reaching my hand out, I stretch from under the bed into the aisle, hoping the nurses don't notice. Nothing but cottony balls of dust, hair, and other detritus. Who's in charge of housekeeping? And where's that damned needle?

The side of my hand brushes something hard. The syringe! Only the cursed thing rolls to the right. Stretch a bit more, Hester. A little further and it's yours! That's right. Now to get out of here. Confound it, is that Hanks walking back to the cart? The only thing separating us is a sagging mattress and a bed skirt.

"Come here!" another nurse yells. "This one doesn't want his shot either. There must be something in the air today."

"Right," Hanks replies.

Holding my breath again, I hide under the bed as two nurses return to the cart for more medication. Minutes seem like an eternity until all of them are busy with their patients once more. I inch out from my hiding place, keeping low, and scuttle to the door. The knob turns in my hand, and I pull it toward me. The sick continue moaning and tossing about, as I sneak back into the hall, disgusted with myself for taking their only means of comfort. Until a wave of nausea rolls through me—then I think only of the craving inside.

Someone steps out of the Incurables Unit. "You there!" Hanks calls, stopping me in my tracks. "I thought I saw the door close just now, out of the corner of my eye. Did you need something?"

I lick the sweat from my upper lip, turn back toward her, and shake my head.

"Then what were you doing?"

She sounds suspicious and annoyed. How do I salvage this situation? I lift my pitch-stained hands so she can see them and mouth two words. Stack. Wood.

"Are you new here? There's *no* hearth or hob in this unit— no need for kindling. *Everyone* knows that." Hanks sighs, as though she's given up on teaching an imbecile. "You really *must* learn your way around."

As soon as the nurse leaves me, I return to the nook under the stairs and grab the sharpened chicken bone from my secret pocket. Will she realize my theft and turn me in? Will Titus be summoned? Reach for me with his hard, bruising hands? But all I hear are the nurses holding down a weeping man. "Let me die," he says. I knuckle the moisture away from my eyes and drop the bone before finding a vein. Breathing rapidly, I tap the syringe barrel as I have heard Faust do on so many occasions and then inject myself, waiting for the hot, stinging rush. And it blessedly arrives. *Fortunatus mea.*

Anna and I are leaving Ironwood tonight. I cannot be a burden to her with my tremors and vomiting. This dose should help me function, at least long enough to reunite Anna with her son.

First task completed, now on to the second.

I leave the asylum by a side entrance, following the path to the woodshed to gather a load of kindling. *Deo favente.* The guards aren't anywhere near the shed. Inhaling, I smell the faint odor of cigarette smoke and hear Titus talking with Roy down near the stables. I haven't been missed, in spite of my larceny. After filling my arms with wood, I count the steps back to the asylum and plead with the heavens in my heart. Forgive me my sins for I am not a thief.

Although with one thing left to take, I am not done stealing yet.

27

Fugio.
I run, flee.

When I finally come upon Titus, he's finished his smoke and Roy has gone off somewhere. Good riddance too. Titus doesn't say anything out of the ordinary, nothing about my appearance. The sweat upon my brow, the bone-deep weariness. We all look like walking death at Ironwood, I suppose. It's a given we're ugly.

"Get that wood inside and hurry up about it," he says. "Doctor's office is nearly empty."

Titus follows me to Faust's domain. He stands near the desk for a few minutes, and I begin stacking the fragrant, sappy pine in the wood bin. I use precise movements, as though I am a kindling perfectionist, and the guard grows bored.

"Pick up the pace," he murmurs before walking down the hall.

I make for the desk as fast as I'm able and pull open the middle drawer, my fingers grasping the locked box. The weight's right. It must be inside. And here I was afraid Faust had taken the thing with him on his trip to town. The doctor is a bit vain and bought a new suit which he must pick up before Miss Honeycutt's visit in the morning. After eating supper at the hotel, he's taking a tour of their best room to ensure that everything is ready for his esteemed guest. Faust isn't expected back at the asylum until quite late, in fact, and I'm counting on it. If he's filled with rich food and wine, he'll want to see his pillow instead of the Book.

Lifting the statue of Plato from its place on the bookshelf, I remove the tiny key that rests under it. I've heard the doctor hide it there during therapy sessions. This small tool unlocks the metal box, bringing its contents into my possession. But the Book is too large for the pocket in my drawers. I tear a strip off my ragged shawl, pull down the front of my shift, and tie the book to the top of my abdomen, where my breasts used to be before my curves diminished and became gaunt planes. Then I draw the shift back up and wrap the shawl around my middle.

Titus stops walking the hall—around the general area of the men's room. Lifting my chin, I gauge the distance. Maybe fifty feet or so to the south? The guard doesn't step all the way into the water closet. I hear him polishing something on his uniform, primping in front of the mirror. He mutters about a stain on his lapel and pulls a towel off the rack. Oh, please. Stay where you are for another moment, won't you? I'm not quite done here.

The metal box feels too light. What to do? Faust will know the Book is missing if he touches it. Turning to the wood bin, I reach inside, taking out a pile of old papers that the doctor uses for starting fires. I lift my hand, balancing the paper stack against the heft of a book.

It will have to do. I've run out of time.

The papers go into Faust's box, and I close the lid, locking it with a soft snick and shutting the desk drawer. Plato finally gets his key back. I then drop on my knees by the fireplace and shove the last of the wood into the bin, hoping it looks neat enough.

As the meal bell tolls, Titus wanders back to the door and looks inside. "Let's go, princess. Supper's on."

He pulls me to a standing position. For a heart-stopping moment, I worry that the Book will fall out from under my shift. I hug my chest in alarm, pressing the leather-bound rectangle into my flesh, but the evidence of the doctor's crimes remains hidden.

I'd be dead if it didn't.

———————— • ————————

"We can do this, can't we?" Anna Loveridge whispers, her voice trembling.

I give her an affirmative squeeze. "Of course," I wish I could say. "All is well, dear Anna. We simply cannot fail."

My hand rests on her shoulder as we creep through the empty corridor in the Violent Unit. Water drips steadily and the atmosphere smells of mold, in addition to a hundred other things that are far worse. Cold air pushes against my skin, and I start to shake. Only men on this side of the compound. How many, I wonder? A few of them mutter in sleep, turn in their beds, snore. It is well past midnight, and Hershel Watts is waiting around the corner to open the door for us in exchange for the necklace and pearls. Hopefully, he won't guess this is the end of his secret salary and imagines that an inmate with deep pockets still resides at Ironwood, planning another job for the future.

Reaching beneath my skirt, I open the secret pocket in my drawers and remove the pendant and earbobs. They represent everything valuable in the world at this moment, and I clutch them tightly. Just a few feet away, I hear Harry Swinton's voice in his cell, whispering his five names. Already distraught, I jump at the sound, and then there's a soft pinging. Something rolls across the floor and plops onto a liquid surface.

"Show yerself," Harry says.

Anna and I continue moving through the darkness, and he laughs. "Oh, I know yer women, sweetings. Come over and visit ol' 'Arry."

No other men at this end of the passage. He must be in solitary, kept away from the other inmates for their protection. Harry rattles his chains, and I push Anna to go faster. We nearly collide with Watts at the asylum door, but he unlocks it slowly, oblivious to danger.

"Necklace first. Then the pearls."

Opening my right fist, I offer the ruby necklace to Anna and she takes it. Earlier this afternoon, we made a pact, Anna and I. The first one out that door runs like hell. No second thoughts, no turning back to help. We do what must be done to get free.

"Bless you, Hester," she says, hugging me.

I hug her tightly in return, my closest friend in the days of my captivity.

During our display of emotion, Hershel Watts inspects the necklace. "Very pretty piece. Better than I thought."

Satisfied with the ruby, he opens the door and pushes Anna out. I listen as she races to the canal and climbs down into it. Good. She'll be with her son in no time.

Then the asylum door shuts with a clang. "The pearls?"

Opening my hand, I realize something's wrong. What? Just one earbob, not two? I give the pearl to Watts and check for its mate in the pocket of my drawers, not caring about modesty or whether the guard is looking. Damn. Nothing there either.

"Need 'em both," he grumbles.

Sitting down, I pull off my boots, checking for the missing pearl inside. My paper and pencil fall out. Watts grabs the old envelope, evidently recognizing it from our many exchanged messages.

"It was *you*? You put all this into action? Scheming and bribing and bossing me around." Watts sounds rather angry, as though everything has been done with the sole purpose of humiliating him.

As he begins to curse, I realize where I lost the missing prize. That pinging sound, after Harry frightened me. It was the pearl dropping to the floor and rolling into the drain. Must have fallen through the iron grating. In the Violent Unit, many of the inmates are beyond reason—urinating and defecating wherever they happen to be. Every so often, the guards rinse the refuse away directly into a grill-covered latrine.

Pulling my boots back on, I do not stop to tie the laces, but reach for the paper and pencil to tell Watts about my misfortune.

"No," he says, locking the door. "No excuses. I'll get what I was promised. You're not going anywhere until I do."

I lead him to the approximate place where the earbob went into the sewer. Hershel Watts hunkers down, makes a brief perusal, and laughs bitterly. "I'm not digging through that mess."

Watts regains his feet and heads down the hall, footsteps echoing. "You find my pearl and we'll do business."

The stench of the Violent Unit makes my eyes water, and I breathe through my mouth, steeling myself to begin the search. Do it, Hester. You must try. Squatting down, I extend my hand toward the grate. I hear chains clank against each other and metal joints creak within the cell to my right. Softly this time.

"'At you, dearie?" Harry asks. "The silent one what took me fingers? We'll let bygones be bygones, 'ey?"

Some snakes cuddle their quarry before squeezing them to death, and Harry is doing the same, cajoling me into trusting him. But I sense that when he is free of his bonds, all good humor will disappear. I could choke on the foul smell of his hatred. I stumble to my feet and run, one hand touching the wall, the other outstretched before me. Harry goes wild at this and works his chains back and forth in a frenzy. A bolt in the wall must have come loose because he is suddenly at the cell door, jerking against it. I round the corner and fall, tripping on my untied laces.

"Careful, Ragamuffin," Harry calls. "Wouldn't want you to 'urt yourself."

The squeaking of metal hinges intensifies. Rusty iron, most likely ignored for years. By the sound of it, he'll have the door off in no time.

Get up, Hester! Run!

And I do just that, until I lose my bearings at the next cross-section of corridors. Which way to my ward? Right? No, left. Left. Not far away, metal whines and gives way under pressure. Sweet blazes. He's breaking free.

Howling in triumph, Harry pushes the door aside and steps out of his cell. Slow footsteps at first, but then, sounding like a ravening wolf, he begins to run.

"Let's play," Harry whispers, turning at the top of the hallway where I stood only minutes ago.

Swinton must be part bloodhound because he follows my trail nearly to the footstep. I take the sharpened bone from my pocket and hold it tight, accidentally snapping the brittle weapon in two.

Bloody hell, I'm an idiot! Now what can I do to defend myself?

The plaster wall under my right hand changes and becomes a split wooden surface—a double door. Applying all my weight, I push through it and enter the room. Everything smells strongly of chemical agents. I feel my way forward into the space, discovering it is much larger than I expected with rows of chairs on several levels. The floor slopes downward, and I follow it until I reach a flat stage.

I run my hand along a broad counter upsetting a stack of gauze, spools of thread, trays of metal tools. Something falls on my foot, and I reach down and gather it in my hands. An apron?

Damn and damn again. This is an operating theatre.

Not the smartest thing I've ever done, leading a murderer who favors knives to a room filled with them. Have I time to sneak out and go someplace else? No. My pursuer is coming down the hall, a hundred yards away. Better to stay here—Harry's not the only one gifted with the blade. I lift a scalpel in my hand and feel its weight. A little light, but if I throw them in rapid succession, they might wound him sufficiently. In any case, the scalpels are far better than my pointy chicken bones.

And what other option is there? I don't trust my new powers—don't know how to summon the heat that wounded Harry before and caused him to lose his hand. I organize my weapons, arranging them on a cart to my right. When Harry enters the theater, I am as prepared as I can be, given my situation.

"Never gets old," he says, moving forward. "Tho' I must confess me disappointment in tonight's chase." He sighs and ambles to the top of the aisle. "Rather anticlimactic, if I'm being 'onest."

That's right, Harry. Keep moving.

But he stays put, pausing for effect. A homicidal showman. "'Ere we are in a mental 'ospital, of all places, at midnight, alone. And there's no pleading or weeping. A travesty, that's what it is."

Must he belabor this? Come now, just another five feet…

At last, Harry walks down the slope. Finally getting on with the actual attack. "Sorry, me lovely. I was 'oping fer better from you."

Far be it from me to disappoint.

I propel the scalpel toward Swinton's shoulder. He cries out and I hear him groping about the wound. The second knife is heavier and reaches its target, sinking harder and deeper than the first.

"Damn witch! Wait'll I get thee."

Harry takes another step, and my scalpels fly fast, a cloud of spikes—hitting him multiple times. He screams and tries to run, but falls as my last scalpel hits. Then I detect a crawling, dragging sound. In a pain laced voice, Harry wimpers and begs to be spared, as he pulls himself toward the aisle.

"All red," Harry Swinton murmurs and drops into a puddle of his own blood.

I cover my mouth, hoping not to be ill or to embarrass myself in front of Jack the Ripper by crying with relief. Exhausted and completely done with being brave, I do not wait for another opportunity of escape and hurry past his twitching body. He doesn't wait either and grabs any part of me he can reach. He seizes my ankle, and I hear a sizzling sound, smell the fetid odor of scorched skin. The contact between us is brief, but I stumble down to my knees.

"Burned again!" Harry cries, outraged.

Light-headed, I get to my feet and make myself walk to the top of the aisle and push through the double doors. Which way am I facing? Breathe and get your bearings. That's right, in and out, in and out. My heart slows to a near-normal rhythm and then a strong hand clutches my shoulder. I jump away, opening my mouth in a silent scream.

"It's me," Davis says, sounding as scared as I am. "You're all right now. Calm down."

His embrace is the sweetest thing I've ever felt. I burst into tears, dampening the shoulder of his uniform. "Why are you so afraid?"

I point at the operating theater doors.

"Something bad in there?"

Intent on investigating the surgical room, Davis enters the theater. Waiting in the hallway is an agony. At any second, I expect a murderous scuffle to erupt but hear only the young guard's footsteps and Swinton's soft moaning.

My friend returns eventually. "How did you do it?" he asks. "I doubt I could have."

New tears form in my eyes—not because I'm sorry for what I did to Harry but in reaction to the awe in Davis' voice. It's so misplaced.

He turns cool and efficient. A new hardness exists in his voice as he begins ordering me about. "I'll take you back to your unit. I know a shortcut. Get into bed and stay there, even if you hear a commotion. I'll handle the rest."

Davis leaves me at the Unresponsive's door without a word, and I tumble into bed. Hiding under the blankets, I begin shivering, colder than I have ever been. The high piercing call of a whistle rings through the night. Each of the guards carries one in the event of an asylum uprising. I pray that Davis is still unharmed.

As the hours pass, I realize he isn't. He does not get away from this unscathed. That sweet boy, that salt-of-the-earth, honest-as-the-day-is-long fellow, compromises himself and lies for me. I listen to the conversation between him and the recently returned Dr. Faust. Davis takes all the blame for the bloody mess I made. He says that Harry tried to throttle him. Even facing a blade, the inmate would not cease his aggression and Davis fought back, resulting in his opponent's stab wounds.

Harry is currently sedated and therefore unable to give an honest account of his injuries. I assume that Davis removed the scalpels from the man's body and wiped them off, putting them away, save one. He cannot explain the burned hand to Faust's satisfaction, try as he may. Sadly, his ruse is all for naught. Titus and Roy know I throw knives, and Faust has experienced my burning touch first hand. They must realize every word out of Davis's mouth is a fabrication. The only successful element of his lie is in the timing. Miss Honeycutt arrives in a few hours, and Faust wishes to look his best for her. He says he needs sleep and cannot deal with the situation now.

It is a temporary respite—until the doctor begins putting the pieces together. Faust will also notice that Anna Loveridge is gone and guess I played a part in her disappearance. Adding to that sin, the Book will come up missing in his office. It's presently hidden under my mattress, but I must find a better place for it. A mattress is the first place the guards would search. Sleep eludes me as my brain darts from one doomed solution to another.

A few birds begin to chirp and sing in the trees surrounding Ironwood, signaling the approach of dawn. I am transfixed by their sweet, throbbing music, so alive and full of joy it makes me ache.

Will I hear it again tomorrow, or is this morning my last?

28

Deus misereatur.
May the gods have mercy.

No food for the inmates today. A messy kitchen is the last thing Matron wants when Miss Honeycutt tours the facility. Many of the patients have been hidden away in the abandoned sections of the basement. While the rest of us—the less repugnant and more able-bodied—are given new clothing.

I wear a gown perfect for a maid in the schoolroom. It barely reaches my ankles and has a wide sash, smocking, and tiny pleats. I shudder to guess at the color. Though I can't be sure, it feels very pink.

"Get walking," Titus yells. "Everybody into the dining hall. Take your places."

A human herd, the inmates file into the great room. I hold back, coming in last to stand at the end of the line, nearest the door where Honeycutt will enter and exit. There is an enormous potted plant to my right, borrowed from a wealthy Ironwood patron to decorate the asylum. I bumped into it an hour ago, before donning the new dress, when I cleaned the fireplace and laid fresh wood. It sits against the wall and has many leafy outstretched arms, like a chlorophyll-driven octopus.

"We expect you to make a good impression," Matron says. "Much is riding on the outcome of this day."

I feel the crowd turn as one, watching her as she walks from my side of the room to the other, spouting advice with each step. The hard outline of the Book presses into my leg, where it rests in the deep pocket of my frilly apron. I must hide the evidence lest Faust search my body and take it from me. Reaching into my pocket, I remove the Book and tuck it into the back of the potted plant, under a thick cluster of leaves.

Latham circles around to the front of the dining hall. "Are you listening, patients of Ironwood? These events will directly affect your lives. Behave accordingly."

I hear the distant sound of pounding hooves and heavy wheels. Then the portcullis being lifted. A coach passes through the entrance of the asylum. It sounds like a well-appointed rig led by strong, athletic horses. Exactly the sort of vehicle that Mama favored when traveling in the country. Matron strides into the vestibule and opens the front door, hissing for Watts to tuck in his shirt.

"And keep your dirty hands out of sight," she mutters to Roy.

Dr. Faust went into Ironwood City earlier to fetch Miss Honeycutt, and he climbs out of the coach first. The mud sucks at his heel when the doctor turns back to help her alight.

"Well she ain't nothin' to look at," Titus whispers.

Roy snickers and Matron thumps him with her fan. "Silence!"

It has been many years since I last met my mother's friend. Yet the sound of Miss Honeycutt's entrance reveals much about the woman here today. She must be layered like a birthday cake, with noisy silk pantaloons and stockings underneath and stiff, heavy material on top. Her step is quick and sure as she tours the dining hall, stopping to speak with the inmates as the mood strikes her. The woman's voice is a contradiction, both kind and remote.

Honeycutt hurries through the throng, as though she is late to another appointment at yet another charitable institution. I sense generosity in her character, but also a love of material wealth that might sidetrack the best of intentions. Sacrifice at war with self-indulgence. The spirit is indeed willing, but just how weak is the flesh? Can I trust her to help me?

I've written a note to Miss Honeycutt on my last scrap of paper. It describes the true conditions at Ironwood and condemns Faust for the murder of Margaret Hotchkiss. I also beg her to contact the coroner of Stonehenge and relay my message. The paper is folded into a small square, tucked inside my right sleeve. With unsteady fingers, I ease it down into my palm. Now if only she'll shake hands.

Honeycutt walks straight past me without stopping.

No, no! I'm Lenore's daughter. I'm here!

But she continues forward, so I step out of line and execute a formal curtsy. It is a ballroom technique universally learned by the daughters of rich men—even those who are blind and mute. The type of honor aging New York heiresses expect from the world. Amelia Honeycutt turns after hearing the surprised whispers of the assembly.

"How charming," she says, coming to my side. "Do you teach them deportment, Harriet? How very open-minded."

"We do not," Matron replies.

Miss Honeycutt lifts my chin, studying my features. "Unusual. You remind me of someone."

Yes, blast you. I resemble Lenore. Your bosom friend.

Faust scurries over. "I cannot think where you would have met her, Amelia. Very sad case."

"Yes, of course, and I have such a difficult time matching names and faces."

"Let me show you into my office," the doctor suggests.

Before Honeycutt can depart, I take her hand and bow over it, like a gentleman about to bestow a knuckle kiss. I push the note under her fingers and curl them around the paper square. Matron draws the older woman away with happy conversation, and I hear Honeycutt's heavy skirts swing toward the door. Yet there is another sound—that of a folded paper striking wood.

The noise echoes through my head, as horrifying as a death knell. Fast! Get the note before anyone else does! I dart toward the place where it fell, bumping against the inmates ahead of me. Drop to the floor, Hester. Reach out your arm.

"Lose something?" Titus asks, his body blocking mine.

Hershel Watts picks up the paper. "A letter maybe? *This* letter?"

"Give it here. I want a look," Roy says from a distance. He's stayed far away from me since I levitated and prophesied his early death. Unfortunately, the other guards show no fear.

Titus forces me toward the stairs, with Watts trailing behind, and I end up in the basement.

In the Pit.

———— ● ————

"Why are you here precisely?" Gabriel asks.

I shrug and cross my arms.

"It *must* be bad for them to put you in with me."

We are sitting on the table/bed, and it's oddly relaxing. I lean back against the warm stones, and Gabriel laughs in the darkness.

"I'd still wager my story's worse than yours," he says.

I think about shrugging again but can't be bothered. We're both dead anyway so what does it matter?

Gabriel leans back, too. Joining me against the wall. "A terrible idea, competing for the crown of sorrow. Forget I mentioned it. Do you know *The Tale of Two Cities* by Charles Dickens?"

A copy of that work sits on my shelf at home, or it did last time I was there. Cordelia and I never got around to reading it.

He quotes, "*It was the best of times, it was the worst of times. It was the age of wisdom, it was the age of foolishness.*"

Both the author and the storyteller beside me are marvelous. Gabriel is an artist with words, summarizing the scenes and breathing life into the characters. I am caught up in the tale of Lucie Manette, her father Dr. Manette and the virtuous Charles Darnay. But my favorite is Sydney Carton. When Gabriel tells me of his final sacrifice, a tear drops from my eye. The martyr's last words echo through the Pit.

"*It is a far, far better thing that I do, than I have ever done; it is a far, far better rest that I go to than I have ever known.*"

The giant pats my shoulder. "Like Carton and his little seamstress, we'll help each other until the end."

Reaching out, I search the wall and find the bold words I carved there.

LEX TALIONIS.

YOUR DAY OF RECKONING AWAITS, FAUST

Failure washes over me, scalding as acid. I am well and truly caught this time, and I have done nothing to help Gabriel or Faust's victims in the Book. There will be *hell* to pay in the after life. Gabriel begins to hum some lilting, gentle tune. It acts as a salve to my worried mind and gives me, if not hope for survival, at least the possibility of redemption.

I straighten my shoulders and turn to Gabriel. Unsure of whether I will survive this kind of sharing, I take his hand in mine and listen to the beating of my heart. His life flashes behind my eyes as it did before and I feel his sorrow and pain, want more than anything to ease his burden. Heat gradually builds in my chest until I feel radiant as the sun. I push the power out toward Gabriel, giving him all the strength I have.

Then I grow weak and feel no more.

"Wake up," Roy mutters, splashing my face with cold water.

I cough and sputter into painful consciousness, wondering where I am. Dead, not dead, or just in hell? I can't decide which. Arms strapped above me, my body hangs and twirls slowly, my weight barely resting on the balls of my feet. Sweet, holy hell. Every part of me hurts! I pull on the cords, but they hold fast, tethered to a high point in the ceiling. Like a macabre ballerina, I swing about on my toes—arms and shoulders aching.

Definitely not dead. Too painful.

The air smells of rotting wood and mold. This must be the basement, though not the Pit. It has a slightly different, more piquant stench. A door opens and several men walk into the room. Titus. Roy. Watts. Faust. A thousand people could enter this place, and I would still pick their footsteps out of a crowd.

"How disappointing, Hester," Dr. Faust says. "I thought we meant something to each other. The message you wrote to Miss Honeycutt indicates otherwise."

No longer afraid now that I am bound, Roy pushes my leg hard, forcing me to spin on my toes toward the right. Titus stops me mid-rotation and sends me whirling back the other way. One of my oversized boots flies off with the momentum. I hear it fall to the floor, dislodging my pencil from its hiding place near the heel. The ridiculous chicken bone knife and lucky pebbles roll out of the boot, too. Faust kicks them aside and removes something from his case. He throws it into the air and makes a snapping noise.

What's that? A *whip?* Surely not—

"I had a dog once who kept getting at my chickens," Faust says. He walks around me, snapping the whip softly. "Wouldn't stop until I threw a bottle at his head, skimmed it right along his skull. Looked like he'd been scalped afterwards."

I keep turning and twisting to face the rambling madman. "One time was all it took, Hester. The dog healed up and learned his lesson. He never touched another of my chickens. Think what a utopia the world would be if people were so teachable. If they could be conditioned with pain to do right. No more killing or war, no crime or corruption."

Faust snaps the whip harder. "Unfasten her gown, Titus."

The guard tugs at the back of my dress, obviously unfamiliar with women's fashion, and the high neckline strangles me. He loses patience and rips away the section of material covering my shoulder blades and spine. The bodice feels intact, held in place by the overhead position of my arms. A cool draft runs over my back, and the whip cracks again.

I bite my lip so Faust can't see it trembling. Perhaps this is only a threat. He's trying to scare me into returning the Book. Roy, Titus, and Watts fear the whip, all right. They scatter like cockroaches hit by the midday sun.

"You were correct when you said that my mother was a stern disciplinarian," the doctor murmurs. "She did not spare the rod or the child. I paid for my wrongs and so will you, my dear. This is for the letter to Honeycutt."

The lash comes with such force that my body arches forward upon impact. No matter how often you've been hurt, acute pain is always a raw surprise. Sharp. Stinging. Agony.

No—air—cannot—breathe.

Gasping for oxygen, I dangle and spin until Titus turns my back to Faust again.

"Aiding an inmate in her escape from this institution. I think that's worth two stripes, don't you?"

The whip cracks and bites into my shoulder like a beast. *Deus misereatur...* Then it sets fire to my lower back. Mercy, mercy. But Faust is consumed with hatred. There is no other smell now but blood—both real and metaphysical. I hear him coil the whip around his arm, a small snake upon a larger one and try to summon Tom's butterflies. They explode within my mind until the world is a cloud of orange and black fluttering wings, the sight so beautiful that I wish to lose myself in it. But the vision does not bring real peace or courage this time. Faust has ruined any magic the butterflies may have once possessed. They are now nothing more than a borrowed memory.

"I really must insist that you return my journal," Faust says. "Where is it, Hester?"

I kick in his direction, causing only myself pain. Nose running, eyes streaming, I gather moisture in my mouth and spit at him. You will never find your damned book.

He unwraps the whip. "My arm is growing weary, but I shall persevere. I'll question you to your last breath, if necessary."

Gabriel's voice echoes through my mind, keeping me company as I bleed. Far, far better thing I do... better resting place that I go to...

Twin blows land on my back, and I lose my footing, swaying back and forth. Oxygen finally enters my lungs. Another breath. Another. And everything fades to black but breathing and pain. S-stop. Stop. Closing my eyes, I listen to my heartbeat and feel something cold in the rooms upstairs. *Death?* But there is only silence. As always, He reaps in His own good time.

My sense of awareness expands, and I hear Faust take a seat, ask for Watts to bring him a drink of water. Then the rhythmic pounding of running horses. Or is my mind gone? Round and around I go, twirling from the rafters, until the nauseating motion slows, a carousel ride coming to a halt. But the sound of the horses grows more distinct. Watts enters the chamber in haste and sloshes water on the floor.

"We have company, Doctor. The sentry outside saw a coach and rider headed this way and lifted the gate."

"I am not receiving at the moment, Watts."

A cheerful whistle penetrates my stupor. *Oh My Darling, Clementine?*

Sir Death glides through the wall like a wraith. *You sent for me?*

29

Morituri te salutamus.

They who are about to die salute you.

T he Reaper's chill presence envelops all. This is the Death I have worked with most, the one who kissed my head and gave me protection from His brothers. All lethal grace, He touches the marks on my body, and I shudder with relief as the pain subsides. The discomfort is gone, but the bleeding continues. Kelly, the whistling horseman, didn't arrive in time after all. This saddens me. I regret that I did not get to hear his whiskey laugh or argue in sign with him again. Smell the sweet mixture of pines and sandalwood that is his alone.

Death sighs and sits down beside Faust. *Do not grow sentimental, Visionary.*

Forgive me. How inappropriate. Thank you, sir.

You're welcome.

Unaware of the Reaper, Dr. Faust stands and leaves with Watts for the main floor. Roy and Titus sit down—one of them shuffles a deck of cards. Up above, the coach and rider pass through the portcullis and stop at the asylum entrance. Faust must have changed his mind about receiving today because he admits Kelly and his companions. Blessing Veritas for my gifts, I extend my hearing to the fullest degree, tuning everything out but the meeting upstairs. I could be standing next to Kelly, so clearly do their voices register with me.

"Welcome, Doctor," Faust murmurs. "This is an unexpected visit. And you've brought the police?"

"Yes," Kelly replies. "I want my wife. These gentlemen are here to see you give her to me."

Faust ushers them down the hall. "Come. I have very sad news to share."

"What are you talking about?"

"As you know, we've been plagued with sickness this winter. I intended to write, Dr. Kelly, but there simply hasn't been time. I regret to inform you of Hester's passing. Her loss affected all of us at Ironwood."

The four men enter the parlor and Faust shuts the door, offering his guests a seat.

Kelly remains standing. "I don't believe it. Show me the body."

"Out of the question. Her corpse has been burned."

The police officers seem to accept my death without comment, but Kelly continues on at Faust. "Let me talk with the nurses who tended her."

"They are no longer employed at the asylum."

"Then show me the surviving patients."

"Regretfully, there were none." Faust walks back to the door, opens it. "I am sorry if I appear unfeeling in regards to your circumstances, but I need to get back to work."

I am surprised that Kelly does not protest. Instead, he seems to completely unravel, weeping and embracing Faust before leaving the parlor. More shocking still, I hear a quick flipping, sliding motion.

Kelly has taken something out of Faust's coat and slipped it into his own. Did he pick the doctor's pocket? "Thank you for doing what you could, good fellow."

Apparently Faust is unaware of the fact he's been stolen from. "Well certainly. You're, um…most welcome. Although, I must insist you leave now. Watts will show you out."

Faust calls the guard, and Watts joins the men in the hall. "Accompany our guests outside, please."

But Kelly begins to cry again, like a man completely shattered. I'd almost believe he meant those tears, if I didn't guess he was conning them all. "Might I have a moment to collect myself?" he asks. "Could I trouble you for a handkerchief? And perhaps a drink?"

Faust goes to collect the requested items. Paper rustles as Kelly takes the stolen note out of his pocket, and I assume, reads it. Could it be the one I sent to Honeycutt? He gets to his feet and steals down the hall. Kelly is almost to the stairwell when the door opens a crack.

"She's in the basement," Davis whispers.

———————— • ————————

Titus and Roy are so caught up in their game of cards, they do not notice the quiet jangle of the door knob, the scratch of some metal tool. Both pockets *and* locks? Kelly is a talented fellow. The door swings open a few seconds later. Then Kelly's at my side, cutting the cords at my wrists. My arms drop and blood flow returns to them, feeling like pins and needles in the flesh. The Reaper's gift of pain relief is beginning to fade.

I try to be independent, to stand on my own, but I sag into Kelly's arms. He examines my wounds quickly and wraps me in his cloak. The pressure of the heavy material resting against my back is agony. Pushing it off my skin only makes things worse.

"I'll get you out of here, sweetheart," Kelly says. "They won't hurt you anymore."

The other language I can't repeat. The curses he mutters as his shoe slides out from under him, when he realizes the floor is slippery with my blood. Kelly picks me up and Titus and Roy move to block the door.

"It's over, don't you see?" Kelly asks. "Your coworker here can attest to the fact that I've come with a police escort."

"That's true," Davis replies. "He did."

"If you're smart, you won't involve yourselves further in this crime." Kelly takes another step forward. "Faust is destined for prison or the noose. Do you wish to join him?"

Speaking of Faust, he enters the chamber in a rush, followed by Watts. The doctor pushes past Roy and Titus. "This does complicate matters," the madman says, advancing upon Kelly and me. "I cannot let either of you leave. That would ruin everything. And some sacrifices are acceptable if they benefit society."

"What benefit?" Kelly asks, holding me closer.

"My research of pain stimulus, of course," Faust says, sounding apologetic. "I'll find my journal, after you're both dead and buried. I am so sorry it has come to this, pet." He takes something from his pocket.

What is it?

Davis shouts and jumps in front of me. "No! Don't."

My head nearly cracks when a gun fires, and then all turns quiet for an instant before pandemonium breaks out again. As Roy, Watts, and Titus run from the room, Kelly lowers my legs to the floor.

In my weakened state, I drop to my knees and crawl over to where Davis fell. Gods have mercy. Why did you do it? I reach for his hand. The skin feels smooth and unlined against my palm.

Kelly charges Faust, who is thankfully slow to fire again, and rips the gun from his hand. He punches the older doctor several times and throws him against the wall. Faust weeps, begging for his life. "*Stop.* I'm *sorry.* I'll be good." The madman sounds like a child who fears he's going to be punished. Amid his pitiful cries, Kelly's policemen join us, demanding that the situation be explained.

The good doctor kneels down at Davis's side and gives a brief accounting to the lawmen as he examines my friend. The sound of snapping metal rings makes me jerk. No cuffs! I won't wear them again! Yet the policemen do not bother me. Instead, it is the asylum guards who are now the ones in irons. They immediately turn on their employer.

I hear all this happen, and none of it matters, for I am cradling a dead boy. I had forgotten Death was still in the room. There is no heartbeat, no breath left in my friend's body as I feel the Reaper take him to the next world.

Versare cum Deo. Be well, Davis.

Holding his cooling corpse, our mingled blood drying on the floor, I hear the policemen drag a screaming Faust away and lock him in the Pit.

30

Sic transit gloria mundi.
So passes away the glory of the world.

The Book was damning for Ironwood as well as Faust. There's talk of closing it down and relocating the inmates to other hospitals. Once the doctor's trial is over and the sentencing done, of course. A month after his own commitment, Faust is stripped of his medical license and living in the same conditions that his patients endured. The spirits of his victims have found peace at last.

Bully for them, though I can't say the same.

Davis is buried in a little cemetery near his family's farm. It plagues my thoughts, imagining the grief his loved ones must feel and knowing I'm the cause. Now two men have died on my account—one temporarily, the other all too permanent.

Lying on my stomach, on a hospital bed, I swim through another wave of pain. My back is completely bare down to the top of my hips, and Kelly is cleaning the lacerations again. It is a painstaking process that we've repeated many times due to infection from the traces of cloth and other foreign matter within the wounds. Damn, he hit an especially raw spot there. Stings like the blazes. Although I'm given plenty of drugs in this place, enough to keep my dependency a secret, it doesn't eliminate the pain of this procedure.

My head is turned to the side, resting on a pillow. "All right?" Kelly asks.

I pay no attention to his question. Instead, I grit my teeth and focus on something else, like spelling the name Jupiter. J-U-P-I-T-E-R. Jupiter. Next it's Pluto. P-L-U—

"You know how to sign, Hester. Do it. I want to know what you're feeling."

But I don't, even when he scrapes another sore place.

"Once your injuries heal a bit, we'll think about returning to Stonehenge, but I don't want to risk it until then."

I've asked Kelly to go home so many times. His daughter Alice is in Stonehenge now. She's been at a boarding school in Boston since last fall. At only eight, the child must be missing her father. But Kelly won't leave me, no matter what I tell him. He rebuts my arguments with "I have it under control, Hester." Or "Alice is in good hands. Don't worry."

His stubbornness drives me to distraction. He's worse than I am.

Kelly pours on the antiseptics, packs the gashes with poultices, and lathers me with salve. After all that, I am shaking like a willow in a high wind. He sits down, takes my hand, and squeezes it. No visions at his touch. No visions at all for weeks. My soul seems to be empty but for the self-loathing and depression.

The doctor remains there until I fall asleep. I do not know if he goes somewhere else while I am under, but his hand still holds mine when I awake.

———————● ●———————

After two months in hospital, we are scheduled to leave on the train today. Kelly has bought a dress for me, which he describes as indigo. Made with yards of soft wool, it fits better than the bespoke gowns my mother once ordered. Then there are the under things, not a single garment missing, and the comfortable boots and gloves, the long, fitted traveling coat and reticule. Our Kelly has a very good eye for the shape of a woman's figure.

And I have a new pair of spectacles. Black lenses again.

We are due at the station in minutes, and my *husband* is in a great hurry. I hope he doesn't notice the slight clicking sound in my case. I just helped myself to a pharmaceutical cabinet, taking as many containers of escape-in-a-bottle as would fit in the little valise. I found the right shelf, the correct medicine. An errant nurse took the same stuff out before leaving the little door open to crooks like me. Eight was the limit, plus a few needles.

Really, Hester, couldn't you have managed nine? It's unlikely you'll have this opportunity again.

Kelly takes my arm, and we leave the hospital, making a clean get-away without the doctor even knowing we're on the lam. The train chugs out of the station a few minutes after we take our seats. He's given me the one by the window although the view is lost on my eyes. A gentleman out of habit.

"How's your back, Hester? Would you like to rest? Use my shoulder as a pillow, if you do."

It hurts when I move, or breathe, or remain stationary, or try to sleep. I do not mention this to Kelly. Instead, I turn toward the glass pane, realizing that this action is a great conversation-ender. One can face a window resolutely and conclude all communication with a traveling companion. Dulling my ears to sound, I lose myself in the gentle motion of the locomotive and awaken sometime later, plastered against Kelly. How mortifying. I hope I didn't salivate or snore.

"Feel better?" he asks. "We'll arrive in Stonehenge by tea time."

Nodding, I again pivot toward the window. This time the doctor does not take the hint. "A shrug *and* a nod both in one day. I am a lucky fellow. Why don't you sign instead, Mrs. Kelly?"

My fingers fly into action before I can stop them. **Not your real wife.**

The doctor laughs. "Legally, you are. The annulment hasn't happened yet."

Our awkward marital state is amusing to Kelly but not to me. Tuning him out, I listen to the train sounds again until we reach Stonehenge. I'm not really upset with the doctor. He has become my closest friend, and I am grateful for all he's done for me. But it is hard to be pleasant when I feel so wretched, when life seems like such a burden. Every bit of food, every kindness, every pleasant word is a condemnation. Surviving one's survival can be difficult.

Once we arrive in Stonehenge, Kelly leads me to the railroad platform. Exiting the station, we take High Street and turn west. The day is sunny and fairly warm, smelling of damp sidewalks, horses, and manure. As if on cue, I recognize the tread of the person walking toward us. Heart, mind, and soul cease to work properly. My first love is using the same sidewalk as Kelly and me.

And Tom's been drinking—a great deal too, by the smell of him. "Look here," he says, slurring his words. "The girl of my dreams, the one who ruined me for all others." He moves closer, blocking my way. "Didn't take you long to move on though, did it? Married now, I hear, and to Kelly no less."

The doctor shoves Tom back a few feet. "Sleep it off, Craddock. Go home."

"I like it better in town, thanks."

Besides the alcohol, I detect the scent of jealousy. Not that Tom wants me back. He's just mad because Kelly has something that once belonged to him. I feel his dark gaze on my face. "Why can't I stop thinking about you?" he asks, sounding truly perplexed. "One minute, I want to break your pretty neck. The next I want to kiss it."

"Shut up," Kelly interrupts. "Don't make me hit you. It wouldn't be a fair fight."

Tom's laughter is cold and hard. "And you're such an ethical man? Won't punch a drunk, but you'll steal his girl." He flicks the brim of his hat. "Good day, Mr. and Mrs. Kelly. I'm off to find a better class of people."

Tom steps around us, and pushes through the batwing doors of a nearby saloon. I listen as he greets the barkeep and a few of the working girls. Grief nearly drowns me when I compare the kind, gentle person Tom once was with the bitter wastrel I just encountered.

"He's the town hellion now," Kelly says. "If it's any comfort, I do believe his current behavior is just a phase."

It isn't a comfort. Or a phase. Tom is still being influenced by my enemy. I felt the supernatural power of Archimendax, heard it control Tom when he spoke. How does one overcome such evil? I must locate that damn Mary Arden and get her help with this. Surely Willard Little Hawk would look for her if I paid him.

Kelly hires a buggy and instructs the driver to take us to The Revels. I do not know where I will live now, but I'd like to get some things from my bedroom. The books Cordie read to me, the china teapot I received from Mama when I turned sixteen, my clothes and shoes. Kelly helps me into the vehicle and then climbs up, taking the seat next to mine. The horse moves forward, and we begin the journey to my old home.

"There's something I haven't told you," Kelly says. "I thought it would be too upsetting, but I'm not so sure now. Might be therapeutic."

What? I sign.

He leans back and tells all. "There was a riot at the asylum last week. Some of the inmates got to Faust. It wasn't pretty. They used the scarificator on his arms and legs, and left the man strapped down. Poetic justice, I suppose, but Faust hemorrhaged and died. Slowly and alone."

I think of the words I carved in the Pit. *Lex talionis*—an eye for an eye. Having killed the doctor many times in my imagination, I am surprised I'm not happier over this development. I feel sick instead.

"Oddly, he was missing all of his fingers on one hand. They appeared to have been removed with a surgical saw post mortem."

The swirling in my belly grows. Was that the work of Harry Swinton? He held quite a grudge against the doctor. And Faust said Harry hated me, too. Even *before* I threw a dozen knives at him. I swallow and cross my arms, hugging myself.

Kelly concludes the gruesome report. "Patients attacked the guards and tore up the place. Caused a fire in the west wing, a massive explosion. With so many bodies hidden under the rubble, it isn't known how many people escaped the blast."

I wonder then about Matron. Watts. Titus. Roy. After fearing my tormentors each day at Ironwood, it's difficult to accept that they're injured or dead. And what of Gabriel? Did he survive? I doubt it. I'm lacking faith at the moment.

The buggy turns left, horse's hooves striking cobblestones. We're at The Revels. I know this place so well and yet it doesn't feel welcoming to me in the least. After the vehicle stops, Kelly gets out and lifts me down. Someone opens the front door. He walks across the porch and the soles of his shoes sound smooth against the stone—evidence of fine leather in action.

"You're a pleasing sight, Miss Hester. It's good to have you back."

Simmons Harrow? I smile, relieved to hear his friendly voice.

———————— • ————————

Kelly hands me my cane, and I take the steps slowly. The first thing I notice is the quiet, the sense of emptiness. No gossiping maids or fussy valet. No Cordelia Collins. I move across the foyer, and reach out to touch the old grandfather clock, but it isn't there. The house even smells barren without the aroma of yeast and butter punctuating the air. Vases of sweet-scented flowers. Dried lavender.

My footsteps echo through the dining room where I ate with my parents last November. Nothing but empty space. I proceed to the library and find it vacant as well. Kelly has followed me quietly to this point, but he walks to my side now.

"What has happened, I wonder?"

I shrug. **No idea.**

Sim hovers near the threshold. I gesture for him to join us, but he hesitates. "I'm not sure where to begin…"

"Get on with it, boy," Kelly says. "Speak your mind."

"Her father lost all his money."

With those half dozen words, it is as though a verbal dam has suddenly broken inside of Sim. He releases a torrent of news all at once. "People are saying he cheated his business partners. That he would have gone to jail if he hadn't sold everything and paid them off. And no one's seen him in weeks—not since he fired the staff. It's just Willard and me here now, keeping watch over the place until the new owner arrives."

I can't imagine Father without wealth. Cheating on his business partners is far easier to grasp. Maybe this was the cause of the desperate drinking after Mama died. He had been exposed as a crook and his carefully built empire was crumbling.

"Must have owed them an enormous amount," Kelly says. "What a shock for you, Hester."

I nod, although I don't agree. After the last few months, I'd be surprised if my father's greed affected me deeply enough to cause shock. I feel nothing. I might even like The Revels more without its riches.

Fate's use of irony in my life again.

Sim clears his throat. "There's a letter for you, miss. I put it in the study."

The doctor and I walk to father's old sanctum, leaving Sim behind in the library. I feel badly for the boy, caught in the middle this way. And where will he go when the new owner of this house shows up?

Once we enter the study, Kelly closes the door and moves toward the nearest book shelf, picks something up. A tearing sound, a paper being unfolded. I listen to his low, dry voice as he reads aloud. It is from my father's attorney, written five days ago.

"In essence, this says that your mother left you a stipend in her will," he murmurs, after the first run-through. "And your father wants most of it."

According to the letter, Mama arranged for a deposit of $2,400 annually to a bank account in my name. It was intended as personal wealth, to spend or invest as I deemed fit.

"John Grayson provided well for you, from birth to the present time," Kelly quotes Father's lawyer. "He has experienced a reversal of fortune, and it is now imperative that you supply him with financial relief as a means of repayment for past largesse."

"*Largesse?* I'll show your father the largesse of my boot when we meet again." He shakes the letter in disgust. "And his lawyer should burn in hell for eternity."

I touch the doctor's arm. He will give himself an aneurism if he doesn't calm down. Kelly ignores me and continues reading. "We ask for sixteen hundred dollars a year, leaving you with the remaining eight hundred. In exchange, your father, John Grayson, will relinquish all of his parental rights. He will have no legal claim upon you, Hester Grayson, or any access to your future wealth."

Did I hear that right? He won't have power over me again? Can't commit me to another asylum?

The whiskey-flavored voice draws me back. "You will be given accommodations at The Revels for the next thirty days, but we advise you to secure your own residence post haste as your family home was sold at auction. Please sign this document, should it meet with your approval, and return it forthwith to my office. Etcetera, etcetera. Have I mentioned how much I hate this lawyer?"

I will sign, I reply.

"Keep your money, Hester," Kelly replies. "Tell him to—"

Want freedom.

"You're a married woman now. Your father can't touch you."

Not real marriage.

"*Yes*, I know. You keep reminding me of that." Kelly wanders the study, counting to himself. It helps him control his temper. After a few minutes pass, he's ready to talk again. "Are you sure? Wouldn't you like some time to consider this? Sixteen hundred dollars is a lot to give away each year."

He watches me for a moment, probably hoping I'll change my mind. "All right," he finally says, flipping his jacket pocket open. "Use my Waterman."

I take the pen and sign the paper against the doctor's back. There must be drops of ink everywhere. On my gloves, Kelly's suit. I don't give a hang. Once the document goes into effect, I won't be affluent, but I'll have enough money to survive. And most important, I'll be free of my father.

Kelly paces the room once more, counting a bit louder. I sense the emotion inside of him—smell the frustration and anger driving each step. He makes one final rotation and comes to a stop in front of the study door.

"Are you hungry?" he asks. "Would you like some supper?"

I shake my head, trying to decide what to do next. Investigate the house further? Unpack? Cry for joy over my newfound independence? For reasons I do not understand, my reticence bothers the doctor.

"A head shake, a few words in sign now and then, a grimace," he says, stepping closer. "That's all I get from you nowadays, Hester. Where's the woman I once knew? Where's your spirit?"

Temper quickens my heartbeat and warms my skin. Just like a man. Putting himself where he doesn't belong. I care for Noah Kelly, damned if I don't. He's worked his way into a corner of my heart—sticking there like a puncture weed—but this is a poor time for criticism. I'm tired, my back hurts something fierce, and I'm in need of a dose of opium.

Kelly wants spirit, does he? He shall have it.

I push up the sleeves of my coat and launch into sign. **Give father money. My life! Not yours. My decision! Not yours. Stay the hell out!**

The doctor remains quiet, leaning against the door, the wood squeaking under his weight. It feels rather good to be mad, even if I am almost screaming with my hands. On fire now, I have another go at him.

This is nothing. *Nothing.* No pain, no cold. Not locked up or dying. Losing money? Easy.

With that, I snap my fingers. My chest is heaving, and I feel radiant, my former weariness forgotten.

"Why hello, Hester," Kelly says, sounding breathless himself. "About time you showed yourself."

I make an obscene gesture, but the whole effect is ruined when I sway a little. In reaction, Kelly pushes off the door, takes me in his arms, and kisses me right on the mouth.

———————— ● ————————

To say that I am unprepared for this is an understatement. More surprising still, I cannot let go of Kelly. I am enthralled by the strong, hard lines of his body, the texture of the stubble on his cheek, his hand entwined in my hair. Vital. Ardent. This man is a new craving, like oxygen, opium, and sustenance, all rolled into one. I push him back to the door, hear him land against it with a thud.

I am undone, utterly destroyed by the kiss. It tastes sweet and clean, the intentions behind it passion-fueled but honorable. If I maintain our contact, will I become sweet and clean and honorable, too? Made whole, as I never was before?

Closer, Kelly. Please don't stop.

But an image forms in my mind, disrupting all physical sensation. Free of revelations for weeks and Fate prods at me now? And with prescience, no less. That rare glimpse into the future of a Visionary seen once or twice in a lifetime. Warning or promise, it's a roll of the dice.

The image shows Kelly and me, waking in a bed together. The room is neat and homely, with calico curtains and a braided rug. We're nestled close—I'm pressed up against his back with my arm around his waist, and one of his feet is tucked between mine. Kelly's darkish-gold hair is rumpled on one side when he rolls over and gives me a crooked smile. Unguarded, lazily affectionate.

"Good morning," he says, caressing my cheek.

His wedding ring glints in the early morning light, and I drink in the sight of him, fascinated by the clever hazel eyes, the beautifully formed face. Who would tire of such a man? Kind, intelligent, funny as hell. A part of me wishes to stay here with him forever. This moment feels so happy, so normal, and what Visionary can deny the allure of that? Our connection has nothing to do with magic or ancient callings from Roman diety. We're just Hester and Noah.

Still prescience is a tricky thing. It allows a small glimpse in time, not the entire picture. What comes just after the incident could be terrible. Tragic, even.

Fate, you treacherous crone. Why do you play such games?

Then all goes dark, blind. Without Kelly knowing I've gone to another sphere, I am back again in my father's study.

The doctor pulls away, just a little. "I've thought of kissing you for some time," he says. "Almost since the beginning."

31

Incendio.
An all-consuming fire.

His words seduce, intoxicate like sweet wine. They distract me from prescience, and visions and make all the poets in the world right as never before. Lord Byron, in particular. Drawing me against his chest, Kelly pulls the ribbon from my hair. It falls a few inches below my jaw, not at all the proper length for a lady, but he runs his fingers through the waves, murmuring, "Beautiful, like starlight."

Ridiculous man. My hair and the word beautiful have never been used in the same sentence. I touch his face, his smiling mouth, seeing without my eyes. Kelly bites one of my fingers. "Come home with me. Be my wife in truth."

Just the mention of truth pierces my heart, and I turn cold. Be his wife? His real wife? No. I cannot. I'm not fit for marriage to anyone, let alone dear Kelly.

"You're shivering," he says, rubbing my arms. "Would you like my jacket?"

I shake my head and he releases me. "Hester, you look ill. What's wrong?

Not a wife. Not now.

"Well, you acted a lot like one a minute ago." He laughs differently this time, sounding anything but happy. "All right. If not now, when? Do you have a time frame in mind? A month, a year, two years?"

We'd fail. Can't you see?

"I *see* that you're afraid of trying, of allowing yourself to be happy."

Stop, Noah. You don't know.

He touches my arm. "Then tell me. Tell me."

The study has grown crowded with just the two of us. Hot and oppressive with the smell of ink and dust and love and fear. I want to leave.

Never understand. Broken inside.

"I'm your friend. Let me help."

No. I fix myself.

Turning my back on him, I find a handkerchief in my reticule and wipe my eyes. I've been so low since leaving Ironwood—nightmares, flashbacks, cold sweats. Sometimes I hear Faust's voice at the most random moments, and I'm petrified, even though I know it isn't real. I loathe confined spaces, freezing water, and most men, present company excluded. Father, Faust, even Tom have soured me on the species, but never Noah Kelly. None of this is normal or right. It's far too great a burden to ask him to bear.

Sim knocks on the door loudly. "Sorry, sir, but the buggy driver outside needs to speak with you."

Kelly mutters under his breath. "Fine. I'll be there in a minute."

"Come here, Hester." He turns me around gently and hugs me, like the true friend he is. There is no ownership in the gesture, just kindness. "We'll finish our discussion another time."

Kelly leaves the house to speak with the driver. As usual, guilt nags, and I worry that the doctor will discover the opium among my luggage out there in the buggy. Really, Hester, you should be ashamed. You steal, lie, utilize drugs. Kiss a man one moment and change your mind the next...

As Kelly said, I am not the person I once was.

Self-examination makes me restless, so I use my cane to cross the foyer, skimming along the wall. My left foot crashes into something heavy. I bend down, rub my painful toes, and touch the hard surface of the offending object. Bulging eyes? Flared nostrils? Snake-like tail? It's Mr. Ming, Mama's Chinese dragon doorstop—my enamel-covered, heart-of-iron friend from childhood. I run my fingers over him, remembering the last time we bumped into each other. It seems like a hundred years ago—the day Mama died and my life took a very different turn. Patting Ming once more, I feel old and fragile. Strange that he wasn't sold with the other household things, but maybe no one wanted him. Cook always said Ming was hideous.

Yet I'm glad he's here. I'll put him in a place of honor. My back muscles protest as I lift the ponderous dragon and carry him to a spot by the window. He settles on the floor with a clang.

Kelly reenters the house. "The driver's pitching a fit. Apparently he has another appointment that he cannot miss. Where can we take you? To visit Miss Collins?"

No, I sign. **Staying here.**

Expecting Kelly to begin counting to cool his temper, I'm surprised when he doesn't. "You're welcome at my house, you know. As my guest, with absolutely no strings attached. Unless you want them to be."

I smile and shake my head. **Need quiet. Time to myself.**

He walks into the hallway and calls Sim, who joins us promptly. "Have you a room for Miss Grayson to use?"

Miss Grayson, is it now, Kelly? My legal husband must not want to explain our marriage to the boy and thereby is still using my maiden name in his presence.

"Yes, sir. I found some furniture upstairs in the servant's wing."

"And you'll lock up each night? Keep things safe?"

"I will," Sim replies. "I promise, Doctor."

Kelly puts his hand on my arm and draws me to the door, lowers his head and whispers, "People will gossip if you stay here alone with him. He's nearly a man."

Let them, I sign. **Don't care.**

"Somehow I knew you'd say that."

The doctor walks across the porch outside but turns back at the steps. "Since you refuse to live with me, you might give some thought to buying a place of your own. We could tour the local real estate together and find something suitable."

My housing options are slim, due to my income, but I try to appear enthusiastic. **Wonderful idea.**

———————— • ————————

And it is wonderful, if one defines the experience as a source of actual wonder, a near miracle. With Kelly's help, I secure lodgings within twenty-four hours, but I cannot move in until the current inhabitants vacate the premises. Therefore, I've been developing some previously non-existent homemaking skills.

A scullery girl comes to The Revels and works with me for an hour or two each afternoon. Scarcely fifteen, she charges a minimal amount for her services but seems to be a wealth of domestic information. I have learned many things under her tutelage. The operation of the big, frightening wood stove, how to gather eggs from the hens without getting pecked, and baking scones. And I've discovered that large kitchen aprons are an excellent invention. Mixing up cornbread and scones can cover even the most skilled homemakers with powdery ingredients.

Yet I am not even close to skilled—thus the ingredients coat both me and the apron like an early spring snowfall. How glad I am today's supper is over! I cooked it all on my own, learning far too late that one should never fry bacon in an over-heated cast-iron skillet. As a result, we had no meat for supper, and the kitchen still smells of smoldering pork.

"Those jacket potatoes were good," Sim murmurs, bringing his plate to the sink. "Didn't fancy bacon anyway."

He lies. Everyone fancies bacon except the pig.

I begin washing up. Sim takes the towel off my shoulder and dries the dishes as I clean them. This is a nice surprise. It seems like I've been waiting on Sim hand and foot since coming home. Not that I mind, particularly. Having someone else to care for distracts me from my own problems.

"Do you know if Little Hawk's left for town yet?" he asks, sliding a dry plate across the counter.

Willard has been in and out of the house for days at a time, searching the woods for Mary Arden. He mentioned earlier that he needed fresh supplies from Hollister's before making the next trip. I gave him five dollars and a shopping list of my own.

Sim adds another dish to the stack. "And the girl is gone? The one who comes in and helps you?"

Nodding in response, I drop our utensils into a pan of hot water, wisps of steam rising to my face. I scrub and rinse the knives and forks before handing them to Sim.

"Willard said you leased a place on St. David's Street. A big old boarding house. When do you move in?"

I hold up seven soapy fingers.

"A week? That soon?" He does not speak much after receiving this information and leaves abruptly when the last mug is wiped dry and placed in the cupboard.

With the kitchen finally tidy, I pick up a large woven basket. It's dark outside, but that doesn't matter to me. The sheets on the laundry line won't un-peg themselves. My back gives me a twinge as I hoist the basket to my hip. Even though the lashes have healed, there are spasms of pain deep in the affected muscles. I injected myself this morning, but it takes more drugs to satisfy me now. I have five bottles left, little more than a dose in each. Just thinking of running dry makes me ill.

When I leave the house, the night air smells of chives and rosemary from the kitchen garden, and a single cricket cheeps its heart out in the flower bed. A soft, gentle evening, and yet depression nearly smothers me as I unpeg and fold the linen.

Knowing my way by heart, I count the steps back toward the house, walk across the kitchen, and down the hallway to the formal staircase. I hold the handrail and proceed to the second floor, turning in the direction of my old bedroom. Sim was embarrassed to admit that my father had given it to him. He offered to move out, but I didn't wish to be a bother. The maid's dormitory isn't such a bad spot, and most nights, I'm too tired to care about my sleeping arrangements.

Sim is packing when I enter my old suite. I hear him drop something on the floor. Is it a shoe? He seems jumpy, like me when the medication wears off. Once he snaps his bag and removes it from the bed, I drape clean linen over the mattress and begin tucking in the corners.

"Might as well leave," Sim says. "Can't stay here forever."

Lifting my eyebrows, I turn in his direction, questioning. What has brought on this sudden restlessness?

He goes downstairs without saying anything more. Sim can't be serious about leaving now. Where will he stay? I've heard nothing about new accomodations and the owner doesn't take possession of the house for several weeks. Perhaps Sim means to take a trip.

I finish adjusting the linens and then open the built-in drawers under the window seat, hoping to find an additional quilt inside. It is as desolate as the rest of The Revels. My hand bumps against a slim wooden panel. I had forgotten about the hidden compartment. In our salad days, Cordelia and I surprised one another by leaving treats in this little drawer. Pushing the right corner of the panel, I hear it release and pop out.

Nostalgic, I reach inside, and my fingers touch something cool. Like links of a chain. A necklace? Stomach fluttering, I trace the edge of a small, rectangular stone and recognize it immediately. It's the topaz—the same one worn by Tom's ancestors. A surge of happiness runs through me until I remember when I last held the pendant. The day a stranger threw Kelly off Settler's Ridge and nearly strangled me. Reviewing that memory in my head, I realize it wasn't a stranger at all.

But Simmons Harrow.

I lean against the foot of the bed, feeling like the air's been knocked out of me. How could I not read him, not know what he was feeling all these years? Even with my supernatural gifts, I never realized the truth. I must have blocked my mind to any clues that brought him under suspicion—the height of the attacker, his build and musculature. Even the smell of beef broth on his skin, now that I think of it—a scent often worn by the oldest children at the orphanage. They earn their keep in the kitchens, separating the boiled meat from the bones and gristle. But I ignored all of this evidence. In fact, it occurs to me that I've never once tried to read his emotions with olfaction. Given his tragic youth, I suppose I felt sorry for the boy, extending privacy to him that I gave to no one else.

A crashing sound on the main floor. I fasten the chain around my neck, hide the topaz locket in my bodice, and step out of the bedroom. Listening carefully, I pinpoint Sim's location. He's in a storage room near the kitchen, arguing loudly. The way he talks to himself reminds me of David Thornhill, moments before he killed Maude Lambson. And Marie-Louise Lennox just prior to her suicide.

As I descend the stairs, another crash comes from the storage room. The sound is painfully close, and I cover my ears. I wish I had a weapon, though I dread the thought of actually using it on Sim. I lift my face and listen. Here he comes, walking toward the front of the house, a container of some kind in his hand. It sloshes back and forth with each step.

Caught out in the open, just beyond the foyer, I'm unsure which way to turn. Don't act scared, Hester. Don't upset him. It's so strange, we just did the dishes together, and everything seemed fine. I can still smell the burned bacon, hear the cricket cheeping outside in the garden. But now Sim's trying to kill me.

He walks my way, the liquid in his bottle splashing against the glass. "Miss Hester—" Sim says. Then he stops and rubs his head. "No! I won't call you that. I won't bow or scrape anymore."

The front entrance is my only hope. I inch backwards, praying the movement is small enough Sim won't notice.

"Do you know what your father did to me?" he asks while opening the bottle. Fluid splatters across my shoulder, the side of my face, coating my hair and stinging my eyes and nose. I wipe at it, using my skirt as a towel, and recognize that sharp, oily smell.

Kerosene.

———— • ————

Sim drizzles the remainder of the liquid across the wooden floor. "He sold my family a worthless mine. Took all our life's savings."

He tosses the bottle against the wall, and it shatters. I cover my ears, but I still hear his angry voice. "It killed Pa. Forced Ma to work at the button factory. But one night she comes home and falls asleep next to the fire. Ever hear the story?"

I have heard it. Everyone knows what happened to the Harrows. How his mother died just months after his father, when a few stray embers popped from the hearth and set her alight.

"Who do you think revealed your father's crimes?" Sim asks. "The partners were shocked when I gave them the record books. Greed cost him this house, all his possessions, his good name, and last of all, his child."

If only Sim knew how little my father cared, he'd realize that this dramatic gesture won't have the effect he desires.

Sim's beyond reason. He scrapes a Lucifer tip and the match flares to life. I run back through the foyer to the front door and twist the knob. Please open. Please.

"No use. Locked it myself."

Turning, I face my attacker, but my thoughts are clouded with fear. Again, I don't know what to do.

Sim remains still. He keeps his distance, the Lucifer—and my fate—in his hand. He wants to watch me burn without risking his own skin. I hear him blow out the match, and toss the stick over his shoulder. Another is struck. It's extinguished like the first.

"Couldn't kill you when I caused the wagon accident in town," he says, lighting the next, putting it out. "Or when I had my fingers round your neck up on the ridge."

My heart sputters as he plays with me. How soon will he tire of this?

"Maybe today's the day." Sim draws out the process of igniting this one, and it sounds brilliant when it finally catches fire. "Let's see, shall we?"

He drops the lit match, and I hear the flame snap against the kerosene. Sim laughs wildly, clapping like a child at a Fourth of July parade. The foyer is a vast octagonal space with hallways branching out to other sections of the house, but I'm cut off from any route of escape. I hear the fire oscillating, forming almost a half-circle as it begins to hem me in. It's moving so fast with all the wood pillars and floors. How long do I have? I track the progress of the fire, counting in seconds how quickly it's eating up the room. I give myself two or three minutes until the flames arrive at my section of the foyer. If the smoke doesn't kill me first, that is. And the roof doesn't collapse. Coughing, eyes already streaming from the hot air, I take off my apron and cover my nose and mouth with it, tying the strings at the back of my head.

One and two and three, I remind myself, counting down the seconds until the fire gets here. Four and five and six. The rhythm makes me think of when Cordelia taught me to waltz. I was bloody awful, stepping on her feet the entire time. Cordelia nearly hurt herself from laughing too hard. Fifteen, sixteen, seventeen.

What do I do? Frozen with panic for a moment, my brain sparks and then returns to full function, pointing out the obvious. The wall behind me has a tall window. Huzzah, thank you brain. I turn around and pound against the glass. Shatter, will you? I don't want to die like this. Yet it doesn't cooperate. Stupid, stupid glass. Thirty-eight, thirty-nine, forty.

My lungs feel dry like the smoky air, and I choke and gag. Losing my balance, I stumble over a hard object. *O di immortales.* Mr. Ming!

Fifty-nine, sixty. One minute gone, two remaining before I go to blazes.

The fire is consuming Mama's painted wallpaper, popping loudly, and the sound waves beat against my ears. One and two and three, I begin counting time again. I tear at my dress, get the buttons undone enough that I can slip out of the kerosene-soaked garment. The corset feels wet too, so I yank the laces loose and it goes as well. Twenty-nine, thirty.

Out of range of the fire, Sim still must be able to see me. "Nice little performance. But getting naked won't save you."

Coughing harder, I ignore Sim, and pull on a velvet curtain until it falls. The heavy panel is lined with wool and has cashmere trim around the sides. Fifty-two, fifty-three. I throw the panel over my body and pick up Ming the dragon. Twisting around, I hurl the dragon with all my might.

Fifty-nine, sixty…

Glass shatters and falls everywhere, hitting my head, shoulders and feet. Flames explode behind me. Jump, Hester. Do it before you burn like the bacon at supper.

The curtain panel that I'm wearing as a barrier to the heat smells hot, as though the tail of it is alight. I throw myself out of the window and land on the ground below. Only a four or five foot drop. Then I roll away from the burning velvet panel, kicking at the heat. Still coughing, I push the apron down from my face and untie it. The grass has bits of glass in it but it feels wet. My legs sting like hell, though. Is my petticoat on fire? Well get it off, you dolt! I untie the ribbons at my waist and shimmy out of the smoldering petticoat. Left with only my camisole, drawers, stockings and boots, I take my leave of the rose garden.

Hide in the maze, I think. *No*, too far away. Go north… This is getting ridiculous. I am sick of running from villains— it's all I ever do anymore. Thorns catch at my skin, and I fall over a small topiary bush, landing on one knee. Damn topiary, never did like it. Scrambling to my feet again, I extend both of my hands and continue forward, hoping to hide in the orchard.

Cordie refused to go there at night. "Black as sin," she always said. But I murmur a prayer of thanks. Darkness is what all hunted things desire. In an effort to calm myself, I exhale slowly, trying to form a sound grid in my mind.

Blast that noise from the fire. Ninety-five feet? Eighty? Who the hell knows?

Flames growl and scream within the house like an angry creature. The Revels is being destroyed from the inside out. I hear a wall crumble, wood hissing. Another window shatters as Sim jumps through it. His blazing monster has gotten away from him, and he's fleeing its open maw, just as I am running from him.

Sixty feet away... Fifty-five... Possibly forty-eight, though I wouldn't bet on it.

Finally, I enter the orchard and cover my face as I plunge between the branches. The aisle grows narrow so I drop to my knees and crawl. Careful now. Keep quiet. Yet my throat hurts from inhaling the smoke, and I want to cough so badly.

A man calls my name. Smooth voice, well-educated. I know him, although we have only met once. "You won't escape this time," he says, using Sim as a mouthpiece. "I'll only lead him to you."

My mind veers back to the vision I had in Ironwood—of the strange Venetian masquerade and the person wearing the mask of the horned beast. It was James Scarlett, so polished and beautiful on the outside, but pure evil within. It's his voice speaking to me now through Sim Harrow's body. The owner of Griffin House is driving people to commit murder.

He is the heir of Archimendax.

<hr>

The grove of fruit trees comes to an end. I crawl out, extend my hands out of habit, and walk, hoping to make it to the corral before Sim finds me. In the barn, horses stomp at the stall doors, kick at the walls. I recognize Jupiter's cry. He's near crazed. Hold on, I'll set you free, old boy. There's a smokehouse between us, and I hurry around the east side of the building and collide with an immovable object. It comes to my midsection and has an open shaft in the center. Something tiny—a piece of gravel?—is dislodged by my elbow and falls, hits the bottom seconds later. A twelve-foot drop, perhaps? This must be the old well!

Last November, my father told Willard to fill it in. But he yelled at Little Hawk that day and made him angry. Willard must have left the job unfinished, bless him. A small, defiant gesture against the tyrant.

Sim pushes through the orchard, cracking branches loudly, but I detect another set of footsteps not far behind him. Is it Scarlett? Here to witness my execution? I sit on the mantle of the well, and throw one leg over the side. The second joins the first, and I turn on my stomach, gripping the overhang with one hand. First the window and now the well, it seems to be my night for jumping and dropping. I ease my body backwards— into open space. Then I take a deep breath and let go. My fall barely warrants the word it is so short, but I land on some gravel and dirt. The wall feels slimy, moss-covered, nevertheless I mold my body against it. In the distance, clanging bells and rolling wagon wheels bash my ears. It's the fire brigade. They won't get to me in time, however.

My doom is nearly at the well.

Scarlett speaks through Sim once more, encouraging the boy to kill. "No, Simmons," he whispers. "Fire is the way it should be done. *Fire.* Just as your mother died, screaming in flames."

As Sim walks toward my hiding place, the person who followed him through the orchard does too. I sense it's a man, small in stature, and with a hitch in his gait. He passes the smoke house, heads directly for the well.

"A flash of light and heat, and the debt is paid," Scarlett says, via Sim. "*Requiescat in pace.*"

Rest in peace yourself, you lunatic.

Something strikes against the rough stones at the top of the well. It flares, like a match tip catching flame. In my mind's eye, Sim has already lifted his arm and opened his fingers. I imagine the match falling into the dark hole and my body igniting like a torch. Instead, I hear several things happen at once, nearly overlapping each other—fast movement, the impact of a hard object against bone, and Simmons Harrow dropping to his knees.

Someone leans over the well, spine creaking loudly. "I said it before and I'll say it again. You're pretty lucky, White Hair."

On the verge of hysteria, I feel intoxicated, giddy with relief. Both smiling and crying, I wave at the handyman. Well done, Willard Little Hawk. You didn't go into town after all.

32

Aut vincere aut mori.
Either to conquer or to die

The volunteer fire brigade arrives, but the men just stand by their wagons and watch the mansion rage. The Revels is a lost cause, and everyone knows it. Noah Kelly is only a few minutes behind them, and I hear the fear in his voice from my place in the well. He calls for me until Willard yells that I'm all right, just stuck in a hole. Kelly laughs quietly at this.

Little Hawk has already bound the still-unconscious Sim, leaving him in a heap by the barn. He also knots a loop in a rope and throws it down to me. The loop feels like a huge noose, but I slip the thing over my head and tuck it under my arms. Kelly and Willard pull me up. The handyman snickers when he sees my camisole and drawers, but Kelly just gives me his coat. After borrowing a bucket from the fire brigade, he dips his handkerchief into the water and washes the ash from my face.

Willard disappears to wherever it is Willard goes, and Kelly takes me home to his housekeeper. She and I become close acquaintances over the next hour as the old woman helps me clean myself. Kerosene is difficult to remove from one's hair, and even now, after so much scouring, I still smell vaguely of table lamp.

My borrowed nightgown and robe belong to the rotund housekeeper and swim about my body like a school of fish. This kindly lady introduces me to Kelly's daughter—a decidedly awkward encounter. Alice seems like a shy child and since her father is over at the jail with Simmons Harrow, the last thing she wants to do is entertain a strange guest. Particularly the person who kept her father away in Ironwood City for two months.

Alice joins me at the kitchen table and asks the housekeeper for a bowl of bread and milk, exactly the snack I'm having. It isn't a companionable meal. No words at all from Alice, even when I smile at her. The only sound is the scooping up of soggy bread. After I've finished, the housekeeper shows me to a bedroom, but I don't sleep well. Now that my opium supply is gone, I long for it. At four in the morning, I think of waking Kelly to confide my drug dependency to him and seek his advice. But I can't bring myself to do it, not when he might think less of me for my condition.

And he probably wouldn't give me any opium anyway, the do-gooder.

I eventually drift into slumber, until the sound of a carriage wakes me up. Is that one of Kelly's patients? Must be. The woman says she's in pain after having a tooth pulled. They talk for a while and then he gives her a small dose of laudanum. He had some? Why didn't I try and find it? Criminy! It's the last in his possession, he says. I hear Kelly toss the container into the trash.

"Have your husband buy more laudanum at the pharmaceutical emporium, if you feel you need more. But if your condition grows worse, please come back."

His patient leaves and Kelly follows soon after to walk Alice to school. I rise from the bed and check a nearby chair for clothing of some kind, but it is empty. I expected one of the housekeeper's dresses, since all my own were ruined in the fire, but there is nothing at my disposal but her cotton wrapper. I open the wardrobe, run my hands over the clothes inside, and find it filled with suits, overcoats, and shirts. Citrus, cinnamon, pine, and sandalwood—they all smell of Kelly. I should have noticed it before. The whole room carries his scent.

At the moment, any odor makes me ill, and I dry heave into my hand. Tremors shake my body, sweat runs down my neck. Damnation. Desperate for relief, I grab one of Kelly's shirts, followed by a pair of trousers, a belt, and some boots. I scramble into the clothes, cinching the belt tight and rolling up the trouser legs. Last night I worried what Kelly would think of me if he knew of my addiction, but I care less now. I scoop a handful of coins from a bowl on the dresser and shove them into my pocket. *Deus miserere.* It might not be enough. I need more.

Leaning against a wall for support, I heave and heave at each step on the stairs, but nothing comes from my mouth except a string of spittle, which I wipe on the doctor's shirt. I regain my equilibrium, and listen for the housekeeper, worried she heard my retching. No. She's humming to herself and baking a cake in the kitchen. This clears the way to Kelly's office.

I am somewhat remorseful as I negotiate the unfamiliar room, hands outstretched, intent on stealing from my friend. But the wildness of Ironwood still remains despite Kelly's efforts to tame me. I'll explain the theft to him later. Another day—when the urge isn't so strong, and I have more control over my body.

Kelly's boots are too big for my feet, and I catch a toe on a chair leg. My arms spin through the air like a whirligig in order to save myself from a fall. I grasp at the corner of his desk, a drowning sailor on his third trip down, but I bump into something on the floor and stumble to my knees. The object is square, tin. The trash receptacle? I shake it gently and hear a clink, the sound of a little bottle shifting within the metal can. In a trice, the bottle's in my fist and a single drop of laudanum hits my tongue. Nothing else, just one blasted drop, even though I whack the bottle repeatedly. Lifting my head, I check that the housekeeper is still in the kitchen. Yes. Working on cake.

After pulling myself up, I hold on to the desk until the dizziness passes. Then I reach for the middle drawer, the one from which Kelly took money for Alice's new school books. I heard him count out two bills and give them to her. The drawer opens smoothly and I reach inside. Papers, a ledger, fountain pens, mints. Where's the blasted money?

My hand brushes something soft. Leather, rectangular—a bill fold. I flip it open and take out all the cash inside. *He has plenty,* a voice says in my head. *He'll never miss it.*

Yet as I am about to shove the money into my pocket, I imagine little Alice stepping into the office. What emotion would I smell on her if she caught me stealing from her father? Anger, loathing? And she would be right to feel so. I'm betraying the one man who hasn't hurt me. Kelly has only been my friend and this is how I repay him.

Filled with guilt, I put all the money back but two bills, thinking of what I'd say if Alice were here and I had the ability to speak to her. She probably wouldn't understand if I told her to stay as she is: a good, sweet girl. To remain as untouched by this world as long as she can.

And never be like this, like me.

Wiping the mingled tears and sweat from my face, I close the drawer and leave the house. The pharmaceutical emporium isn't far, just down the street. Nausea twists my stomach, and I gag again. I extend my hand before me, trying to keep pace with the people on the sidewalk. Horses and wagons pass by at a fast clip, and I can't gauge the distance of the oncoming traffic. Everything is loud, too loud. Stepping off the curb, I move forward cautiously and a carriage nearly runs me over. So close. A gust of air whirls around my face in its wake.

The smell of headache powder and liniment is strong up ahead. Finally, the Emporium. I walk inside and bump into a man standing a few feet from the door. His inner happiness is sickening. Damn my gift of olfaction—the scent of flowers makes me retch.

"Ill?" he asks. "Take my place in line."

I shake my head. The brain inside feels larger than the skull, as though it's pushing out through my ears. Leave me alone—too cheerful. Someone on my left keeps talking to his coworker about taking a dinner break. Can't you be quiet? Go to dinner, or not. No one cares either way.

Nausea strikes again, nearly knocking me to the ground. I move in the direction of the employee's voice, and run into a marble countertop. Kelly's money in hand, I rest my head on the cool stone.

"This station's closed," the clerk says.

I wave the two dollars, without moving my head from the marble, but he gets up and leaves.

Don't need you, blasted clerk. I'll find it myself. Feeling woozy, I stand upright, climb up on the counter and lean over it. I can't make my body move. Someone stands behind me, hands on my leg. Is it the police? Are they taking me to jail for stealing the money? No. I won't go with you. I kick at the person holding my leg but strong hands lift me off the counter. My feet hit the floor, yet I can't move or run away. Still gripping my arms, the hands draw me back until my shoulder blades press against a solid chest. I smell citrus, pine, and sandlewood.

"Never mind," Kelly tells the returning pharmacy clerk. "We don't need your assistance after all." The doctor turns me toward the door and half-carries me outside. "I must admit, you look better in my trousers than I do."

He's trying to be funny, but I'd choose hitting him over smiling. I want assistance even if Kelly doesn't—that damn clerk needs to get the bloody laudanum. We walk along the sidewalk for a moment, back toward his house.

No, I sign. **Stop.**

Kelly continues pushing me forward. He doesn't understand the gnawing inside. I'd do anything for relief. My lips move, forming word shapes as sweat drips off my chin. I can't, throat feels so tight. "P-please."

He stops in his tracks. "Was that you? Did you speak?"

I feel Kelly's surprise. It ripples through me like an electric current on a telegraph wire. He pulls me closer, hands on my hips—his ear next to my mouth. "Do it again."

We are standing in the center of the sidewalk, people passing us at random. My throat burns, constricting painfully. Don't want to, Kelly. Don't make me. "Please," I finally beg. "Need—"

Kelly steps back a pace and gently takes my hand. "Sweetheart, I know exactly what you need. Let's go home and see you get it."

The doctor leads and I follow, without any further thoughts of rebellion. I cover my aching head with my hands as he asks his housekeeper for a jug of drinking water, a ceramic basin, and towels. Then Kelly takes me upstairs to his room.

He removes the hat from my head. "Sit on the mattress."

I do as he says, and Kelly slides his boots off my feet.

"Lie down, Hester."

I curl up like a babe in the womb, and a soft blanket is draped over me, ripping the skin from my bones. No, not true. My flesh is still intact, it just feels as though it's being scraped asunder. And cold, so cold. *O di immortales.* I'm back in the treatment room at Ironwood. No, never again. I'll die this time. The icy liquid covers my face, and I claw it away, coughing and sputtering. "Answer my questions," Faust whispers.

The waking nightmare ends, and I grow lucid, back in Kelly's bedroom. I shudder and retch into the basin. When the nausea passes, I hear him pour a small amount of water into a cup. "Rinse your mouth and spit," he says, holding the glass to my lips.

Soon he is wiping my brow as someone weeps and gags. "Don't worry. I won't leave you, Hester."

My journey through the valley of the shadow of death takes nearly a week, and Kelly is with me every step.

———————— • ————————

Shivering is one of the worst symptoms—and the hallucinations, the constant, sickening stomach ache, the veering from hot to cold, the chattering teeth and muscle spasms. At my sickest, Kelly whispered things I cannot utter, words so kind the mere memory of them causes me to tear up, filled with a gratitude so raw as to be painful. No man has ever spoken to me so, and I doubt one ever will again—including Kelly himself. Some situations call for a heroism never to be duplicated thereafter.

During my coherent moments, he described how the toxins of a bad drug are flushed from one's system. Nevertheless, I will always be tempted in varying degrees as time goes on, my body yearning for the poison it loves.

This morning finds me in low spirits again. I sit abed, wondering whether I want to leave Kelly's room. I haven't for days, just staying in and napping, but the doctor keeps waking me up. He has brought me flowers that Alice picked from their garden and just-baked biscuits. He's lain down on the other side of the bed and read to me. Sometimes *Robinson Crusoe* or *The Three Musketeers*, always stopping at the most exciting part. The man is utterly diabolical.

Alice sometimes visits. Mostly she just peeks into Kelly's room for a moment and then scurries downstairs without a word. The housekeeper has the day off today, which leaves the child in a perpetual state of boredom. She doesn't trust me yet. I'm still the unwanted guest, stealing her father's space, time, and attention.

Listening for Kelly, I hear him in his office, telling Alice she may indeed look at his encyclopedia of North American waterfowl. Alice drops in front of the crackling fireplace, the book's spine creaking a welcome as she turns its pages.

What month is it? The end of April? Beginning of May? Wearing a borrowed gown from the housekeeper, I lift the long skirt, climb off the bed, and walk to the door, hoping I do not trip. I descend the stairs, gripping the handrail until I reach the bottom, and then exit through the door by the kitchen. The garden smells of growing things pushing clear of the wet soil. I kneel down and touch a tender shoot. The tiny leaf feels delicate against my palm, the dirt heavy and oppressive by comparison. It occurs to me that plants are rather brave, growing blindly toward the light.

How pathetic, a voice whispers. *Where has bravery ever gotten you? It didn't save Davis.* The whisper is like a brief thought, an impression, but I am profoundly sad again. Weary. Hopeless.

Kelly walks out of his house to find me kneeling on the grass. "What are you doing out here? It's going to rain."

I've lost my voice again, now the drugs are gone. But I have nothing to say to Kelly's remark so I just shrug in response. He sits down on the bottom step. I hear him reach forward, and pluck a blade of grass.

"Do you enjoy spring?"

My favorite, I sign. **As a child.**

"Really?" he asks. "But not now?"

Older. Feel ancient.

"At twenty-two?" Kelly plucks another blade of grass. "Bah! Your life's just beginning. My Irish mother often told me—the sun may hide behind the clouds in May, but the roses will bloom come July."

I can't help smiling. Of all the absurd advice. **What does that mean?**

"How should I know? The woman gave enigmatic counsel. She expected me to work things out for myself." He tosses the grass aside and stands. "I don't blame you for forgetting, Hester, but the future holds wonderful things for you."

Kelly climbs the stairs, and enters his home, calling for Alice. She meets him in the hallway and jumps into his arms. I hear him laugh softly, swing her side to side. My mind grows dark at their happiness, and the whispering voice returns. *What do they know? They've never truly suffered. Not like you.* I drop the little leaf I've been twirling, surprised at my thoughts. I love Noah Kelly, and Alice is just a timid, lonely child. I wouldn't want either of them to suffer.

Those words didn't come from me.

But I have a good idea who was behind them. All these miserable days I didn't realize what I was hearing, *who* I was hearing in my head. And I *didn't* kill Davis. His death was not my fault, even though I've been accepting the blame and hating myself for it. Wanting to die.

Ah, Visionary. At last you see.

I rise to my feet, violated by Scarlett's evil presence. *Leave my thoughts, liar. I know what you are.* He whispers terrible things, things my father often said to me, things I've said to myself. Negative, hateful words that sound like my own voice. *Get out. You've taken enough of my time. I won't give you more.* My body trembles, but I remain resolute. I don't give in when he pushes and then the voice grows softer, until it completely disappears.

Wrapping my arms around myself, I smell the wild sage from the mountains on the wind. Thunder booms and rain splatters on the paving stones, the roof. I tilt my face to the heavens and water bathes my cheeks, runs through my hair. I smile at the sky and feel cleaner than I ever have, awash in the tears of the gods.

———————— • ————————

I don't have many possessions to pack. Besides the new dress I'm wearing, I have a second-hand night gown, a few toiletries, under clothes, and an extra pair of wool stockings. Truth be told, I wish I could sneak away unnoticed. I hate goodbyes. But I can't remain any longer and involve Kelly and Alice in my conflict with James Scarlett. I would never forgive myself if harm came to them.

I carefully fold my petticoat into a neat square and place it in the suitcase. My hair brush, a set of combs, and a cake of soap soon follow. Last of all, the night gown.

"You don't need to go," Kelly says. He is just outside the door. I lift my head and smile at him.

Yes, I sign. **I do.**

The doctor crosses the room and sits on the bed. A small, soft thud comes next, like a leather flap dropping into place.

Closed my suitcase?

"I meant what I said. Don't go. Stay with me."

Reopening the bag, I feel a tingling warmth begin at my hairline and move downward. I haven't been embarrassed in some time, certainly not around Kelly. Next to Cordelia, his housekeeper, and a few other females, this doctor's viewed more of my body than any being on earth. I've vomited all over him and shown him the worst side of my character. Why am I discomfited now?

Kelly closes the suitcase again, and reaches for my hand, grazing me with his fingers.

Stop!

"Which?" He laughs lightly. "Shutting the bag or touching you?"

Both.

The doctor grabs a handful of my skirt and hauls me into his arms. "Stay, and don't sign the word *annulment* again. Not this time."

I feel like one of the waterfowl that Alice so admires, when it's caught in the crosshairs of a hunter's rifle.

"I'm not him, if you're pining for Tom," Kelly murmurs. "Hell, *he's* not even him at present. The boy you loved is gone."

Anger pulses through me as I pull away and reach for my luggage. Tom may be a troubled, dissolute rogue, but I won't hear him disparaged.

"That's what he is, you know—a boy. Whether you realize it now or not, Craddock was never your equal."

My spine goes ramrod straight. **Watch what you say.**

"You mistake my candor, madam. I mean no offense to your friend—rather, I think so highly of you that I deem most men your inferiors." Kelly exhales and steps back. "Forgive me, Hester. For pressing you with another proposal at such a difficult time."

Cursing myself, I realize I've done what I hoped never to do.

I've hurt Noah Kelly.

33

Aequat omnes cinis.
Ashes make everyone equal–Seneca

Jupiter is eating oats when I arrive at the house on St. David's Street. I hear the horse blowing softly into his feedbag as he chews. Resident handyman and new tenant, Willard has converted the old shed behind the garden plot into a chicken coop, but the hens are outside scratching dirt, searching for feed. I purchased quite a few birds from Hollister's and plan to sell the excess eggs back to them. In addition to the chickens, I have a young milk cow. A gentle bovine, Molly is near the fence, working her cud with her teeth.

These common sounds are a symphony to my ears. I hope to leave the day-to-day management of the animals in Little Hawk's capable hands, but I think I will enjoy having the creatures about.

"Here we are, Hester," Kelly says. He climbs from the wagon and helps me down. "Would you like to open the front door or shall I?"

Me.

My newest cane swishes back and forth just ahead of my feet. It came from the dusty lost-and-found collection in Kelly's office on Black Swan. The handle is carved with oak leaves and acorns and there are nicks in several places at the tip. Seems rather adventurous, like the cane of an alpine hiker, and I feel the shocking urge to purchase lederhosen.

Kelly and I take the short pathway to the house. Inside, the scent of polished wood and fresh paint lifts my spirits. All thanks to Cordelia Collins! Her parents, a cousin, and a couple of aunts live a block from me, and she enlisted their help. They opened the stale-smelling house and prepared it for my arrival—going above-and-beyond the call. What have I to give in return? Fresh milk and eggs, I suppose.

I cross the parlor to the kitchen. The table is made of rough pine, and I touch the corner carefully, afraid of splinters. What is that smell? Freshly baked bread? I discover a warm loaf sitting near me on the table, covered with a tea towel. What a lovely surprise. Upon further inspection, I also find a crock of butter, preserves of some kind, a corned beef, and an apple pie. Kelly reads the names from the tags attached to each gift. I don't recognize even one.

Last December, I considered St. David's to be the slum of Stonehenge. Was I really so ignorant and callow?

"Miss Collins left a note," Kelly says and reads it for me. "She fixed your room herself. For old time's sake."

He leaves me in the kitchen and looks over my main floor bedroom. "Nice," he calls out. "Dresser, curtains, a pitcher and basin." I hear Kelly circle the space. "Rather impersonal as yet, but you'll have a cozy home given time."

After putting my suitcase down, he returns to the kitchen. "You're sure about this?"

Yes, I sign. **Sure.**

"That's what you told me when I left you at The Revels. Can I trust your judgment?"

No choice. Not my boss.

Kelly laughs. "Well, legally I am your husband. I could always throw you over my shoulder and lock you in the attic at home."

He says this in good humor and to most people it would have been funny. But I was locked up too long in Ironwood. I can't even pretend to smile. **No. You wouldn't do that.**

He sobers instantly. "You're right, sweetheart, I wouldn't." The doctor coughs, and turns toward the kitchen door. "I'll have a word with Little Hawk. He's in the garden, I believe."

We stroll outside together and find Willard planting potatoes. I rather like their starchy, home-cooked meal smell. Kelly reminds the handyman to check on me from time to time during the day.

"Let me know," he says, "if she needs anything."

The doctor wipes his feet on the mat at the door, and I follow him back inside. "All right then. Good luck, Hester."

He doesn't want to leave. I sense his distress, smell the sharpness of worry. He'll miss me. I'll miss him, too.

I take off my spectacles and put them on the kitchen table. Then I reach over and hug Kelly. We pull apart when Willard enters the room. He takes some food from the table and goes back outside to eat.

Thank you, Kelly, I sign. For saving me, for seeing who I am, for loving me.

The doctor is quiet for a moment. "Perhaps we can resume our lessons, Hester. After you've had time to settle into your new home, of course. Those Braille manuals are still on my desk, just waiting to be read."

Dear man, ever the taskmaster.

Wouldn't miss it.

I smile and walk with Kelly to the door. Once he's gone, I decide to explore the garden out back. Willard comes out of the shed-turned-coop, carrying something in his arms. "Make yourself useful, Silver Eyes," he mutters and shoves a basket at me. "Feed the chickens."

The corn is hard and dry and has a dusty fragrance. I take a small handful and throw it into the dirt and gravel. A group of birds come over and peck around my feet, clucking and cooing. I listen to the intermittent patter of falling corn and flapping wings. A sense of correctness expands within me, and I know I've found my place. I can belong here.

Kelly's right. I will have a cozy home, given time.

●

Willard and I share a quiet meal. He tells me to expect a visit from Mary Arden and resumes eating, saying nothing more. At all. Even when I write questions on my slate asking the date and time, his impressions of the witch hermit, etcetera.

Don't know…Don't know…Don't know.

Getting details from Willard is like squeezing blood from a turnip. He, alone, could have stymied the entire Spanish Inquisition.

If the conversation leaves much to be desired, at least the corned beef and bread are tasty. I linger over the apple pie with a cup of tea, long after the handyman retires to the basement bedroom. I am just finishing my last bite when there is a knock at the front door. Taking up my cane, I leave the kitchen, cross the parlor, and open it.

"I'd like to rent a room," the man says. "Have you any to spare?"

That distinctive, almost musical voice. I *know* this person. How could I not, we went through hell together. It's Gabriel, my arch angel! And he isn't crushed under the rubble at Ironwood but standing right here on my stoop.

Gabriel seems as surprised as I am by our unexpected reunion. "Hester?" he asks. "Is it really you?"

I smile and nod, gesturing for him to enter the house.

"They told me at Hollister's that I might find lodging here, but I expected an old widow."

Using the chalk and slate, I write—JUST MOVED IN. SO GLAD YOU ARE WELL.

"And you? I heard of what you endured from Faust. All to expose his depravity and free the inmates."

GETTING BETTER NOW.

"That is a relief to know," Gabriel says. "I've never forgotten how kind you were to me at Ironwood. I'm a stronger man because of it. Less aches and pains, fewer sorrows."

He sounds bemused, as though the times that I healed him still remain a mystery. Gabriel's just too polite to have me explain how the miracle occured. Caught up in the happiness of our reunion, I push the chalk too hard against the slate and it squeaks.

Gabriel laughs, but my face flushes while I write. DO YOU LIVE IN STONEHENGE?

"In the woods just outside of town."

WOODS?

"I left Ironwood City and wandered for a time, until I took work at the forge here. I've tried to find accommodations, but people fear my face."

Again I scribble quickly on the slate. WELCOME TO STAY, GABRIEL.

"You may wish to reconsider. I don't want the townspeople to shun you for housing me."

NONSENSE. COME LOOK AT THE ROOMS.

Gabriel follows me to the stairs. We reach the second story landing, and he sets his luggage on the floor. "I've always wanted to ask," he says. "How did you know that my name is Gabriel? Everyone called me Lazarus at Ironwood."

I am slow to write an answer now, wondering how to explain about magic and ancient powers. The tiny space allotted me on the slate would not do such a message justice.

GOOD GUESSER?

Gabriel laughs. "No one is *that* good."

WOMEN'S INTUITION?

Another chuckle. "Never mind. Keep your secrets. I trust you."

I offer him his choice of the four rooms upstairs. Mrs. Woodrow, the former owner, left behind some pallets and mattresses. They are broken in places, and a little saggy, but Gabriel doesn't care. He is happy to select the bedroom with northern exposure—even if we do need to carry in another mattress and frame to oblige the length of his legs.

I go downstairs and take one of the blankets from my bed. It is soft and smells of lavender. My new tenant is delighted. ARE YOU HUNGRY? I ask him.

"No, thank you, madam."

My fingers are growing stiff after all this enthusiastic chalk work. BREAKFAST AT SEVEN. HOPE YOU LIKE OATS.

Gabriel steps into his room. "There's nothing better in the morning," he replies before closing the door.

⸻ ● ⸻

Willard sits down next to Gabriel, a bowl of hot oatmeal before him, and begins muttering holy words in Arapahoe. A shaky start, but I'm sure it won't take long for Little Hawk to warm up to our new roommate.

The afternoon is chock-full of housewifery. It is a success, excluding the temporary misplacement of my cane, tripping over a chair, and a kitchen towel catching on fire. Carver, the old gambler ghost, fades in and out for several hours. I enjoy his visit, despite the fact he's mourning the loss of his favorite deck of invisible cards. At my urging, Carver summons his ghost-sight and I make him tour my new home. Looking at the rooms through his eyes, I'm rather pleased overall. The house is a little run-down, but it has potential.

I haven't seen Carver for some time, although this isn't unexpected. It's feast or famine with the old gambler—he's either constantly underfoot or completely removed for months. Where does the ghost go? Is there another Visionary in his life?

An hour before supper, Kelly shows up, claiming he needs a cup of Earl Grey above all else—although I know it's really to check on me and confirm the latest gossip.

"He really does look like Frankenstein," Kelly says after Gabriel goes to his room.

I act as though I didn't hear that and sip my tea.

"Is it wise, having him around? What do you know of the man?"

Quite a lot, I sign and pour him another cup.

Fortunately, Kelly moves on to a different topic. "Have you heard that Miss Collins is now engaged to Mr. Baker?"

Lovely!

"I noticed the announcement in the *Gazette*—wedding's in September." The biscuit jar rattles as Kelly pilfers it. "Oh, and I saw the mysterious Mary Arden as well. First sighting I've ever had of the woman."

Mary Arden? In town? It's taken her long enough.

I sense a sudden reticence in the doctor, as though his thoughts have veered in an unpleasant direction. **What's wrong?**.

He takes a bite of the oatmeal biscuit. Chews slowly.

Well?

Kelly washes down his biscuit with tea, and sits back in his chair. "Apparently, the Craddock's have lost their ranch. That's what the rumor mill is saying anyway. The whole family is moving to California to live with relations."

The whole family? Does that mean Tom's leaving? I spill my entire cup of Earl Grey and Kelly begins mopping it up with a napkin. He takes the sodden table cloth to the sink, giving me a moment to myself. I cross my arms, imagining a life without Tom's presence. Though we are not now what we once were, it has been a comfort knowing he lives nearby, alive and well but for the drinking. I can't imagine not hearing his voice again, not passing him in town by chance. Yet those are selfish reasons to keep a man around, because he reminds you of his former self. Perhaps it's best Tom go to California. If he leaves town, Scarlett may forget about him and leave his poor mind alone.

Kelly returns to the table, sits down quietly. **Thank you,** I sign. **Didn't know.**

"You're welcome, Hester. Though I dislike causing you pain."

It isn't long after Kelly leaves that I hear chickens flapping around the back yard, making a terrible ruckus. A fox, perhaps? No. Sounds bigger. Maybe it's Mary Arden.

I wait for Willard to go outside to check on the poultry but he doesn't. Did the handyman leave while I was having tea with Kelly? Gabriel doesn't stir from his room either. After a tiring day at the forge, he often takes a nap before supper. The snoring has already begun.

Stepping out onto the back porch, I listen, but the rain from this morning makes it difficult to deduce much from a person's footsteps. Who is it? The wind gathers force and the shutters slam against the house. I cover my ears with my hands. Something flies through the air behind me.

<hr />

I wake up in the arms of a stranger. The fellow is walking at a fast pace, as though carrying an unconscious woman is no trouble at all. "Scarlett's leaving on the last train," he says. "We're to drop her in the box and put the lid on. Clean and simple. Insisted it had to be done tonight."

Drop *who* in the box? Me?

Another man is walking on the right. He smokes cheap cigarettes, and the odor of old tobacco smoke has permeated his being. "Well, I prefer a bit of notice," he says. "Professional courtesy and all that. What if I had plans for the evening?"

"Exactly right. Our personal lives count for something, don't they? We're more than just hired muscle."

Sensitive hoodlums. Men like these bring out my violent tendencies. I punch the face of the one holding me prisoner and kick at his side. It doesn't seem to bother him a bit. What in tarnation? A right cross is usually quite effective. Without breaking stride, the oaf adjusts his grip on my body, pinning my hands against his chest.

"A little she-devil, ain't she? A regular hoyden."

"At least this one can't scream," the other criminal replies. "I hate when they do that. My ears ring for a week."

"You really should think about using cottonwool plugs. It's changed my life as far as work is concerned."

"Would the boss spring for them? Since it's a job-related expense?"

I sigh to myself. Must I *always* get the stupid kidnappers?

A long drawn-out creaking hits my ear, as though an old door is being pulled open. We enter a building that smells of dead flowers and incense. Even though I fight them, Scarlett's men follow his directions to the letter, and drop me into some kind of box. My head hits the bottom, and I lose consciousness once more. Yet the cold stone under my body revives me. Marble, I think. I slide my fingers along the sides of the box, only to discover a heavy lid above. I push and push to no avail. How I dislike being confined. Especially since this isn't actually a box—it's a sarcophagus. An above ground coffin kept in a crypt, usually locked away and forgotten.

James Scarlett, I despise you. *Loathe* you to eternity. You're a vile, monstrous creature!

Oh, stop ranting, Hester. *Think* while the oxygen lasts. Where are you? Stonehenge only has one cemetery with a crypt. Holy Trinity. Am I in the Grayson death chamber? If so, Mama is just across the room in her own marble box. And I must be trapped in the one meant for Father—unless the bank has foreclosed upon it.

Damned irony. Is there any other kind?

Growing light-headed, I pound my fist against the stone, livid once more that this, my murder, has played out so conveniently for Scarlett. And with so little respect. Couldn't be here to kill me himself. Oh no, he has a train to catch. I'll slap Death in the face when He comes for me —

Something heavy hits the sarcophagus and sound waves rumble over me. The marble box and I both quake under the impact. *Oh* the pain—the cold sharpness that crisscrosses my skull. And I'm nauseous, I have no equilibrium. It sounds as though the world is underwater, as if a lake swirls within my brain. I cover my head and find a sticky wetness about the sides of it. Blood.

My eardrums have burst.

34

Quid est veritas?
What is truth?

The underwater sensation dissipates quickly, leaving my hearing raw and exposed, even more sensitive than before. Each noise is a hot poker. I try to shut off my ears, but I lack control over my own body. The blows against the marble continue, and I think I might die from the vicious sound waves until a gust of air rushes over me. The stone lid must have chipped, creating a small hole. I suck the beautiful oxygen into my lungs, and hear my rescuer breathing heavily outside. He must be strong to rain down such wrathful strokes.

"Not long now," the man says. "And you'll be free."

Tears fill my eyes, and I wipe them away. 'Not long now and you'll be free?' These are the nicest words he's ever said, and one of the few times I've heard my father speak directly to me.

Eventually he creates a big enough divot in the marble for him to stick his hand inside and take hold of the lid. He pushes with all his might and moves it back a bit—then he reaches inward. I feel him grip my feet and pull. My body scoots along until my legs are draped over the side of the sarcophagus. Father puts his hands around my waist and draws me out like an ungainly calf being extracted from its squalling mother.

He sets me down and moves away quickly. "We're even now," he whispers.

Even? What is he talking about?

My father dusts off his clothes. "No more, Hester. I did what I could, and that's the end of it."

How did he know I needed help?

I reach toward my father, and he flinches, smelling strongly of fear. He drops something—his hammer, maybe—and turns for the door. I step to the side, right into his path.

"I said we're square. Move."

My entire life, I've wanted him to explain our relationship, to reveal why he couldn't love me even a little. I step closer, and he sucks in his breath, as though he's afraid I'll hurt him.

"Never much of a parent, I'll admit that," he says. "But you can imagine what it was like."

I shake my aching head. I still don't understand.

"Having your little girl tell you such horrible things. You'd talk about dead people with *that voice*, and it always came to pass. Always."

What's that twitching sound? Is Father so scared he's shaking? I breathe deeply and decide to take action. Powers above, don't fail me. I'll never get this chance again.

Reaching out, I touch his cheek. "No!" he yells. "Stay back."

One of his memories fills my mind, not an image of murder or death. This experience happened long ago at The Revels, when I was very young. My present-day adult self stands at the door of the old nursery, watching the five-year-old me. The child I was is ill and feverish—her silver eyes glazed as she licks red, cracked lips.

People within the house are weeping, mourning the loss of several servants to the sickness. Typhus, they say. Everyone fears for Mama's survival. Scared and weak, Little Hester calls for her mother, but no one answers, so she switches to her father's name. Grown me watches him stop at the nursery door. He observes the suffering five-year-old for a moment. The pillow under her head is wet with perspiration, and she begs Father for a drink.

He doesn't move, a look of revulsion crossing his angular features. "Get it water," he says to a passing maid.

Little Hester and I simultaneously inhale a coppery scent, and she begins to cry, knowing what it means. Father smells of blood. Of hatred. Of *his* hatred for *her*. The tears leave wet tracks upon her face, and she grows quiet.

Mute from that day on.

This is the reason I have been a prisoner of my own silence? The obstacle preventing me from having a voice all these years? Truth rattles through the adult me, settling in my heart. The vision ends, and I leave the psychic realm, plummeting back into the crypt.

Father is still talking. "Blame myself, of course. Bringing such a creature into the world."

I shake my head. What a waste, Hester. Allowing one so unworthy to control you.

Almost like a key being turned in a lock, I feel a small click in my throat, and I know without even trying that I can speak. Something inside me has broken loose and been healed at the same time. I'm free of more than a tomb.

"Step aside," my father says. "I won't do more."

I turn my iridescent gaze in his direction. "You've done quite enough," I reply in *that voice.*

He dashes out the door, scared as hell.

———————— • ————————

I eventually find his sledgehammer. It's a smaller version of the tool than I imagined. Heavy but not unmanageable, considering the adrenaline coursing through my veins. I heft it to my shoulder, step out of the room of death, and begin my journey to High Street. The churchyard smells mossy and the grass is wet beneath my boots. Walking carefully, I turn east and ascend a small hill, banging into a wooden structure at the top.

Drop the hammer, and check inside, you dunce. Get yourself a stick.

After entering the shack, I nearly fall over an axe. I feel my way around, finding shovels, long-handled clippers, and rope. It's the groundskeeper's hut, it would seem. Discovering a half-broken rake, I stomp on the handle, until the rod separates from the tines. Voila, a cane! It prevents me from falling over tombstones, but my progress is still slow. Especially with the added weight of the sledgehammer. I test my hearing ability as I walk—it's better, almost normal now. The extreme sensitivity has faded and I can extend reception and subdue it. *Deo favente.* Sometimes it's good to have a Roman goddess on your side.

I sense a presence behind me, smell chimney smoke and unwashed skin. Definitely a woman—part Beelzebub, part wilderness-dwelling peasant. "Mary Arden," I croak, throat sore.

"Good," she replies. "You're speaking at last."

Gesturing in the direction of the train station, I take a step forward. "Help me. Scarlett's getting away."

"He doesn't leave for a while yet. Let's talk a spell."

Mary Arden links her arm with mine, her stench wafting around me. We follow a path that intersects the city park. "You're in my debt now, dearie. My old friend Carver told me you were in trouble over at the crypt, and I sent your father right away. Didn't want to go at first, but I made him do it. I'll expect a favor for that one."

Did she say Carver, as in Carver the gambling ghost? *My* Carver is her old friend? Blast him! He's more like her spy, I'd warrant. Well that explains his absences over long periods. Confound it, I knew he was seeing someone else.

Swallowing against my burning vocal chords, I turn away. "No favors. Father said we're square."

Mary Arden laughs. "John always was squeamish, even as a child. Likes things easy and explainable. Magic's to be avoided at all costs."

"You know him, too?"

"Of course I do, ducky. He's my brother."

We reach the park gazebo where this whole episode began for me on All Hallows Eve last year, when David Thornhill touched my wrist, and I saw him throw Freckles to her death. Mary Arden follows me into the vacant structure. I prop the cane and sledgehammer against the wall and cross my arms. "Let me be sure I heard correctly. You are… my aunt?"

She seems amused by the question. "We're quite a family—all of us endowed with supernatural talent."

I can't help snorting at this. "Father's *not* supernatural."

"John doesn't like to admit it, but he has the Gift of the Phoenix. He will always rise from the ashes and reinvent himself—find new success and prosperity."

She turns telepathic in an instant. *All true words, daughter of Rome. You know it, too.*

Wishing her out of my head, I stick to speech even though it's painful. "How did you make him save me?"

"Why, by Compulsion, dear. You know that as well. I have a smattering of gifts, some less than benevolent."

"Dark skills?"

Mary Arden pats my arm. "Don't worry, Hester. I won't use them on you. I'll need your help one day."

"Why does Scarlett want me dead so badly? Don't say it's because of my gifts. I won't believe it."

"Your relationship goes much deeper than you realize. Before Scarlett's mother married Mr. Lennox, Marie-Louise had a brief affair with a Welsh miner who'd struck it rich. A man we both know quite well."

I reach for the gazebo railing and sit down on a bench, letting it all sink in. My father, the same John Grayson that I've grown up with, had an affair. With Marie-Louise Lennox, the woman who committed suicide last November. The idea of him having an illicit affair with anyone seems ludicrous. And a trifle repugnant. But having met the vulnerable Marie-Louise, my heart goes out to her.

Mary Arden continues with her narrative. "Their liaison began before he met your mother. John told Marie-Louise he would never marry a poor girl like her, and when she found herself in the family way, she wed Lennox. He was a cruel man and abused Marie-Louise and her son terribly. James Scarlett isn't one to forgive and forget—especially where his parents and half-sister are concerned."

I'm his half-sister? "But he's descended from Archimendax, not Veritas."

"Oh you're wrong, Hester. He's descended from *both*—Veritas, through your father, and Archimendax, on his mother's side. A unique and lethal mixture."

It makes sense, actually. Why Scarlett is so difficult to read...and so powerful...and why he has a vendetta against me. Truth heats my bones, and I know Mary Arden is right. Although I do not trust her beyond the basic facts of the story.

"Fine," I say, picking up the sledgehammer and cane. "We should go—"

"I cannot, Hester. Scarlett has shielded himself against my powers. Whatever magic I cast upon him will be thrown back at me a hundred fold. I will not help you in this fight, but the shielding has cost Scarlett dearly. His strength is less than before."

He was stronger? His abilities greater than they are now? Well, that's just bloody wonderful. I nod and make for the stairs of the gazebo, feeling the weight of my burden. She walks with me to High Street.

"What can he do?" I ask, unsure I want the answer.

Mary Arden sighs sadly. "It's not that Scarlett has a large number of gifts. But truth and falsehood each have great power, don't they? Mix them together and you've got a dangerous weapon. Beware the Serpent's Tongue, Hester. Unlike Compulsion, it's subtle and can be sustained indefinitely. And he has some elemental powers."

I drop my pitiful sledgehammer and rake/cane on the sidewalk, lean forward and rest my hands on my thighs. Don't throw up. Don't have an apoplexy. Breathe.

"No reason to fret, child." My aunt whacks me on the back. "Fragile nerves never won battles of magic! It's boldness that's called for." She picks up the hammer and cane and pushes them into my hands. "Now where was I?"

No place good. "The Serpent's Tongue?" I reply.

"Oh, yes! Scarlett mixes reality and illusion, lies with half-truths. Beguiling, coaxing. He can have no happiness of his own, and therefore, seeks the misery and dominion of others. Strike him now, or he'll kill all those you hold dear."

As he did mine, she whispers in my head.

The impact of her words hits me. I turn toward Mary Arden. "Will you teach me how to shield them? Keep my friends safe?"

"Triumph today, and shielding will be unnecessary. There's quite a price involved, anyway. I'm not sure you'd be willing to pay it."

Her words cause a shiver of alarm to run the length of my spine, and I wonder if she's using Compulsion on me. Maybe it's her hope that Scarlett and I kill each other. Two birds with one stone.

"What about those elemental powers you mentioned he possessed?" I ask.

But the old woman seems not to hear my question and leaves me without saying farewell. Just a pat on my shoulder and a vague reminder. *Remember that favor you owe me. I'll be in touch.*

A gust of wind tosses my skirts, thunder rumbles, a few raindrops fall. The air crackles with supernatural energy as I hasten toward my fate. As though they sense a whopper of a storm brewing, the people of Stonehenge scramble inside. I hear merchants pack up their wares, and shoe-shine men gather their brushes. The usual crowds head home to supper, or to the Red Rooster for a drink. Tourists take refuge in their hotels.

Wishing I could hide with them, I cross the nearly deserted street. I extend my hearing despite the noisy weather, and determine the number of souls at the station ahead. Thankfully, only a handful of people are waiting for the last two trains. Rounding a corner, I bump smack into Tom. Of all the places for him to be. Why here and now?

"I'll be damned," Tom says, half drunk. "Come to give me a goodbye kiss?"

I push him away with my rake/cane. "No."

"Heavens lass, you spoke. Soft-like but I heard you." He whistles, takes a step closer. "Dress covered with dust and carrying a hammer. Trouble at home, *Mrs.* Kelly?"

"Not your business anymore."

Tom grabs my hand. "Don't run off just yet. Let's shake at least."

The sledgehammer strikes the ground, but I barely notice. Memories are being passed to Tom through our old telepathic connection. I cannot move an inch—we are grafted together at the palm. He sees our childhood, the time we spent together growing up, the cases we solved, his death, and revival. The vision ends with my visits to his hospital bed last December, and then I pull my hand away, barely daring to hope. Is this the answer? Will the old Tom return?

"What in hell?" he says, breathing fast.

Beneath the liquor, Tom smells of fear and confusion. No love, no happiness at being reunited with me. Instead, he seems like a bewildered stranger observing another man's life, not his own past. I sense that this other Tom is a decent person despite the drinking and bitterness. Scared he's delusional, not entirely convinced that what he saw was real, but good deep down. I could try telepathy. That might convince him of his history, make him believe.

And then he'd insist on helping me fight Scarlett.

Let the man go, Hester. He needs to leave Stonehenge before it kills him for good. My chest feels hot and jumpy inside. I once imagined our names figuratively carved there on my heart. Like the initials Tom whittled across tree trunks when we were little.

"You're a Visionary," he mumbles. "And I'm the Interpreter."

Tom takes something from his back pocket. A flask? Yes, smells like gin. He has a healthy swig. "Am I crazy? Did I imagine all that?"

Let him go now. You can. "Imagine what?" I reply a moment later. "You're not making any sense."

"The vision. It happened when we shook hands. You had to have seen it."

I gasp, pretending offense. "Does it *look* like I have visions? It isn't very kind to tease a blind woman."

A door in the station house opens, and Mrs. Craddock calls for Tom. "Go to her," I rasp, picking up my hammer. "And stop drinking so much. It's addled your wits."

He doesn't follow when I walk away. As the distance between us grows, I hear the entire Craddock family board their train and head for California.

Goodbye, Tom. *Deus benedicite.*

35

Veritas lux mea.
The truth is my light.

Two people are waiting on the platform with James Scarlett. Standing a good distance from my enemy, they laugh together and puff on expensive cigars—their reward for a job well done. I know these charming fellows—they kidnapped me. Over the fall of raindrops, I gather a picture of my surroundings through sound, graphing even the tiniest details. An insect flutters its wing, water runs down a broken pipe inside the depot wall, a mouse crawls near the tracks. I memorize the space in my head, and slip my cane under an empty bench. This is the farthest platform from the station, for the privately-owned railway cars. We shouldn't be disturbed here.

Still laughing, the first brute doesn't even notice I am behind him until I slam the sledgehammer into the side of his knee. Bones and cartilage snap and pop, sounding like water on a hot skillet. The man gives a shriek and crumples. Before the second fellow turns around, I hit him on the head with the handle and he goes down as well. Oh shut up, will you? He's crying so loud, I hit him again, and the kidnapper loses consciousness. Heart's still beating, breathing's all right. Recovery is likely. I point my weapon at the fellow with the knee injury and he turns quiet, crawls over to the wall. Smart man.

Footsteps, soft clapping. "Brava, Hester," Scarlett says. "I was going to fire them anyway." He stops several feet from me. "Never took you for the violent type, but I must say, you handle yourself in a scrape."

No scent or emotion coming from Scarlett. Just like the night we met at Griffin House, he has no tells.

"It's come in handy lately," I say.

My half-brother laughs at my hoarse voice. "Baby sister, that's marvelous. You're speaking again."

Would people *stop talking* about my talking? "Spare me your false praise."

"It's not false at all. You have my respect. I've had fun, hearing about your escape from Harrow, Faust, and Swinton. Why, that sounds like a law firm."

A droll villain, just what I need. The connection with Harrow is obvious, but how does Scarlett know the two from Ironwood? I lift the hammer to my shoulder, listening for his goons, making sure they're still down. "Why not leave me alone?"

"Can't oblige. Archimendax's heir, remember? It's my job to stir up trouble."

I detect a faint stretching sound and the smell of leather, as though he's removing his gloves and shoving them into his pocket. "I knew the exact moment you came into the world, Veritas. I was eleven at the time, and even then, all it took was a whisper in John Grayson's mind, and he turned against you. Because I told him to do it."

Arrogant ass. I track his movements and pivot to the side as he steps toward the sledgehammer. The humidity in the atmosphere feels like ribbons of silk winding around us—binding us together in our circle of hell.

My new brother lifts and drops the sash on my gown. Too close. Get away. He must know I despise being touched by a certain kind of man. And that I loathe tight spaces—must be why he chose the sarcophagus. Exploring my fears, is he? What's next, an ice bath?

"Scared of a little cold water, pet," Scarlett whispers against my neck, sounding exactly like Faust. "How sad. I planted the desire within Grayson to send you to Ironwood *years* ago, and it grew, and grew. Until it became an obsession, and he acted upon the idea."

I spin toward him. Scarlett? *Scarlett* was behind my commitment to the asylum? The hunger. Addiction. Endless work. Faust's bloody whip... And I had thought I couldn't hate my brother more. "You failed. I came back."

"Like a bad penny. I obviously underestimated my opponent. Don't worry, it won't happen again." He slips out of his coat, dropping it on a bench or something. "This is my corner of the world. No room for you, baby sister."

"Move, then."

Scarlett rolls up his sleeves. "Not an option, I'm afraid."

So Stonehenge is his seat of power, too. We can both visit other parts of the world, but we must always return. Damn, I should've guessed. If I die today, a new Veritas will take my place, and if Scarlett falls, another heir of Archimendax will arise. I was foolish to waltz in here and expect to dispose of him as easily as I did his employees. Think ahead, Hester. You're always too impetuous.

A terrible sport, my foe tries to belittle me before the game even begins. "It isn't as though you're a great threat, with those *scary* magic ears, that *smelling* ability." Scarlett imitates my rasp next, saying, "I can't see you, but I sense your emotions and hear like a owl.'" He returns to his own voice. "Your feeble ways are amusing."

In a sense, Scarlett is beginning to sound like an actual brother. The kind who tattles, dips your braids in ink, and burns ants with a magnifying glass. Except that he won't think twice about destroying me or killing good people.

"David Thornhill," I say. Scarlett seems like the bragging type, habitually crowing over his victims. "Why did you make him murder Freckles…I mean, Maude Lambson?"

It sounds as though Scarlett is untying his precious cravat now, the popinjay. He pauses, as if weighing whether he wishes to indulge my curiosity. "Stalling, sis? All right. I'm game. Thornhill worked for me until he met his wife. She awakened his conscience, I presume, and my employment was no longer to his liking. He needed to be taken down a peg."

"And Miss Lambson?"

"You met her. The woman was obnoxious. Surely you have better questions than these? I'm getting bored."

"About Marie-Louise—"

"What has *she* to do with *anything?*" Scarlett asks, sounding angry for the first time.

Do I smell perspiration? Perhaps he isn't as impervious as he seems. I may have broken through his armor and hit a nerve.

"I suppose I'm just puzzled that you killed your own mother but merely ruined Father."

"Because she married Lennox, of course. You really are stupider than I thought." Scarlett takes off his hat and tosses it. "It's in my nature to strike where it hurts most. Father loves money more than life, so it didn't make sense to kill him. I took his riches instead."

"But he'll rise again and get it back."

"And I'll destroy him again. For the rest of his life, he'll never have time to enjoy prosperity, always looking over his shoulder for the next crisis, just waiting for the other shoe to drop. As soon as he reaches the zenith, I'll plunge him back to the depths. Another Sisyphus with his boulder, if you care to borrow from the Greeks."

"Hmm," I say, enjoying the fact he's riled. "Hat, coat, gloves, cravat. Are you going to remove any other clothing before we get on with this? If so, I'm glad I'm blind."

The air freezes. Oh, that poked the bear a bit. Vanity, thy name is James. Suddenly, a great force pushes me. It winds around my legs, abdomen and arms, squeezing like a python, rubbing the skin raw beneath my dress. I struggle against it, but I lose ground, feet slipping backwards as my body slides closer to the tracks. I am picked up like a rag doll and flipped on my back, suspended in the air.

"A taste of what you're up against," Scarlett whispers.

Whistling loudly, the train comes round the bend and speeds toward my head. *O di immortales.* Please help me. The air around the top of my skull is terribly hot and sucks my body forward as the huge machine screams past. My hair is ripped free of its pins, flying about my face. Then I am thrown back to the platform, skidding across the hard surface on my knees. I try to stand, but my legs buckle, weak from shock and fear. My bladder nearly empties itself. What the *hell*, Mary Arden! Scarlett has some elemental power, you said. He can mix reality with illusion, you said. You never mentioned anything like this! Sweet blazes, when I get my hands on you…

Scarlett's at my side in an instant. "Your great weakness, baby sister, is that you care about others. How foolish to make yourself so vulnerable." He laughs regrettably. "I will stab you in the heart, but not with a blade. Miss Collins will be the first to go, and then Willard Little Hawk. It's been fun playing with Craddock's mind, but I'm undecided on the order of disposal between him and Kelly—you're attached in different ways to them both. And that hideous monster who just moved in with you? I don't know what I'll do with him."

You'll never save them. It's your fault they die. He whispers the words in my mind and desolation fills me. I grow desperate to do myself harm. *Worthless freak. Unlovable.* Weeping uncontrollably, it is all I can manage not to dash my brains against the station wall. *Do it, Hester. Throw your life away.*

With Scarlett's power still wrapped around me, I push myself up. *No. I won't, liar's spawn.* The pressure is crushing, but I stagger like a drunkard across the platform. *Not for you.*

My defiance must surprise Scarlett, enough to make him lose focus for a moment. Blinking back tears, I raise my hand, fingers separating to form a V, for Veritas, goddess of virtue and truth. My brother's dark energy bears down upon me, and heat builds inside my body, igniting my own power. Drawing on the inner blaze, I physically push against Scarlett's might, until a scream tears from my throat. The force weakens slightly and then dissolves.

I stumble back a step and drop my hand. Lungs aching, I inhale deeply, free to breathe at last. The oxygen stings my throat, but I savor it. Yet there isn't time to recover. Echolocation tells me Scarlett is now standing on the south side of the platform, fifteen feet and six inches away.

Lex talionis, brother.

Following the sound of his black heart, I run directly at Scarlett. *Boom. Crash.* Lightning splits the heavens as we collide. The sound stabs at my head, and we tumble apart. A whirlwind arises and pushes me upward, a sensation similar to the one I had when I levitated at the asylum but much more powerful. The strange wind lifts both Scarlett and me from the ground so that we're high above the train station roof. We spin faster and faster within a vortex. Bile in my mouth, I hear the humans below cry that the moon has covered the sun. An eclipse! Is it a miracle or the end of days, they ask and huddle together within the station house, praying in the darkness.

I sense the black fog—impenetrable, boiling and writhing like a living thing. It forces its way into my lungs, and I cough like I am choking on molasses. The viscous air doesn't move when I push against it with my hands. How do I fight this?

"You cannot win," Scarlett says, as the fog rolls back.

His voice is like crashing waves, and sound pummels me from all sides. Continuing to spin, I scream, covering my bloody ears, and once more turn off the power I have always relied upon, my greatest gift from the Lady Veritas. Never have I shut down my ears in a situation this dangerous. All is speed and terrifying silence. I fly round and round, not knowing what's coming next. Up, up, I go. Then I'm jerked side to side and plummet down again.

The faces of my dearest friends fill my blind eyes. I see Cordelia cold and still as marble, Willard broken and torn. Then Tom. Kelly… Scarlett said he would strike me in the heart, and he will. Maybe I shall lose. The courage I previously demonstrated has deserted me. I cannot summon it, not when I imagine my loved ones suffering on my account.

Where are the immortals? Have they turned away in my moment of need? *Deus miserere.* Help me.

As I continue to whirl in the vortex, I think of the people I served as a Visionary, those who passed from life in violence, searching for justice. I remember when Tom and I struggled with our first investigation. Odds stacked against us, evidence slight, but he said something that made all the difference.

Now I say it in my darkest hour, and offer the words to the universe in supplication. *"Veritas vos liberabit."*

The truth will set you free.

Once the words are spoken, light fills my mind, but it's the opposite of the hot fury I expected. Peace and assurance flow through me, like a blessing from the heavens. I open my ears to sound and the earth shakes, but the spinning grows less turbulent. More light fills me, beginning at my toes and moving upward. Particle by particle. Cell by cell. Enough that it would not surprise me to have rays shooting from my eyes. A voice comes out of my throat, but it isn't mine. It belongs to the Lady, the ancient one. She must have heard my call for aid. After all these years of labor and sacrifice, I am at last receiving help from above.

Terrifying, wondrous, the voice rends the air. "My wrath is stirred, James Scarlett. Release my servant or we shall do battle. Do you think yourself greater than I?"

My half-brother may have inherited some power from the goddess, but it has become polluted by his deeds. I feel her anger over this, her desire that Scarlett be punished for abusing the gifts she gave him.The blazing light which fills me is pure, not the warped illusion of truth Scarlett uses to deceive. I would be a fool not to capitalize upon this godsend. Down, down, down I fall. My feet land lightly on the railway platform, and Scarlett drops to earth a moment later. Veritas has left my body, but I feel her strength running through me.

I wipe the blood from my ears and smile at my brother. "You will not touch Cordelia *or* Willard. The same goes for Kelly, Tom and Gabriel."

A growl forms in his throat and Scarlett launches himself forward. His hands clutch at my neck, but an awful burning-flesh smell drifts around us, followed by wild shrieking. He releases me and stumbles back to examine his wounds. Perhaps I am getting the hang of that new power of mine. Simple, really. The key is to touch evil people when one is righteously indignant.

As I am right now.

Lunging forward, I rake Scarlett's face with my bare hand. The cheek and eye-socket dissolve under my fingernails like honey in hot tea. A vision of his death flies through my mind as he screams again. I know the location, the method, and the perpetrator.

My half-brother is backing up. "What have you done, you stupid girl? How could this happen?"

He falls off the platform to the train track below, and a bone in his leg shatters beneath him. Oh, ouch. From the sound of it, Scarlett has a compound fracture. Searching about the floor, I locate my sledgehammer near a pile of debris and return to the edge of the platform. My foe still lies whimpering on the tracks. With his defenses weakened, I smell the terror inside him. He does not wish to go to the other side, to meet Sir Death. He knows the punishment that awaits him. Evil as he is, I almost pity my brother. Almost.

The sledgehammer feels solid in my hands. It would be so easy to finish Scarlett, but I shrink from it. Maybe it isn't in my nature to kill, having represented the rights of the dead for so long. I am Veritas of Stonehenge, after all, not one of the Furies. Or it could be that I saw him die a moment ago in my mind, and it wasn't here and now. And my old friend Death does not lurk about the train station but reaps elsewhere. Who am I to defy that old hussy Fate?

People begin to stir. I hear them talking of the terrifying weather—the eclipse, earthquake, and tornado. A brave few venture out of the station house. They find Scarlett, and his wounded henchmen, and call for help. The rake/cane is not where I left it under the bench, so I turn and walk away, hand brushing against the station wall for guidance. No one seems to notice the impaired Grayson girl as she heads back toward High Street.

I drop the sledgehammer into some bushes near the cemetery, but my shoe dislodges something small from the dirt as I turn away. I bend down and pick it up. It's a smooth, flat stone, similar to a dollar coin. There are no heads nor tails on either side of it, but I flip the stone into the air like it's a silver dollar. Feels different than my lucky pebbles, more solid. It certainly wouldn't represent the best day of my life like the pebbles did, the day when I learned I could escape.

Yet it might symbolize something else—the day I survived. When I learned I could stay and fight, and the heavens came to my defense.

While tucking my new lucky stone into the pocket of my skirt, I change my mind about the sledgehammer. I remove it from the bushes and hoist it over my shoulder. Could come in handy some day.

Lilacs scent the air as I walk toward my house on St. David's Street. The winds settle into a gentle breeze, promising that summer is not far distant. I am not so optimistic I imagine Scarlett is gone for good. He'll be back to settle the score, but I doubt the Lady Veritas will stop him then. She helped me this time and that, in and of itself, was a miracle. I'll see to it my loved ones are protected. Have Mary Arden show me how to shield them, regardless of the price.

Hopefully, Tom will stay in California and have a long and happy life there, his need for alcohol overcome. I imagine him as an old man, great grandchildren as far as the eye can see. He has a head of snowy hair and black, shining eyes. Wearing his cowboy duster, Tom rides out each day and surveys his cattle ranch at the base of the Sierra Nevadas. The image makes me smile.

With Tom's future decided, I focus on Noah Kelly. He must let me go, for his own good, and find another woman to wife. She'll be a loyal, maternal lady who looks upon Alice as her own daughter. Kelly will teach their future children many things. Sign language first and then how to whistle. They'll name every pony that comes into their lives after Jupiter.

Melancholy settles over me as I think of Kelly marrying again. The sledgehammer slips a little on my shoulder, and I move it to a more comfortable spot. My limbs feel tired, and I yearn for the old copper tub I once used and a steaming, hour-long soak. But there's no copper bath in my new home. Almost there now, I hear my St. David's neighbors bustling about, preparing for the evening ahead. For a moment, I fantasize I'm one of them. But some daydreams are too much even for me to entertain.

None of these good Welsh people carry a sledgehammer as a weapon. They don't levitate above the train station or have visions of James Scarlett's demise. I sit on my front step, drop the hammer between my feet, and review the scene in my mind. Experiencing it all again.

He stands before the fireplace in the parlor of Griffin House, and the mirror over the mantel reflects the room behind him. I cannot discern his age, for the lamps are turned down low, but he wears an eye patch and the right section of his face is missing, the bones barely covered with a thin veil of skin.

Sir Death lurks in the hallway, winding his watch as he waits for his cue. A figure enters the parlor, lifts a small pistol, and shoots Scarlett in the head. I see the killer in the looking glass, and it's the most disturbing revelation of all. I've learned something about visions, however. They are but a fragment of time and truth and what is done with this knowledge is left up to each Visionary. Even demigoddesses are allowed to choose who they will become.

Although I spared my brother today, I cannot speak for tomorrow.

Pale skin. Platinum hair. And silver eyes in the mirror.

Acknowledgements

My children were fairly young when I first started this project and now most of them are approaching adulthood. Back in those days, it was especially difficult for me to find the right balance between parenting and writing. Yet I could always count on a night out with my critique group to help me improve my craft and keep my sanity. I owe so much to these talented ladies. They have been a constant source of support, writing advice, and wisdom. Many thanks go to: Ruth Craddock, Adrienne Monson, Jennifer Greyson, Rebecca Rode, Angela Brimhall, Karen Pellett, and Karyn Patterson. I also appreciate Jenilyn Freestone, Kristy Peterson, and Kay Haynie for reading through early drafts and not letting this painful experience effect our relationships. You are all the best!

Angela Eschler of Eschler Editing has shared valuable insights with me on this story and several others. Her knowledge of writing, and the whole publishing industry, is outstanding. I use what you taught me on a daily basis, Angela.

And I owe an enormous debt to Kira Rubenthaler, editor extraordinaire at Bookfly Design, for taking so much time on my manuscript. Working with you has been a wonderful experience, Kira. I highly recommend your services to anyone in need of awesome story insights and precise grammar.

My thanks to James Egan of Bookfly Design for this amazing cover. I loved watching Hester come to life under your skillful hand.

I greatly appreciate Bob Houston at Bob Houston eBook Formatting for answering my questions and coming to my rescue time and again. You have been a true example of graciousness and professionalism.

About the Author

Quinn Coleridge grew up in the Pacific Northwest, where she learned to love rain storms, green, growing things, and reading books by a crackling fire. As a young adult, Quinn ventured across the pond to England, another green, rainy place. While there, she met a man with the prettiest eyes, and they later got married and had lots of kids. (She blames the eyes.)

Now their family of eight lives in a place with little rain or greenery. They have two dogs and two cats which the man with the pretty eyes never even remotely wanted, although he's a good sport about it. Crackling fires are a rarity at Quinn's house these days, but it's seldom boring. And she still loves books.

Reader friends, if you are so inclined, please leave a review of Veritas at Amazon or Goodreads.

Cheers!

53097589R00240

Made in the USA
San Bernardino, CA
06 September 2017